SHADOWS & SIDESHOWS

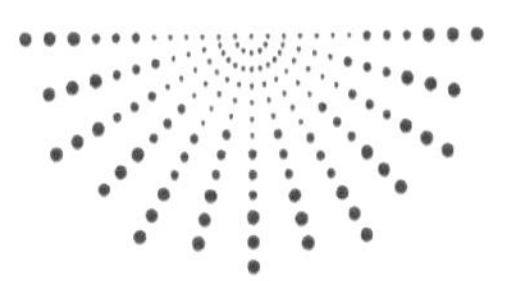

SHADOWS & SIDESHOWS

FINNEGAN FAMILY SUPERNATURAL HUNTERS
VOL. 1

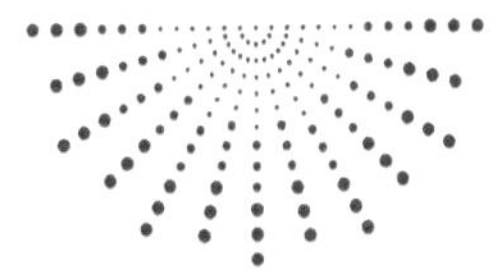

JUDY BLACK

To the family I was born into and the family I've found along the way

CABINET OF ABERRATIONS

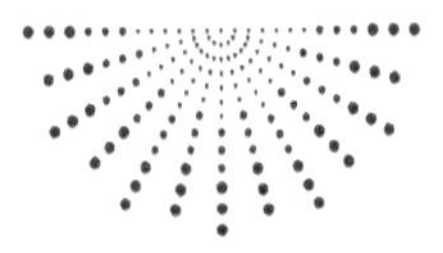

CHAPTER ONE

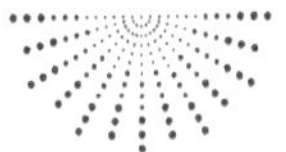

Despite the troll currently doing its best to crush me between its fingers, I had zero plans of dying in the middle of nowhere Arkansas. My backup hadn't shown, and the time to wait for the cavalry of my dad and brother had long passed, but I didn't need them. I could handle this all on my own.

I twisted in the crushing grasp and managed to pull one arm free through the gap between his massive fingers. All I needed was a distraction. The tattoos on my skin glinted in the first peeking rays of dawn as I focused on the tiny pair of wings inked onto my wrist. Each picture held a story, but mine contained more than just a thousand words. Behind every design on my skin dwelled the spirit of something supernatural I'd killed and captured or that Dad had gifted me. Now was the time to put those marks to work and save my skin.

The summoning tingled all the way up the base of my spine as the ink vanished from my skin, leaving a patch of bleeding flesh behind. A small Faerie with missing teeth and a cigar in hand appeared. Standing at just over three feet tall with the body of a toddler and the face of middle-aged regret, Puck looked at me, then to the troll crushing me.

In my mind, Puck's fear pounded against me, but I easily conquered his will with one command: *Get me out of here now!*

As I tasted the long drag of his cigar in the back of my throat, my mind fell into Puck's body, controlling. Seeing through the eyes of the Faerie, I focused all my will to overcoming Puck's own instincts and sent him charging straight to the troll's face. Puck blew some smoke at the massive beast then threw the cigar straight into its eyes.

Instantly, the hand released me, and I crashed into the ground, knocking me from Puck's head and back into my own. Choking for air, I scrambled to my feet and limped across the plains to get some distance between the howling, raging troll and me. It swung wildly at Puck with one hand and clawed at the burning ash in its face with the other.

As soon as I could breathe without pain, I let go of my hold on Puck. His presence blew from my mind like a summer storm rolling through. The inked wings returned to their place on my now blood-tinted skin. I glanced toward where the rest of the caravan was setting up shop and half-expected to see Dad there, judging me.

He'd told me I wasn't ready to go out hunting on my own, but if I didn't stop this monster soon, it'd flatten me, my family's sideshow, and all the nowhere towns around here.

For my first solo hunt, I might as well go big. I squared my shoulders back and tore off the bottom half of my dress. If I was going to die crushed by a troll, I'd at least do it without crinoline in my way.

I took off away from where my brother would be getting our sideshow tents set up. "Hey, you duffer!" I yelled, waving my ripped off skirt like a flag as I ran.

The waving fabric caught its attention even through its watering eyes. The troll roared and stomped after me.

I took a deep breath, steeling myself like Dad had taught me: *anything you summon can't hurt you so long as you stand like a fort in body, mind, and soul.* I didn't know what the hell that meant but better to give it a try with a full belly of breath first.

My thigh burned with white-hot pain as I focused on the tattoo there, a swirling mass of teeth, fangs, and hollow black eyes that knew only hunger. As the mark began to take shape in front of me, the tattooed spot on my leg pooled blood that floated through the air from my skin into the shadowy shape blooming at my feet. The blood leaving my body and forming the shape burned through my muscles and brain like an oil lantern catching flame on a show curtain.

Long, lean, and hissing at me, I swallowed hard as the wendigo, created of blood, shadow, and magic, stood in front of me. I tried to not think about the wendigo den Dad and I had cleared out. We'd lost track of the number of human skulls deep in that cave. The creature hissed again and stepped closer to me, skinny arms raised high with claw-like fingers ready to strike.

The wendigo's spirit twisted against my mind, hungry for human, not troll, flesh, but I closed my eyes and forced my way into its body, turning the wendigo's hungry eyes toward the towering beast. It screeched before lurching at the troll like a spider.

Pulling out of the wendigo's head, I let out a deep breath and tried to ignore the blood seeping down my leg. I dealt with blood between my legs once a month, so this I could handle even if it burned like a fire trying to cut a hole to my bones. As long as I could keep the wendigo focused on the troll, I'd count that as a win.

The wendigo leapt onto the troll, crawling up its body, as I yanked out my satchel of daggers and readied them. Ignoring the pain, I moved closer as the wendigo slashed into the troll's back, cutting out thick chunks of skin and attempting to devour it, though the flesh just fell straight through the summoned monster and splashed onto the ground in rotten chunks.

With the troll distracted, I moved up behind it. Taller than a building or not, the anatomy was similar enough to a man, and I knew the best way to bring a man down. With my dagger, I struck. The unicorn blood-forged blade sizzled through the back of the troll's ankle, cutting through tendon, muscle, and bone.

The wendigo's hunger spiked through me, nearly bringing me to my knees as the smaller creature crawled down its back to me. The troll howled, scrambling to reach the wendigo as I ran to the front and drew my arms back as if to shoot a bow. The mark of Lady Death over my heart stuttered out of rhythm as Death's gift materialized from my blood and appeared in my hands. The bone and sinew bow weighed nothing as I drew back the string made of darkness.

I released my hold, and the arrow shot forward, a streak of blood following its path, connecting me to its target as it burst through the troll's chest and out its back, shattering the wendigo spirit too. The wendigo slamming back into my flesh dropped me to my knees, and I nearly vomited with the pain burning white-hot against my skin.

I found my feet again and followed the tangled web of blood tying me and the now still and silent troll together. I'd never had anything as big as the troll try to make a home among the ink of my skin, but I'd figure out what to do. I was a hunter for Lady Death, and no troll would beat me. Death had chosen my family to capture the souls of the supernatural on Earth, and I had to trust that I knew what the hell I was doing.

I climbed up onto the troll's leg and walked up its body to stare into the hollow cavity of its chest. Swallowing back the bile that burned in my throat at the smell, I spotted it, the glittering piece of soul I needed.

The small stone, just the size of a river rock, flickered and pulsated, wrapped in the magic that would tie me to this corpse. I plucked it from the goop, and the second it touched my hand, I felt the troll's spirit roaring before latching onto me with a crushing blow around my left forearm, squeezing so tightly I worried that a spirit could break bone.

Rage. Blind rage slammed into me faster than a steam train, and I stumbled back. In that instant, we were one, and the same as screaming vibrated through our combined bodies.

"Hazel!"

My name jerked me out of the blind fury. I blinked a few times, shaking my head and dropping to my knees. The troll still burned in the edges of my mind, but I looked up and spotted my brother running toward me.

"What the devil are you doing?"

"Keeping you from getting crushed. You're welcome," I snapped as I looked down at my forearm where the troll's spirit had gripped me.

A large black ink handprint circled my entire forearm. Great, that'd be a good look.

"Where's Dad?" he asked.

"Not here," I said, putting my daggers away.

"What do you mean?" Marshall frowned, looking from me to the skeletal troll remains.

"Just that, he wasn't here. Just me and a troll."

"You're covered in blood."

"Part of the job. Did anyone see anything?"

"The show heard some of the screaming. But I doubt it got far as town. You really dealt with that all by yourself?"

"Don't look so surprised." I picked up the lower half of my skirt and tied it around my waist, so I, at least, had a little dignity walking into camp. Not that the rest of the show hadn't seen my full business before, but I still had to play at being a proper lady.

Marshall wore his traveling clothes, and by the dirt stains on the knees of his trousers, I'd wager the show was all set up.

"Are you okay to perform tonight?" he asked.

"Maybe after a wash."

Marshall looked at the skeleton, walking around the entirety of its massive body. "Dad missed a troll fight?"

"I know. His favorite."

Marshall frowned, then looked at me. "You captured it?"

"Yep. It won't be coming back," I said waving my new tattoo at him.

"So what happens to the body?" he asked.

"Dad usually tries to burn 'em up or toss 'em into the ocean or a river or something. Bones are powerful things."

Marshall touched the femur of the beast. "I can't believe you killed this. It's huge, Hazel."

My brother looked like someone from our audience during a show; he couldn't believe what he saw.

"You know, we're down an act… Think these bones would work?" I asked.

"What?"

"I bet people would pay to see this," I said.

"How are you even going to get it back to the show?" Marshall asked.

"I can figure something out. Come on, I can even talk it up."

"You're not going to go on about where this came from," Marshall said.

"I won't even have to lie about it!"

"No one wants the truth Hazel, we both know that." He patted the femur. "Fine, I'll ask Alma about getting it to camp. We've got a backup tent we can set up around it."

"Perfect, I'll get it tonight once the show's over," I said.

I walked with Marshall back home, the Finnegan Family Cabinet of Aberrations, currently on display in Arkansas. "Dad hasn't shown up at camp yet?" I asked.

"Not yet, but I hear the weather's been real rotten lately. He might've just gotten held up. We're here for at least a week anyways, so we've got time for him to arrive," Marshall said.

"You aren't worried about him?"

"No, I'm worried about getting us set up and ready to start the show."

I rolled my eyes. That would be what Marshall focused on when it came to anything.

Getting into the camp, I found everything mostly set up. A few people worked at getting the main tent up, but all our performers sat eating dinner.

"What did you do to your dress?" Temperance looked from her dinner to me.

"Nothing you can't fix," I said with my best smile.

"We don't work as your seamstress," Constance said, not turning from her meal.

Sitting at the table, the two looked like sisters just sitting close together, but at the hip, they fused into one woman held up on three legs.

"No, but you're good at it," I said.

Temperance laughed. "Not till Sunday or until we get back on the road."

"I'll hold y'all to it," I said.

Constance shook her head, but the corner of her lips tilted into a small smile.

"Do you want me up front with you?" I asked Marshall.

He shook his head. "No. Heard the cops might come by. I was going to have the Duncans showing off up front."

"I'll wear the short slip then."

"If you want."

"People aren't paying to admire my tattoos; they're paying to see some leg."

"Then you better clean up. You're bloody," Alma said from her seat.

Our strongwoman looked like a statue brought to life in dark brown marble. With a giantess mother and a mortal father, Alma grew up taking after her mother. She'd been one of the first acts to join when she was just fourteen and I was twelve. Even then Alma had towered over most grown men—she'd made Dad look downright delicate in stature.

"We still have work to do," I said.

"Get your daddy to help," she said.

"He isn't here," Marshall said.

"What do you two want?" she asked.

"There's a troll skeleton. We need help getting it back here," Marshall said.

"You're crazy if you think I am carrying a skeleton all the way back here," she said. "You don't pay me enough to add being a mule to my show."

I looked at Marshall, and he frowned but didn't say anything. My arms crossed in front of my chest, my fingers ghosted against my new tattoo… What better way to move a troll body than a troll?

"I can do it," I said. "But it'll have to be when no one's around."

"How do you suggest we do that?" Alma asked.

"Just before dawn's usually quiet enough," I suggested.

"And how are you planning to do that?" he asked.

"I got my ways, but we need to get ready or there isn't going to be a show."

He shook his head but left to go get himself ready for the show.

"Your daddy really hasn't shown?" Alma asked once Marshall was gone.

I shook my head. "He probably just found the bottom of some bottle in town. He'll show. I'll check town tomorrow and find him."

"So, you went off on your first hunt, huh?" she asked, motioning to my arm. "How'd that go?"

"I think I need about a three-hour bath to get that smell off."

"Well, we got a river and some soap, so get to scrubbing." She passed a bar of soap to me. "I'll keep an eye out and make sure those singing tiny people don't come over here peeping."

"Thanks," I said as we made our way to the small river.

I jumped in, clothing and all, before stripping out of everything and giving the remains of my dress a good washing that didn't quite get the blood out of it, but this was my hunting dress, so that didn't matter much. Now that the skirt was ruined, I'd just steal some of Marshall's trousers to use. Manners or not, dresses were a pain to wear during a fight.

The cold water stung, but getting the blood and grime off my skin felt like luxury. I worried about my hair, knowing the brown mess would take ages to dry, but I could perform with it tucked up.

"Hurry it up," Alma called from the shore.

"I'm finishing now," I said, getting my wet dress back on.

"Good, we gotta get ready for round one of fun and games."

Alma and I walked into the tent set up for the lady performers. Constance and Temperance already sat in front of the mirrors. "One of you girls want to lace us up?" Temperance asked as Constance took a long swig from a bottle of whiskey.

"Y'all aren't supposed to drink before the show," I said as I went to help get the twins into their custom dress.

"There isn't enough whiskey in the world to get us drunk, darling," Temperance said as she pulled the bottle from her twin and took a swig.

Alma walked to the other side of the tent to start getting ready, leaving me to deal with the twins alone. Their dress hung open at the back exposing the point of fusion between the base of their torsos and top of their hips. Two spines running parallel to each other with a vast expanse of pale, sagging skin between them.

"Keep staring and we're going to have to charge you," Temperance said.

"Sorry." I found the laces of the dress and began pulling the edges together.

"What'd you hunt down today?" Constance asked as Temperance drank from the bottle.

"A troll."

Both the twins whistled. "Your daddy let you take that on?"

"My daddy ain't here," I said as I got the last loop of their dress tied together. Now paisley fabric covered their fused bodies leaving just the obvious: two women, two arms and three legs from one body.

"Then who's been talking up the show?" Temperance asked. "We better have an audience."

"We will," I said.

"Drink for a good show?" Constance offered me the bottle.

I shook my head. "Y'all good getting your makeup done?"

"Honey, we've been putting makeup on two faces since you were a screaming babe. We're fine."

I didn't say anything else and moved to Alma's side of the tent to start my own getting ready process. My show dress might have been the only clean, nice looking thing I owned. The color of fresh milk with a few lace details, the dress was more slip than anything else. It hid all the bits it needed to, but a proper lady would never have worn that out into public. But tattooed ladies got a bit of a leeway. I wasn't a respectable lady. I was a freak made by my own hands.

Shoving pins into my hair, I managed to get into some semblance of respectable before I worried over my makeup. Deep red lipstick, blush, and powder so I matched the billed "tattooed beauty," not that most of the men in my audience spent time looking at my face with the rest of my body so exposed.

Beside me, Alma wore no makeup. She wore a skimpy get-up, although hers wasn't anything nice or elegant, just an animal hide covering all the important parts.

"Places!" Marshall called from outside. All of us girls pulled on long robes to hide our bodies as we walked into the main exhibition tent.

The long tent had five small display areas arranged around each side to make up our ten-under-the-big-top show. Everyone filled into their designated spot: Constance and Temperance sat on their stage in a chair with all three legs swinging as Temperance knitted something; Alma hopped into her display, more cage than stage, and picked up a massive club. Her area held all kinds of heavy objects, anchors, barbells, and, if anyone was brave enough, she took volunteers to pick up. The singing Duncans, a troupe of kobolds, tiny faeries about the size of Puck, tired of housework, adjusted bowties and smoothed down dresses as they headed to help drum up business out front with Marshall.

Near the back of the tent, Jonah, our armless wonder, sat in a chair reading the newspaper. The only thing that made people stare was the lack of arms and his talent for doing just about anything with his feet. He'd demonstrate rolling cigars, reading, drinking, eating, and playing poker with his feet. He nodded as I walked past to my area in the back of the show.

Velvet curtains lined my stage, and the whole thing looked like a scene out of one of those burlesque shows. Mine wasn't quite a peep show, my dress never came off, but the men would want to see some skin, and that I could deliver on. I hopped onto my stage and settled onto the swing that Marshall had set up for me. I was no acrobat, but I'd learned a few basic tricks from the troupe that traveled with us back west. All I needed to make a happy customer was flash a little leg and maybe a hint of undergarment. Easy money from worthless people.

Marshall stopped by all the exhibits, poking his head into the back. "You good? We already got a crowd."

"Let them in," I said, idly swinging.

Marshall's Adam's apple bobbed as he swallowed repeatedly. The nerves rolled off him in heavy waves. "Marshall?" I called.

He stopped by my exhibit. "Yeah?"

"Show time," I said with a smile.

Marshall nodded before he disappeared to the entrance of the tent.

Audiences always sounded the same, idle chatter and rambling, the same stupid questions, comments, and requests. No matter how far we traveled, the people all seemed to have the same reactions to seeing someone looking different than they were used to.

Beside me, our band started warming up. The group of four men was a new addition and one of the best musical groups we'd had. Across from me, I saw Alma leaning at the edge of her display area looking toward the band, and I grinned. She had her eyes on the trumpet player, Creole.

The usual talkers took their places around the exhibits. We freaks weren't supposed to tell our own story; we had to let someone else speak for us. Ruth, a man about my father's age, had been my talker for years. More than that though, we needed someone to keep the audience away; last show someone had decided Constance and Temperance were a fake and had thrown a bottle at their shared leg. Dad had taken that man down harder than he'd knock down a vampire. Maybe the Arkansas folks would be a little nicer, but I doubted it. No matter what monsters I hunted, people always remained the worst.

"Wonders from around the globe, the strange, the frightening, the beautiful, we've got it all right here under this tent. Ten cents, a single dime, gets you the chance of a lifetime! Come closer folks, that's right!" Marshall's voice echoed even into the back of the tent. Hearing the same spiel show after show made it easy to memorize Daddy's usual speeches. Marshall's voice lacked that burn of charisma. Daddy had something that just drew people to him like a moth into a candle.

The telltale clack of a dozen pairs of tiny shoes hitting the stage gave away the arrival of the Duncans onto the stage with Marshall. The group began singing some songs from their home in Ireland. They were no Arthur Collins, but they could carry a tune way better than I could. Besides, their appeal wasn't the tone of voice but the novelty. Most people had never seen someone as small as the Duncans before, let alone a whole group of them singing a hymnal.

"Right this way gentleman," Marshall said as he opened the flap to the display tent and let in a group of about a dozen men. I put on my performance smile, flirty and welcoming. Around me, I saw everyone else flip that same switch: from everyday life to suddenly something extraordinary.

"Hello there, boys," I said as I started a slow swinging pace on my stage.

A few of the men adjusted their jackets as they walked closer. For a moment, none of them spoke, so I just kept swinging slowly. "Don't be shy, you can come in a little closer."

A few of the men moved closer to the stage.

"Why is a beautiful lady like you all…" A man gestured to himself, apparently struggling with the word tattooed.

"Hazel, our tattooed beauty, was captured by a savage tribe in the Indies. She and her father were shipwrecked and alone, they were taken captive and tortured by being tattooed for ten hours a day!" the barker, Ruth, at my stall said with gravitas.

I'd never been anywhere near the Indies and neither had any of these men. No one would believe the actual truth, so we made a tale that let them all take comfort that no "self-respecting woman" would deface herself like this. Not that any of them really cared. They liked the chance to ogle this much skin on a woman not married to them. I adjusted my legs to let my slip slide an inch farther up.

People always thought what a terrible fate to be put on display like this, but the truth was, with groups like this, I held all the power. They'd listen to any word I'd say and have no frame of mind to do anything else. All we had to do was keep them enthralled enough to feel they got their money's worth. If hunting my monsters was my real calling, then entertaining men was my hobby that paid the bills. When no one really knew monsters existed, no one paid to get rid of them.

"Your father should have protected you," an older man said.

"He tried," the barker said. "But he was tied to a tree for the whole two years. He thought Hazel dead, and she thought the same until they were rescued by the Finnegan Family and brought home to America."

I looked away and tried to fake demure, not one of my strong suits.

A few of the men shook their heads, tutting about what a poor thing I was, but most of them just moved their heads to the speed of my swinging.

"I've seen a woman like you before. The second you touched her skin, every bit of that ink came off," a man said.

My swinging stopped immediately. "Are you calling me a gaff?" I asked before my handler could respond.

"I don't think any woman could live through that. Women are too delicate."

I got off the swing and walked to the edge of the stage with a smile.

"Sir, I assure you all of our acts are one-hundred-percent genuine. The realest show on Earth. No fakes, frauds, or phonies here," Ruth said.

I hopped off the edge of my stage and beckoned the man closer. "Well, if you have so many doubts, why don't you try to rub the ink off of my arm?"

The barker looked at me with a frown that said he didn't approve, but he couldn't control what I did in my own act. If this man was going to call me a fake, I'd give him something real to complain about.

The man shifted uncomfortably, and the crowd around him murmured. I ran my hand down my own arm and leg. "I'm perfectly confident you will find nothing fake about me."

The man reached out with one finger and poked the newest mark. I barely resisted wincing and forced myself to keep smiling. He began inching his finger up my arm and toward my shoulder, trying to get an extra treat for his price of admission. From the small mark of a moon along my inner thigh, I summoned the smallest Faerie I could. Barely the size of a nickel and easy to control, the sleep Faerie appeared in the air behind the men. She found her way to the man with his hands on me and crept up his pant leg like a spider. I let the Faerie take control of her own actions, and her tiny dagger teeth sank into his leg.

The man jumped, slapping at his leg and with a pain like a paper cut, and the moon returned to my skin.

"Are you alright?" another man in the audience asked.

"Mosquito," the man muttered and then looked at his hand that had run along my arm. The other men crowded around him, all of them looking for some speck of my tattoos on his skin.

"You are one of a kind," the man finally said. "My apologies for doubting you, miss."

"Of course, all forgiven. We have nothing fake here at Finnegan's. Everything you see is real enough to touch," I said as I climbed back onto my swing. I hoped her bite had drawn blood.

The men stayed around another few minutes, but finally they left. I smiled and made a bet on how many proposals I'd receive by the end of the week. Most of them would have asked Dad for my hand, but now they'd have to talk to Marshall, and I couldn't imagine my brother taking that in as much stride as Dad had.

We shut down after midnight, and I hopped off the swing and stretched. My butt had gone numb from sitting, but judging by the crowd, we'd made good money.

"You can't be doing that with the guests!" Ruth snapped at me.

"I didn't do anything." My innocent act only worked on rubes, and I knew it, but that didn't stop me from trying.

"Don't be talking to them, and don't let them touch you! One of them grabs you in a bad spot, it's my skin going to get cooked."

"I can take care of myself and tell my own tragic backstory, you know."

"Not-uh. We tried that, and that ain't happening again."

"Just go get dinner. I'll try to behave tomorrow, alright?"

He sighed but stomped off.

Alma shook her head. "You give that man too hard a time."

"Someone has to. My mouth still works. I don't much care for sitting up there to be ogled."

"Honey, you're in the wrong business then. That's all we're supposed to do."

I sighed. "Yeah. Reckon so."

Alma's eyes drifted to the band packing up their instruments. Their laughter rang like music through the halls, a sincere sound after hours of pretend.

"You keep looking like that and someone might look back," I said with an elbow to Alma's side.

"You hush. That boy don't even know I exist."

"You're kind of hard to miss, Alma."

"Hush," she hissed as the boy in question, Creole, turned to us.

"Good show tonight, ladies," he said.

That French lilt to his voice gave all the weight to what everyone called him. Music men and tent men didn't stick around long to learn their names; they got named by what they did or who they sounded like.

"Thanks," I said. "Y'all play a pretty tune."

He smiled. "Eh… Miss Finnegan… where do my boys and I eat? I didn't see a separate tent for us."

"We don't have the manpower to keep separated here. We all eat together. You're part of the Finnegan family now. Alma, you want to show the band where the mess tent is?"

The look Alma shot me could've frozen the ocean, but it didn't matter a lick as she nodded. "Sure thing. This way, boys."

The genuine smile burned my cheeks after hours of faking it, but as they walked off with Creole and Alma talking, the pain was worth it. I headed back into the dressing room tent.

"Good show?" Marshall asked as he came in carrying the same old dinner of rice, beans, and hard tack. We ate like real kings here.

"Yeah, only a few talked all poppycock," I said with a shrug. "How was it out front?"

"Not quite a penny-lot day, but close. Don't know if Dad even made it here to talk up the show. We aren't going to turn any kind of profit if it keeps like that."

"Well, once we get that new addition to the show, we'll be rolling in it."

"What new addition?"

"The skeleton. That ought to bring in some big money. We just got to collect it."

"You've got a skeleton to collect," he said. "I don't have anything to do with that."

"At least come with a horse and lantern or something. I don't need you to carry anything."

"Hazel, I'm going to town to look for Dad. You do whatever you want with the skeleton."

"Fine, then get out so I can change. I'm not wandering through the woods in my slip." If Marshall wanted to leave the hard work to me, then I'd be taking the credit for it once Dad got back.

Marshall gave an exaggerated bow before he left. I rolled my eyes before dressing in a pair of Marshall's pants and one of his shirts. The town folk wouldn't much care for a woman in a man's outfit, but what they didn't know wouldn't ever hurt me.

I grabbed the oil lantern and headed for the horse stable, grabbing one of the old mares, good at hauling. If I couldn't get something together to bring the skeleton back, then I'd have to spend my whole night dragging it back piece by piece.

But I was sure I could do it. I just needed to focus. I didn't need Dad here. I could show him I could do anything I wanted without him having to worry about much of anything. He didn't need to hold my hand and tell me what I could and couldn't take on. I'd dropped a troll by myself and now I was going to turn a profit on its bones.

I ran the horse a bit harder than I should've, but we made it to the clearing, and the lantern gave just enough light. But even if I'd been in pitch black, I could follow the feeling of the troll against my mind. Spirit and body might have been separated, but they, sure as the devil, were aware of one another. Like a homing pigeon, the spirit of the troll pointed me straight and true to the bones.

I hopped down out of my saddle and circled around the skeleton. While all the muscle and tendons piecing it together had rotted away with the loss of the spirit, the bones remained. Trolls were made of earth, so their physical bodies didn't always melt away. At least that's what Daddy had always said about trolls. I'd never run into one before, and that meant all this was uncharted for me.

Most of the other bodies I'd seen had been faeries or sprites, a few nymphs and animal-sized critters but nothing that was anywhere the size of this. We always just buried the bones and gave it a prayer to set it to rest. But I got to do my own thing this time. That meant no more hiding what I could do, what was out there in the world. We showed off the extremes of nature, and I'd be a fool to not profit off the ones I hunted.

The troll wasn't hard to hear. Unlike most of the other spirits, it hung close to the surface, filled with rage. The second I reached for it, it lurched back with a hunger that ripped my skin open as the troll rushed from my tattoo, spilling more blood than anything else ever had. I caught myself on the tree and winced as I looked up at the spirit looming over me.

A trail of blood ran from my tattoo to the monster now above me. I took a deep breath. "Pick it up," I commanded.

My voice sounded a lot firmer than I felt leaning against the tree, bleeding.

I felt the resistance slam into me like a chair in a bar fight. Wheezing, I stood up straighter and pictured my mind like a steel beam just like Dad had taught me. Nothing was stronger than me. Certainly not some troll dumber than a splat of mud.

"Pick it up," I said again, gritting my teeth and digging my feet into the ground. "You listen to me now."

It lurched toward me with a roar, but I didn't budge. Slowly I felt it give, and the troll moved, beginning to collect its pieces and bundling them into its arms like a broken baby doll. It struggled with holding all the parts, but I managed to get the smaller ones gathered up on the wagon I'd brought with me. Now we were in business to get back to the camp in one trip.

The troll wobbled slowly across the uneven wooded ground. Every few steps, the troll would drop something, and we'd have to work on it all over again. I sighed and finally hopped off my horse and looked at it. If only I could just…put the bones back inside the spirit.

Could I do that?

First, I had to figure out how to get this big troll to listen to me enough to do the impossible.

I took a deep breath and stood up straight and tall as I could. Any time I pressed too hard against the troll's spirit hanging around my head, I could feel the blood seeping faster out of me. Not a sensation I was real keen to keep happening.

Its soul hung in the corner of my mind, heavy and sulking like a kid who just dropped his last piece of candy. Maybe this thing really just needed to be treated more like a toddler than anything else. I wasn't great with kids, but I could make an exception for thirty-foot-tall, foul-smelling, supernatural one.

Looking up at the spirit, I pointed at it. "Put that down."

The troll looked at me for a second before dropping its arms, and all the bones clattered down to the ground. I jumped to the side to avoid a falling femur but managed to keep my footing and took a breath.

"Put your bones back on," I said.

The troll titled its head and that angry fullness slammed into the edge of my mind. It wanted to destroy—destroy me and everything around me. It didn't want to listen, to do anything I had to say about any of this, but I still had to try.

I closed my eyes and forced my mind to concentrate on what I wanted. I imagined the bones returning to their right spots and played that image on loop in mind. Every time I felt the troll's rage rise, I focused harder on that image until it turned into a looping photograph in my mind. Not even the pain flaring in my arm could do much to stop my focus.

My will is stronger than anything you can do to me.

When I opened my eyes, the troll's spirit stood in front of me. But this time, through the transparent body of the beast, I could see the outline of a skull bone, a rib cage, a series of bones all floating in spirit goop built from my magic.

I got back on my horse, and we started back for the camp. The troll's footsteps rumbled but stayed steadily behind me like a thirty-foot shadow made of blood and bones. A strange thing to see and I hoped that the rest of the camp would forgive my display, and better yet, I hoped most of them would be sound asleep and not see a thing. Most everyone knew about me and Dad's line of work, but I didn't fancy a lecture about not doing this kind of thing without Dad here to help.

With this system, we moved a whole lot faster, and when we got nearer to the camp, I tried to get the troll to quiet its steps, but there wasn't a whole lot that would quiet something that big slamming into the ground.

As we made it to camp, I decided to give it up. My arm burned, and I could feel wooziness creeping up on me. "Release." I waved my arms.

The troll looked at me and didn't vanish immediately. Instead, it began charging me.

"Release!" I said again, firmly picturing the spirit falling apart in front of me even as I closed my eyes and braced to be crushed.

I didn't have to open my eyes to confirm it'd worked. The slamming of bones to the ground answered that for me. I felt the spirit slinking back into my skin. It oozed slowly though, not like Puck or the other small spirits. It moved with the speed of a traditional ink and needle tattoo. The bleeding had stopped, but the mark had only partially returned.

I shook my head, no time to worry about whatever was happening there. I had to get to town and find Dad and give him a talking to.

CHAPTER TWO

Back in my cabin, I washed off the blood, wrapped the new tattoo, and got out of Marshall's old clothes. I put on a clean dress and boots and was off to town in just a few minutes. With my high collar and long-sleeves, I looked like just any other woman from the area. My disguise let me walk in both worlds.

I found Marshall in the only bar in town, sitting with a bunch of men in a den filled with cigar smoke that hung heavy and thick. I walked to the table and cleared my throat. The men looked up from their cards; a pile of money sat in the middle of the table.

"Well, hello there, darling," one of the men said with a leer. "Come here all on your own?"

"I came here to give my brother some company," I said, and took a seat up beside Marshall.

Marshall glanced at me.

"I ain't playing with a woman," another of the men said.

"I'm not playing, just watching," I said with a smile. "You don't want to show me what you can do?"

He sat up a little straighter. "Well, you're going to see the game played right then."

Men were always predictable when it came to responding to a

pinch of ego stroking. They always moved in whatever direction I pushed, and I wasn't even wearing my lipstick tonight.

The men dealt out a new hand, and I leaned back to look over Marshall's hand.

"Where's Dad?" I asked Marshall.

"Your brother was just asking that, too. We saw him just about a week ago, I reckon. He headed east on a train in a hurry."

"Headed to where?" I asked.

"Didn't get the chance to ask him. Left so fast he didn't even grab his case."

"Where is it?" I asked.

"Hotel down the street."

"Well, we should go collect that then. Marshall folds," I added, tugging on Marshall's arm.

Marshall groaned, and the men on the table laughed as he followed after me.

"I was going to get it," Marshall muttered.

"Before or after you lost your wages?"

"I know how to play poker." He shoved his hands in his pockets. "I thought you had work tonight."

"Already done. See? I work fast."

Marshall snorted as we walked into the same hotel Dad always visited when we came through here.

"Mister Finnegan!" The desk clerk greeted Marshall as soon as I walked in. He didn't even glance at me.

"I heard my father left some things," I said.

The man looked at me, then to Marshall like I hadn't just said something. "Is there something I can help you with, Mister Finnegan?"

"I believe my father has a case he left behind."

"Of course. I'm happy to release that to you once his account has been settled."

"Dad never leaves something unpaid," I said.

"This is a civilized establishment and not a place for unchaperoned little dears," the man said, glaring at me.

I bristled and took a deep breath, but Marshall patted my hand. "Hazel, wait outside."

"Marshall—"

"Hazel. This isn't a place for a lady," he said. "Now get out. I'll see you out front."

I reached for the moon Faerie along my thigh, but the sting flickered, and the spirit didn't rise to my call. *What in the blue damn?*

I didn't say anything to Marshall or that man and walked out front. I traced my hand ros my sleeve where the troll tattoo lingered on my skin just out of sight under the cotton fabric. I tried again to free Puck, but nothing flickered to life in my mind. Could I run out of power? That'd never happened before.

I paced the front of the shop before Marshall walked out carrying Dad's trusty steamer trunk. He never left without it, but something clearly had chased him off in a hurry.

"What's in the case?" I asked.

"Haven't looked yet. Didn't want that clerk looking over my shoulder."

I snorted. "Yeah, thanks for sticking up for me in there."

"Making an enemy of the man with Dad's case don't seem like a bad idea to you?"

I fell silent as we started the trek back to the show.

"You don't think he'd put anything dangerous in there, do you?" Marshall asked.

"Dad carried weird stuff. There's no telling."

Marshall dragged case straight back to his wagon. We crowded around the small table, and Marshall popped the lock.

On top sat Dad's journal, the thing he took notes about every supernatural thing we ran across. Then there was a pack of clothes and a strange container that looked like it was filled with ash.

"Ever seen that before?" Marshall asked me.

I took the bottle from him and examined it. "Nope. Never. Where did Dad even get this?"

"Don't know, but he thought it was important enough to keep in here."

"Not important enough to take with him wherever he went, though."

"Must've been in a hurry. Maybe trying to beat a storm?"

"He would've left us a message at the hotel. Besides, he was supposed to meet us and get Ruth all trained up to take over being front man so Dad could travel with us. We need to go after him."

Marshall sat on the edge of his bed. "We're committed to finishing our shows here, Hazel. We aren't going on some goose chase."

"This is just an all-around muddle," I said as I dug through the rest of the trunk.

I flipped through the journal but just saw the same old sketches and notes that'd been in there for ages. "There's no way he just left for no reason," I said, looking up at Marshall. "He wouldn't have left this behind."

Marshall looked at me. "What is that?"

"Everything Dad knows about monsters is in here. He doesn't go anywhere without it."

"Well, maybe something came up at home."

"He would've left us a note."

"You got a book in your hands. That looks like he left a note to me."

I thumbed to the back of the book and the most recent entries. There was a whole section on the gowrow we'd run into last time we'd visited Arkansas and then a few new notes.

"Smell and tracks look like a troll is out here. Need to locate its den."

Done and done, Dad.

Below that, in a corner of the page, he'd scribbled, "Found charred bones. Teeth marks burned into the bone. Not natural."

I flipped the page over and found a sketch of the woods around us and then some basic directions. His sketch of the woods contained what looked like a magic circle someone had made with rocks and thick black marks. Strange symbols I'd never seen before. Dad had drawn them out to the side and even he had a few question marks around most of them except for the rune in the center of the circle. Beside that one, he'd simply written, "hell."

Was someone trying to open some kind of Hell portal in the

middle of the woods? Trolls weren't Hell-based—they were all about earth—so that couldn't be connected, could it?

"Find anything?" Marshall asked.

"Dad found a circle in the woods."

"And? He probably dispelled it."

"I don't think so." I turned the book toward Marshall.

He picked it up, and his frown soon matched mine. "Is that...you don't think someone was trying to open a hell portal, do you?"

"I don't know. It's possible," I said.

"But why?" Marshall asked.

That I didn't have a real good answer for because I couldn't think of any reason anyone would want to give the devil a ring.

"I've got to go find it."

"Not tonight," Marshall shook his head.

"Marshall."

"Look, I'll go with you at first light. Christ, we'll have Jonah come, too. But not tonight. If someone's playing with circles and Hell, walking into that in the pitch-black night ain't a real good idea."

I had to admit he had a point.

"Fine. First thing when the sun comes up."

"Yeah, yeah. I'll get you up with coffee. Morning's aren't your strong suit."

"I didn't become a hunter for the early morning hours."

"I don't think we are going to figure it out just from his case. We don't have enough information for that. We just have to keep on the path he's planned out for us," Marshall said.

"We need to find out where he's going," I said. "Something's wrong, and he probably needs us."

"If something's wrong, he might need you, Hazel. He doesn't need the whole show."

The big bone between us. He wanted to be the hunter, but Death had picked me from the moment I was born. We'd been together ever since then, and somehow fate had very different plans for us, even though we were twins.

Sometimes I wondered if Constance and Temperance had their own troubles as twins. Then again, I couldn't imagine being connected to Marshall always and never having a second alone. That probably explained the twins' drinking habits. I'd sure drink until I forgot everything if I spent every day sharing the same space with the same face every single second of my life.

"So what? You want me to just hop on a train and leave you out here alone? You know those monsters are attracted to places of magic. Our show draws those things, and if something shows up without me here...I don't think Alma and the singing Duncans are going to be much help."

"I've got a pistol and silver bullets."

"You want me out of here that bad?"

"We leave now and take off after Dad and we lose money. No one gets paid. We already live on hard tack. I don't want to stretch that anymore."

"Well, that's why we've got a genuine troll skeleton to show off now."

Marshall leaned back in his chair and pulled a cigarette from his coat. He lit up and let out a slow smoke-filled breath. "Charge an extra nickel to see the bones?"

"At least."

He chuckled. "If we can get that, we'll be doing good."

"The big shows don't come around here much. We're the best entertainment these folks are ever going to see."

"We're the best something alright," Marshall said. "Now, go on out of here. You ought to sleep if we're going hellhole hunting in the morning."

"I'm taking Dad's journal. If I find anything else, I'll let you know."

"Don't stay up all night reading," Marshall said as he put out his cigarette.

"Goodnight." I tucked the book under my arm and headed into my own wagon.

Unlike Marshall's wagon filled with ledgers, weapons, bandages, and clothing filled mine. I went through clothes fast, most of them bloody from hunting trips. Then I had all the fancy slips and swimsuits to wear for the show themselves and then the dresses for when I had to go into town as a normal woman and not get all the attention of a freak. So far, the spirits had been kind, and nothing had burrowed home above my collarbone or past my wrists.

I poured myself a finger of whiskey from a bottle the twins had given me and downed it to help get me to sleep. Dad always said the more color my skin got, the harder it'd be to sleep, but until tonight, none of the spirits had ever really bothered me. Now here I sat with a pissed off troll annoying the hell out of me when I just wanted to sleep.

After another few fingers of whiskey, sleep snuck up on me like a chair to the back of the head. I woke up with Marshall standing above me. "Jesus, how much did you have last night?" He looked at the bottle.

"Enough to sleep," I muttered, trying to ignore the pounding in my brain. At least the headache seemed to be beating that troll quiet.

Marshall passed me a cup, and I sipped at the warm coffee and sighed.

"Let me get dressed," I said.

He tossed Dad's suitcase at me. "Dad's got a whole wardrobe for you in here. Borrow his clothes. I don't have time to get mine washed up after you bleed all over them."

"I'll meet you at the horses in a minute," I muttered.

Marshall nodded and left me alone. I got dressed in Dad's clothes, the smell of tobacco, smoke and blood melded into his singular scent, and I let out a long breath. I felt like I wore a piece of his soul with me in those clothes. They hung bigger than Marshall's, but the looseness felt comfortable, and it wasn't nothing a good belt couldn't keep up. I got on boots and finally headed out to meet Marshall for some circle hunting.

CHAPTER THREE

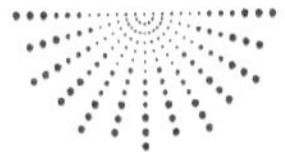

Beside my brother stood Jonah, our armless wonder.

"Morning, Jonah," I said.

"Oh, good morning, Miss Hazel," Jonah said and bowed his head.

He wore boots, one of the only times I'd seen him in shoes. His performance in the show meant displaying all the dexterity in his toes.

"I thought Jonah might be a bit of help today."

"Yeah?"

"If you want someone who knows the Lord's word frontwards and back, he's your man," Marshall said.

A flush of pink rose to Jonah's cheek. "I wouldn't say that."

"You alright hiking around with us? It might get dangerous."

"I'll be fine," he said.

Since the Bible wasn't exactly my first language, having someone who knew about Heaven and Hell probably wouldn't hurt when hunting down a hell portal.

"You think you can find this place?" Marshall asked.

I looked at Dad's journal. "Easy. We'll be back before lunch."

Marshall and Jonah didn't look convinced. We all got onto our horses, Marshall and Jonah riding together while I took the lead.

Thankfully Dad had always been pretty good at directing the way, so his maps pointed us right. In a few places, I even found scraps of fabric tied around branches, pieces I recognized from Dad's travel pack. He always said you could never have too many things to mark a trail. He hadn't skimped, and I resisted my urge to pull the fabric from the trees. I'd need to find my way back here, and that meant leaving up the pieces of my father to mark the way.

"Dad definitely came through here," I said.

Marshall nodded. "Yeah but look how faded these are. They've been here through at least a storm."

"Maybe," Jonah said. "But that doesn't mean a long time. It is summer, storms come out of nowhere."

"They're recent," I said. I didn't really believe that, but I needed to say it, to put the words out into the universe and hope that it listened.

Following the trail with Dad's markers was easy, and we made better time than I thought. At this rate, we'd be there just after the sun finished rising. Thankfully, not many clouds blocked the sun, so we had a clear view of where we were going. If it kept up like this, I bet we could be home in time to get some help setting up the bones into something that would be worth a nickel. We had to abandon the horses when the woods got too overgrown, but we made good time. Soon we found the clearing Dad described.

Most of the markings were starting to fade, but for being at least a week old, they were darker on the ground than they had any right to be. Up close, the markings looked clearly like burns as though something had scorched set patterns across the ground.

I let out a long breath and knelt down to touch the markings. "It's warm." I looked at Marshall. The warmth felt like the fevered brow of a kid, like something alive.

"What? That doesn't make sense."

"Well, you can come tell it that." I stood up.

Jonah sat down on a rock at the edge of the clearing and began kicking off his shoes.

"Hey, you're going to get splinters being barefoot out here," I told him.

Jonah smiled. "I have soles of steel, Miss Hazel. Besides I want to feel these markings."

"Suit yourself."

The boys walked to the markings, sticking to the edge of the circle. None of us had chanced crossing it yet. We all knew better than to enter a strange circle.

Marshall knelt down and put a hand on one of the marks. "You're right."

Jonah moved his feet with an elegance that made me feel oafish; he had more grace in his big toe than I'd been blessed with in my whole body. He frowned as he traced the mark. "This does look like an old sign once used as a greeting."

"Great. So, we've got a circle just saying hello." I crossed my arms.

"The markings inside, however, those are clear markings of the devil." Jonah pointed.

I pulled Dad's book out. On a blank page near his drawing, I began sketching out the other symbols.

"You haven't seen anything like this before?" Marshall asked.

"If I had, I wouldn't be letting you bully-rag me," I said. "Anything else, Jonah?"

"I believe this was made by someone trying to reach into Hell."

"Alright but did Hell reach back?" Marshall asked.

"Those markings are warm. I'm guessing the devil stopped in for dinner," I said.

"Those who sup with the devil best have a long spoon," Jonah said.

"Do what?" I asked.

"The devil doesn't grant bargains in anyone's favor but his own. Anyone willing to make this kind of summoning best hope the light of God protects them."

"Right." I rubbed the back of my head. "Dining with the devil's not my thing."

"Who would know more about these, then?" Marshall asked.

"I don't know. Dad...only took me to things based from the earth, not Heaven or Hell or wherever."

"The devil could be loose in Arkansas and you don't know?"

"I doubt it's the devil, Marshall. We'd probably have run into him by now."

"The devil doesn't work in regular ways, Miss Finnegan," Jonah said.

"Yeah, but I doubt the devil is going to make it real far without generating some attention. We'd have heard something!"

"Maybe," Jonah said. "But the devil plays a long game. If he is here, then his presence will be known eventually."

"Okay, but right now, we can get rid of this, at least," I said.

"Breaking a circle that's not yours isn't a great thing to do. Isn't that what Dad said?"

"Yeah, but leaving it like this? Stones all warm and probably still active? Worse idea."

"I can try to help," Jonah offered. "A prayer, perhaps?"

"Sounds good," I said.

I didn't much care for having the Lord's word tossed around like some kind of shield, but I'd never dealt with a summoning, let alone something from Hell, so might not be a bad time to call in some bigger help.

Any help you've got to offer, Lady Death, would be real welcome right about now.

But, as usual, my benefactor kept silent. The closest I had to anything heavenly was Cupid—fat, balding, and a terrible shot—but better a cherub than nothing.

The little Cupid on my shoulder pinched as it fled my skin and materialized at my side. Jonah took a breath and stepped back.

The cherub, for once, focused straight on the task at hand. I closed my eyes and let my mind slide into the cherub's body. Together, we moved forward, flying to the edge of the circle. I braced as the barrier was crossed.

Fire flared out from the center of the circle.

The cherub vaporized immediately, and I slammed back into my body, dizzy as flames licked my arm.

"Hazel!" Marshall yelled, but I'd fallen forward, into the circle, and fire flared around me, separating me from Jonah and Marshall.

I winced and moved toward the center of the circle. Trapped by my own poor planning, the story of my life. In the center of the circle burned one large stone with a sigil in it I didn't recognize.

The fires circled in tighter, closing in around me. Burning alive would be one hell of a way to go.

"I am not dying here," I said clenching my fists.

Some circle cast by a demon would not be the end of Hazel Finnegan. I let out a long breath and raised my fist. I barely felt the pain or the blood drip down my arm as I slammed my fist, my fist backed by a troll, into the stone. It shattered as I pummeled it into the dirt.

The fires died around me as I panted for air.

"Hazel."

I turned to Marshall who looked at me with something I'd never seen on his face before: fear.

The power fled my body, and I hit the ground on my knees. Blisters popped along my hand from ripping through the fire, guess troll skin didn't translate into spirit form.

My breathing hammered through me as I brought my hand to my face, wiping blood dripping from my nose.

"Hazel!" Marshall rushed to my side, Jonah just behind him.

"Are you alright?" Jonah asked.

I nodded. "All a treat."

Jonah moved over to me and made the sign of the cross with his foot in front of me. When I didn't burst into flames or scream in pain, he seemed satisfied I wasn't possessed or something.

"We should get back. We've got to get ready for the shows," Marshall said.

"Yeah, alright," I said, looking at the cracked stone in the center. The symbols had faded to almost nothing by now. Hopefully that had gotten rid of whatever might be going on.

We walked back to the horses, and the ride back happened in silence.

CHAPTER FOUR

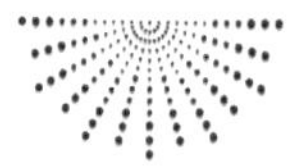

Back in camp, I headed straight to the skeleton to make sure it got laid out right for the afternoon shows.

"What did you do to bring this thing down?" Alma leaned against an arm bone. She looked downright petite next to the troll remains.

"Little bit of this, little bit of that." I shrugged.

Alma shook her head. "That I would've liked to see."

"Maybe next time I'll see if you want to tag along," I said.

"Yeah, I don't know how much that would have helped. Picking up a man, no problem. Dealing with whatever that was?" She motioned to the bones. "Not really my thing."

"Well, you at least got to help lay it out. Foot bone connected to the leg bone?"

"Yeah, putting it together wasn't that hard. It might be big, but it looks close enough to a man."

"You seen a lot of skeletons?"

"Don't you want to know?" Alma smiled. "Good showing yesterday?" she asked.

"Good enough. Only one called me a gaff."

"I haven't had any try that here," Alma said. "Which is a damn shame. I could use a new volunteer to pick up."

"Oh, I'm sure some fool will open his fool mouth, and you'll get your wish."

"Maybe. But, unless there's anything else you need moved around…" She motioned to the bones. "Then I'm going to start getting ready. You ought to, too. You don't want any of them townsfolk seeing you dressed like a man."

I looked down at my pants and sighed. "Yeah, yeah."

"Look at least you get something that looks like regular clothes. I got to wear that animal wrap the twins cooked up."

"Well, you'd have a hard time lifting anything if you were wearing a full skirt."

She shook her head. "It's all for the show of it."

"We sell people things they want to believe. Whether it's true or not is up to them."

"See, I don't quite believe that."

"That's because your act is real."

"Yeah but the story behind it sure ain't."

"Neither is mine. Prisoned and tattooed against my will?"

"It's different."

"I know," I said and patted Alma's back. I couldn't quite reach her shoulder to offer a comforting hand there.

"How many marriage proposals you got this time?" she asked.

"I haven't asked Marshall yet. No one's asked me."

"They'll go to your brother first."

"And that's why they never get a yes." I smiled.

"One of these days the brother of yours might just surprise you."

"And he'll be dealing with a runaway show if that happens. I ain't the marrying type."

"Yeah?"

"Course. Never have been, never will be."

"See, I been thinking that it might be time for me to put this up and settle down."

"Yeah? With someone named Creole?" I asked with a smirk.

She laughed then shook her head. "It's hard being out here like this all the time. Being gawked at all the time, by everyone."

"Well, it's just the show—"

"No, it isn't just the show for me. See, you put on a pretty dress, and you're just another lady. It doesn't matter what I wear, it doesn't change my skin; it doesn't change my height. I live with everyone looking at me."

I put my hands back and took a breath. "Yeah...well, at least at the show they got to pay for it."

She snorted. "That's at least something."

"If you really wanted to leave..."

"I would. I didn't say I was packing up and leaving right now. I just said I'd been thinking about it. It might be nice to not always have to be a spectacle. Settle in some cabin somewhere. Have a farm maybe."

"You'd get bored."

"Yeah, but that might be nice. It's never boring with you around, that's for sure."

"And you like it."

Alma laughed and elbowed me a little before she stood up straighter. "Alright, but really, I got to go get ready. You ought to—you got dirt on your face. Can't have the tattooed beauty with smudges on her check."

"And can't have the African Giantess in a full dress."

She smiled and nudged me again before she left for her wagon, the biggest on site to accommodate her height.

I headed into my wagon and got myself cleaned up. Changing into a swimsuit, I looked myself over in the mirror before finishing up my makeup, adding the perfect, slightly scandalous amount of red lipstick before I declared myself done and went to find Marshall.

He stood in the tent with the skeleton, staring at it.

"Impressive, right?" I asked.

Marshall looked at me. "When you said it was big...I didn't think you meant this big."

"Don't know what part of troll you were misunderstanding," I said, crossing my arms.

"How are we going to transport this anywhere, Hazel?"

"We'll figure it out. We'll make a killing with it! We can even get one of Dad's old professor buddies to come talk about it once we get near New York."

"Aren't we supposed to not reveal this kind of stuff to the world? Keep the magic hidden."

"The bones don't have any magic in them aside from being big. It's not like they're going to sit up and curse someone all on their own, Marshall. You just need to come up with the story to sell the tickets."

"That's my job. You did yours; now it's my turn." Marshall ran a hand along a rib bone. "Dad would be impressed."

"Yeah, I think so."

"Got some of the guys painting up a sign for it. Nickel to see the giant."

"I could stay here, talk it up."

"Not happening."

"I can tell the best story about this," I argued.

"Go on and get into place. The show's about to start," Marshall said, opening the tent flat for me.

"Of course, boss," I said and stomped to my designated spot in the main hall.

Outside, Marshall's voice rang clear as he instructed our roustabouts to get a tent up high enough to block the skeleton from view.

I stood on the stage, pacing a bit as Alma took her place across from me. She offered a smile, but I was pretty sure she was aiming it at Creole. Temperance and Constance staggered in looking like they'd lost a fight with the sandman. The circles under their eyes needed their own luggage. I'd seen the twins enough to recognize a hangover when I saw one.

Jonah stopped in front of my area as I hopped onto my swing.

"Did you find out anything else about that circle?"

"No. Haven't been back out there since I broke it up."

"I was just looking over my Bible this morning. If you want to go back out there, I think we could try to bless the area."

"Chase out whatever bad's hanging around?"

"Maybe."

Jonah nodded and hopped into his area, sitting in an old chair and picking up the paper to read. After seeing it for the three years Jonah'd been traveling with us, seeing him turn pages with his toes looked normal.

Everyone here was normal to me. Some days I had a hard time even keeping a straight face during the grand stories told about us all. No regular histories allowed, we all lived in a fairytale book that sold tickets to the show. But hey, people liked our stories, and we all made enough money to survive by slinging lies, so it worked out for the best near as I could tell. I did always wonder how a righteous man like Jonah was alright with peddling lies, but I wasn't about to ask.

Marshall's voice rose above faintly rumbling thunder. "Ladies and gentlemen, we have the show to end all shows for you today. Ten, count them, ten attractions, bizarre, beautiful, and strange, all waiting for you. For just a dime, yes, one dime, all ten attractions are yours. And for the strong of stomach and brave of heart, we have a once in a lifetime creature so monstrous we had to hide it away. For just a nickel, you can see this once in a lifetime mystery: a true giant."

Since our tent stayed empty, I peered out between the seams and watched the small crowd start slapping down money to get their tickets to head inside and see my handiwork. Mostly men, like usual, but they seemed more buttoned up like they might be running to church right after this. Not that those shiny shoes would last for a second with the rain building outside. It thundered against the tent, and I prayed that the tent would hold. The last thing I wanted was buckets of rain pouring down on me. I might have worn a swimsuit to show off my tattoos, but I didn't want any part of putting that to actual use in water.

When people began spilling into our tents, Alma's handler began his spiel to the crowd in front of her as Alma demonstrated her strength with a few of the weights around her stage area. I hoped one of the men would say something, call her some kind of gaff. Those were the best to watch as she'd hoist them up and let them squirm in the air as she proved her point without a word.

A small group of men meandered my way, pausing in front of the stage. I offered a smile. "Hey fellows," I said in my sweetest voice.

"What's a lady like you doing all marked up showing yourself off like some animal?"

Ruth stepped up, but I just put a hand to his shoulder.

"Well, it's for fine men like yourself. You came here to see me, didn't you?"

A few of the men cleared their throats and twisted the rings on their fingers. The guilt of a married man made this job more fun than it had any right to be.

"Did you want to see all of the tattoos?" I asked.

"This isn't all of them?" one man asked.

I smiled. "No. Did you want more?"

A few of the men shifted like something tickled the bottom of their feet. Guilt and lust made men do some strange things.

"Is that extra?" the youngest-looking of the men asked.

"Not for y'all," I said in my sweetest voice. Draw them in with honey.

Ruth eyed me, but he kept quiet. The youngest man nodded, and his earnestness was almost charming. I almost felt bad, but I slowly turned around. "See? More on the back."

I could practically hear the sound of disappointment flooding out of them. Had they really thought I was just going to strip right here in the middle of the tent just for their enjoyment? Men.

"That's it?" one of the older men asked.

I felt a hand graze my thigh and turned around. "Not a one of you have permission to touch me."

I saw Alma stand up straighter and make eye contact with me. Funny how we could say so much without a single word being exchanged. *I'm good*, my eyes said, but Alma kept watch, waiting for a chance to come mess up some cocky man.

Ruth rolled up his sleeves and grabbed the man.

"Well, that was hardly the show you promised!" the man argued.

"The show I promised? That I had more tattoos to show you?" I asked, and leaned back. "If you're looking for a peep show, you have come to the wrong tent," I said. "We don't offer those kind of shows."

"Well, I never! I don't attend such…debauchery!" the same man argued.

"That isn't any way to speak to a lady," Ruth said, the threat clear in his tone.

"You're lovely. What's a girl as lovely as you doing here?" a younger man asked.

Aww, the sweet type wanting to save me from this terrible life. Sweet and annoying as hell. I would have to ask Marshall if this one came with a marriage request.

"I'm working," I said. "There are nine more acts for you to enjoy in this tent, gentlemen, and the skeleton of a giant. I suggest you keep moving."

"Do you want to get out of here?" the younger man asked.

"I'm real happy right where I am. Keep moving," I said and stepped back from them. Conversation over.

Ruth moved the men on to Jonah's show next. They didn't say a word about him being too handsome to be doing this type of thing.

I leaned against the edge of the stage and sighed. It was going to be a slow and annoying type of show that I hated. The kind of day that dragged forever without enough guests showing up to really make a difference and keep it from dragging into the whole lot of nothing that made some days unbearable. I didn't hate working at the shows at all, but days like today made me question if it would even be worth it if the weather kept up like this.

The rain continued, and the day dragged by slowly. But by the afternoon, the weather finally cleared. I could hear the people outside Marshall's tents, and the growing sounds of astonishment. Fewer and fewer people came into our tent, and eventually, I hopped off my stage and crept to the entrance. A crowd gathered around the tent with the bones of the troll. I knew it would do well and, boy howdy, was I right. I'd never seen a line like that before for any of our shows. Had word gotten into town about this already? There had to be something all about the amazing display that we'd just added. If we made it a permanent part, we'd be doing well for the whole thing and rolling it in. We just had to figure out a way to carry the bones from state to state. I couldn't very well summon up a troll to carry its whole skeleton across the country, though what a display that would be.

I crept up to the stage and hopped on to join Marshall. "And our lovely tattooed woman has come to help us with this crowd. Jewel of Ink, what do you have to say about this astounding exhibit?" he asked.

I half-glared at him. This whole selling thing wasn't my thing. My words weren't made of silk and lace; they were more made of blood and punches.

"It's something unlike anything you've ever seen."

Marshall nodded. "That's right. In fact, our delicate jewel here collapsed on the first time seeing it. So, this is only for the strong and brave men in the crowd."

I nearly punched Marshall right off the stage but instead forced a strained smile. That brought up a roar of activity as people paid for tickets and plowed into the tent. I glanced at Marshall, and he smiled. "Better than anything we've ever seen before," he said half to me and half to the audience.

I could tell from the crowds that we wouldn't need to worry about having the money to cover Dad's expenses and pay for the camp. We would be making bank. At this rate, we could probably cover a train ride back toward the east coast and not have to sling it along in our wagons. If that happened, we could follow Dad's path exactly, since he'd left on the train anyways.

I stood near the back of the stage, showing off my body while Marshall talked about the wondrous giant skeleton. Behind me, I could hear the groups gasping and then falling silent. Except for one older man with a voice like a rusty saw.

"This is a sign straight from Hell," the man said. "Like those damned hounds. The devil travels in these shows."

The devil might be performing with us, but I wanted to hear more about these hounds. Before I could follow after and eavesdrop further, Marshall called me over to display more of my skin.

Marshall enjoyed the crowds and handled them well, working the groups well through the afternoon and into the evening. It wasn't until late that the crowds finally left, heading back to their little homes in the city and we were left to count the money.

Marshall whistled low as he looked at the mounds of nickels and dimes. "Damn. Damn. This was the best show we've had, I think. The best by a long shot. I know that we are working on getting this thing all upgraded, and we're halfway there with just today's money. If we get another day like this, without the rain…then we have made more than we did all last month."

I whistled. "We could retire early with that kind of money."

"Yeah? You finally going to settle down with one of those men proposing?"

I rolled my eyes. "How many today?"

"Only two. I think only one was really serious about it, but…"

"And you told them back off?"

"Not in those words, but I'm not real fond of the idea of you marrying some man who just paid a dime to see you."

"I'm not marrying any fool," I said.

He laughed, and we shook hands. "Deal and I admit this was a good idea. Why didn't Dad do this stuff?"

"He wanted to keep all this whole monster thing not real obvious."

"Yeah, people were pretty freaked out about seeing this."

"But it's amazing. If we can keep displaying things like this everywhere? We'll have another tent at the next show that's nothing but bones of monsters."

"Not a bad idea…but I don't think you'll have ten new things by the time we head out of here. Not unless this place is just crawling with stuff."

I shook my head. "Nah, Dad was just here, so he couldn't have left too many things behind."

"He left that troll behind. Maybe testing you?"

"Yeah, I doubt that. Trolls aren't great first test material."

Marshall laughed. He looked like a new man, all light and air tonight instead of the usual heavy, earth-filled man who walked with the weight of a thousand worlds on his back.

I just was happy that he seemed to be relaxing a little. A tense, angry brother made for a terrible salesman, and that's what we needed more than anything right now. I could hold off a horde of demons, but selling tickets to a show? Not my thing at all. I needed him to help on how to do that and what to do to make townsfolk come in to see us working on our show.

"In the morning, we should get by the train station, see if we can figure out where Dad headed," I said.

"And see how much it'd be to take the whole circus with us on a train."

I looked at the pile of coins on the table and motioned to it. "I'm betting you're looking at using most of this."

"Well then, we'll have to double it tomorrow, and we'll be good to go," Marshall said. "When we go into town, we could take some of the acts with us, drum up some business."

"You can do that, but I'm just going to the train station and finding out what happened with Dad."

Marshall nodded like he heard me, but I could tell he was already deep in thought about what acts would make a good impression in the town and what he could get away with bringing into public. Me displayed in one of my show outfits would probably get me arrested for being indecent, Alma would cause all kinds of problems on account of her skin, and so it'd probably be Jonah, a safe, fun and a good attention-grabber.

"Well, you can do that and drum up some business, and I'll go by the train station. Want me to go tell Jonah he's going to town tomorrow so no wandering the woods tonight?"

He shook his head and stood up. "No, I'll talk to him." He smoothed his hair down. "But can you set up something to watch over those bones tonight?"

"What?"

"Just something little, so none of them walk off in the night?"

"I can do that," I said, not at all sure I could.

Marshall stood up to kiss my forehead. "Goodnight, Hazel."

"Night, Marshall."

I headed to the tent with the bones and walked around them. In the near pitch black of night with only the lights of the circus around, the bones looked even more otherworldly. Taller than some of our horses, the whole thing looked like an alien landscape.

I ran my hands along the femur and shuddered to think what that thing slamming down on me would have meant. I had killed this. Me, by myself, and if that wasn't worthy of celebrating, then I didn't know what would be. I couldn't wait to see the look on Dad's face when I told him about it. He'd probably be mad, but proud too. Besides, it's not like I went out looking for a troll to kill. Not my choice to get into it, but I sure as hell finished it.

I stepped into the center of the creature's rib cage and took a breath. In my mind, I reached out to Puck. He responded almost immediately. The benefit of being the first caught was that we'd gotten used to each other. Puck felt like family, or a pet, more than anything else by now. Puck flickered into view, sitting on top of a rib bone and looking down at me.

"Guard this tonight," I said.

Puck looked from me to the skeleton before floating down and crossing his arms. I could feel the resistance in my mind, but Puck was easy to navigate. "Don't wake me unless something happens," I said.

Puck began floating around the skeleton in waving patterns, criss-crossing the whole body, floating over, under, and through the massive remains.

I headed back to my wagon but paused by Jonah's door. Marshall'd probably gotten distracted counting money, and I didn't want to spring a trip to town on Jonah first thing in the morning.

My hand hovered at his door as I caught Marshall's laughter from inside the wagon. Who knew Jonah had a sense of humor? Shrugging my shoulders, I headed back to my place, hoping Puck as guard would work. The pain in my arm barely registered, and the blood barely flowed. Puck no longer cost as much of me. More like a paper cut than anything major. The closer I got to the spirits, the less blood they required. Dad could summon some without bleeding at all, and I knew one day I'd get to that point. One day soon if I had anything to do with it.

After hopping into my pajamas, I sat down on my bed with Dad's book. Thumbing through it, I looked for any kind of information about Dad fighting with a troll, but I didn't find any entries on that. Thinking over the patchwork of color on Dad's skin, I couldn't remember anything that even halfway resembled the mark the troll had left on me. Had I finally done something not even Dad had accomplished? I hoped so.

Flipping to the beginning of the book, I traced my fingers over Dad's name written at the front. A note from Mom, and the only piece of her I still had after she died giving birth to me.

My dearest,

May this book hold all the wonder in the world that you see at your fingertips and hold on your skin.

Love always,

Maggie

Dad sometimes told stories about Mom, but they might as well have been fairytales. I had no memory of her to draw on. Nothing. She'd died before I'd even entered the world. They'd had to cut me out of her to save me. Marshall, at least, got to live in a world where she existed, even if just for a little while. Not that he remembered it at all. It was hard to mourn someone you'd never met.

Dad blamed himself. If he hadn't been cursed with Lady's Death touch, maybe she wouldn't have claimed another soul from him. Whatever happened, Lady Death left her mark on me from the moment I was born. There was never a doubt about what I was and what I could do.

I closed the book and shoved it onto my desk before putting out my lanterns and closing my eyes. Trying to sleep with Puck still floating in my mind was challenging; he kept nudging at my mind just as I was about to drift to sleep. It was going to be a long night if I had to deal with that. Maybe I should have put out a more docile spirit, rather than one made of mischief and trouble. None of this worked really well, but I'd be damned if I told Marshall I couldn't do it. I closed my eyes and tried to force Puck to stop bugging me. Eventually, I managed to drift off.

A jolt of panic ripped me from sleep, and I dropped out of bed wheezing for air. I coughed and tried to catch my breath. For a second, I couldn't figure out what had happened before I scrambled to my feet.

Puck!

CHAPTER FIVE

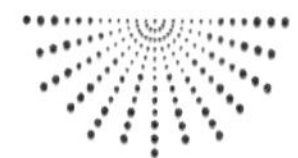

I scrambled out of my wagon and to the tent with the bones. Blue o'clock in the morning before the sun had even come out of the horizon. Bursting into the tent, I found no sign of Puck. At first glance, I didn't see anything wrong; nothing looked out of place. I rubbed my eyes and groaned. Had Puck just been joshing with me?

I stumbled around the entire skeleton, but finally, when I got to the hand, I noticed one of the finger bones missing. So now we had a four-fingered troll. I ran out the back of the tent but only found a faint set of paw prints that tinged the dirt black and almost burnt around the edges. Had some dogs gotten in here somehow? Puck wouldn't be great at defense against them.

I paced around before I moved to the other hand and adjusted the bones there too. If it was even on both sides, that should be fine. No one would ever know there were supposed to be two five-finger hands—they would only see the four fingers and never be the wiser. I just needed Marshall to not lose his mind about the change in anatomy.

I let out a long breath and groaned. I might've screwed this up... but no one would know any different aside from me and Marshall. I headed back for my wagon with the finger bone. Then I got dressed in some of my more appropriate clothes, a dress that hid all my tattoos.

"It's alright," I told myself as I looked over myself with my hand mirror. I tucked my hair back into a bun and sighed. I looked like a different person in this outfit, like I ought to be someone's wife, not a performer. I hated it.

Sitting and eating breakfast, I saw Marshall walk out of his wagon and into the tent with the troll bones. When he left, he headed straight for me.

Great.

"What happened?" he asked.

"I think a wild dog or wolf or something got a finger bone. I just evened it out. No one will know anything's wrong, okay?"

Marshall ran a hand through his hair and sighed. His telltale sign of being annoyed as sin.

"Alright, well we still need to go to town."

"I know. I'm ready whenever you are."

"Let me bring Jonah some coffee," he said.

I went back to my wagon and looked over Dad's book until Marshall was ready. It took about an hour. We fashioned up a wagon, and I sat in back with Jonah as Marshall handled the horse.

"Did you find anything else about that circle?" Jonah asked as we climbed into the wagon.

"No. Nothing else in Dad's book. You find anything in the Bible?"

"There's much to read about the devil in the words of the Lord," Jonah said. "But nothing about the thing you found."

"Well, seems to me I broke it, and that's all done now."

"The devil's reach is a spider web, not easily gotten rid of."

"Well, the easiest way to get rid of a spider is to crush it, so I think we're good," I said.

Jonah shrugged his shoulders. The gesture looked strange with no arms moving along with it, but it translated well enough.

"You sure it's alright to be showing off the show without charging?" I asked.

"We've got a skeleton to motivate people to come visit."

"Don't want my company?" Jonah asked.

"What? No, it's fine. You boys have fun wooing the crowds. I've got a train station to visit."

"We traveling by locomotion now?" Jonah looked to Marshall.

"We might. Mainly just need to see where Dad's gone."

"He's not following our route?" Jonah sounded concerned. We really didn't need to be bringing one of the performers into whatever was happening with Dad.

"Just figuring some things out," I said as we arrived to town. I barely let the wagon stop before I hopped out.

"See you fellows later," I told Marshall and headed off without waiting for a response.

The small train station held only one counter with a bored, balding man at the window. I took a breath and walked up to the counter. "Morning," I said.

"Hello, miss, can I help you?"

I put on my most charming voice. "I need your help."

"That's what I'm here for, ma'am," he said with a smile that oozed sleaze. *Great, just my luck.*

"My father left from here last week. I'm trying to find out where he went."

"I might have records of that," he said

"Oh, thank you. He left in a hurry, and I just want to make sure he's alright."

The man pulled out a massive book. "Your father's name?"

"Charles Finnegan," I said.

He put on a pair of glasses and ran his finger down the pages. "Dates of travel?"

"I think he left last Wednesday or Thursday," I said.

He looked down the list. "I see a C. Finnegan traveling the morning of Thursday."

"Great, where was he headed?"

"Memphis."

"Memphis, Tennessee?" We weren't supposed to be heading that far east for another month.

"Yes. ma'am. Did you want to purchase a ticket to the Memphis station? We have one leaving this afternoon."

"Uh no. Not today, sir," I said.

"Is there anything else?"

"Not right now. Thank you."

"Anything for you, ma'am. You come by and visit again real soon."

I forced myself to keep a smile as I backed away and hurried out of the depot. Marshall could deal with figuring out the cost of putting the whole circus on a train to Memphis.

But what was Dad doing? What had gotten into him? He couldn't be heading there to start advertising just yet; it was way too early.

I found Marshall easily in the city square. A small crowd had already gathered to listen to the elaborate origin story of Jonah. I made my way over to Marshall. He smiled, and I scooted closer as Jonah demonstrated rolling a cigarette.

"You can go talk to the train depot about transportation," I said.

"Why?"

"That counter guy gives me the creeps."

"Everyone gives you the creeps. Did you find anything out about Dad?"

"Bought a ticket to Memphis."

"What?"

"I know. I'm just telling you what the man said."

"He could have gotten off before Memphis."

"He could have," I said, but something in my gut said he'd ridden the train the whole way. Something about Memphis tingled against the back of my skull like I knew it was true even if I didn't want it to be. Dad always said being touched by Death gave you a second sense; maybe I ought to start finally listening to it.

"So we head that way?" I asked.

Marshall sighed heavily. "If Dad's not going ahead and telling people about us, we aren't going to have an audience. I'll figure out what to do."

After Jonah smoked a freshly rolled cigarette, Marshall took back to the stage. "Thank you all for watching our display. If you want to see more extravagant, amazing, incredible wonders of the world, our show begins at one this afternoon. For just a dime, you get to see ten wonders of the world right in your own backyard. From the tattooed beauty to the bones of a giant, our show will leave you in amazement."

I got back on the wagon in silence, and Jonah sat beside me, offering a cigarette. I took it, and we smoked during the ride back to camp.

When we got back to the camp, I let Marshall deal with getting the wagon unpacked while I went back to my room. I looked through Dad's book and tried to find any clue, but so far, there was nothing I could find that pointed to why Dad would go to Memphis.

I didn't care what Marshall wanted to do. My instincts screamed to go after him and not to just leave it well enough alone. Dad wouldn't have gone off for no reason and left no message. There had to be some clue somewhere, something pointing to why Dad left in a hurry, and I'd bet my whole season's wages that something was the circle I'd punched to pieces.

I didn't bother to change out of my dress as I grabbed a horse and headed back toward the circle. Despite not being familiar with the area, the path seemed almost ingrained in my mind.

Soon enough, I found the forest too thick to manage on horseback. I dismounted and tied the horse to a low tree. Patting her side, I promised to be back soon and headed deeper.

It felt like something else moved my feet. I didn't even stumble over roots or rock, as though I already knew the path.

The circle had faded more than the last time I'd been, but the main difference, aside from the center stone I'd cracked: the missing finger bone from the troll. Something had dragged it all the way here, and that couldn't be a coincidence.

I looked over the bone, spotting teeth marks burned into it. The marks were big, bigger than a about the size of a big wolf's, but wolf teeth didn't burn into bone like fire, whatever bit this, whatever dragged this to the circle, wasn't something natural. Now I wished I'd gotten the chance to follow that man talking about hounds from Hell at our show.

Another monster lurked around, and it was hungry for bones. I knew what I would be doing tonight, not leaving Puck to be my guard, but spending the night with the bones of a troll and watching to see what monster would be there. I'd have to check the book and see if Dad had anything about something that left burn marks like this.

I decided to leave the bone and not let this thing know I was onto it. It probably could smell me being here, but whatever it was didn't need a reason to come hunt me down just yet.

My plan decided, I headed straight back to the horse and pointed her back for the camp. I might be a little late for opening, but Marshall could get over it. I wasn't the star attraction by any means.

CHAPTER SIX

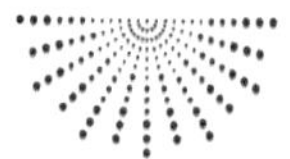

When I got back into the camp, crowds had already started to gather. The look Marshall shot me could have melted steel, but I didn't react to it as I went into my wagon and changed down to my slip before rushing into the tent.

"Cutting it a little close, aren't you?" Alma asked as I walked past her stage and to my own.

"I had stuff to do. Miss anything?"

"Nope, Marshall hasn't let anyone in yet. He's probably right angry with you."

"Yeah, what else is new?" I asked as I got onto my stage.

I could hear the telltale exchange of dimes for tickets, and then the crowds began wandering in. It felt like the same thing all over again, the gawking, the comments, the accusations of not being real, everything playing on repeat. Despite being on display in different cities across the country, the only thing that changed was the location and accents. People, no matter where we were, were the same. The questions, stares, comments, and requests rarely changed. There was always someone out trying to prove a point, to show off for the rest of the crowd.

By the time the shows were wrapping up, my cheeks hurt from

forcing a smile onto them for the whole day. All I wanted was to hide in my wagon and not speak to anyone. But that wasn't an option; instead, I had some bones to look out for. I grabbed a quick dinner, avoiding Marshall, and ate in my trailer.

After eating my dinner, I grabbed Dad's book, headed to the bones, and sat down on top of the femur. Not the most comfortable seat in the world, but being uncomfortable would help keep me up for the night. Dozing off wouldn't do to try to get rid of the monster, whatever it was.

I flipped through Dad's book and found a small section that talked about burning monsters. Fire spirits were an option, but I didn't think they had teeth like some kind of dog, and they usually existed in hot areas. While summer in Arkansas could be brutal, it wasn't exactly volcano-level hot. So that didn't seem like a likely choice. Then there was an option of some kind of wolf spirit. There were a lot of animal spirits that took on the shape of a wolf or a large dog, but none of them looked like they dealt with fire damage or burning just from their touch.

Great, a whole lot of nothing in Dad's book. For as long as Dad had been at this, I had hoped he'd have had more answers in there. Then again, Dad had never been the best at keeping up with his notes and works. I sighed and started writing in information about the bone and the burned bite marks. If Dad wouldn't take notes and keep things helpful, then I could at least work on that.

"What are you doing?" Marshall's voice jerked me from my bad sketch of the finger bone.

I closed the book and looked up. "Keeping an eye on things tonight."

"You can't stay out here all night."

"Unless you want us to be ending up with a three-finger troll skeleton, then someone ought to, so here I am."

"I can keep watch."

"Marshall, whatever is taking the bones is some kind of monster, not something you can deal with, so just go on to bed."

"I'm not leaving you out here on your own."

"I'm fine, Marshall. I don't need you."

He didn't answer and leaned against the other leg bone. I groaned and rolled my eyes. Why did Marshall think I was so incapable that I needed supervision? I'd been doing this with Dad for almost two years now. I knew what I was doing. Well, I knew more what I was doing than he did, and that was more than enough for me. I shook my head and went back to sketching.

"We made good money today," Marshall said after several long minutes of silence.

"That's good."

"Look, Hazel, I know you're mad."

"I'm not."

"Stop. Look, going to Memphis is going to put us off our whole planned tour. We don't know if we'll even have a spot to set up our camp."

"That's where Dad went."

"That's where he headed. We don't know if that's where he actually is now."

"I can feel it, Marshall. That's where he is."

Marshall sighed but didn't argue. He knew better than to question my feelings. I had the gut of the family while Marshall had the business sense, but my gut almost never led us astray. Even Dad trusted me when I said I had a feeling about something.

"Hazel…"

"Look, you don't have to go, but that's where I'm heading, with or without you and the rest of the circus."

"You're going to make Alma mad if you do that."

"She'll get over it," I said. "We've got to find Dad. You know it's not like him to just disappear like this. Even when we were living with Grandma and Grandpa, he would send us letters about where he was." I knew I was right, and I didn't care if Marshall didn't want to be part of that. I could take care of monsters on my own, but I didn't want to just leave Dad alone with whatever had sent him running.

"Fine, Hazel. Fine. We'll go to Memphis, but if this screws us, and we lose money…"

"We'll be alright," I said, sure that it wouldn't go quite like I planned, but I was committed to finding Dad if nothing else.

Marshall sighed and shook his head.

"You don't have to stand guard out here with me," I said.

"I'm not leaving you out here alone," he repeated.

"Whatever took the bones is probably not some normal animal."

"You don't know that. They're bones. Some normal wolf could be going after them."

"And I can handle a normal wolf. Just because you've got a pistol doesn't mean we need to be waking up everyone nearby with you firing it off."

Marshall crossed his arms and stayed where he was. Looked like I wasn't getting him out of here without a fight, and I didn't have the energy. Honesty, I'd love nothing more than going to bed early and calling it a night, but I needed to get to the bottom of what was going on.

"Marshall, go to bed."

"After you."

I sighed and flopped down on top of the femur.

I heard Marshall hoisting himself up and looked over to see him on top of the other femur. When the silence hung for a little too long, I broke it.

"Why do you think Dad took off like that?" I asked Marshall.

"Chasing something?"

"If he was chasing some monster, he'd be on a horse or something. Not train tracks."

"Unless he got word about something back east."

"But why wouldn't he wait for us?"

"I don't know," Marshall said. "But Dad knows what he's doing."

I looked at the book in my hands. "Yeah…" Some of the lack of information in there made me wonder just how together Dad really was. I'd always considered Dad able to handle anything, but in his book, he seemed almost as clueless as I was. Had he just been winging it this whole time? Guess I had a proud family tradition to uphold with making stuff up and making things work. I wondered if Lady Death ever regretted giving her gifts to the Finnegan family. Was she watching and just shaking her head regretting ever meeting my father?

In the back of my mind, the troll still lumbered around, heavy against my thoughts, but now I'd gotten used to it there, waiting and hanging in the corner. It felt like I had a large bear who had taken up residence in my mind, but in time, I bet I could get that bear to dance and do tricks just like I'd seen at the Ringling shows.

"I can't believe you killed something this big," Marshall said.

"I know."

"Dad would be impressed."

"Oh, he'd probably have some comment about a better way to do it."

"Yeah, he would. I'm sure he'd have all kinds of things to say about the way I'm doing things."

"When doesn't he have stuff to say?" I asked.

"He means well."

"Intention doesn't always mean a whole lot."

"You sure whatever it was that stole the bone will be back tonight?" he asked.

"There's not a guarantee, but I think it will."

"Why?"

I chewed on my lip about to tell Marshall about finding the bone in the middle of the hell circle when a branch snapped near the tent. Marshall and I both sat up. I looked at him, and he nodded. Every once in a while, our twin powers flared up. It wasn't like the summoning; it was subtler, more like a whisper than anything else.

I called Puck. He floated down to the floor and landed. His unease burrowed in my skin as he moved around the bones and toward the sound.

CHAPTER SEVEN

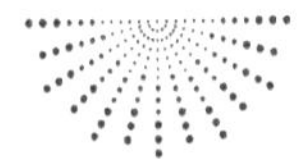

It barely took a second, but something snapped, and Puck slammed back into my body. I groaned, and Marshall hopped down. Shit. Whatever just got Puck had grabbed a bone and sprinted for the woods with Marshall right behind it. I caught a glimpse of is a large, bear-sized shadow. I scrambled down from the bone, grabbed the lantern, and took off into the woods after Marshall and the creature. If that thing hurt Marshall…

The trail sounded like an elephant making a drunken stampede through the forest. Trees, branches, and dirt snapped and cracked, spewing everywhere as Marshall pursued the thing and I followed.

The darkness pooled around me, broken only by the swaying lantern at my hip. "Marshall!?" I called.

"Over here!"

I shoved through the tree branches and found my brother on a stump with his hand on a scratch along his forearm. It didn't look too bad.

"What did that?" I asked.

"Wolf, I think."

The edges of his cut looked a little singed.

"Get back to the camp," I told Marshall.

"What?"

"Get back to camp," I said, pulling out my dagger.

"Hazel—"

"Go!" For an instant, I felt like I sounded just like Dad.

I needed to deal with this and get answers without having to worry about Marshall.

"I'm not going anywhere," Marshall snapped.

"Then stay out of the way at least," I said, continuing on the path without waiting for Marshall.

Whatever this thing was, it left a path clear as day even in the dark of night. The bone it dragged left a solid line, pointing the way exactly where it'd gone. Even in the brief spots when the line disappeared, there was still damage to the trees around it. This thing wasn't even bothering trying to be sneaky. Not that we were either. Between the lamps and our running after it, the forest sounded real alive right now. The poor, normal, nocturnal animals were getting a show tonight.

Marshall fell behind as I moved through the woods. I was a lot more used to running after monsters in the dead of night through weird obstacles than he was, and it showed. I resisted every protective instinct I had to fall back to his side. Instead, I just had to hope that he would give it up and go home. I didn't have time to watch my brother, just because he still thought I was a baby girl that needed rescuing by him because he was the man of the family now.

Dad had gotten over that the second time we went hunting together.

Marshall's lantern light started fading out of sight as I kept moving. I could hear the creature running along faster through the woods, but its pounding steps started to slow.

I hit a clearing with a gap of trees was just wide enough for me to catch sight of the creature. Its massive shoulders hunched forward, and it lumbered like an ape, but the face had the long teeth-filled snout of a wolf. Not any creature of God I'd ever heard of. If its shape hadn't given that away, the fact that its eyes blazed with literal fire definitely made it more than obvious this thing didn't belong in this world.

It spotted me, and a low growl rumbled like thunder around me. It dropped the bone in its mouth and snarled as it turned to face me, long claws digging into the earth beneath its massive feet.

It's going to be one long night.

"Hazel!" Marshall's voice rang out.

The creature's pointed ears turned in that direction, and it ran its tongue across its teeth before bolting toward Marshall's voice.

I reacted instantly, springing after it. I summoned Cupid from my shoulder and took a breath, hoping I'd be able to find a chance to get a shot in before it found my brother.

"Marshall, get out of here!" I yelled.

If he heard me, he didn't answer. But the silence, at least, meant that thing hadn't found him yet. I doubted Marshall would be silent while some monster tried to rip him to pieces.

I ran faster, pushing past the burning in my lungs and of my skin as the cupid bow stayed over my shoulder, waiting for me to take a shot.

"Hazel!"

I pushed faster for the source of Marshall's voice and finally reached him. I spotted him half up a tree, standing on a thick branch, pointing his pistol down.

Beneath him, the creature rammed itself into the trunk. The bark began splintering, and the trunk eventually wouldn't be able to handle the weight slamming into it.

I aimed the bow and shot, hitting the creature in the middle of its back. "Hey!"

It roared before charging me. I hadn't thought this out at all.

I scrambled back into the woods, weaving through trees to try to put some kind of distance between the two of us.

The creature lunged for me; then a deafening boom cracked the sky as the creature stumbled backward.

Smoke billowed up from Marshall's raised pistol.

"What are...you idiot," I snapped but ran to the wolf to try to finish it off.

"Wait, Hazel, can you contain it?"

"Can I what it?" I asked.

"Contain it. We could put it on display."

"It's a monster. It's going to hurt someone."

"We needed the money to go to Memphis. Something like this, we'd make hand over fist."

I knew he was right. We needed to make more money than we'd ever made before to be able to put the whole circus on the train.

I took a breath and summoned up one of the fairies of Knock, the land of dreams, from the moon tattoo on my leg.

I moved her straight to the creature just coming back to after the shot had knocked it down. The wolf creature snapped at her. She just barely avoided it and began spreading sand all over the beast. It roared and fought against the powder. I'd never seen so much knock out dust before, but eventually the creature hit the ground in a slumber so deep, I had to check it was still breathing.

"Go get a wagon," I told Marshall.

For once, Marshall didn't argue or try to tell me how to do anything. Instead, he did exactly what I asked as I kept the Faerie at the ready. We'd have to clear out an old cage to put it in, but the cage that had once held our lion might work for this thing. I wasn't sure it'd be big enough, but then again, a monster like that probably wouldn't be happy in even the nicest of cages.

I didn't know how long I'd be able to keep it knocked out, but for now, everything seemed to be working. I just had to keep it up for at least another day or two, and that meant I'd be the one showing off the monster. The world would get to see what I was capable of, not just a canvas of skin to be ogled.

Marshall returned, the wolf was still out, and the Faerie slept on top of it. Marshall and I struggled but managed to get it loaded it in; then we tied it up real tight and headed back for camp.

The empty pen took a quick sweeping out before we got the creature locked up. The cage had barely enough room for the beast to spin in a circle, and I felt a little guilty locking it up like this. Containing a lion was one thing, but a monster was something else entirely.

"Do you really think that's going to hold it?" Marshall asked me.

"I don't know," I said. "I don't even know what it is."

Everything in my mind screamed to kill the thing and get rid of it...but Marshall had a point. We needed the extra money, and if the skeleton of a troll had brought in that much money, what would a live supernatural specimen do? Especially one with fire for eyes.

For now, the sleeping spell kept it slumped on the ground with a slow, almost peaceful breathing to its chest. The rising and falling looked natural enough, but even sleeping, the thing posed an impressive figure, looming against the bars.

"I'll have to be in the display with it," I said.

"That thing will eat you alive," Marshall said. "Absolutely not."

"Better me than anyone else off the street. I don't think our clients being eaten would do too well for business, do you?"

Marshall crossed his arms, and I knew I had him. He knew it, too, but didn't want to admit it. But right now, I was the authority. At least when it came to monsters like this, and Marshall knew it.

"You'll have to wear some more covering than your usual show clothes."

"Sure," I said. I knew that no amount of clothing would stop those claws and fangs, but I didn't need to tell Marshall that.

"Fine. You can be the wolf tamer...what are we going to say this thing is?"

"Hell hound?" I joked.

"No." Marshall leaned back and closed his eyes in thought. "What about a Tasmanian devil?"

"The what?"

"It's an Australian thing...I think. I read about it once when we were little."

"Ever seen one?" I asked.

"Nope, and I'm willing to bet that no one in Arkansas has either."

"Does that mean I have to be Australian?" I asked. "I can't do an accent to save my life, Marshall."

"Well, just grunt or something. You don't have to talk. How are you going to keep your magic hidden?" he asked.

"In a full dress, no one will see the marks, and some of the faeries are small enough to look like bugs."

"We can't keep it asleep the whole time. No one will believe it's real."

"I don't know if I can keep it awake and contained, but I'll figure something out."

"If I give it just enough sleep powder to keep it...half awake. Maybe."

A theory, but that was about all I had to operate under at the moment, so theory it was.

"As long as you think that will work."

"It'll have to. We need the money," I said.

"I'll go by the train station in the morning to get tickets booked."

"Sure we can fit everyone on?"

"We'll figure it out."

"Like we always do?"

"Like we always do."

"Well, go on to bed, Marshall. I can keep an eye out here," I said. Not to mention I had to be the one out here. After Puck did nothing to stop the original bone theft, I didn't really think I would trust an unsupervised Faerie to manage to keep this devil asleep.

"I'll bring you breakfast in the morning."

Marshall disappeared back into his wagon. I sat out in front of the pen and sighed. "What am I going to do with you?" I asked.

The beast, thankfully, didn't have an answer. So, instead, I yanked out my dad's notebook and began sketching out this creature on a new page.

"Hell Hound," I wrote out in slow letters.

Fire eyes.
Steals bones.
Large, stealthy, aggressive.
Can be put to sleep by Faerie sand.

That was about all I had on this thing right now: some monster that stole bones, had burning eyes, and didn't like people. That looked like most other monsters I'd run into...not that I'd done many actual monster hunts. Dad had taken me on less dangerous missions or hunts, that's why most of my ink was filled with more faeries than monsters, but already that'd changed. No matter how much money this thing might make us tomorrow, we weren't going to be taking it on a tour of the country. It'd end up on my skin eventually.

Then again, I felt a little guilty about trying to kill something pinned in a cage, unable to defend itself. That felt like shooting fish in a barrel, but monsters didn't play fair either. If the tables were turned, this thing would rip me to ribbons and not even think twice about it.

The creature shifted in its cell, and I sent another blast of sand toward it. Its snore rumbled like a growl in its chest, and I took a step back. Even in sleep, it still lurked like a threat. I had to make sure this thing didn't get a chance to go after anyone else.

I nearly drifted off a few times, but the sound of growling always snapped me back to alertness. Nothing like a sharp bolt of fear in your heart to keep you up all night. By morning, I was ready for a nap, but there wouldn't be too much of a break for me. Marshall delivered breakfast, then headed to town. Alma walked over with her breakfast and looked from me to the pen.

"What is that?" she asked.

"Tasmanian devil."

"That's a Tasmanian devil as much as I'm an African princess."

"We're making some money with it..."

"With a drugged giant...bear wolf?" She arched a brow.

"People pay to see weird things," I said.

"They do pay to see us," Alma said.

I laughed; it felt good to relax for a moment after a night spent on high alert. For the moment, we were okay. The thing was still mostly sleeping. But I didn't think it was just sleep deprivation that kept a sick twist in my stomach.

"So, you won't be joining us in the tent?" Alma asked.

"No, I'm going to be a Tasmanian devil tamer today," I said.

"You need a different look for that."

"Well, we don't have the outfit for it, so a dress will have to do for right now," I said with a shrug.

"I'm sure the twins could whip you up something pretty quick," she said.

"After today, I don't think we'll be worrying about this display."

"Right... So, seriously, what is this thing?" she asked.

"I don't really know," I said. "Maybe some kind of werewolf?"

"Don't those things turn back into people at dawn?"

"I reckon so," I said. "But I've never actually met one to ask all about how that works."

"Yeah, I'm sure they would tell you all their secrets. Especially if you kept it locked in a cage drugged all night."

"It's just sleeping," I said.

"I'm sure it loves that."

"Can you watch it while I go clean up?" I asked.

Alma looked a little uneasy but nodded. "Just hurry it up."

I rushed to my room and put Dad's book away before giving my face a quick wash up. I changed into one of my nicer dresses, khaki and brown with some dirt stains that seemed to have become a permanent part of the fabric at some point. I smoothed down the dress and hoped the look would sell as some Australian monster tamer. That was the one part of the shows I never really got used to, working on the stories, the fake things that Marshall spun to hide the truth. No one liked the truth. Even on real exhibits, like the twins. There always had to be some story about how their mother saw a horrible monster when she was pregnant and that's why they ended up born like they were. No one wanted the truth.

I put a wrap over my marking for the sleeping Faerie to absorb the blood from staining my dress at least. Little things like these faeries didn't take much effort at all, so I should be able to keep it up for the day.

All I had to do was manage to keep this thing under control until the show closed tonight. I could do that. Then we could get out of here and work on getting back to finding Dad.

I took a breath and did my makeup very simply before coming back out to the creature's pen.

"Miss anything?" I asked Alma.

"Oh yeah, it woke up, told me it was a werewolf and hated you, then turned back into a wolf just in time to keep fooling you," Alma said.

"Sure, great. Good to know," I said. "You should get ready. Marshall wanted to start a bit after noon today."

"Where is that boy?"

"Town. He's getting us train tickets."

"We're taking the train?"

"We're giving it a try."

"That will be nice. I do not enjoying traveling in the summer. It's way too hot out here."

"It's not the heat; it's the humidity," I said, a long-held Southern saying of the weather.

She laughed. "Yeah, I've been living in the South longer than you have, so don't start that with me."

I smiled as Alma headed for her wagon to start getting ready. I sat back down and sighed. Thankfully, the last dose of sand seemed to have knocked that monster on its butt for the time being, but I knew it would only be temporary. I took a breath and tried to just relax a little without actually falling asleep on my feet.

Relaxing against the bars of the pen, I could feel the sweet lure of sleep and had to force myself to stand up straighter and not give in. Tonight. Tonight, I could get a full, lovely night's sleep without having to worry about this thing or if we'd be able to go after Dad. We'd get the money, I was sure of it. Marshall had to be drumming up a crowd to come and see this monster, and that money would pay our way as long as we played our cards right. I just had to put the rest of it under control and keep things contained for the day. I could manage that.

CHAPTER EIGHT

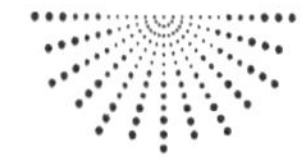

After what felt like ages, Marshall returned with a crowd of people trailing behind him. The thing was still knocked out and not looking real convincing. I glared at Marshall, trying to telepath him to slow down, but he didn't seem to get the message, so I was left just glaring at him on my own without a response from him.

Wonderful.

"Welcome to the Finnegan Family Cabinet of Aberrations!" Marshall waved his arm like our camp was some majestic thing to be displayed. I could see some of our acts scrambling to their tents.

"We have mysteries and oddities from across the globe. For just a nickel, you can see the giant found right here in the heart of Arkansas," he said, leading the crowd to the tent first, instead of straight to me.

Thank goodness. Maybe he had gotten my message about slowing down. The twins ambled by, moving faster than I'd ever seen their shared three legs move. I was surprised they didn't trip and topple over. Everyone else stumbled to their places, Alma helping get some of the stragglers into the tent and onto the stage.

That just left me to figure out how to wake this thing up just enough for it to look scary but be harmless. That was a mighty thin line I needed to walk. I swallowed hard and freed Puck from my skin and sent him into the cage. The troublesome Faerie resisted at first but finally moved into the cage. I urged the Faerie to poke the monster. The beast growled softly but stayed sleeping. Puck looked at me and glared but poked the wolf in the ribs, harder this time.

This time, the eyes popped open, and with a snapping of teeth, Puck slammed back into my skin. I lurched back and took a breath to shake off the blow. The monster stared at me through the bars, eyes flaming as it roared, the ground shaking. Almost instantly, Marshall and the crowds burst out of the giant tent to look at me.

"For a dime, you can see the fierce Tasmanian devil and nine other incredible acts," Marshall said.

The crowds looked silently toward me before a rush moved to Marshall for tickets. Our eyes met, and we both smiled. This was going to be easy.

The crowds moved quickly, although the number of people who wanted to touch the monster surprised me. I had to slap away hands, or gently step between people and their stupid decision.

Trying to keep the balance of sleepy and awake was a delicate tightrope. Several times, I had to pull Puck back out to poke the wolf awake. As the day went on, it got harder and harder to keep things evened out.

The crowds kept growing in size, more people than I'd ever seen at the show before. These kinds of crowds didn't usually happen except for on a real good day in a place like New York City, but to have these numbers here in Arkansas? That was something amazing.

Marshall eventually passed ticket selling over to someone else, and he moved to my side to talk the display up.

"Ladies and gentlemen, what you have here is one of the rarest creatures on God's green earth. An embodiment of the devil himself: the Tasmanian devil. Found only in the most savage parts of Tasmania, this beast lives on flesh, hunts in the dead of night, and can smell fear. Only the bravest should approach!"

I made a show of grunting or making gestures but not speaking, which took a whole lot of willpower when people kept acting like total idiots. The men especially made all kinds of comments when they didn't think I could understand the words coming out of their mouths.

When a lull in the crowd began slowing sales, Marshall announced, "We will be taking a fifteen-minute break. Please wait by the ticket booth."

It took a few minutes for the townspeople to move along. When Marshall and I were alone, he asked, "How you doing?"

Exhausted, sore, so tired I could sleep standing up.

"I'm fine." There wasn't really another option.

"Go wash up a little. I'll keep an eye on things."

I nodded and went to pee before washing my face and hands. I stopped by my wagon and began rewrapping my leg when I heard what sounded like a yelp from Marshall.

Heart in my throat, I ran back to the pen and found the bars melted and the monster forcing its way out. Marshall stared at it, then to me, as I scrambled to get the sleep Faerie back out. I threw it toward the monster, and it swallowed her whole.

Playtime was over. I tried to reach for Puck, for anything, to stop it from breaking out of the cage. But nothing appeared as I ran to Marshall and tugged him away as the beast broke free.

"The exhibit has gotten out of its pen," Marshall said, sounding like he was just announcing that a storm was coming. "There's no need to panic. We have everything under control," he said, but his voice was drowned out by the completely panicked crowd.

The crowd swarmed like a mass of ants just disrupted by rain. They clumped and stumbled in a multitude of directions to try to get away. Some of them ran to where the exhibit had been held, but they didn't even seem to care about any of that. They moved with blind panic steering them, nothing focused or controlled about any of their activities.

I'd never been trapped in a crowd like that before. All I could think of was seeing herds of buffalo stampeding. These people were going to destroy our whole tent if we didn't get them out soon.

Time for crowd control. I focused on a fire Faerie, and he sprang forth easily. The crowds screamed as the Faerie sent up a blast of embers. We'd be kicked out of town for this, for sure, but at least we'd get out without massacring the townsfolk. I kept up the Faerie figure, multiplying his image into several other places, steering the crowds away from our things and back to the town.

Finally, all the townspeople disappeared, aside from a few stragglers. Marshall and Alma took care of them. Marshall glared at me. "That was not helpful, Hazel. You could have burned us down!"

"Oh really? I don't see our tents ripped to pieces, do you?"

"Just go catch it," Marshall said.

"Kill it you mean."

"Go!"

I let the illusions fade away, and the burning pain around my leg stopped. "Alright, keep people away from the woods. I bet it went back where it was supposed to be."

"Yeah? Back to Hell?"

"No, back to the forests we found it in."

"Just go," he snapped.

I grabbed one of our horses and took off for the woods.

The orange glow of sunset made the woods almost appear to be on fire as the edges of the leaves caught the sun. It felt a lot like wandering straight into Hell to catch a missing dog sent out for the purpose of death and destruction. The horse shimmied at the edge of the woods, and I didn't push her to go in farther. Horses were too nervous to do well around the supernatural. A big anxiety-ridden vehicle I did not need adding to the fun.

I hopped off and slapped the horse's rump. It bolted back toward the circus. Most of them were bright enough to make it back to the camp. We were close enough the smell ought to serve as a guiding light straight back to the safety of the stables. I couldn't say I blamed her at all.

I pulled out my dagger and wished I'd thought to grab a lantern, but I'd just have to do this fast before I lost the little light still hanging onto the sky. In the dark of the night, I'd be in trouble.

"Here puppy," I cooed, hoping it would work although I doubted an actual hell hound was anything like a stray dog I'd feed scraps to on the road. No, if it was out here, it was hunting me, hungry and angry. I was sure it remembered who caught it, who put it into the stupid pen, who made its life miserable. I bet they could hold a grudge as well as they could hold a scent, and I must have smelled like the best two for one deal it'd ever heard of.

"Blue damn," I muttered and tightened my hold on the dagger as I began moving into the inner parts of the woods. With the sun rapidly disappearing behind the horizon, I knew this had to be a death trap. I didn't really like the odds. Hunting a black dog in the black woods in the black of night was a recipe for me turning up dead.

I squared my shoulders and took a deep breath. I didn't have a lantern…but I did have a will-o'-wisp. One of the very first things Dad had let me catch, the little floating light wouldn't be anything like a spotlight, but it was a lot better than wandering in darkness.

The tiny tattoo on my hip barely burned as I called the spirit forth. The small spirit ghosted like a fall breeze against my mind. The wisp swirled around me before settling just in front of me, lighting far enough ahead that I could avoid the roots gnarled and curled out of the ground like hungry fingers. It moved like a Faerie, swift and delicate, but when things went south, this wisp wouldn't be much use. It was strictly meant to lure travelers, not fight demon dogs.

In the distance of the trees, howls echoed and multiplied. I just prayed that this thing didn't have friends. One was bad enough, I didn't want to think about how a whole pack of them would go, especially since I didn't much fancy dying in the middle of Arkansas and leaving Marshall to deal with the show alone. If Dad was gone, we were all we had, and I had no plans on leaving my brother to deal with everything. If I died, Lady Death would make a bargain with Marshall, and these summonings would eat him alive. I'd give my soul before I let anything touch a hair on his spoiled little head.

The howling got louder, and I held tight to my dagger like it would help. I wasn't sure how well a knife would do in a dogfight, but it'd never served me wrong before, so I held onto my old friend.

The wisp floated a little higher, and the shadows cast shapes in the pale light as the last of the sun dripped from the ground in a slow puddle of blackness that consumed it all. One moment there'd been light in the world, and now it'd been swallowed whole by the hungry night.

"You can do this, Hazel," I muttered and forced my legs to move against the shackles of fear tied to my ankles.

The light of my wisp looked like a floating star against the sky with no sign of any other person around. Even the lights from the show's camp had been swallowed whole.

A shot of fear hit me from far away as I realized the wisp had stopped moving and seemed to turn to face the west. I swallowed hard and gripped the handle of my dagger. I hoped that unicorn blood-forged blades worked on things straight out of the gates of Hell that I might have accidentally cracked open when I lost control of a troll spirit and smashed a circle to bits.

The howling grew louder, and before I could react, a set of teeth flashed through the dim light. Then the wisp vanished. It snapped back onto my hip, and I winced at the flare of pain of an unexpected spirit release. I didn't have time to register it too much before I started running. If it got the wisp, I was next on the menu.

Tearing blindly through the forest, I ignored the twigs grabbing and clawing at me. Instead, I used them as a hand up and took to the branches, moving upward. If these hounds were anything like regular dogs, climbing wasn't their strong suit, so I just had to get up before they found me.

The thundering of paws I heard had to belong to at least three of them, not just the one that I'd caught earlier. Once I'd found a solid perch far enough up a tree to feel a little safer, I pressed my back to the trunk and looked down.

Now that my eyes had had some time to adjust to the darkness, I could make out the shapes circling me. Occasionally, the whole tree shuddered as one threw its body against the trunk. As big as those things were, I had no doubt they'd take me down eventually.

Great, a whole pack for me to deal with. My lucky day.

I swallowed hard and summoned Cupid. The familiar spirit felt comfortable, and his fear matched mine. But where I had a flesh and blood body to worry about, Cupid didn't have that problem anymore. I looked at the little Faerie as he rolled his eyes and shook his head. He resisted, his fear and mine blending together, but I forced my will to be stronger.

GO.

He obeyed, floating down the tree and whistling a tune. Instantly, I could see the wolves shifting, looking to this new thing moving and making sound. I drew another breath and drew on Cupid again, drawing the bow back. I closed my eyes, forcing my vision into Puck's head. The Faerie's eyes saw through the dark with more clarity as I counted three wolves, all very near to ripping Puck right out of the sky.

With my eyes still in Cupid's head, I pulled my bowstring back and aimed.

The first shot hit one of the wolves in its side with a hollow *thunk*. I drew again immediately and fired, hitting that same one straight in the eye. It dropped, dissolving to shadows. The other two wolves rushed me, circling the tree I'd taken shelter in. They snarled and slammed their bodies into the trunk, shaking the entire thing.

When everything stilled for a moment, I chanced looking down and found the two remaining wolves digging at the base of the tree. With those massive paws ripping the dirt out from around me, I'd be hitting the ground very soon.

Damnation.

I sent Cupid back closer, keeping him whistling. The wolves looked up, ears swiveling as they spotted him, but instead of pursuing him, paws kept ripping up clumps of dirt and roots. With a wince, I released Cupid, feeling the tattoo come back to my skin. I had to get out of this tree or I was going to wind up dead before I even had the chance to fix breaking a hell circle.

I drew Cupid's bowstring back again. The tree shifted, and I took a breath as I aimed and fired. The first shot missed, but the second one found a home between the shoulders of the larger of the wolves. It growled up at me as I fired again, hitting the other wolf square between the eyes. It dissolved to smoke.

The way the other two had vanished so easily made it clear this creature could make illusions of itself, but the one bleeding at the base of the tree had to be the real creature. It slammed into the tree, and I could feel the tree starting to drop down to the ground.

Taking a breath to try to steel myself for the fall, I gave my arm a shake, summoning out Cupid once more; he couldn't fly much, but I just needed a slowing of my fall. Cupid screeched as I grabbed his feet as the tree tipped out from under me. Struggling with my added weight, he dropped to the ground, but the fall slowed enough that I landed on my feet, rolling like my daddy taught me, before I sprang up with my bow at the ready. The wolf was nowhere to be seen.

I released the Faerie and squinted through the forest. Wherever the hell hound had gone, it couldn't have been far. Not with an arrow between its shoulders. I closed my eyes and listened. The woods were almost silent, a strange thing for a forest that probably teemed with life any other night. Animals had a way better sense for monster than most people did, and they probably all hightailed it out of here before any of this mess started.

I crept toward the tree I'd just jumped from. It'd ripped straight from the ground and laid on its side, supported by a few other trees, but it wouldn't be long before it found its way to the ground too, taking some of the smaller trees with it. I guess hell hounds hated nature, too. Then again, they seemed to hate everything there was, so that wasn't too much of a surprise.

"Here puppy," I cooed and hoped my voice sounded braver than I felt.

Marshall had claimed the Tasmanian devil could smell fear, and if this thing really could, then I bet I smelled like a nice home-cooked dinner. My heart ran a race inside my chest, and sweat beaded along my skin. But Daddy always taught me that fear only matters if you let it tell you what to do. Fear might have been along for this ride, but it wasn't in the driver's seat. Besides, any person right in the head would be a little worried about going after something straight from Hell.

A branch snapped to my left, and I turned to face it. Before I could even react, the hound charged straight at me. I jumped to the side, hitting the ground, barely dodging the snapping jaws as it lunged at me. I scrambled to my feet and dashed into the woods, bobbing through trees, and past the unkempt ground where roots and weeds threatened to grab my ankles and jerk me down. The hound's feet slammed after me, not slowed by any of the obstacles that threatened me.

A claw grazed across my back and ripped through my dress but didn't cut through my skin just yet. If it got a second attempt though, my back would be ribbons, so I switched directions, moving faster and trying to get some distance between the two of us.

I didn't think any doctor would appreciate having to manage that kind of wound, not to mention that scars would really mess up some of those tattoos back there, and I needed them all intact so I could still summon them. I didn't know for sure if a scar would mess things up or not, but I didn't really want to have to find out the answer.

Switching directions, I made a hard left, spinning past a massive tree trunk. The hard breathing of the hound still felt like it was right on my tail, but I knew there had to be hair of distance now, and that was all I needed.

I leapt over a grouping of roots and rolled to the ground to pop back up facing the hound as it barreled toward me. Ripping my dagger from my boot, I gripped the handle in my hand and dug my heels in. My skin tingled against my bones, like even it didn't want to be here, but we were all in this together, bad plan or not, there was no turning back now.

The hound dove at me, and I plunged my dagger to slam into its heart but missed, and instead, the blade sank deeply into the monster's shoulder. It roared before clamping its teeth onto my forearm. I screamed, dropping the dagger as the teeth cut into skin, twisting and ripping. The pain burst like an explosion through my body.

Sheer stubbornness cut through the pain. If I could handle a troll on my own, I could handle an oversized dog. I jammed my thumb into the dog's eye, and it released my arm.

I scrambled to grab the dagger and cut for its throat. I nicked it, but the thick alligator-like skin stopped deadly damage. Blood dripped down my arm, and something like tar oozed from the dog's shoulder and the small cut I'd given its throat. For the moment, we stood staring at each other, neither of us moving until I made a charge to stab at it.

The wolf dodged and sank its teeth back into my arm, and with a twist of its teeth, I felt the real danger of my arm about to be ripped clean off. With teeth twisting into my wrist, I couldn't get an angle enough to stab it. But Daddy hadn't raised no fool, and I had two hands for a reason. I dropped the dagger, and as the wolf tightened its grip on my right arm, I slowly leaned in and grabbed the knife from the ground with my left hand. Moving slowly so the wolf wouldn't notice, I picked it up, then plunged the blade straight into the wolf's right eye.

It roared, jerking back, and this time I didn't wait for it to recover as I jumped on it, slamming my dagger into its chest with both hands. I shoved straight through the thick skin, and the wolf gave a loud screech before it dropped to the ground, still.

Panting for air, I kicked it with my foot then jumped back when it burst into flames. The fire stayed centered on the wolf, sputtering in red, orange, and black that licked through flesh and blood. As the shape of the hound faded slowly to nothing more than a skeleton, I saw its soul.

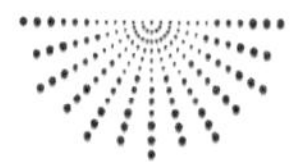

This wasn't right. I hadn't even summoned Death to separate out the soul. It ripped through the fire and charged straight at me. I held up my arms to block it, and then the flames rushed into my bleeding arm. I screamed at the searing pain consuming me from the inside out. Fire engulfed the bite marks on my arm, twisting and burning into more and more agony.

I sank onto my knees and shoved my arm into the damp earth of the forest. The dirt consumed the fires as I panted for air. I looked back to the wolf as it tumbled into a pile of a skeleton made of ash that faded into nothing. None of the other souls had ever hurt like that. None of the other souls had ever hit me, consumed in fire and brimstone.

Slowly, I freed my arm from the dirt and looked down at the damage. The gashes were all closed up, my skin healed as though nothing had happened, aside from a new tattoo patterned in the shape of the teeth that had clamped on my arm. The marks were all in orange and red, the shape more abstract than anything concrete. But how was I not burnt to a crisp?

Dried blood still caked over my skin and dress. I looked like I'd run through Hell, and I guess I'd at least been pretty close to it with the wolf fight tonight. Brushing myself off a little, I headed back out of the forest.

Summoning the will-'o-wisp to help with some light, I had to focus to keep it going the direction I wanted and not toward the center of the forest. Grateful that I had my mom's sense of direction, I managed to find my way out of the forest and whistled. It took a few minutes, but I was grateful that my horse had waited for me instead of returning home. I climbed on after dismissing my wisp. Leaning heavily on her neck, I let the horse lead the way without much input from me. She knew the way, and exhaustion weighed heavily on me.

"Hazel!" The voice of my brother snapped me upright, and I nearly fell off the horse.

"Hazel, are you alright?" he asked, offering his hand.

I took it and hopped down, leaning on Marshall for support. I didn't even argue when he began to lead the way to his carriage. Inside, I dropped into his desk chair and let out a long breath.

"Hellfire, Hazel."

"Exactly that," I said. "No sign of Dad still?"

Marshall shook his head.

"I reckon we head on back east like we'd planned. He's got to be ahead somewhere."

"Yeah," Marshall said, but he didn't sound so sure of it. "You got the wolf?" he asked.

I nodded and held up my arm.

"Hazel, you look a mess."

"Yeah, well, fighting a thing from Hell doesn't go real smooth all the time," I said with a sigh. "I just need some sleep."

"You need a wash."

"In the morning."

Marshall didn't look sure before he nodded. "Alright, I'll walk you to your—"

"Can I just stay in here tonight?"

Marshall looked surprised. We hadn't shared a bunk since we were younger. We'd had different wagons most of our time in the circus. But tonight, I didn't really want to walk across the camp alone and deal with the darkness of my own bunk.

Marshall nodded. "Of course." He pulled out some extra blankets and a pillow and got himself settled on the floor.

"You take the bed," I said.

"Goodnight, Hazel," he said.

I sighed but didn't have the energy to argue any more as I climbed into his bed and closed my eyes. Sleep washed over me like a wave.

CHAPTER TEN

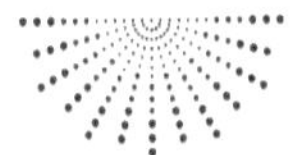

"So, you got rid of it?" Marshall asked as we sat eating breakfast the next morning.

I nodded.

"Good. I got us tickets out of here today."

"Today?"

"We stick around any longer, and we're going to get run out. We're out on the first train today."

"What about the wagons?" I asked.

"Leave 'em. Pack only what we need," he said.

"You tell everyone that already?"

"Yep. Jonah's got everyone on a wagon to town with their chests. I started packing up your stuff."

I slowly got out of bed and groaned. "Do I have time to wash up?"

"Yeah, I left out a dress for you, but we got to get moving."

I stumbled down to the washing hole and splashed myself. Washing the grime, soot, and blood from my skin felt heavenly, even with exhaustion still weighing on my entire body. The newest marking still burned, and the tattoo felt hot to the touch. I wrapped it with a thin layer of gauze before climbing out of the water and putting on the dress.

After I got dressed, I didn't head back for camp. Instead, I walked back toward that circle I'd busted up. Moving fast since I didn't want Marshall to know what I was up to, I reached the stones in no time.

The remains of the circle had faded away to almost nothing, and I'd bet with one more rainstorm, there'd be no sign of it left. I walked to the smashed center stone and picked up a jagged piece. It felt warm in my hands. I looked around for any other signs, but nothing stood out. Keeping the rock in my hand, I returned to Marshall and the camp.

"Ready?" he asked.

"Let me just double check my wagon. What are we doing about the troll bones?"

"We got most of them loaded on a wagon and on the way to the train station this morning."

Marshall waited outside as I packed up as much as I could, making sure to shove Dad's notebook into my chest. We got loaded up, and I watched as the remains of our circus faded behind us.

Somewhere east, Dad had to be waiting for us, and I got the sinking feeling that this summoning circle and new demon mark on my arm were just the beginning of a whole lot of new trouble.

GRAVEYARD RIDE

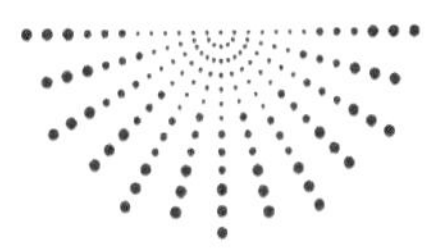

CHAPTER ONE

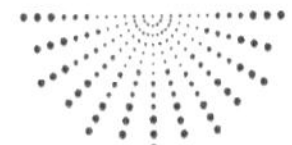

The trainmaster looked from me to my brother then to the giant troll skeleton we'd brought to join us on our trek to Memphis. I had my sweetest smile plastered on my face even though the heat trapped in my dress made me feel like a human bonfire.

"That isn't going on my train," the oily-skinned man muttered, his voice seeming to travel right past his bushy mustache and come straight from his overly thin nose.

"We can make it fit," I said, not sure that was true, but we needed it to come with us. I wasn't about to abandon this thing in the middle of the city.

The nasally man shook his head. "That is of the devil, and I am not bringing any more demons on this train than the rest of you lot."

"We can pay for the inconvenience," Marshall said with an easy smile though I could see the muscles in his neck twitching with irritation.

Leave it to Marshall to try to make peace with the biggest human jerk we'd dealt with in months.

"It's not coming on my train," the man said with his arms crossed.

Marshall looked at me like I'd have some bright idea to get this man to accept a troll skeleton, but to be honest, I had nothing. I couldn't shrink the bones, and I sure as hell wasn't going to summon the troll spirit to put on its bones and run after the train all the way from Arkansas to Tennessee. That'd be very subtle and definitely not cause any problems for us. Besides, I wasn't the one who was good with words. Marshall had the "snake oil salesman" voice in him; I had the "punch it until it stops moving" in me.

"If I may intrude on this conversation?" A woman's voice joined our discussion.

All of us turned toward her. She wore a flattering and slim-fitted dress showing the clear shape of her silhouette. Her pale brown hair had been curled to perfection, and she looked like her makeup was part of her face, not something extra added on. Her gown was made of a fine silk, nothing like the cheap cotton and khaki dresses I wore. This was a woman with money, someone with no reason to be in a town like this.

"Can I help you, ma'am?" Marshall asked.

"I think we can help each other. I'm Madame Eclipse... You may have heard of my small traveling show?" She produced a postcard and offered it to me.

I looked at Marshall, he looked at me, and we both shook our heads. Even the train master shook his head—seemed like they needed to work on the advertising for their little show. I took the card and ran my fingers over it: a rush print job still warm from the press with a lot of red ink all over the card making it almost look bloody.

"Well, I was on my way to see your show. I came to see this remarkable display of yours and hurried as soon as I heard you were leaving," she said.

"We don't have time to give a walkthrough of running a show," I said.

"What suggestion did you have?" Marshall asked. "You said we might help each other."

Everyone wanted something, and this woman was being way too polite to not want anything. I'd not met a woman running a show before, and I didn't have any problems giving some advice to her if that was all she was after, but we didn't have the time.

"If I am hearing this conversation right, you're unable to bring this fine specimen to the railroad," Madame Eclipse said.

"It's not coming on my train," the trainmaster said again. "And if you aren't on when it leaves in..." he paused to look at his watch, "ten minutes, then you ain't coming either." The man marched away.

"You've got an idea for it, I assume," Marshall said, crossing his arms.

"Well, I am in the process of acquiring showpiece items as it were. And I travel by carriage or truck, no railroads for me."

"What'll you give us for it?" Marshall asked.

I stared at him. "We aren't selling it!"

"Hazel, it isn't coming on the train. It's either this or we leave it behind for nothing," he said.

I didn't want to admit it, but we needed the money. I wasn't really up to trying to summon a troll to carry the bones across state lines. It seemed like that'd be breaking a couple laws and every sense of self-preservation I had in my body.

"I understand parting with your beloved items can be hard some-times," the woman said. She pulled a purse from her side. "I can give you three-hundred dollars."

I stared at Marshall as his jaw went slack. Three hundred for a sack of oversized bones? That was more than we made at most every show we did; this kind of money would set us up for months. Marshall and I looked at each other, and I gave him a subtle nod. The cost of putting the show on the train had drained us dry. This would give us some money to survive in Memphis. It still stung, but the sight of the money eased the loss.

"Done," Marshall said, then looked to me. "We can get another set."

I shot him a glare. Unless he planned on going out troll hunting in his free time, that was a big ol' "no way." I had no plans to deal with one of those things again if I could help it. I certainly wasn't going to be going after them while we traveled. Not unless I absolutely had to, but going out looking for trouble was not any part of my goals. We'd make due with something else on display, and I'd deal with figuring that out once we got to Memphis.

"You got yourself a deal, miss," Marshall said and offered his hand for a shake.

The woman smiled and shook his hand. "You're a very wise businessman. I can see why your shows do so well. Where do you ever find such amazing oddities?" she asked.

"They find us," I answered.

She looked at me, and her smile grew. "A woman after my own heart." She offered her hand to me.

We shook hands; her grip squeezed strong and warm against my palm like she'd just taken something out of the oven right before coming here.

She pulled the money out of her purse and counted three hundred dollars before depositing it into Marshall's hand. "Thank you, it's been a pleasure, but it seems like you'd best load up or miss your train."

Marshall tucked the money into his coat and nodded. "Come on, Hazel."

I followed after him as the woman turned to the bones with a gleeful grin. I didn't like someone else getting credit for my work, but getting rid of the damn things would simplify traveling for sure. She had a few burly men already moving the bones from the caravan we'd rented and onto her own set of wagons. Watching them go twisted uneasily in my gut, but we didn't need any extra complications while we still tried to hunt down Dad.

"Hey, there wasn't anything else to be done," Marshall said.

"I know, it's fine," I said, and I mostly believed it. I hoped that Marshall did too.

I moved down to the end of the train to make sure everything got loaded up all right. Our wagons were being pulled onto some flatbed cars, and our horses were resisting getting onto the train at all. I couldn't blame them; I could only imagine what terror something this big and metal seemed like to something as jumpy as a horse.

Some of our tent builders helped finally get the horses loaded up and locked into some basic stalls for the trip. They stomped around, and I heard more than a few annoyed snorts, but the animals eventually settled down. I let out a long breath and thanked the guys before we all hopped on board and found our seats near the front of the train.

We both settled into the main riding car, and Marshall loaded our small travel bags under the seats. Compared to our show, the train oozed normalcy. The shabby interior looked well-worn and well cared for; the seats were patched but still in good shape. Everything had been cleaned, and I could imagine the seats filled with regular folks, but instead, we'd rented out the whole thing, and it would hold no one but us until we hit Memphis.

Glancing out the windows, I saw the last glimpse of the skeleton being loaded onto a series of carts. Around us, two other trains were boarding with well-dressed people all saying goodbyes on the platform.

Constance and Temperance had lowered down one of the beds so they could sit. Their shared backside wouldn't fit in a single seat, not comfortably anyway. A carriage might be slower, but we'd had every-thing made to fit us right. I sighed.

Jonah sat with his Bible in his lap. Occasionally, a foot popped up to turn his page, but otherwise, he seemed engrossed in his reading. The Duncans sat behind Jonah with several of them squeezed into a single seat. It was hard to even think of them as individuals because they kept to themselves and always together. I wasn't sure if that was something all German faeries did or something with our group of them. They were like Constance and Temperance in a way even if they did have physically distinct bodies.

Alma's laughter hit the air, a strange but welcome sound. I glanced behind me and saw her and Frenchie sitting close together with a book half on each of their laps. I hadn't seen Alma smiling that much in a long time. I turned to find Marshall to sit with but, to my shock, found he'd settled into a seat beside Jonah. That left me the seat behind the Duncans.

I'd rather pull out all my hair than sit by the Duncans. They took every chance to show off their singing talents, and their serenading me for the fourteen-hour ride across the country didn't sound like a good time to me.

"I'm going to the dining car," I said.

"They won't be serving anything yet," Jonah said as he turned the page of his Bible.

"That's alright, just need some place to write," I said.

Jonah didn't respond, and Marshall nodded as he pulled out a newspaper, lit up a cigar, and leaned back into his seat.

The dining car was only one car forward, and like Jonah had said, there wasn't anyone manning it yet. I found a seat by a window and pulled Dad's book from my bag to read over and update. I'd make sure Dad knew everything he'd missed by doing whatever this vanishing trick was.

I made a few notes about the woman who had bought the troll bones from Marshall. Madame Eclipse certainly seemed like a character I wanted to remember. I didn't know a woman could run a show all on her own, but I hoped she'd succeed and let the world know it could be done. I'd have to keep an ear out for her and see what tale they came up with for the bones.

I wished we could use the truth, I could stand over that skeleton and tell everyone, "I did this. I killed this to keep y'all safe." I didn't want adoration but hellfire, some respect would be nice.

A jerking motion and a train whistle screaming announced our departure as the train began chugging forward. I looked out the window and watched the city start to fade away. The sun inched up toward its noonday peak as we finally gained solid speed and rolled along. I leaned against my hand as I watched the scene zip past. This was a lot faster than horses, but it wasn't nearly cozy enough.

I bet the Barnum and Bailey guys had their own custom-built train so they didn't have to worry about any of this. We needed a few more big shows, then maybe we could have our own little train. The three-hundred dollars from Madame Eclipse was a nice start toward that. The idea of a Finnegan Family train chugging across the country made me smile. That'd be a sight.

We just had to worry about how to get from the train to a fairground space and if we would even be welcomed. There was no telling what else was going on in the city, and no one would have even heard of us yet, especially if Dad hadn't been traveling ahead to spread the word of mouth.

We'd be in a struggle from the moment we set foot in the city, let alone that Memphis was a bigger place than we usually ever visited. Those kinds of cities got the big shows, and we didn't bother competing. We specialized in small, isolated towns. Not to mention that made my job a whole lot easier. When it was a tiny town, there were fewer people wandering around at night to catch me in the middle of a hunt.

I looked back to Dad's book and kept writing out everything that had happened: the hellhound, the mark, and all the rest of it. The new mark still burned, and I kept glancing at it, expecting blisters would spring up at any moment. It felt fresh as the day I'd gotten it, and that made me nervous. Usually the pain vanished pretty quickly after the ink settled in my skin but not this time. It didn't comfort me the hound remained quiet. Eerily silent.

Most things weren't as obnoxious as the troll with the lingering feelings melting into mine, but none of them had taken up residence with no note. Even the tiniest of faeries had made some kind of impact on me in the days after their first arrival; a newly arrived spirit often made its presence known, but this hound... I couldn't even hear it at all. Not a whisper. It made no sense.

Maybe I needed to learn what to do to coax it out. Perhaps hell-creatures acted differently. I traced my fingers over the vibrant flame tattoo on my arm and hoped I hadn't made a big mistake taking on a demon, not that I'd chosen to do that. It had charged for me and chosen to join me whether I wanted any part of it. I had to figure out how to deal with it.

Looking over at the glowing orange of the sun setting over the horizon, I clenched my fist. Having fire on hand might be useful if we ever ran into any other devils trying to get a foothold in this world. Our agreement with Lady Death hadn't specified demons, but apparently the law of possession and absorption still held.

I had a demon spirit now and no instructions on how to handle that in any way. But I'd been doing a pretty solid job with winging it so far, and I had best keep that up.

When the dining car door opened, I expected to see one of the workers coming to take my order or at least open up the bar, but instead, Marshall looked in. "Hazel! Come quick!"

I shoved the book back into my bag and pulled out my dagger as I got to my feet.

"What is it?" I asked.

"Conductor's about to throw a fare-dodger off the damn train."

"What?" I paused, not at all ready for that. I'd been ready for a fight. Why did Marshall think I could help with a stowaway at all?

"Just come with me," my brother said as he grabbed my arm and pulled me along to the back of the train.

CHAPTER TWO

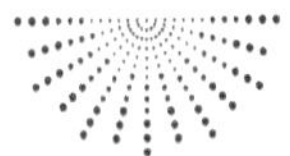

We scrambled through the train and to the caboose where the crying of a little girl pierced the air.

"Stowaways get kicked off trains!" the conductor said, dragging a small girl in a dirty dress down the aisle.

The girl looked like she was only five or six, and she clawed at every seat they passed to try to keep from getting to the end of the train, but even the scrawny conductor was stronger than this tiny child.

"What the hell," I said before moving and grabbing the girl by her shoulders to hold her steady against the man's grasp.

The man's moustache twitched, but he didn't let go of her. "Excuse me, this is a stowaway, and I am not allowing—"

"You're about to throw a child off the train!" Marshall yelled. "A kid in the middle of nowhere when it's basically dark!"

"This girl should have thought about that before she chose to steal a ride on my train," he snapped as he tried to pull her from my grasp.

The little girl had her arms wrapped around my waist, and I had no problem resisting him. His strength against mine wasn't even a contest.

"This is unlawful!" he yelled.

"This is our train," Marshall said as he pulled out his wallet and fished out a few bills.

He thrust the money out to the man, who finally let go of the girl. She sank sobbing into my dress.

"There, her fare is paid," Marshall snapped.

"You freaks are nothing but trouble." The man glared as he took the money and stormed out of the car.

Marshall knelt down by the little girl. "Hey, shhhh, it's alright. You're not getting thrown off of anything, alright?"

She sniffled and finally peered out from my skirt. Her skin was nearly ghostly white and dotted with a jumble of freckles and wide green eyes. Taken with the bright red hair, she looked like the picture of every Irish kid I'd seen in our brief visit to New York last year.

"Mmmmm sorry!" the girl finally said as she wiped her eyes.

"It's alright," Marshall soothed. "Here, how about we get you something to eat, does that sound okay?"

She nodded but took hold of my hand and not Marshall's offered one. Great, I had never been any good with kids, but somehow this little one had decided I was the better offer than my brother. I was not the best at providing any kind of comfort, and I didn't even know what to do as she sniffled and rubbed her eyes.

Marshall looked at me and motioned back toward the front of the train, and I picked the girl up to carry. I didn't trust a kid's balance walking between cars, and besides, she weighed almost nothing at all.

She quieted down to only the occasional sniffle as we walked back up to the sleeper car.

"You two wait here, and I'll bring some food back for everyone," Marshall said.

I sat the girl down and then sat beside her.

"What in the world have you done, Hazel?" Alma asked as she looked between me and the girl.

"That gaff of a man was going to throw her off!"

"A kid?" Alma asked, shaking her head. "There is no sense in that man's head."

"Sense doesn't have room with all that ego he's got shoved up his a

—" I stopped myself and cleared my throat. "Are you okay, kid?" I asked.

"What's your name?" Alma asked.

She wiped her nose on her sleeve before answering with a very soft, "Rowan."

"What a pretty name," Alma smiled. "I'm Alma, and that's Hazel."

"Hi," Rowan said.

"Where's your momma?" Alma asked as she knelt in front of the girl. Even kneeling, Alma was much taller than the small child.

"She died."

"Your daddy?" I asked.

"He died too," she said. "I got no one but Red."

"Red?" Alma and I spoke at the same time.

"Yeah, he's my stuffed doggy... I don't know where he went." Tears started to well up in her eyes again.

"After dinner, we'll go look for him. How'd you end up on this train?" Alma didn't lose a beat.

"I saw the circus... I wanted to go with the people. Are you the circus people?"

Oh lord, a kid with no family running away to join the circus by stowing away on a train. We hadn't run into one that young pulling this stunt before, and with no parents, where were we supposed to even send her?

Alma and Rowan spoke softly as I leaned back in my seat. There wasn't anywhere we could bring her. She was coming to Memphis with us, and once we got to the city, there had to be some kind of orphanage or somewhere we could take this girl.

Marshall returned with sandwiches, and a few of the other train workers followed behind him with carts of fruit for the whole group. The workers didn't stick around long as we all got it all distributed. Rowan only ate a little before she curled up with her head in my lap and dozed off.

"I think she likes you." Alma smiled.

"She's got bad taste," I said with a sigh. I could not be having a tiny shadow following after me, but here on the train, it was safe.

"Get any information out of her?" Marshall asked as he pulled a blanket over Rowan.

"Lost her parents and jumped on the train to join the circus," Alma said, shaking her head. "A right sad story for such a little thing."

"Everyone's got a sad story," I said.

"Yeah, she really picked a nurturing soul with you." Alma laughed as she got up and got food.

The ham sandwiches tasted like the meat had been boiled for way too long before it'd been tossed between some bread, but it was still better than the hardtack we had on the roads. It didn't seem like the cooks here had put in much of an effort, but the carts did have enough food, so I didn't think we'd be going hungry for a bit. Marshall sat across from me, frowning as he watched her sleeping. His eyebrows drew together, and he worried his lower lip between his teeth.

"You got your thinking face on. What are you stuck on?" I asked.

Marshall shook his head. "Just trying to figure out what to do with her. What's her name?"

"Rowan. You know they got to have orphanages or something in Memphis. It's a big city."

"Those places are awful," he said.

"We are not dragging a kid along on our show, Marshall. You get that right on out of your head."

"But—"

"No, absolutely not. We get into too many dangerous situations to have a kid around," I said.

"Hazel—"

"Look, whatever you got in your head, you need to drop it. We're a show, not an adoption agency," I said.

"What's your deal? We take in the strays no one wants all the time. We could come up with an act and—"

"We are not taking in a kid and putting her to work. What is even wrong with you?" I groaned.

"We have to do something."

"Taking her to an orphanage is something," I growled.

"Shh! Y'all are going to wake her up," Alma whispered, pointing at the sleeping child. "She must be exhausted; she barely ate anything before falling asleep. Poor thing."

I glared but crossed my arms and kept quiet. This kid would just be another distraction when what we needed to focus on was keeping the show together until we found Dad. I wasn't sure why Marshall was willing to adopt a stranger anyway. We had enough going on.

Marshall looked out the train window but kept glancing back to the sleeping child.

Not wanting to continue in the weird silence, I started eating my lunch and ignoring Marshall. The texture of the boiled ham on bread with butter felt sour in my mouth, lukewarm and like eating pudding, and I had to force myself to eat the whole thing.

I'd finished eating when the Duncans began singing an old tune and the girl jerked awake.

"Gunther!" Marshall snapped.

The short leader of the group looked confused. "What did we do?" he asked.

"It's okay, that was pretty," Rowan said as she rubbed her eyes. She got out of her seat to walk over to the Duncans. "Do you know more songs?"

Gunther's chest puffed up with pride. "Of course we do, young one. Shall we sing for you?"

Rowan looked to Marshall, and my brother joined her side as I crossed my arms over my chest.

I didn't really want to be serenaded the entire train trip, but I supposed if it kept the kid entertained, it would be all right. There were other cars I could hide in and not have to deal with the singing all the time. But I had to admit this was the most animated I had seen the Duncans outside of their performance. Usually they kept to themselves, so it was easy to forget they existed, but with Rowan, they seemed to come out of their shells a little bit.

I got comfortable in my seat as the singing started up again with Rowan clapping along, slightly off the beat. The kid didn't have much of a sense of rhythm, but she certainly was trying, and I supposed that counted for something.

I didn't know why Marshall was so intent on bringing this kid into our show when we really had no place for her and no one to look out for her. I had no idea how we would even manage taking care of her. Everyone had jobs already, and no one had the free time to play babysitter. Our work was dangerous in the best of times with town folks who didn't take kindly to our kind of entertainment. That wasn't even including things like trolls and the hellhound that were part of our show too.

I absolutely would find a way to make sure Marshall knew we were not taking this kid anywhere with us once we got off this train.

"That was great!" Rowan said with a clap as the song ended.

Marshall nodded like he hadn't heard that song a million times before. "Yeah, good work, Gunther."

Gunther beamed with pride.

"Could you teach me those songs?" Rowan asked.

Gunther looked to the rest of his little troupe, and there were a few murmurings in German before Gunther nodded and offered his hand to the girl.

Rowan smiled and took his offered hand. Their hands were almost the same size, and Rowan actually stood about a head shorter than most of the singing group. I bet they enjoyed having that brief moment of having someone look up to them.

"How about the singing lesson happens in a different car?" I suggested.

Gunther looked surprised and hesitated for a moment before he nodded. "We can practice in the storage car."

That sounded great to me. Had I always been this much of a crank or was this a recent development? The girl and the Duncans left the car with Marshall escorting them.

"I didn't know you hated kids," Alma said.

"I don't hate kids," I said.

"So just the one girl?" Alma asked.

"No. We can't be taking in orphans now too," I said.

"I mean, we take in every other kinda stray, so why not?" Constance spoke up.

Was the whole group really excited about the idea of adopting a kid? How had I missed that decision?

"Look, the work I do is dangerous. It's no place for a kid. Y'all know that."

"That doesn't mean we leave her out on the streets," Alma said.

"I never suggested that!" I protested. "Look, there are places and people out there whose whole job is to take care of kids who don't have nobody."

"We abandon her?" Temperance asked. "That's cruel, even for you."

"We aren't abandoning something that isn't even ours!" I groaned. "Why are y'all so excited about adding a kid to the mix? She ain't even got an act!"

"It's the right thing to do," Alma said simply. "Your daddy would have—"

"Oh, don't you even start," I said as I held my hand up. "Don't you even start trying to guilt me into anything by bringing up Dad. In case y'all have forgotten, he's missing! Excuse me if some kid I just met isn't the most important thing in the world right this second."

I didn't wait for an answer as I grabbed my bag and stormed out of the car. What was even happening? Why were all my friends teaming up on me? Was I really that heartless?

CHAPTER THREE

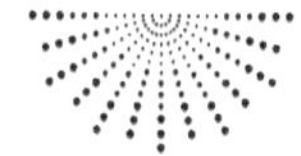

I sat down at a table in the dining cart, barely noticing as a waiter brought over a pot of coffee for me. I poured myself a mug and drank the taste of that sandwich away as I stared out the window with the world slowly being painted in the final orange and purple strokes of evening. We'd be in the pitch black of night soon. At least on this train we didn't have to worry about people having to take watch. Maybe a good night of sleep for everyone would be what we all needed.

We'd been traveling a lot more than usual, and that was clearly taking a toll on everyone, and we needed to take some time to relax and get some rest. Then everything would be normal again.

I glanced at the door, slightly surprised no one had come after me yet. I was starting to feel like the outcast of my own show. How could everyone else be so convinced adopting this kid was the thing to do? Any time we even tried to bring on a new act, it was never this unanimous a decision.

I shook my head and pulled out Dad's journal. I started sketching out Rowan, the red hair, freckles, and wide eyes. Her teeth were all messed up, jagged and crooked, and those gangly arms made it clear she hadn't been eating right for a long time.

I groaned. I was not getting drawn into this thing. I could feel sorry for her and know letting her stay with us wasn't the right thing. Why did everyone else have such a hard time with that?

What was I missing that everyone else got? It was making me feel like a monster. I rubbed my arm over the hellhound mark and took a deep breath. Was this thing somehow getting to me? I didn't imagine hellhounds were known for their sympathy; what was happening?

"I wish you were here, Dad," I muttered.

I felt like I said that every day, but it remained true every single day he was gone. Much as I wanted to be, I wasn't sure I was ready to be on my own as a hunter or in this show without him.

The silence of the dining car was soothing in its own way, and when no one came to find me or try to talk to me, I decided to make myself comfortable. I laid out in the booth seat and let out a long breath as I closed my eyes and drifted off.

When I woke again, the world was dark. The dining car grew dark, and the world beyond the windows held only the moon as a dim source of light. My eyes slowly adjusted as I stayed on the dining car booth bench, not quite ready to move yet.

No one had come to find me or ask me to come back to the rest of the group, and I must have been asleep for a few hours. How had I been so easily replaced by a little kid? I didn't understand how everyone could ignore me, but then again, what did it really matter? We were all stuck together as a show and a makeshift family whether we liked it or not. There wasn't a lot that would change that.

That didn't mean it still didn't hurt like hell and piss me off that I had been tossed out. I'd have thought my own brother and Alma would've cared a little more than to leave me alone.

I sat up and stretched. My back popped a few times in protest of sleeping on such a crummy "mattress," but it was nothing that wouldn't fade in a few hours. It's not as though the beds in the sleeper cars had much better mattresses, and our wagons didn't have anything comfortable enough to warrant missing.

Through the window I tried to spot some kind of landmark or something to give me a hint about where we were, but all I got was a whole lot of darkness. Not even a light from any nearby towns showed up. We really were in the middle of nowhere, but I knew we were making a lot better time than we would be on the carriages. Here we could travel through the night. We all needed the rest; I knew I did for sure.

I finally got up from the booth and stood up before deciding if nothing else, I didn't want to keep sleeping in my dresses. I slipped out of the dining car and back to the sleeper.

With the pale light of the moon outside to guide me, I fumbled around under the seats until my hand hit my rough burlap sack where I'd thrown clothes for the trip.

I started unlacing my dress, not too worried about anyone seeing. None of these seats looked too comfortable either, and I was considering heading back to the dining car to sleep some more when screams sliced through the dark and quiet train.

CHAPTER FOUR

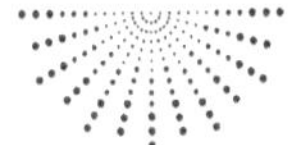

At the sound of the screams, I immediately took off at a run. I couldn't tell exactly where they were coming from, but they were loud and towards the caboose. Pushing back through the sleeping car, Marshall and Alma blinked awake but most everyone else remained asleep. I didn't wait for them to get up as I ran through the room, jumping over Marshall as I bolted across the connection between cars and into the next one.

I found several of the singing Duncans scrambling through the room, the screaming coming from them as they all barreled forward, past me.

"What's going on?" I asked, trying to get any kind of answer.

"Monster!" was the only answer I got before they scurried out of the car. I pulled my dagger from my garter and kept moving. The next car was quiet, but the air smelled of blood. It wasn't heavy in the air yet, but I'd been around enough death and violence to know what that smelled like even at a bit of distance. What the hell had managed to get onto the train and how?

I'd have time to worry about all of that later after I'd dealt with whatever this thing was.

As I sloppily re-laced my dress, I summoned Puck out to serve as a second set of eyes as I moved through this train car and to the next. The smell of blood and death hung heavy in the air like a blanket. How had some monster gotten on board? Before I could ponder on my own question any more, a roar ripped through the air, nearly shaking the car. A horrible gurgling punctuated the screams as I rushed forward with my dagger out and ready to summon whatever I needed to deal with this threat.

I tugged at the door, but it didn't slide open like all the others had. Something heavy blocked it from moving. Balancing on the connector piece between the two cars, I got a little speed and rammed my shoulder into the barricaded door. It slowly began to budge as a noise tore through the back of the car. I finally managed to shove the door open enough for Puck, and then I squeezed through. Tripping on the remains of a large trunk that must have been the barricade, I landed on a blood-splattered floor.

Huddled in the nearby corner of the baggage car, Rowan curled herself into a ball, crying and clutching a stuffed toy, dripping with blood.

"Rowan? What happened?" I asked.

Rowan cried more, and I moved past her to try to find the source of the blood. Behind a pile of our crates and trunks of supplies, I spotted it and felt bile rise up my throat. Dangling from the ceiling by a scarf, Gunther hung upside down with his throat split wide open. Under his body, a bucket laid on its side with blood running out of it and covering the floors. My shoes were already saturated and sticking to the floor.

Knowing it was useless, I still moved to Gunther's side and tried to check for a pulse, but he was entirely still with all signs of life splattered around the floor. Behind me, the door creaked open and I heard a sharp intake of breath before Alma's voice said, "What in the blue damn?"

"Get Rowan out of here," I said. "And don't come any farther into the room."

Alma didn't argue with me, and Rowan's crying got quieter as the door closed behind them. I was left alone with the body of Gunther, our lead of the Singing Duncans.

I moved across the train car and through toward the caboose. I found a few claw marks along the floors, nearly ripping through the metal, but even with Puck helping me on the hunt, there was no sign of any kind of monster. Something with claws that could cut metal had hung someone from the ceiling and drained them dry? That didn't make any kind of sense.

Vampires didn't hunt like that, neither did wendigos or trolls. Most of the monsters weren't smart enough to have this kind of hunting strategy—their whole goal was to eat, not create a pool of blood.

As I walked back up toward the bloody car, I heard Marshall's voice and the damn train conductor.

"You are all under arrest!" the man yelled.

"You can't arrest us. You have no authority, and we had nothing to do with this." Marshall, somehow, sounded calm and collected even while standing in a room filled with gore.

"As soon as we get to town, you are all going to get locked up and dealt with like freaks should!" Red splotches flashed over his pale face as his nostrils flared with each heavy breath.

"And how is that?" I asked as I walked closer.

The man jumped then glared. "You! You're responsible! Stay back, murderess!"

"I didn't do anything. I'm trying to find what *did* do this before it gets a chance to do it again," I snapped.

"What?" The man frowned as if the thought hadn't dawned on him.

"Whatever did this is probably still on the train," Marshall said.

"You mean *whoever* did this? Because I am looking at her!" The man nearly shoved a finger into my chest but caught himself before he touched me. Lucky for him and his finger.

Marshall cleared his throat. "What my sister means to say is that we will take care of this and ensure there is no further harm to any person or your train."

"You aren't getting any of your security deposit back!" the man said, waving his finger in Marshall's face.

"A man is dead. My *friend* is dead. Have some decency," I snapped.

"It's you freaks' fault. I'm going to the sheriff soon as we hit town," the man muttered, walking away. "Don't come near the front of the train. I've got a pistol and I'll use it."

I barely hid my eye roll as the man finally left. Marshall turned to me, and I noticed the faint green color to his cheeks—he looked like he was about to heave up every bit of the sad dinner we'd had a few hours ago.

I wrapped an arm around his shoulder and moved him out of the blood-soaked room. "Deep breaths," I said.

"That's Gunther," Marshall said.

"It is."

"He's…"

I nodded. "He is."

Marshall ran a hand through his hair. "Damn it all."

"Yeah, basically." "

"Do you know what did this? Where is it?"

"I don't know. I looked farther down the train, but I didn't see it."

"Did it leave? Jump off maybe?"

"Marshall, your guess is as good as mine. I got no idea. I saw some claw marks in the metal, but whatever killed Gunther I think had some brains…it wasn't like an animal or beast attack."

"What are you saying? That conductor is right and this was something a person did?"

"I'm saying we're dealing with something I've not run into before," I said.

"How are we going to tell Helga and the others?" Marshall asked.

"I don't know." I sat beside Marshall and let out a long breath.

"Shit," Marshall said.

That seemed like about all there was to say about the current state of affairs. Had that Eclipse woman sent something after us to destroy our show? Was she following behind somehow, ready to loot the remains of the train for more goodies for her show? No money in the world was worth whatever was happening.

After a few moments of silence, Marshall got to his feet.

"Where are you going?" I asked.

"We need to tell the others," he said.

I really hated when he was right.

We quietly walked back to the rest of the group. There were no words to make sense of what happened, and it felt useless to even try.

"What is going on? That damn train man came in here and said we were all under arrest!" Alma said as soon as we walked in.

Everyone was awake, every set of eyes stared at me and my brother, and for the first time it really hit me that, for better or worse, Marshall and I were running the show right now.

Marshall cleared his throat. "There's been an incident."

Rowan sniffled loudly, and Constance wrapped her arm around the girl.

"Where is Gunther?" Helga, one of the Duncans' sopranos, a bright young faery with flaming red hair, said.

"Helga… I'm sorry to say…" Marshall's voice cracked.

"Gunther is dead," I said when it became obvious emotions stole Marshall's voice from him.

The impact of the words rippled through the room. Half of the group sank into their seats while the other half seemed too stunned to move. For a second, silence lingered, and then multiple voices exploded all at once.

"Dead?" Helga stared at us.

"How?" Constance asked.

"What happened?" Temperance snapped.

"Who did this?" Alma asked.

"What did the train conductor mean we're all under arrest?" Jonah asked.

Marshall swallowed hard and held up his hand. "We are trying to figure it out," he said.

"What should we do?" Alma asked.

Marshall looked at me.

"Stay in here. We're going to figure this out… Give me and Marshall some time."

"Are we all going to die?" Helga asked between heaving sobs.

"No!" I promised. "Absolutely not. No…wait here for a few minutes."

I grabbed Marshall's elbow and pulled him into the dining car.

Marshall sagged into a booth and wiped his face with a handkerchief. "Hazel, what are we going to do?"

"You're going to deal with our people, and I'm going to hunt down whatever killed Gunther."

Marshall nodded but didn't seem convinced. Hell, I wasn't convinced either, but what choice was there? We were the only ones who were able to deal with whatever kind of monster had done this.

"I'll go look and see if there's anything else in…the room where it happened. You talk to everyone else?" I suggested.

"Somehow I think you're getting the easier end of the deal here," Marshall grumbled as he got out of the booth and offered his hand to help me up. He paused and looked down.

"You maybe ought to change clothes; you're getting blood every-where with those shoes."

"Alright, go check on everyone, then bring me my bag so I can change."

Marshall nodded and left the room.

I ran my hands through my hair and winced as I remembered all the blood I'd walked around in and that likely splattered over my skin. I'd need a hose down and then some once we got to the city.

Whatever else happened here, I had to make sure nothing else got to my family. No other attacks, no harm. Dad had never let a creature through to hurt the show, and here I was already messing up that track record.

Marshall came back in and passed over my bag.

I pulled Dad's book out of my bag. Flipping through it, I didn't even know what to look for. Something with claws that could string a man up and collect his blood?

I could match pieces to things. The claws matched one part and the stringing up matched something else. Was I dealing with two different monsters or one very different kind of thing?

I ran my fingers through my hair and sighed. I'd wanted a relaxing trip where I could catch up on my sleep, and here I was on a hunt in a confined space.

"How is everyone?" I asked.

"Well...as alright as can be expected. The Duncans are...struggling."

"I can't even imagine what they're going through," I said.

"But I think they might know something. Helga keeps saying, '*Die kleine Roth-Kappe*' and panicking. I can't get her to calm down enough to talk to me."

The name sounded familiar, like something Dad had read to us in a legend once. "They think another faery did this?" I asked as I wracked my brain for translation.

I'd never learned German, but being around the Duncans had taught me a few things. The little red hat? That sounded like a bad joke, not a dangerous monster.

"I don't know. But I think you ought to talk to her and see what she might have to say," Marshall said.

"Even if it is some faery, what am I supposed to do? We can't really tell the police, 'It's fine. It was a faery. Don't worry about it.'" I groaned. That conductor really had it out for us.

"We have to convince the trainmaster to not drag us off to the police. We got until we get to the next station in a few hours. We need an answer by morning."

I scoffed. "Oh, plenty of time."

"It's a train. If there is some monster thing here, it can't have gone far," Marshall said.

"It could have jumped off. It could be invisible. It could be the size of a dime. And if you've forgotten, they can fly. Faeries don't play by the same rules you and I do."

"Look, Hazel, we got to sort this out or we're in trouble."

I knew he was right, but God above, I didn't want to be dealing with this. "Fine, I'll talk to Helga and go on this wild goose chase."

CHAPTER FIVE

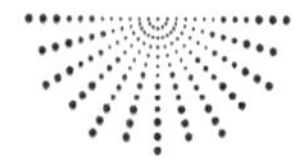

I headed straight over to the Duncans. The remaining four of them were huddled around Jonah, who seemed to be offering a prayer of some sort to soothe them. Funny, I hadn't figured faeries for the type to listen to the Bible.

I walked over and stayed silent as Jonah finished his prayer. A few of them wiped their eyes while Helga looked stone-faced and determined.

"Are you here to help?" Helga asked me. Her voice wasn't as accented as the others. I felt a little guilty I'd never spent much time talking to the Duncans before, and now they were lost and hurting. I'd been a terrible friend to them. Maybe I should have made more of an effort.

I cleared my throat. "I'm here to listen."

"Hazel can help," Jonah said.

Helga nodded and looked from Jonah to me. "Alright. Then help. You cannot bring him back."

"No. But I can try to figure out who or what did this and make sure nothing happens to anyone else," I said.

"It was *Die kleine Roth-Kappe*," she said with no hesitation.

"The red hat? I don't know about killer hats anywhere in America," I said.

Helga's glare could have melted the very steel railroad we were riding on. "Not a hat. A faery. He wears a red cap."

"And you think this thing killed Gunther?"

"It did. You can smell it in the blood."

"What?" I asked, staring at the little singer in front of me. Had they been able to smell blood the whole time and I was now finding out about it? If that was the case, I could only imagine what they all must think about me constantly smelling like a bloodbath.

"Okay, you can smell this red hat?" I asked.

"Red Cap. No. I can't smell it. Just recognize its work."

"Can you find it?" I asked.

She shook her head. "No, no. I like my head and my life. I will not go look for this monster. That is death."

"But you'd like me to go look for it?" I asked.

"You hunt these kinds of things. Your job, not mine."

"But you can smell it!"

"No, I cannot smell where it is. But on your shoes." She pointed. "There is the smell of faery blood. Gunther."

"And you think it might be this thing because…?"

"I saw enough. I saw Gunther in the air over a bucket…" She wiped her eyes.

"Can you give me any kind of clue about where this thing might be? What it looks like?" I asked, trying to keep my voice gentle.

"It is murderous old man. Same size as we are. Once was like us but no more. It lives in shadows."

Charming. This sounded like a great time for me.

A tiny old man in a blood-red hat hiding in the shadows… Should be a piece of cake to actually find, especially on a train. I couldn't imagine something the size of Helga here would be too much of an issue to deal with, murderous or not. I dealt with deadly things all the time; I might as well not worry about it too much. I wasn't sure Marshall's idea of finding the creature responsible was going to keep us from getting kicked off.

"Great. I'll take care of it."

She nodded but didn't look convinced as she headed back to her group all huddled together. Jonah returned to their side, offering some comfort. I still didn't know how Jonah hadn't been able to become a preacher... Well, I did know. No one wanted a preacher with no arms even if he was the Godliest man I'd ever met. People were the worst sometimes.

"Alright." I looked to Marshall. "I need to examine the body again. You coming?"

Marshall swallowed hard before Jonah spoke up. "I'll go with you."

I looked at the preacher man, but when he didn't back down, I nodded. "Then let's go."

The smell of blood rang like a bell, loud and clear. At the entrance to the car, the makeshift blockade laid mostly toppled over. I began disassembling that to clear up space enough for Jonah to more easily get in.

The dead man still hung from the top of the car by his foot. One rope bound his wrists together where they dangled uselessly above his head, and another rope wrapped around his ankles then up through one of the car vents. A deep slice across his throat had nearly totally detached his head as he swung with the movements of the train.

I let out a long breath. I'd seen a lot of dead things in my life, but this one hit up there as one of the worst. Beneath the hanging man sat a large, rusted bucket. The liquid in the bucket had already congealed and turned dark as maple syrup, but the smell was clearly blood. That wasn't the fastest, easiest way to kill anyone, even if this madman faery did want the blood.

The wolf tattoo lurched at the rancid smell of blood, and heat poured from my arm. I wrapped my other hand around the mark, ignoring the burning of skin. The wolf struggled to get free, and I bit at my lip to focus on my own pain and draw my focus to my own body.

The hunger twisted and lurched almost out of my control. Heat pooled around my arm and burned through the skin. I groaned and bit harder at my lip, the sharp taste of the blood against my lips soothing the hunger for a moment.

Slowly the fire shrunk back to a small but all-present burning, the heat that had been lingering since I'd captured the wolf. Taking a deep breath, I took another look around the room without the hunger changing everything into pain and struggle. I shouldn't have complained it was too quiet before.

Around the bucket there were splashes of blood, like the bucket had been knocked or jostled around and spilled somewhere along the way. I let out a long breath and looked at Jonah, who had a decidedly green tint to his skin.

"Either the Duncans are right and this is some murderous faery, or we have a regular murderer loose," I said.

"Considering it's basically our show on the train, I'm inclined to believe the Duncans on this front."

I shrugged. "You saw how much the ticket inspector doesn't like us. Who's to say he wouldn't do something like this? He's got the access."

Jonah cleared his throat. "Yes, but how about we start with why would anyone be back here?"

Guilt slammed into me. "I asked them to go sing somewhere else," I said softly.

"It isn't your fault, Hazel," Jonah said in his entirely too preacher-like voice.

I didn't say anything and started looking around for anything I might have missed.

I started poking around the trunks and crates for any information and found a few things that didn't seem to belong to any of our people. How they had gotten on the train seemed a mystery, but I had one person in mind: the woman from the platform, Madame Eclipse. No one else had really been around the train at the time we loaded up, and if Rowan had managed to sneak on without being seen, then how hard would it have been to put something else on the train? Something dangerous.

The question was, where was it now?

"Okay, if the Duncans are right and this is some murder faery, how do we find it?" Jonah asked.

"How do *I* find it. You've got no part in this but being a second pair of eyes for me."

The only thing out of place looked like the trunk I'd spotted earlier. "Jonah, you know this thing?"

Jonah tiptoed past the bucket and over to me. "That's not ours. How did—"

I walked over to the trunk and shoved my dagger between the lid and the box and began prying.

"Hazel!" Jonah hissed.

"What? You want to know how a monster got on board, and we find a strange box in the room with the dead body. Looks like our answers could be right here. That damned woman probably did this."

"What woman?"

"The one who bought my skeleton. Knew it was too good to be true," I muttered.

"Hazel, just 'cause she was around doesn't mean that she—"

"Then where did it come from?" I asked.

"Well, maybe Rowan saw something. She was stowing away."

Not a bad idea. I nodded before returning to picking open the locked chest.

Jonah shifted on his feet. "Be quick about it. We don't need to get caught breaking into stuff that isn't ours."

The trunk was old and not in great shape, so it forfeited eventually, and the lid popped open. Inside was a collection of strange leather caps. They all looked like the ones all those newsboys yelling on the corner wore. They didn't look anything like something the posh Eclipse woman would wear. A few had strange fur stuck to them. But why would anyone have a trunk of only hats?

I picked one up, and moisture stuck to my fingers. I dropped it immediately, and it slid down my dress. A thick brown sludge smeared along my khaki dress. Great. Another dress ruined out of respectable daily wear and into a hunting outfit.

"What is that?" Jonah asked, looking around my shoulder at the caps.

"Well, Helga did say it was called a Red Cap so... I guess we found its hat collection."

"What's it doing with this many hats?"

"Jonah, if I knew, I wouldn't be staring at them like this. I don't know what a trunk full of caps means or why anyone would have them. All I know is clearly this ain't our chest, and how it ended up here is a big problem we need to figure out."

Jonah sighed. "Yes, this does seem a mess."

"Let's get out of here." I closed the trunk, glad it didn't look too obviously pried open.

Jonah didn't need me to tell him twice as he headed out the open door. I followed behind him with one last glance toward the body.

"I've got to figure this out," I said.

"We will," Jonah promised.

I didn't bother correcting him again; this was not a group problem. This was a me problem to solve.

Marshall looked slightly less green as we returned to our car. He lingered on the back of our sitting car and pulled out a cigarette and lit it up. That seemed to soothe his shaking hands and uneasy stomach. I watched him to make sure he wasn't going to puke up his lunch, but he looked better at least.

I felt guilty I wasn't more shaken up by the death of someone who had been part of our show for several seasons. Months together, and his death barely seemed to faze me. We all were a troupe, but some of us had made tighter bonds than others. The Singing Duncans had always stuck together and not really been interested in letting anyone else involve themselves in their lives. It didn't help that only a few of them spoke any kind of English aside from the songs they'd memorized. The language barrier made it a challenge to have any kind of relationship happen. But now, the Duncans were all huddled together dealing with their loss while I stood on the outside trying to save the whole troupe from getting hit with more trouble. If some supernatural thing was hunting and killing people on the train, we needed to be dealing with that immediately.

I sat back in my seat while Jonah paced, trying to get rid of whatever images lingered after wandering through the room of death and blood. Pulling out Dad's notebook, I thumbed through and found a blank page to start making notes on.

Dad had really been terrible at keeping track of much of anything in here. It looked like he hadn't updated it in years, but I needed to keep this information somewhere. I wanted to have some way to show Dad what I'd been up to while he was gone. If his little disappearing act didn't do anything else, it would show him I could be a hunter all by myself and he didn't need to hover around like a shadow all the time. We needed someone to lead the show and not be trying to manage a show and a hunting job. Marshall and I worked because we could split the labor, but Dad tried to take it all on and only managed to do it all really poorly more than anything else.

So far all I had were pieces of information that wouldn't do me much good to make a whole picture of what I was even dealing with. There was always some mystery of "I don't know" when dealing with monsters. Most of them didn't come with informational postcards you could review like our acts did; it was a lot of figuring it out as you went. My method meant a whole lot of trial and error. This thing sounded like that kind of strategy wouldn't work very well.

Usually I dealt with monsters hunting people, not faeries, but it had killed one of the Duncans, and they weren't humans, so did that mean only other monsters were at risk or had it acted for another reason, maybe been trying to silence someone outing them? Was this a monster trying to live unnoticed as a train hobo and then got caught and exposed? Somehow, I doubted anything called a Red Cap that had drained the blood from a body was something looking for a quiet, anonymous life. I imagined the only life it looked for was a life it could drain out over a bucket.

I didn't know where to begin here, but the best leads I had were the Duncans. They clearly had some idea of what this thing was and, grieving or not, I needed answers and I needed them fast or else we were all out on the streets without wagons or money and potentially some monster would stay on this train doing who knew what once we left.

I walked back over to the huddled, crying group. "I'm sorry to bother you—"

"We have nothing else to say," one snapped.

The woman who had originally talked to me, Helga, stepped from the group with a sigh. "We can speak, but privately."

I led her to the car behind us. Perched amongst the pieces of our show, I said, "Thanks. I need some more information to try to help out."

"I don't know what more you can want. I told you what did this."

"Yes, you did, but what is a Red Cap?"

"It's a horrible creature that murders for blood."

"For blood?"

"Its name isn't for looks. The hat it wears, it's dyed in blood to keep it bright. That's what a Red Cap does."

The trunk of sludgy brown hats suddenly made a lot more sense than I had originally thought.

Creepier than I originally thought too. Great, creepy, my favorite. Now there'd be a little man hunting down people to dip dye a hat.

I rolled my shoulders. I needed to figure out how this thing hunted before it tried to go after someone else. Killing things was easier to figure out if you knew the when and where first. Otherwise, you stabbed in the dark and hoped you hit something.

"How does it hunt?" I asked.

She shrugged her shoulders. "I don't really know. Like anything else, I suppose. I don't work on its schedule."

"Nothing?" I asked.

"It likes dark and being alone. It lures creatures with a hint of treasure then kills them."

Great, that'd be easy to find on a train. There'd be nowhere dark and full of hidden treasure to work with on this train. Absolutely not anything.

"Thank you," I said. "I'm sorry for your loss," I added.

Had I apologized already? How could I apologize when I barely felt the loss? It felt like it hadn't hit reality yet, like the death somehow hadn't connected with the rest of the world. Time on the train felt different, like it didn't match up with reality in any way, shape, or form.

I couldn't imagine what this all looked like from her angle, how strange it must seem. What would a proper answer be to an apology for her loss? That didn't bring anyone back or change what had happened. Why did I even apologize for something that's not my fault? Did this somehow make it my fault?

She nodded her head, and we returned to the rest of her group. I glanced at Marshall, and he sank back into his seat beside Jonah. Hopefully the preacher man could give Marshall and the Duncans some semblance of peace in one way or another. That was what the Bible was supposed to be good at, right? It'd never given me much of a comfort, but I didn't need to worry much about that. Comfort didn't do a whole lot of good in a fight anyway.

I adjusted my dress and headed into the storage room car again. If it had been in here to begin with, then maybe it still hid somewhere in the strange boxes.

I started with the largest boxes. The first few held tent parts, stakes, poles, and other large items, no sign of dried blood or hints of any kind of tiny man hiding in them at any point. Next, I went through the twins' things. Their double-person dresses made their wardrobe the largest aside from mine, but it turned up nothing again.

"Just rifling through everything?" Alma's voice came from behind me.

I spun around and found her hunched over to fit through the doorway.

"Spying on me?"

"Better than sitting around. I wanted to grab a book from my things," she said.

"Thought you said reading while we were moving made you sick." I moved over to Alma's things and opened her small box, looking for any sign of a killer man.

Alma leaned over me and rifled around until she found the book, a thin book of verses. "It's not for me. Besides that's in a carriage, not on a train. They move totally different," she said.

"Who's it for? If you're reading a bedtime story, then I—"

"It's for Clarence. He never learned to read, so I figure now's a good time to start teaching him," Alma said.

"Clarence?" I asked.

"Frenchie," she said. "His name is Clarence."

Alma had gotten to know his name and not what we called him at the circus; that sure boded well for how they were getting on. Not to mention Alma wanting to teach him how to read. That definitely wasn't something happening for no reason for sure.

"You're not on board to help me figure out where this thing is?" I asked.

Alma hesitated for a moment, and I hastily added, "Alma, I'm kidding. Go read with Fren... Clarence. I've dealt with enough murderous critters to handle it on my own. Just teasing you."

Alma's shoulders relaxed a little as she held the book to her chest. "Anything we should do to keep this thing away from us?" she asked.

I couldn't imagine something the size of the Duncans really posing much of a threat to someone as tall as Alma. If its whole thing was draining blood into a tub, I couldn't imagine it'd be able to hoist Alma anywhere in a train.

"Stick with Clarence. Don't go into the dark and don't go after any strange boxes that show up," I finally said. "Don't think it'll be a problem for long, so don't worry."

"I'll keep an eye on Rowan. Might teach her to read too."

I nodded. That painted a nice little family picture right there.

"Alright, I'll head over to talk to Rowan in a little bit."

"Do not tell me you are interrogating that child."

"She's a stowaway. Maybe she saw something, that's it." I held up my hands.

That seemed to placate her.

"Alright, we'll be in the sleeper car." Alma nodded and took her book and left. I smiled to myself. Alma was getting quite smitten with this musician. I hoped he stuck around long enough to see where this would go.

I turned back to the boxes, finally diving into my own things, and immediately I found a torn dress with smudges of brown dried blood along the tears in the fabric. Had my dress become a napkin? I glared at the ruined fabric, one of my only good dresses I could wear into town, all messed up because of a homicidal faery. For being so little, they sure caused big problems.

The side of my crate had a hole ripped into it, and from there, I found a track of small, bloody footprints leading to the door heading toward the back of the train. I doubted the little thing had abandoned the train quickly. I followed after the footprints and out the door, but from there, I lost sight of it. There was no blood in the next car, nothing obvious until I looked to the side and saw the blood on the ladder.

Great, it'd gone up.

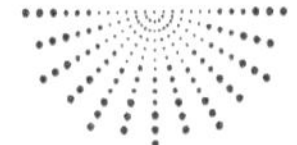

I hesitantly climbed up the ladder, pausing at the top and looking ahead. The track looked clear, no trees nearby and no tunnels immediately visible. If I gambled, I'd probably make it okay.

Taking a deep breath and hoping luck might be on my side for once, I moved up to the top of the car. The air whipped past me, cool but humid with nothing but blurred shadows whipping past the train. The footprints were spaced close together but all of them smeared like they'd been made in a hurry. Whatever this thing was, it moved fast. I tried to not think about what that meant for me. As I crossed over the passenger car where I knew Marshall was, I swallowed. This thing had been right above us and none of us had noticed. Jumping to the next car, I followed the blood that dripped back down the ladder and into the next car, the dining car.

I followed after and stepped inside. No one sat at any of the tables, and even the bar was unattended. I didn't know why, but I guessed the middle of the night didn't count as a peak time or that lead train inspector had shut down everything as punishment for us having dared to have someone murdered on his train. It wasn't like any of it had been done on purpose, so what did it matter? It wasn't our fault.

Well, it might have been. Our show did seem to attract trouble no matter where we went. Probably all part of the agreement with Lady Death. I really wished Dad had shared the details of the contract with me. I wanted to know what exactly I had signed up for by doing this. Not that it mattered. I didn't think there were any take backs as far as deals with supernatural beings went, whether the devil or Death, a deal was a deal for as long as you lived and then some.

With no one at the bar, I took the chance to sneak behind the counter, but I didn't see any blood anywhere. The trail vanished as soon as I got into this car. It couldn't have disappeared, but the blood could have been cleaned up by this point, and with that went the best lead I had. I knew it was quiet, fast, and sloppy. Not a great or very helpful list of traits to have at the moment, but it was more than I'd started with.

I couldn't wait for it to attack again because this thing didn't injure people, it killed them, and no one else was going to lose their life to this thing, not if I had any say in it, and I was inserting myself into the conversation right now so that was the end of that as far as I was concerned.

With no sign of the creature, I headed back to the sitting car. Maybe Rowan had seen something while she was hiding.

The Duncans had all settled into seats near the back of the car and sat alone speaking quietly amongst themselves. I didn't know how to help them feel better aside from killing this thing, and even that might not be enough. Nothing I could do would bring back their lost boss, and that was the real pain of loss. It was permanent.

I headed to Jonah, surprised to find Marshall sitting beside him again. Since when had the two of them been this friendly? I sat across from the boys, and they both looked up from their papers.

"Find anything?" Marshall asked.

I shook my head. "Not yet. Whatever it was took off toward the dining car."

"And you were following that trail from the roof?" Marshall asked.

"You heard me?" I frowned. I'd tried to be quiet.

"It sounded like a horse above us," Jonah added.

"Yeah, well that thing went by roof earlier and you didn't hear anything?" I asked.

Marshall looked at Jonah and frowned. "No."

"If Miss Helga is right and it is something similar in size to their troop, that would make it harder to hear," Jonah said.

"Which is going to make it a pain to track," I said with a heavy sigh.

"You've tracked worse. Those little sleeping faeries of yours were smaller."

The sleeping faeries… If I really wanted to keep everyone safe…

"Yeah but they had obvious homes to find, fairy rings and that sort of thing. This Red Cap guy hides in random dark places, and that's not easy," I said, shifting the topic away from my tattoos.

"We are on a train with limited hiding spots as opposed to in a large city," Jonah said.

He had a point, and I knew I really had to deal with this thing before we got near a city. This monster loose in a big city like Memphis meant big trouble for me and for anyone who lived there. I really couldn't have that happening.

"Jonah, you know anything about this creature?" I asked.

"Why would I?"

"You know about all these demons and Bible things. This thing sounds like it'd fit right in with that."

"That may be the case, but no. I am familiar with the Word of the Lord, and this Red Cap is not a part of any Bible verse."

He had a point.

"Right, thanks," I said before heading over to where Alma sat with Clarence on one side and Rowan on the other. Alma looked up when she saw me and offered a smile.

"Hey… Rowan, can I talk to you for a minute?" I asked.

Rowan looked to Alma, who nodded.

"Okay." Rowan got up and took hold of my hands. Her tiny grasp was a lot warmer than I'd expected.

I carried her across the gap between our car and the dining car. Sitting her at a booth, I slipped into the kitchen and made her a small cup of hot chocolate.

"What's going on?" Rowan asked.

"I'm figuring that out. Rowan, did you see anything when you got on the train?"

"There were a lot of boxes, so I hid with them." She hugged her stuffed red dog to her chest.

"Okay, but did you see anyone else getting on the train? Any other boxes being brought on?" I asked.

"Oh, I think I heard a woman and a big thud like something heavy got dropped." She sipped on her hot chocolate as she thought.

"But I couldn't see anything 'cause I didn't want anyone to see me so I stayed hiding."

A woman loading something onto the train? I was right—that Eclipse had done this. But how had she gotten a murderous faery or monster or whatever this was, onto the train?

"Are we going to get hurt?" Rowan asked.

"What? No, nothing is going to happen to you," I said.

"Mr. Marshall said we would all have to help keep each other safe tonight," she said.

"Did he?" I frowned.

Glancing out the window, I guessed it had to be nearing midnight. This thing hunted at night, and I needed to make sure no one else got hurt.

"Do you want to help me pick up snacks for everyone?" I asked.
Rowan nodded.

I went to make sandwiches before spotting my hands then Rowan's. We were both filthy. "First we gotta wash our hands," I said.

"No!" Rowan pulled back.

"Rowan, you're covered in blood," I said.

She wrestled against me. "No! I don't like water!"

"Rowan, stop!" I struggled with her, surprised by how wily a six-year-old could be.

"If you want dinner, you have to wash up," I said. "The water isn't going to hurt you."

When it became clear to Rowan she wasn't getting away from me, she went limp in my grasp. I washed our hands together even as she made whining noises. Her little stuffed toy was filthy too, and I shoved it under the water.

"No!" Rowan screeched, trying to grab for her toy as I washed some of Gunther's blood from it as Rowan cried. She clawed at my arms, actually managing to scratch me up a little bit, and I finally let her take the damn toy.

Children.

Washing myself off took a little time, especially since the stupid fur from the damn dog toy clung to me and my dress. When we both were mostly clean, I set to making sandwiches. After Rowan finished glaring at me, she helped too.

We carried the food back to the sleeper car, and Rowan passed it out to the group.

I chewed on my lip and looked around at my show. If I couldn't find this thing, then I would set a trap for it. If there was no one out but me, it'd have to come after me, and that was exactly what I needed.

CHAPTER SEVEN

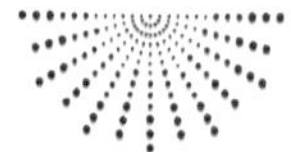

You look worried," Marshall murmured softly to me as everyone ate.

I shrugged but didn't say anything. Marshall always could see through my lies, much better for me to keep my mouth shut.

"Do you think whatever this thing is will be out again so soon?" he asked.

"I mean, I hope. If it's not out to hunt soon, we're in trouble with getting kicked off the train and unleashing a murderous monster into a city," I answered after thinking about it.

"You'll find it," Marshall said, but I wasn't sure if he wanted to convince me or himself of that.

"If it dyes its hat with blood…then I bet it will be looking for more. Gunther can't have given it much."

"It's a hat," Marshall said. "That can't take a lot, right?"

"There was a whole trunk full of hats. I don't think it's got just the one," I said.

"So it will be after a human?" Marshall asked.

"That's what I reckon," I said.

"Well, I'll go with you tonight and help," he said.

I nodded even as I let the sleep faery from the Land of Noct slide from my skin. The faery moved quickly to the ceiling out of notice and began her work moving from section to section of my sideshow family.

I tried to not feel guilty. This was the right thing to do. I wasn't going to lose anyone else to this thing. Slowly people began dropping to sleep. Marshall noticed and turned to me. "Hazel?"

"Sorry, Marshall," I said as the faery slammed him with dust.

His eyes got heavy, and I helped ease him into the seat beside Jonah before sleep fully washed over him. The faery curled up on the headrest behind him, and I let her stay there to keep everyone sleeping for the night.

Rowan curled up by Alma and Clarence, her stuffed toy on the floor at her feet. Constance and Temperance were sagged into their seats snoring like a train engine.

I let out a long breath and reminded myself this was the right thing to do before I slid out of the car, locking the door behind me. I headed back to the storage car to start the hunt.

I found my bags and rifled through until I found an acceptable hunting dress. I couldn't get to Dad's stuff to put on a decent pair of pants since the trunk was under a pile of parts for the tents. I changed right there and strapped my dagger to my side. I didn't even bother to hide it. Probably be in my best interest if someone did see it. I'd rather scare someone away from me because if the train employees left me alone, they'd probably get through the night in one piece.

Hand on my dagger hilt, I climbed onto the roof and nicked my finger, hoping the smell of blood would draw this bastard out.

I figured if the thing had taken to the roofs after its first kill then it probably would use that way to get back to the action tonight. I could find it and deal with it quickly before we ever got to Memphis. But even if I dealt with this thing, would that really fix anything? The conductor still planned to throw us off and report us to the police once we hit town. That wouldn't do at all. We couldn't find Dad if we ended up in prison.

If the Red Cap got ahold of that annoying man, you wouldn't have to worry about a thing.

The thought flickered across my mind in a rough, growling voice that was definitely not my own. I swallowed hard then shook my head quickly. Almost as soon as I had asked the question, I knew it belonged to the hellhound, and demons speaking into my head was not a great thing to be happening.

I shook my head and kept moving. I would not be doing anything that let anyone get killed, especially not a random human who, while a jerk, really didn't deserve to be murdered by a little goblin type thing. No matter how much easier that would make my life.

I would fix this and make the man see reason. Maybe if I didn't immediately kill the Red Cap but instead captured it, I could be able to prove what had happened and get the whole thing taken care of. Surely the inspector would believe something right in front of his eyes. I certainly hoped so because I didn't fancy having to break anyone out of jail if that man didn't believe me, and there were too many of us to make a run for it.

The top of the car was quiet, but ahead I could see we were moving through mountains with tunnels. I wouldn't be able to be out on top for very long tonight, not without being on all fours and maybe losing the skin on my back. Not something that sounded like a good idea to me. I climbed back down and walked into the dining car.

"The kitchen is closing down," the man at the bar said.

I didn't recognize him. He was polishing up glasses and not making eye contact with me. What on earth had that terrible conductor been telling the employees about us? Had they all been avoiding us?

"That's fine, I came in to read and enjoy the view," I said and quickly sat down before he could notice the dagger at my side.

The man left me alone as I sat and pretended to be engrossed in my dad's hunting book. I flipped through the pages slowly, skimming the words until I got to the most recent pages I'd added about this Red Cap thing. Soaks hats in blood, what a gross, messy thing to do.

"Good night, miss," the man behind the bar finally said. "The dining car is closed."

"I can still be in here?" I asked.

He shrugged. "I don't really care what you do, but no one will be making anything else for you."

"Where are y'all staying?" I asked.

The man narrowed his eyes at me. "Why?"

"Just curious." I raised my hands.

"We'll be up near the engine. I don't suggest you go any farther than the kitchen car if you don't want to get a taste of a bullet," the man said.

The man didn't even look back at me, and I kept my eyes to the window watching his reflection in the glass until he vanished from my sight.

CHAPTER EIGHT

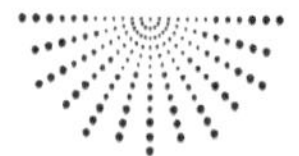

I took a deep breath and wished I'd at least gotten a cup of coffee or something else to help keep me up for the night. I supposed I could always sneak behind the counter and brew myself a cup. I didn't imagine they would worry about it too much.

I decided to not wait and went ahead behind the counter and got the coffee brewing. I filled a whole pot and hoped that would be enough to keep me up through the night. How did Dad do this? Hunting all night and then working on the shows all day. I was ready to drop, and it hadn't even been that long since I'd taken over his hunting duties. I guessed maybe Dad had more experience or something. Hopefully I'd figure out how to make this work for me too without having to worry about trying to force myself to stay awake.

Sipping the first cup of coffee, I glanced out the windows. Was I being paranoid about Rowan? She'd had me alone here in the kitchen and hadn't really been able to do a thing to me even when I was washing her stuffed toy clean. I thought back to the fur I'd seen clinging to the hat collection in the rotten trunk. Just because her toy shed a similar looking fur couldn't mean... Surely if she was actually a Red Cap, she would have attacked me. Little kids weren't monsters, right?

Rowan had appeared on the train right when we left the station. A stowaway arriving at the same time as a bloodthirsty monster was a big coincidence, but kids ran away to join the circus all the time. I wasn't sure what to believe.

I didn't know how I was going to handle this but felt like I had no choice but to project confidence. There was no one else ready to fight these monsters, and the job was mine to work alone if I wanted to keep everyone else safe.

I could do this. I didn't really have any other choice in the matter but to make it happen. I needed to work on making sure I didn't get myself killed in the process because I didn't much fancy dying on a train. If I was going to go out, I wasn't dying at the end of the knife of a little pissed off faery. That would be embarrassing, and I could imagine Lady Death wouldn't take too kindly to that happening no matter how much she admired our family or whatever. Besides, if I died, Marshall would take up the mantle, and that wouldn't go too well for anyone. He'd make a terrible hunter.

I sat down my mug and walked through the door into the next train car. The kitchen looked pristine and clean, nothing sat out in its own juices. It was filled with cabinets and large boxes of supplies. This was the perfect place for a Red Cap to be. I might set up for the night here.

I didn't see any signs of anything disturbed, but I didn't know the kitchen well enough to know if something was out of place. Even with it all clean, it wasn't clear what needed to be here and what pieces might not belong; I started opening things up and hoped no one who worked on the train came in and found me looking through everything.

Most of the cabinets were filled with various seasonings or other dried goods. A few held cleaning supplies, towels and the like, but I didn't see anything distinctive. In the back of the room, a large ice chest sat. I opened it up and found bits of meat packaged away nicely. My stomach lurched at the sight, but I reminded myself this meat had nothing to do with the murder earlier—this was food for more sad sandwiches.

The cool air from the icebox soothed my heated skin. Ever since

I'd taken the hellhound onto my skin, I felt like I constantly burned at a higher temperature than I should. My skin felt warm, my dress felt too hot, and I was hyperaware of any changes in temperature. I hoped I got used to this damn dog soon or I'd be in big trouble. I imagined it would make performing feel better; the little amount of clothing I wore to show off my tattoos would feel nice and cool.

I moved on to the next car but found the door locked and turned back. That must be where the staff was. I wondered if they'd locked themselves in the front few cars to avoid being near us. To be fair to them, I knew what had happened was upsetting, especially for people not used to monsters. I couldn't totally blame them for being scared and especially for being worried about us. I knew none of my folk would hurt anything that didn't deserve it, but we were freaks at our core, and that made for some scary judgments about what we were capable of and what we would do.

No one trusted a freak.

I sat back in the dining car and poured myself another cup of coffee with a heavy sigh. When we came out of the tunnel, I barely noticed a difference in the world outside the window. The train ran through places where no light lingered, no towns or people lived. Instead, we traveled through darkness all around. This would be the perfect night to hunt, and I was ready to prove I was by far the better hunter.

I couldn't get the worry about Rowan out of my head. I put my cup of coffee down on the bar and tiptoed back for the sleeping car to check on everyone. Had I knocked out everyone I was trying to keep safe and left them locked in with a monster?

I worked the door open and carefully stepped inside.

Glancing around, everyone was where I'd left them. Jonah's head had fallen onto Marshall's shoulder, and Clarence was laying on Alma's chest. Nothing looked out of place until I realized there was no redheaded little girl anywhere.

CHAPTER NINE

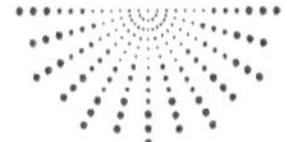

I searched around the room, but there was no sign of Rowan or the little red dog toy. Shit. I'd left a tiny murderer in a car of people knocked out with sleeping dust. Why hadn't the dust worked on her?

Checking the back door of the car, I rattled the padlock the conductor had used to lock us out, but it held steady. I moved back to the door leading to the kitchen. The ladder leading up to the top of the cars had a tiny smudge of red on it, and it smelled like blood.

I climbed upward but could barely get my head up before a tunnel forced me down. Someone Rowan's size could make it around up top but not me. But I had someone who could.

I pulled Puck from my skin and sent him up to the tops of the train cars. Puck stayed low to the metal roofs and floated quickly around. I closed my eyes to focus entirely through his vision.

For several long seconds, I saw nothing, but then I spotted it, a tiny fragment of a torn dress on the ladder leading down into the kitchen.

I pulled Puck back to my side and headed into the dining car.

Checking my dagger, I kept my hand over the hilt, ready for anything. A strange sensation tickled at the back of my mind, from Puck. Fear. I'd never felt Puck show this much fear before, but it seemed like this Red Cap was a well-known horror for the other faeries; I couldn't imagine he was particularly happy to be summoned to deal with it.

A cigar appeared in Puck's hand, and he took a long drag of it. I glared, and Puck waved it out. I didn't want to be screaming out my location because of some cigar smoke.

"Go check the kitchen," I instructed Puck.

He resisted for a moment but then turned and floated out the door. I closed my eyes and looked through Puck's vision, guiding him. The kitchen looked the exact same, and I didn't think anything had changed. Maybe the Red Cap wasn't there now, but my instincts kept pointing toward the kitchen.

I squinted out the windows and in the pale light of the moon, saw the silhouettes of buildings. Memphis. We'd be there in the morning, and if I didn't have an answer by then, we were in big trouble and someone was going to end up in jail for murder.

I was about to command Puck to return to my side when panic flared against my mind from my grumpy Fae companion.

I bolted from the car, dagger in hand, and ran straight for the kitchen.

Charging into the kitchen, I had my dagger up and ready for the little murderous bastard. What I was not ready for was the train inspector pointing a kitchen knife at Puck and chasing him around the kitchen. I waved my hand and dismissed Puck as I tucked my dagger behind my back.

The inspector stared at me. "What was that?" he demanded.

"What was what?" I asked, playing dumb.

"I know what I saw. What was that?"

"Nothing. Looked like a big bat or something to me. It's dark in here; how can you see anything?"

He glared at me. "I know what I saw."

"What are you doing in here?" I asked.

"I work on this train, what are you doing here? Customers are not allowed in the kitchen."

"I heard you in here and you sounded upset; I came to check," I said, glad I thought quickly on my feet some of the time.

"I was fine."

"Yeah, after what happened earlier…I wanted to check," I said.

For a second, he looked like he believed me, but then he shook his head. "I know one of you freaks did that. And you are all getting dealt with as soon as I get the chance to talk to the authorities. We'll be in Memphis in the morning, and the police will be meeting us there," he said.

Somehow I doubted that. There was no way this train could communicate with town without stopping. We'd have a little time, even if we didn't get to work on much else but getting out of Memphis before we got arrested for causing problems again. I already knew how it'd go if we had to defend ourselves to the police; that never went in the favor of traveling shows. Dad used to warn us that the most dangerous thing to us freaks wasn't any kind of monster: it was the police.

"I promise you, we had nothing to do with his death. He was one of our own."

"None of my staff would have done that, so it had to be one of you," he said.

"What if there was a stowaway?" I asked.

"What?"

"The murder happened in the storage car, right? We do occasionally have people try to sneak after the show, run away with the circus. What if that happened?"

"The little redhead girl you wouldn't let me throw off!" He pointed at me. "You're trying to blame a kid. Your type really are monsters."

I resisted rolling my eyes, but only just barely.

"Get out of the kitchen. You're not allowed in here," he said.

I exaggerated a bow and backed out of the car. That idiot was going to get our whole show shut down. If any of us ended up arrested, that'd be the end of the show and hunting for Dad. I had to find some way to make sure that didn't happen.

I sat back at the dining table and waited. If the conductor came through this way, I'd have to stop him from going farther back into the cars. I couldn't figure out where that monster could have gone.

Maybe back onto the roofs and back? What was Rowan planning anyway?

I was about to pull Puck back out when I heard a strange thudding noise. When the car didn't rock, I realized the sound hadn't come from the tracks. Drawing my dagger, I crept past the bar and back into the kitchen.

Inside I saw the inspector face down on the floor, not moving. I rushed over to him. He didn't look badly injured aside from a big bump on his head.

"Watch...out..." he wheezed as his eyes opened.

"What?" I asked.

Before he could tell me, I got my answer when something slammed into my head and I hit the ground beside him.

CHAPTER TEN

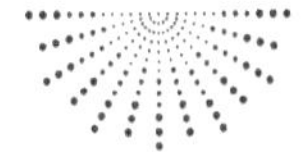

Coming to, I realized two things immediately: wires bound my wrists and I dangled from the ceiling by a something tied around my ankles. If I hadn't already hated dresses, this would have solidified it. My skirt fell down around my head, blocking most of my vision. I could see a large pail under me, and another shadow swung.

"Hello?" I whispered.

"We are going to die," the inspector sobbed beside me.

"Shhh, what is going on?" I asked.

The man sobbed again. Useless.

I summoned Puck and hoped that whatever bound me from the ceiling was made of rope like what bound my hands. Diving into Puck's head, I tried to not groan at how ridiculous I looked hanging here like a stained bell no one wanted. Skirts really were the devil.

Puck lit up the cigar and pressed the burning end to the rope binding my feet to the ceiling. This fall wasn't going to be fun or quiet.

As the rope began to give out, Puck grabbed my feet, flying with all his might. He managed to swing me from hitting the pail, and I caught myself without any kind of grace.

I sat up and saw we were still in the kitchen car. Getting to my feet, the man beside me whimpered as he saw Puck again. "He's here to help," I tried to promise the man, but he honestly didn't look like he believed a word I said.

Puck flew over to press the cigar to the rope around my hands. He'd barely even touched the rope when there was a sudden sharp flair of pain and Puck popped back onto my skin. A blade sliced my arm right over my hellhound tattoo, but I rolled away and avoided any deeper damage.

I backed up but couldn't see exactly where this thing was coming from. The blade vanished back into nothing. Hellfire, could this thing turn invisible?

"Behind you!" the inspector yelled, and I moved as the blade slashed through part of my skirt.

Well, that was helpful. With the tear started, I yanked at the fabric. Not wanting to get tangled up in the half-dangling fabric, I ripped it off and tossed it into the pail.

"Hey, Rowan," I called, trying to not feel useless without the use of my hands. What could I summon in here that would fit and not also kill the inspector? A sleeping faery might not be the best bet, but what choice did I have?

For a split second, I considered getting the sleep faery to throw some dust in his face, but I could use another set of eyes to help me out. Besides, if he saw this going down, he'd know who the murderer was and maybe not get all of us arrested. If he kept yelling where the attacks were coming from, he'd make himself somewhat useful.

The blade charged at me again, nicking my knee as I instinctively kicked. This time I felt my boot connect with something solid. There was a grunt then a clang as the Red Cap slammed backward with a flash of red hair. I rushed toward the sound trying to stomp the devil out of the little thing. Instead, my feet hit air and I groaned. This was like trying to kill a cloud.

I pulled Puck back over to my hands and had him start working on trying to get through the binding. He'd only gotten through part of the rope before a knife ripped through him and he slammed back onto my skin. But the blade that had finished the faery off also hit the rope around my hands and my wrists. With the weakened rope and my hands slippery from blood, I pulled my wrists free and grabbed for my dagger, only to find it nowhere on my person.

Was this thing really attacking me with my own knife? Devil's luck and my own!

Sliding backward, I grabbed a butcher knife from the kitchen counter. I'd much rather the blade I knew, but I could make do with the one I found if it meant dealing with this brat and getting out of this alive.

"What is that thing?" the inspector yelled.

"That's the murderer you've been yelling at me about."

"It is one of you freaks! I knew it!"

"That is not one of ours! It's the stowaway!"

"It's a freak!"

"Look, I'm going to get you out of this alive and you're not going to breathe a word about this to the cops, got it?"

He hesitated, sniffling a little. "Just get me out of here!" he yelled.

I moved over to him, kneeling down to cut through the ropes binding his hands. I'd gotten his wrists free when pain exploded in my back.

I kicked backward, knocking the creature back from me. Blood seeped from the wound in my side, and I prayed it was something Constance and Temperance could fix. I was not going down to a tiny murdering jackass.

The pain boiled against my skin, and the smell of blood overwhelmed my senses.

"You're going to have to untie your own legs," I told the inspector.

For once, he didn't argue or say anything; he nodded and crawled up toward his legs. Hopefully he had enough muscles to manage that angle. I kicked the pail out from under him so he wouldn't crash into it.

"Alright, come on out, Rowan. I know it's you."

Shocking no one, the orphan girl kept her advantage by staying hidden, but I kept moving and summoned Puck back out. Bleeding from my leg, wrist, and side, I was running out of blood quickly. Summoning anything bigger would be a challenge, but after all these years together, Puck took almost no effort, and he could watch my back.

The inspector thudded to the ground, and I caught glimpse of a shadow darting for him. I ran over and kicked with all my might. I connected with the tiny girl I'd been making sandwiches with just a few hours earlier. Rowan growled and slashed at me, barely missing the sole of my foot.

"Go!" I screamed at the inspector.

He scrambled for the door, but the creature moved faster than I could and slashed at the man, cutting across his shirt and drawing a thin but steady stream of blood. My stomach lurched at the sight and scent of fresh blood that wasn't mine. When had I gotten so squeamish? My stomach rumbled, and I realized this wasn't nausea at all.

This was hunger.

I dove for the little brat with my kitchen knife, and Puck was right behind. Rowan darted around with a speed I could barely follow. She was faster than anything I'd ever run into before.

The inspector looked at his bloodied middle, then to me, then promptly passed out. Great, so much for him being any help at all. I sent Puck over to the man to attempt to stop the bleeding with some kitchen towels.

I twirled the knife in my hand, starting to get the feel of the unfamiliar blade. My stomach continued growling and lurching loud enough it felt like it might rumble right out of my body. Pressing my hand to the cut on my forearm, I jerked back when I realized the wound was burning hot to the touch and the wound itself had all but sealed back together. What the blue damn?

While I stared at my tattoo like an idiot, Rowan dove from a cabinet, slamming down on me and sinking the blade into my shoulder. I screamed in pain and jerked around, flinging the faery off of me.

With a deep breath, I pulled my blood-drenched dagger from my shoulder and moved for the creature.

My hunger boiled, and the smell of blood melted into the rage of battle. This time when the hound pounded against my brain for freedom, I didn't resist. Fire rushed around my arm, and in the smoke and flames, the hellhound appeared.

CHAPTER ELEVEN

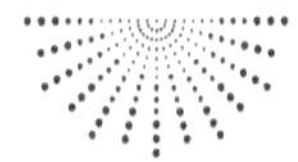

The hound and I moved as one, each of us stalking the darkness and following the smell of blood, the smell of fear, the smell of a soon to be very dead faery. The hound rushed forward, and I moved with it. This time I didn't care if I captured the soul. I just wanted her dead.

The hound found Rowan first, and the shrill scream she let out as the hound's jaws clamped over both her legs made me smile. Animal instinct overcame anything human in me, and I felt like I watched my own body from a great distance. Red flames continued dancing along my arm, latching onto my dress in a great ball of flames, but my skin didn't burn.

The wolf held the creature still as I descended on her.

Rowan clutched her toy dog close to her chest, dark black eyes wet with tears, but the blood around her mouth and down the front of her dress ruined any illusion of innocent little girl.

"You killed Gunther," I snarled.

"I do it to live!" Rowan spat.

I pressed the blade of my dagger to her throat. "How did you get on the train?"

"I saw a chance and I took it," she said.

I didn't see her little hands moving to drop her stuffed toy until the hound beside me gave a low growl and I found myself staring into the face of a wolf with no skin, just pure muscles, blood and fangs standing over Rowan and baring its teeth at me.

My hellhound knocked me backward as the jaws slammed toward me, barely missing me as I tumbled. Around me the kitchen was fully engulfed in flames, the heat bursting the two small windows, as Rowan and I sized each other up while our two monster dogs growled with ears low.

Puck gave an alarmed squeak, and I glanced toward him, seeing the faery trying desperately to move the inspector from the flames. I couldn't summon anything else to help him, and I didn't know how long rage would keep me standing against blood loss.

The hound moved intuitively, putting itself in front of me as I backed up toward the inspector, my eyes never leaving Rowan.

"Leaving so soon, Finnegan?" Rowan called.

I froze, one hand on the inspector.

"How do you know that name?"

"Oh, we are all out for your blood." She grinned, running her hand down the skinless wolf at her side.

"Guess you're going to have to wait," I said. "I'm busy."

I grabbed the man under his arms and began pulling him from the room.

The wolf stepped toward me, but my hound intercepted it as I dragged the man out of the kitchen car door. I could barely keep him in my arms as I balanced across the landing between cars and into the dining area.

I shoved him onto the far side of the car and tried to catch my breath. I felt the fight exploding in front of me, hound against wolf. Puck stared at me and shook his head, trying to block my path to the kitchen, but with the sun rising and Memphis coming into view, I didn't have time to rest for more than a second.

I shoved back into the room, the flames ghosting around my body as though I were already a part of them. My hound limped but stood strong while the monstrosity Rowan had brought out was feeling the heat. The exposed tissues bubbled under the flames. Rowan coughed and hid her face as she tried to grab for her dog.

I threw my dagger, and it slammed straight into the dog's eye. For an instant, everything went still before Rowan's scream ruptured the stillness.

The wolf didn't drop into nothing like any other spirit I'd gone after; instead, it fell to the ground as a pale pink, almost colorless stuffed toy again.

Rowan scrambled for it, but I grabbed it first, holding it to the flames. Rowan screamed. "I am going to make you suffer for this, Finnegan," she sobbed before she climbed up to one of the windows and out onto the roof.

I pushed after her, shoving the toy into my garter, about the only scrap of fabric that hadn't burned up, to keep it with me and rushed out the door and up the ladder after her.

Beneath me the train lurched and began to slow as the station began to flicker into view on the horizon. We were about to hit Memphis with a flaming train car, a bloodthirsty child, and me mostly naked. I sure knew how to make an entrance.

Up on the roof, I could make out Rowan's shadow scurrying up toward the front of the train. I lurched after her, but my movements dragged slowly, awkwardly. The hound leapt after her, but as I began to slow, piece by piece, it vanished into nothing but smoke.

I watched as her shadow leapt an impossible distance, landing at the edge of the station and vanishing from sight. I scrambled after her, but as I hit the front of the train, I realized I had no hope of making that jump. I was screwed and she'd gotten away.

I managed to climb down the ladder and stumbled into the engineer's room. The engineer stared at me as I dropped to my knees and wheezed out, "Fire in the kitchen."

The weight of blood loss hung heavily over me, weighing down every movement. The edges of my vision grew fuzzy, like the world was fading away into a dream. I knew I was passing out, and once the intensity of moment began to fade, I didn't resist it.

CHAPTER TWELVE

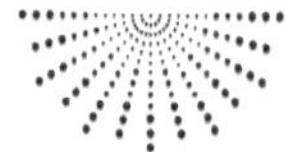

azel!"

I woke with Marshall, Constance, and Temperance around me. I was wrapped in a blanket but totally naked under that.

"What?" I blinked as the pieces slowly clicked back together—the hellhound, Rowan, the fire.

"Is the train okay?" I asked. "Is the inspector okay?"

Marshall let out a long breath. "He's fine. Said you saved him from the kitchen fire. He's not calling the cops on us anymore. That train car is pretty much gone."

At least one good thing had come out of this in that we weren't going to be arrested.

"What happened?" Marshall asked. "I was going to help you and then… I fell asleep. All of us did. Strange it happening like that. Almost like magic." He crossed his arms.

I was busted and I'd already known it. It didn't make the disappointed face any easier to deal with.

"I had it under control."

"Hazel, you almost died!"

"It's an occupational hazard, Marshall."

"What happened?" Marshall asked again.

"Where's Rowan?" Alma asked. "If that thing got that child—"

"Rowan was the Red Cap," I said, slowly sitting up as much as I could.

My hands wrapped around the little plush dog, and I held it up out of the blankets wrapping around me. "This was the thing she dyed. I don't know about the hats, but this damn dog that turns into a monster too."

Alma stared at me. "That little child could not have been—"

"You think I'd make that up?" I snapped at her.

Alma stared straight through me. "Hazel, I don't rightly know 'cause I didn't think you'd use some magic to knock out your own people either."

"Look, you can yell at her all you want in a minute, but we need to see if she's hurt. There's a lot of blood on her," Constance said.

"We need to know what's going on," Marshall protested.

"We need to make sure she don't die! You saw all that blood on her. Quiet down, boy, and get out so we can get her undressed," Constance said as though I had any modesty left. Damn near everyone in this show had seen everyone naked at some point—bath day meant everyone got washed all at once.

"I got stabbed a lot," I said.

I vaguely remembered. Gingerly I moved my hand to my shoulder and traced over where I'd plucked my dagger from my flesh, but no hole greeted my fingertips, just solid, slightly too warm skin.

"The hell?" I muttered.

"Get!" Temperance shooed Marshall, and he finally left with a last glare at me.

The twins pulled the blanket from me and together the three of us examined me for any wounds, but everything was healed up. Constance and Temperance pulled around a big washbasin of water, and I climbed into it. The water turned a hazy pink almost immediately as I started washing the blood from my skin. The twins started scrubbing my hair while Alma moved around the car to pull the curtains over the windows so I didn't give anyone a real show. Then my giant friend walked out without a word.

"You said you got stabbed," Temperance said.

"We looked over every inch of her and didn't see anything. She's fine," Constance argued with her twin.

"I remember pulling my dagger from my shoulder." My fingers touched the spot again. "And a knife to my back and hands and legs…"

I felt pulled too far and woozy still like I'd stretched myself too much. I'd been injured, I knew it happened, but how had all that healed up? I'd never been able to heal any of my injuries before.

"We've got to get off the train soon. You need to get dressed, can't have you going into town indecent," Constance said.

"And for the record, young lady, you ever send that little sleeping faery after us again and there's going to be trouble," she added. "Marshall told us what you pulled."

I nodded. "Yes ma'ams."

"See, I don't think you need to do it again to already be in trouble," Alma said as she walked in. Her arms were crossed over her chest, and the muscle in her neck twitched as she clenched and unclenched her jaw. "What in the hell were you even trying, Hazel?"

"I wanted to make sure the Red Cap didn't get anyone else," I said weakly. Saying my reasoning out loud made me feel ridiculous. No one had ever done anything that made me think they wouldn't really listen to me, and the Lord knew I could have used backup last night.

"You sure Rowan was what killed Gunther?" Temperance asked.

"She admitted it. And she damn near killed me."

"You thought knocking us all out in a room with the monster was the best plan?" Alma asked.

"I didn't realize what she was! You didn't either, did you?" I said, too tired to even snap at her. "It should have knocked her out too. I know I messed up."

"You sure did," Alma said, but finally walked over closer to me. "I brought you a dress to wear. I'm tired of looking at your naked ass."

The twins cackled, but I didn't even have the energy to be any kind of amused or embarrassed. The dress was one of my traveling dresses, something Alma must have pulled from the top of the bag. The heavy cotton clung to my still wet skin, but it was better than being nude.

"Seriously, Hazel, you alright? You been acting strange since…" Alma trailed off. "Oh, your daddy."

"I'm fine, alright?" I snapped then took a breath. "Just feel like I've been dragged under a train for the whole night. How long was I out?"

"A few hours at least. It's nearly noon," Constance said. "We've been at the Memphis station a bit letting them get the fire sorted out. But it's time we get out of here."

I got decent in something not charred and bloody. Hopefully some word of our arrival had gotten here, but I doubted it. We'd be in for a hard sale in the big city, and that wasn't even the worst part. I wasn't sure I had it in me to fight a single more thing after the train ride, but with a Red Cap out loose in the city, I'd have to find a way.

The twins had to support me getting out of the tub to keep me from falling over. Some of the anger fell from Alma when she saw me struggling to do much of anything, and she came over to brush my hair out while the twins helped dress me.

"We'll get you some rest before we start the show tonight," Alma said.

Sitting in the car, the twins offered me whiskey, but Alma slapped it away and gave me a cup of tea and a sandwich to eat. Time moved around me, but I felt totally separate from it, barely aware it had passed when the twins helped me out. Me, Alma, and the twins climbed into a carriage. Some of the tent assemblers held big blankets to block us all from the sight of the curious onlookers, but Alma's head still stuck up above the blockade.

When we got to a small site outside town, the twins got out of the carriage to get cleaned up, but Alma stayed inside with me. "Hazel, lay down before you pass out."

"I'm—"

"I swear to the Lord Almighty if you say you are fine one more time, I am going to pick you up and carry you to a bed myself. Lay. Down. Now."

I slid down the carriage seat and sprawled out over the seat bench with a sigh. "Alma?"

"Go to sleep, Hazel."

"Alma, I think there's something wrong with me."

"Yeah?"

"That hound…" I said and trailed off, not knowing what to say. How did I explain what it felt like to have a spirit of a demon somehow take total control and burn everything to the ground? Revulsion curdled the sandwich in my stomach. "Could I get some more tea?" I asked instead of finishing my thought.

Alma frowned but nodded. "Yeah, I'll be right back."

She stepped out of the carriage as I closed my eyes and drifted off.

CHAPTER THIRTEEN

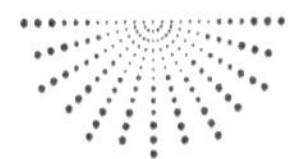

I knew I was dreaming right away. The show was all set up, but it was much bigger and nicer than any display we had. Everything looked new and pristine, not third-hand donations and scrapped together pieces we'd had to make fit what we needed.

"Yeah, boys, put that down right there!" my daddy's voice boomed through the camp.

I ran toward his voice and saw Dad standing in the center of all the set up. Tears poured down my cheeks as I rushed toward him and threw my arms around him. "Dad, where are you?"

"Hey, my little huntress." Dad ruffled my hair and smiled. "Look at all those new markings on you. You're doing great."

"Where are you?" I asked again.

Dad sighed and pulled a cigarette from his pocket. He lit it up and let out a long breath. The warm smell of tobacco, cloves, and dirt, the smell of Dad, drifted around me like a trip back home. "I'm working."

"Where? I can help."

"This is something I got to fix myself, Hazel."

I frowned and looked around. In the distance, I heard the rolling of a river and a train whistle. Mountains to the north of me looked smoky and hazed in purple and gold. I recognized it almost immediately. "This is Robbinsville!"

"Hazel, darling, this is where I need to be. You need to stay with your brother."

"Dad, no. We hunt together. Whatever this is, I can—"

"Come on, places, everyone!" a woman's voice called.

Dad kissed my hands. "Get out of here, Hazel, and don't come looking for me. I'll find you when I can."

"Dad!"

Dad gave me a push, and I woke with a gasp on the carriage seat.

"Hazel?" Alma sat across from me, her brow furrowed.

"Hi… Is that tea?" I asked as I sat up and wiped my eyes.

She passed over a cup of lukewarm tea. I sipped at it in silence.

"Bad dreams?" Alma asked.

"Mmm," I said softly.

Alma leaned back in the carriage. "Did I ever tell you about the dreams I had when my momma died?"

"What?"

"After she died, for months, I'd dream I was visiting her. I'd be right there back in her too little for me house. She'd always be working in the kitchen, and I wanted to help her, but I couldn't fit through the kitchen door to get to her."

I looked down at my tea. "What happened?"

"One day I realized it was a dream…made the kitchen door bigger, got to go in and see her again. We cooked together, made my favorite, and had a big ol' meal. The biggest one I'd ever seen."

"That's nice."

"Woke up trying to eat my pillow."

I blinked before laughter burst past my lips. "You what?"

Alma smiled. "Yeah. But after that, I don't dream about Momma anymore."

"Oh…"

"Look, I'm just saying I know you're missing your daddy, but don't get stuck there or you might end up eating pillows."

"Thanks, Alma. Camp set up?"

"Mostly. Our tent's ready."

"How long till show time?"

"Hour at most. Marshall's in town trying to drum up some business. But…"

"But what?"

"Looks like them Ringling boys are here too."

"Great," I said.

"We'll be alright."

"I guess we better get ready to go then." I sat back up, glad when the world didn't turn topsy-turvy this time. I still felt like I might be made of paper and anything could blow me over. But I was a hunter and I had a job to do.

Alma helped me to the tent, then she went to get herself ready. Nothing at my makeup table was laid out right, all the brushes haphazardly thrown every which a way. I found the one hairbrush I always used, the only thing of my mother's I owned anymore. Holding it tightly in my hands, I brushed out my hair, imagining each stroke held some comforting energy to it, something to get me through the night. I was unsteady but managed to change into my bathing suit for the show. That boded well for tonight. The last thing I wanted was collapsing while being gawked at.

I managed to get my makeup done without it looking like I'd been hit by a truck and melted in the summer heat. My hair, on the other hand, despite my attempts with the brush, was a bit of a lost cause and hung limply down my shoulders.

If I didn't have the energy to even get my makeup right, how on earth was I going to find Rowan before she killed again?

"That isn't going to do, dear," Temperance said as the twins walked up behind me.

"Yeah, but it's what it's going to be," I said.

Both twins shook their heads, and before I could say another word, they had their hands in my hair. I'd never seen either of them doing anything resembling deft work, even their stitching was sloppy and messy, but as their fingers worked over my hair, a French braid emerged. Constance smoothed down the front of my hair, then they pinned my hair up so my neck and back were clear and free for viewing. For that second, it felt a little like I'd found a mother. Granted, a two-headed one who drank too much, but a mother's touch none-theless.

"Thank you," I said.

Together we walked to the exhibition tent as all the display signs were hung out front. The tent guys sure could move fast when they needed to. I'd never seen the show go up that quickly. Our dressing room area was close to the big display tent to make sure we didn't have to walk far. It worked the best so people couldn't get too much a chance to see us before the displays opened.

I sat on the swing in my area and let out a soft sigh. The support beams above me creaked as I swung gently back and forth. The smell of the city, coal smoke, and horse manure, overrode the stale familiar musk of the show. I hadn't adjusted yet and wanted to hide in my wagon and sleep. Just a few hours and I could get to bed. Swinging idly, I let the show drift into the background. The world around me turned hazy and soft, nothing in sharp focus around me as I looked around at the familiar shapes. Until I glanced at the Duncans' tent. Empty. The stage hadn't even been set up.

I looked to Alma. "Where are they?" I asked.

Her hesitation played over her face. "They quit."

"What?"

"Left the station and said they weren't coming back," she said.

"But..."

"Don't worry about it right now. We got to get through tonight's shows, okay?"

I took a breath and nodded. One of our troupe was dead, and it was my fault. If I hadn't stepped in to keep Rowan from getting tossed off the train...if I hadn't suggested they go sing somewhere isolated. Guilt rang her hands around my heart and crushed me.

I took my place and focused on nothing. With the show melting to the back of my mind, I felt like I was sleeping with my eyes open. Stacey looked at me but didn't have any smart comments to make; he looked like he knew I wasn't at full thrust today. I couldn't even bring myself to swing back and forth.

The crowds trickled in with a slowness that made the time drag on. With only a few people in at a time, time all but stood still with a constant low-level boredom. I think I drifted off at some point. I blinked awake and aware of the world around me when someone cleared their throat.

Outside Jonah's exhibit, I saw a tall man with long blond hair. He looked to be speaking with Jonah, but both of them talked quiet enough I couldn't really make out anything they were saying. The man glanced at me, and our eyes met; he looked taken aback, like something about me shocked him. He looked back to Jonah and didn't look back my way.

I knew I was intimidating to a lot of men, but I didn't need that kind of reaction. At least he'd paid to come in, if nothing else, I could take pleasure in that even if he couldn't handle looking at all the exhibits.

"You look a little pale. I'm getting you water," my handler, Stacey, murmured to me before stepping out of the tent.

I felt fine. I wanted to sleep.

"Tattooed woman, hm?" The blond man finally made his way over to me.

"Brave enough to come over?" I asked, not caring if it was rude.

"I was startled by your beauty. Most of these shows advertise nothing but falsities."

"If you want fakes, then Ringling's in town. You can get your fill there."

He smirked. "I'd much rather the real experience like meeting a lovely woman like yourself."

"Yes, well now you've met me," I said.

He looked surprised I hadn't fallen at his feet. Had he tried to do this with other women and had any measure of success? I arched a brow. "Did you need something?"

He stammered as Stacey returned, passing the cup to me as he turned to the stranger trying to woo me.

"Well, it certainly seems you have quite the tale," he said, bowing his head to me as he turned away.

I scowled after him and looked at Stacey.

"I was gone for a second. He didn't do anything did he?" Stacey asked.

"No, the usual trying to sweep me off my feet and doing badly."

"And I'm sure you let him down graciously." Stacey couldn't even say it without a smirk.

"Oh, of course."

He shook his head and smiled.

We only had a few more people head into the show that night. It was the slowest show I'd seen in a long time. We could have made more money if we'd not even opened our doors. We couldn't compete with a big organization like the Ringling's circus. We had no hope of beating out their shows.

Everyone was quiet at dinner, aside from Alma and the twins checking on me about every damn second. I sighed and let them fret. When Alma headed to bed, she nearly dragged me with her, but I waved her off. "I need to talk to Marshall. I'll be there in a few minutes."

"I will come find you if you aren't."

I nodded. "I know."

CHAPTER FOURTEEN

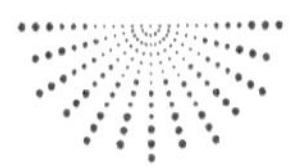

"What the hell were you thinking?" Marshall paced his tiny caravan. "You could've died. Almost did!"

"I was trying to keep y'all safe. I didn't know that damn kid was the monster I was looking for! I didn't know her stupid dog toy would turn into a damned monster!" I snapped. I didn't have the energy to argue with him, but here we were.

"And where is that little kid then?" Marshall asked.

"She jumped off as soon as we got to the station."

"So this Red Cap thing is loose in the city?" Marshall stared at me. "What the hell, Hazel?"

"I'll handle it."

"Yeah and how are you going to do that? Memphis is huge, and we don't have time to stick around. We're losing money. We're going to be using most of the money from the troll skeleton to make sure everyone gets paid for today."

I frowned as I remembered Madame Eclipse. Had she put the Red Cap on our train? Rowan hadn't said anything, and I hadn't seen anything connecting her to the train, but the timing was strange. We'd see if we ever ran into her again.

"I've got a plan."

"And how long is this plan going to take?"

"How long do I have?" I asked.

Marshall crossed his arms. "We ought to get out of here tomorrow. We can't compete with those Ringling boys."

"And where are we headed?" I asked.

"We'll hit up Murfreesboro. We had a show planned there next month anyways, so they might have heard of us by now."

"Alright. Well, plan on lunch time leaving. I'll deal with Rowan," I said.

"Don't get yourself killed, Hazel, alright?" Marshall's tone softened a little.

I waved my hand and headed out of his caravan and back to my own. I changed into some of Dad's clothes and pulled out the scant remains of the bloody clothes Alma and the twins had stripped off of me on the train. Most of them had burned up, but wrapped inside what remained was the little plush toy Rowan had carried with her.

It was almost colorless and didn't look threatening at all, but somewhere in this toy was a horrible monster. I figured the best way to catch a monster was to use one.

I shoved the toy into my pocket, grabbed my dagger, and made sure my hair stayed up and out of my face. I wasn't sure I had the energy to do this, but time wasn't on my side.

The camp was quiet and engulfed in darkness, making it hard to see much of anything but my hand in front of my face. I took a deep breath of the warm, moist summer air. Summer always felt like getting out of a warm lake, steamy, muggy and miserable with enough mosquitos and screaming cicadas to turn things sour. At least there weren't love bugs here like they had in Florida. Those things were the worst and got everywhere no matter how much you tried to get rid of them.

The noise of the city around me reminded me we were not in our usual middle of nowhere location. That made me all the more aware of what all was at stake. I didn't trust myself to summon anything or work anything out with my tattoos. If I'd lost control in the train, then what did I hope to accomplish trying here where the stakes were even higher? If I lost control here, I'd destroy more than stuff—I could burn a whole place down. Who knows how many people might die if I lost it again and ended up letting a hellhound loose.

But because of me, there was a Red Cap out in Memphis, up to who knew what. I couldn't walk away and leave these people to be bled dry. I had to do something, and that consisted of a vague hope this toy dog would be the answer to my problems.

I stretched out my hand and sighed before going to find a horse.

"What are you doing, Hazel Finnegan?" Alma's voice came from the darkness.

I nearly jumped out of my skin and steadied myself on the sturdy flank of my horse.

"I'm dealing with this problem," I said as I found a saddle and started getting my ride ready.

"You have got to rest." Alma didn't sound angry at all, worried more than anything else.

"I can't let that girl run through this city."

"And how are you going to deal with her? You think she's gonna come running?" Alma crossed her arms.

"Yeah, I do. I've got her friend," I said as I held up the dirty plush toy.

"You held onto that ratty thing?"

"It's all she cares about, I think. She'll come and I'll deal with her for good."

Alma sighed. "There isn't any way I'm talking you out of this, huh?"

"Not tonight, Alma. I gotta do this so we can move on and find Dad."

She shook her head. "If you aren't back by dawn, I'm going to hunt you down myself, got it?"

I smiled a little as Alma helped get the bridle situated over the horse's head.

"I got that," I said.

Alma pulled me into a nearly-bone-crushing hug before letting me go. "Be safe, Hazel."

"I'll try," I promised, about the best I could offer.

Alma watched as I got up into the saddle and headed away and into some fields out to the west and hoped this worked.

When I got far enough out that I hoped the city wouldn't hear most of what was going on, I stopped my horse and tied her to a small tree and continued a bit farther out on foot. I wasn't doing this to immediately have my horse get eaten or killed; my stupidity had killed enough people.

Once the horse had faded from view, I pulled out the toy and dropped it to the dirt. Staring at it and waiting for it to move didn't grant much action, so I pulled out my dagger and hoped this weird "cuts sealing themselves up" trick I'd recently discovered still worked.

I drew my dagger down my arm and pressed the toy into the wound, letting the blood trickle into it. I wouldn't be able to give it as much as an entire body, but after being dried out, I hoped anything would wake it up.

It only took a few moments for life to spring from the toy. The hound in my skin immediately reacted, growling against the back of my mind.

I dropped the toy to the ground, watching as the tiny fluffy shape stretched and transformed into the skinless beast I'd seen on the train. This time though it was weak, barely able to support itself, snarling at me from the ground but helpless.

Glancing around, I hoped Rowan would magically appear, but so far, the area stayed still and silent. I took a breath and stepped closer to the wolf on the ground. It growled low in its throat and snapped at me but missed.

Twirling my dagger in my hand, I almost felt bad for the anemic beast limping along the ground, teeth biting uselessly toward me. Pity or not though, I knew the way to get to Rowan was through this beast. I raised up my dagger and aimed straight for the chest.

Just before my dagger plunged into muscle, sharp teeth ripped into my arm.

I jerked backward, stumbling a few steps away and glaring toward the small shadow of a little girl standing in front of the wolf.

In the pale light, her silhouette still looked human, but when the light glinted onto her face, she couldn't pass as a kid anymore. Her mouth spread from ear to ear with row after row of sharp teeth dripping with blood and saliva. Her eyes reflected back pure unnatural gold, and the tips of her fingers ended in sharp claws.

"Stay away from him," Rowan snarled.

I kept my dagger up and stopped retreating. "Sorry, but that ain't how this is going to work," I said.

Rowan hissed at me.

"How did you get on the train? How do you know my name? Did Eclipse send you?"

The Red Cap shook her head. "Stupid Finnegan. You think we don't know who you are? What your family does? We can all smell the blood on your skin."

"So what? You came looking for me? All by yourself? What about the woman you said you saw loading stuff onto the train?" I asked.

Rowan sneered as her clawed hand gently pet the head of the monster at her feet. "You think I owe you the truth? You and your family have been destroying us. We have always been coming for you," she said.

The clouds in the sky shifted overhead, and more light poured down. As more details became clear, I saw Rowan's clothing tattered, her feet bloody, and her body covered in a dark liquid.

I stepped closer, not the smell of blood…but of… "Gas."

"You won't be wearing our skins, Finnegan. We go together without you taking us prisoners." Rowan produced a small box of matches.

"Rowan, put it down," I said, looking around the field.

If she lit herself and the dog on fire, this field would be ignited in seconds.

"Goodbye, monster," Rowan spat. "I won't be another decoration on your family's skin."

As she struck the match across the box, I threw my dagger. It slammed into her chest but not before the strike lit the match and flames exploded around her small form. She wrapped her arms around her dog, and it curled into her touch.

Instinctively, I tried to grab for her as she slumped to the ground still and silent before the flames consumed the pair and, in seconds, had taken over the field around me.

CHAPTER FIFTEEN

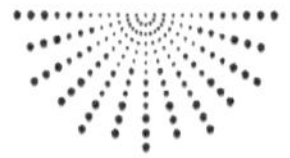

As fire licked along the edges of my pants and shirt, I stumbled back. I'd nearly burned up every pair of clothes I had in the last few days. Every direction I ran in seemed to be nothing but a sea of fire, and as the smoke got heavier, I lost all sense of direction. I ripped off part of my sleeve and tied it around my nose and mouth, trying to keep low to not breathe in too much smoke. Everything around me started to spin. I hadn't been doing great when I got here, and I was in no shape to get through this.

I didn't know if I had the strength to do it, but I pulled the hellhound from my skin. I grabbed onto it, hoisting myself onto its back as it growled and bristled at being used like a horse. The hound began running through the flames, and I held on tight as I could. I didn't know where we were going because every time we turned, we found nothing but new flames waiting to consume us.

Consciousness kept trying to flee from me, and with my body giving out, so did the hound. I crashed to the ground, my arm bleeding from the hound mark and from Rowan's bite. My mouth filled with smoke and heat blistered along my skin.

With no other options, I started crawling. I couldn't die like this, but I swore at the edge of my eyes I could see her. I could see Lady Death waiting for me to join her.

"Not going nowhere," I muttered to the specter.

It didn't react.

Keeping low and dragging myself forward, I caught a cool burst of air and moved toward it with everything I had. I caught a glimpse of a patch of dirt free from fire, but my body wouldn't move another inch.

I closed my eyes and kept my face against the ground to breathe and try to find the energy to keep moving.

"You alive?" a voice called.

I looked up and saw a man moving through the fire and straight toward me. The flames seemed to bend away from him as he got closer to me. I got onto my knees as he reached out for my arm. I grabbed his hand, and he tugged me to my feet. With his arm around my waist, I limped alongside him. The flames retreated from us, and within a few moments, I took a desperate gasp of cool air.

The man let me sag to the ground and wheeze as he turned to look at the fields. Flames had consumed most of them, and the fire lit up the sky like a hellish dawn. Overhead, a rumble of thunder promised the potential for relief.

"You're damn lucky," the man said.

I didn't feel lucky. I felt mostly dead.

"Thanks," I said as I tried to get to my feet but swayed heavily.

The man steadied me then wrapped a coat around me. "You've lost most of your clothes there, miss."

I was too exhausted to even blush as I wrapped his jacket around myself and the scraps of burnt clothing still hanging on my body. How had I ended up in a fire, burnt nearly naked, twice in the past twenty-four hours and still didn't have a mark on me?

"Let's get you home," he said, starting to get us walking.

"I've got a horse," I said.

"Well, let's start by getting there," he said.

I stumbled along with him for a few moments as the smoke cleared my brain and rain began pouring from the sky. The fire hissed and sputtered, slowly being beaten down and out until nothing but smoldering ash remained.

"I'm at Finnegan's show," I said.

"I know," the man answered.

I frowned and looked at him a little closer. "You're the weird guy from earlier," I said.

The blond man who had come over and tried to flirt me off my feet with the worst lines I'd ever heard. Was this guy really trying to help me or take me off somewhere else? I reached for my dagger and froze.

"My knife," I muttered.

"What?"

I pushed from the man and stumbled back into the burning fields. My dagger. I had to have that. My only piece left of my dad could not be lost because of a bloody faery.

"What are you doing?" The man moved after me, catching my arm.

I jerked free. "You can get yourself home," I snapped.

With everything burned up all around me, nothing looked familiar, but I had to have this dagger.

The man swore and kicked at the ground as I hurried from him and into the smoldering fields.

I quickly lost sight of the man who'd saved me as I scrambled through the ashes for my dagger. Summoning Puck from my skin sent me tripping to the ground, and the grumpy old faery looked more concerned than I'd ever seen him. Puck floated over to me, putting a tiny hand on my shoulder.

"Dagger," I said.

Puck frowned but nodded and floated from my side and through the field. I managed to get back to my feet and continued shuffling through the ash that was quickly turning to a thick sludge in the rain.

"Hazel!!"

I barely reacted to my name as Puck floated over, the glint of a blade in his hand. He dropped it at the ground in front of me, and I scrambled to get it back into my hands. The familiar weight of having what felt like the only piece of my father I still had soothed the panic rising in my chest.

When I was suddenly jerked into the air, I instinctively reached out with the blade only for a familiar voice to still my hand.

"I swear to the Lord Almighty if you cut me, Hazel Anne Finnegan, I will end you," Alma said.

I went limp in her grasp as she set me onto my uneasy feet.

Marshall stood beside her with the man from the fire watching me with an amused grin on his face and my horse's reins in his hands.

"I told you I'd found her," the man said.

"Thank you," Marshall said. "We owe you a great deal of gratitude. We don't have much in the way of financial rewards but…"

"That's alright. I'm not much after gold."

"Why were you out here?" I asked.

My voice felt a lot firmer than I felt, with Alma's arm around me the only thing keeping me upright.

"I came out to your show earlier this evening to see what kind of group you were. I returned this evening to offer my services."

"You came back in the dead of night?" Alma asked.

"I didn't want to disrupt the crowds. I was certain someone would still be awake. When I got to the camp, I saw someone grabbing a horse and running off. I pursued and arrived with the fields on fire and you burning, Miss Tattooed Beauty. What exactly were you doing out here?"

"Not your concern," I snapped.

"We need to get you back to camp before you kill yourself, Hazel," Marshall muttered. "Alma, can you carry her?"

"I can wal—" I didn't even get the dignity of finishing my sentence before Alma had scooped me up over her shoulder and carried me off back to the camp with Marshall and the strange man following behind. I was grateful the stranger's coat at least hid what little dignity I had left.

Alma took me straight back to my tent while Marshall and the blond man went to Marshall's caravan.

"Hazel, you have got to stop this running off on your own. You look paler than a bucket of milk. You ain't immortal. I told you to be careful."

"I tried," I said as I peeled off the remains of my clothes and tossed them into a bin. There wasn't much of them left, but they could get patched together into something in the future. We didn't throw much away here.

"You need to get some sleep," Alma said.

"Yeah, I will. I need to return this jacket." I held up the man's coat.

"I can," Alma said.

"Alma, please. Let me do this and see what this man saw tonight and then I will go to bed. I swear on my momma's grave."

Alma sighed heavily. "Fine, but if you aren't in this bed in an hour, I will be carrying you there myself."

I nodded and headed to Marshall's caravan to figure out who this man was and how he had walked through the fires unscathed.

CHAPTER SIXTEEN

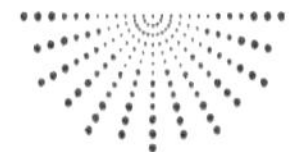

ou're wanting to join our show to do what exactly?"
Marshall was asking as I walked in.

He shot me a sharp look. "Bed, Hazel."

"I was returning this jacket to Mr....?"

"Luther," he smiled as he took the jacket from me.

"You're wanting to join our show?" I asked, sitting on the edge of Marshall's desk.

Marshall glared at me.

"I know I can bring something you've never seen before," he said.

I snorted. "We've been doing this since we were babes. There is nothing you can show us we ain't seen before," I said.

"Step outside and I'll show you," he said. "Bring a light."

He ducked back outside, and I looked at Marshall.

"You need to go to bed," he said.

"You're not making this decision by yourself." I crossed my arms.

Marshall let out a long breath. "Then come on, let's get this over with."

Luther stood in a clear spot between the mess tent and the main entrance. "Ready to be amazed?" he asked.

"Stop talking and get to impressing," I said, crossing my arms.

He tossed his jacket back at me. I caught it out of instinct. No man had ever stripped for me before, so that was an interesting development, but we weren't in the market to become that kind of show.

Luther rolled up his sleeves, pulled his gloves off, and that's when I noticed his arm. The skin along his right arm was a bright red color like a fresh burn that had only started to heal. Maybe he hadn't gotten through the fires unscathed.

I peered a little closer but couldn't see anything as he proceeded to hold his arm up and moved it around to show the solid red coloring. I had to admit he either had spot-on instincts for being a showman or he'd done this before, and I was beginning to think he was an old pro at being on display as he moved with a confidence and grace that came with time and not just skill.

"Can I borrow a light?" Luther asked.

Marshall offered a lighter, and Luther took it. He smiled before bringing the flame to his arm. As I reached forward to stop him, his arm ignited like a paper tossed into a bonfire. In a flash, his entire right arm was engulfed in flames.

My mind raced through the catalogue of ink on my skin, but I didn't have anything with water to help stop the fire from consuming this poor idiot man who had lit himself on fire for us. I didn't have the energy to summon anything anyway. The flashing orange and red colors sent me right back to that train car, to the field. It was starting to feel like fire was personally after me.

"What are you doing?" Marshall demanded, stepping back from the man.

"Showing you what I can do," he said.

He raised his arms, and the flames moved to concentrate in the palm of his hand.

"How are you doing this?" I asked, moving a hair closer.

I couldn't see any obvious trick to it, and the heat from the fire was real enough to burn against my skin in an all too familiar way. The hellhound on my arm seemed to coo in my mind, pleased with the warmth and the man in front of me.

"That's enough," Marshall asked.

"I was getting warmed up," Luther said with a smile, but he waved his arm, and the fire vanished.

Before I could stop myself, I grabbed his arm, tracing my fingers over the skin. No burns or marks of fire lingered there at all, nothing but the strange red skin, which felt stiff and hot under my fingertips.

"I'm alright, promise," Luther said, patting my hand.

I pulled back and looked to Marshall, who had his arms crossed over his chest.

"Well? Interested in hiring me on?" Luther asked.

"It's your right arm?" I asked.

Luther nodded. "My mother saw my father burn alive when she was pregnant with me. Left me touched by the fire."

I snorted at the obviously fake story. We had come up with enough of those to recognize the poppycock when I heard it, and this guy was full of it. But he had a unique skill, for sure, and as much as I hated to admit it, he was right. I'd never seen anything like him before.

"It'd be hard to display," Marshall said. "Lots of risk to the tents."

"I can control it, I promise."

"Smoke would be a problem too," Marshall said.

"We could display him out in the back of the tent," I suggested.

Marshall shook his head. "People would be able to see it."

"The fire obeys me."

"That's all very nice for you to say, but reality doesn't always match those nice promises," Marshall said.

"It's true, Marshall," I finally said. "He got me out of the field. The fires didn't touch him."

"Wait out here for a moment," Marshall said.

"Of course. Could I have my jacket back?" Luther asked.

I tossed it back to him and joined Marshall in his caravan.

"Well?" Marshall kept his voice low.

"I know he can control it," I said.

Marshall frowned. "He could burn us all. And with all the issues we've been having with fire—"

"It might be nice to have someone who can control it," I said softly. If fire kept coming for me, it might be nice to have some backup.

"You tell me. You're the one with the experience in this realm."

I shook my head. "He's human, Marshall," I said, not that I had any kind of ability telling me what everyone was, but nothing about this strange man screamed supernatural other than his showing off his ability to light his arm on fire.

Marshall sighed and pulled out the big binder of ledgers. I didn't even want to know what our numbers looked like right now.

"He looks like he's worked a show before. He knew how to display himself," I said. "We won't have to train him."

"And that's what makes me nervous," Marshall said. "What happened to it?"

I shrugged. "Shows go under all the time."

"We're gonna check some references or something," Marshall said. "You saw him in the fires in the field?"

"Yes. He pulled me out."

"And what were you doing out there anyways?" Marshall asked.

"I was taking care of the mess we left," I said.

"Hazel, you cannot keep disappearing. You could have died!"

"I got rid of the Red Cap!"

"You almost died!"

I crossed my arms. "This is my job now, Marshall. Dad would vanish—"

"You're not Dad!"

We both sat in silence for a moment, Marshall breathing heavily and me still under the weight of too many expectations.

"Are we hiring him or not?" I finally asked. "I want to go to bed."

Marshall ran a hand through his hair. "Fine."

We walked back out of the tent to where Luther waited. He'd slid back into his jacket but not put his gloves or hat back on. Even in the pale light of the closing show, I could see the red color of his right hand. I wanted to spend more time studying him, but I couldn't figure a way to do that without making it inappropriate.

"Well?" Luther asked.

"Welcome aboard," Marshall said and offered his hand.

Luther grinned and shook Marshall's hand. "Happy to be here."

"Well, we're happy to have you on board. You'll be sharing a tent with Jonah right now. We're working on getting carriages ready to go in the morning."

"Anything I can help with?"

"Just staying out of the way. Hazel, show Mr. Luther here to his tent on your way to bed?" Marshall asked.

I barely hid my rolling eyes but nodded. "Sure, this way."

Luther followed behind me as Marshall walked back into his wagon. I didn't much care for my brother letting a strange man walk alone with me. I'd stab him if he tried anything, but sometimes I realized how little Marshall understood about what life was like as a woman.

"Miss Hazel, is it?" he asked.

"Hazel is fine. We'll be working together. You ought to think of a show name or else Marshall will come up with one for you."

"I think that might be for the best. I'm not too quick with words," Luther said.

I didn't believe that for a second. He'd sold himself on the show and on his abilities with the ease that came from having a silver tongue and knowing how to use it. No one in a side show was truly bad with words when it mattered. We sold stories for a living; there was no way you could get by with not being able to think on your feet. Not with all the ridiculous questions, comments, and naysayers that showed up at every show.

I might not be the best with my words, but I could hold my own in the court of making up a story. Thinking on my feet was a skill taught on a stage, and there was no better place to learn than with a live audience paying to see you.

"Anything I ought to know?" Luther asked.

I shook my head. "We run a clean show. Don't be swiping anything from anyone, no girlie shows, and no fighting. Unless the fight comes to you first."

He nodded. "Yes, ma'am. I can."

"Where were you before that?"

"Oh, I worked out west on a few ranches."

"What show were you with?"

"I didn't perform in any show—"

"Bull. You got your spiel down to a memorized set of lines. You've done this before, and I don't much appreciated being lied to right after offering you a job. Saving my life doesn't mean you can lie to my face."

For a second, he looked surprised, and my hand moved to the dagger at my side. Surprised men were the most dangerous animals there were.

Then he laughed, long and hard enough he stopped walking.

I turned to stare at him. "What?"

"I didn't expect that to come out of your mouth," he said. "Yes. I worked in a small show out west, but it didn't survive a season. I turned to cattle work."

"What was the name of the show?"

"Barnaby's Circus."

I frowned. That didn't ring a single bell, but we rarely made it out past the Mississippi River. I didn't know anyone active over there that I could get a letter to verify this guy was who he said he was. Then again, if he was lying, he was doing a piss-poor job at it, and he wouldn't be the first. We'd had a lot of guys join the show to get away from a bad past or a lifetime of expectations. What was one more of those hanging around?

Besides, I doubted Luther would stick around for long. He seemed like he was on the lookout for something, and I bet as soon as he got whatever it was, he'd be gone faster than a snowflake in Georgia.

"Here's your tent. There ought to be an empty bed in there. Jonah's probably already sleeping."

"I'll be quiet then," he said with a smile and held out his hand for mine. I let him take my hand, but when he pulled it toward his lips to give it a kiss, I jerked it back. "Night, Mr. Luther." He wasn't getting anything more than formal greetings and words from me.

I turned and walked away before Luther had a chance to try anything else or say much else. I was too tired to be dealing with flirty men trying to make an impression.

When I got back to my tent, I climbed into bed. Alma had dozed off on her side of the tent, and her soft, steady breathing was the only sound aside from the cicadas screaming in the night to announce the height of summer. I'd always thought the sound of them seemed more like a mass murder happening than anything else. Nothing relaxing or peaceful about it. But despite the screaming bugs, I managed to drift off for a few hours of desperately needed sleep.

I woke to loud noises coming into the camp. This time I got dressed before wandering out, not wanting to give another nightgown show, especially with the sun up and the day wide awake.

Marshall led the horses to our wagons, getting everyone hitched up. Our carriages were old, but they'd work to get us out of here. We could get away from the city and back out to the boonies where people were more likely to come see us and we weren't competing with the Ringling Brothers and their show. Really, I wanted to put all of Memphis behind us.

Marshall waved at me. "Ready to get loaded up?"

"You bet."

Marshall whistled, and the tent team set to work. Our boys were fast, and by early afternoon, all signs of the show were packed up into the new fleet of carriages. Clarence and his boys played some music to keep spirits up, and I tried to not smirk at seeing Alma sitting not too far away watching the band.

Marshall supervised for a while before he went to get his things packed up. I tagged along behind him.

"Need something?" he asked.

"I dreamt about Daddy," I said as I idly put together some of his documents.

"Hazel, you've had a hard go of it. I'm sure it was just—"

"I saw him," I said. "I know it was him. It wasn't a dream."

"And what do you want me to do about it, Hazel?" he asked.

"He's in Robbinsville. That's not too far away from where we're already going. If we could swing by there—"

"Hazel, that's way out of the way."

"We're already off our schedule!"

"Hazel—"

"Marshall, he needs us. Please."

Marshall ran his hands through his hair and sighed heavily. "Fine.

But we're only staying a few days. That's it. Then we have to get back on schedule or we're going to be out of money."

I nodded. "Thank you." I squeezed Marshall's hand.

My brother pulled me into a hug. "And stop going off and doing stupid things by yourself. I can't be losing you too, you hear?"

I wrapped my arms around him and nodded. "I'll try."

He patted my back before slowly stepping back. "Good, hop into a wagon with the girls and let's get on the road."

I squeezed his hand once more before leaving to get into my own cart. I rode in the car with the other ladies. Alma, me, Constance, and Temperance passed around a bottle of whiskey, though the twins drank most of the bottle themselves. I didn't want to spend the trip puking, and alcohol plus a carriage ride tended to make me a little more nauseous than was safe.

"Where we heading anyways?" Alma asked as she passed the bottle.

"There's a little town a few hours east of here we're going to go visit. We were supposed to be there next month, they might have heard of us."

"Oh boy, another nowhere town," Constance cheered.

"You know that's where we always go."

"Yep, we're queens of the places no one wants to live in," Temperance said, taking the bottle from Alma and drinking heavily from it.

I sighed. The drunk twins were never fun to deal with, especially not when I was stuck with them for hours while we rode to the next spot. I looked out the window of the carriage, relieved to see the town had already faded from view, and I felt like I could breathe again. Memphis felt like it crushed down on my entire body.

"Who's the new boy?" Temperance asked.

"New performer," I said.

"He's handsome," Constance cooed.

"Guess so," I said.

I hadn't had the thought to weigh in on his looks. I still wasn't sure if he could be trusted. He followed after me last night, and something about that still seemed all kinds of wrong to me. What man went out this late to get a job? The whole thing seemed strange.

"What's he going to be doing? Taking care of us?" Temperance grinned.

"Knock it off, you dirty old ladies," Alma said.

The twins both laughed, and Alma shook her head.

"He'll be performing. He works with fire," I said.

"That sounds like something to see. Think he'd put on a demonstration for us?" Temperance asked.

"I bet you'll see plenty of his show during performances," I said.

The twins chuckled as Constance finished off the bottle. I tugged some bread from my bag and passed it around, grateful when the twins both ate a few pieces of the loaf. I didn't need them too drunk to walk by the time we stopped—trying to move their joined bodies wasn't a job I wanted to try to manage ever again.

Alma leaned back and pretended to be asleep, probably not a bad plan. As Temperance launched into a tale from their childhood, I followed Alma's lead and closed my eyes, but this time, I dozed off and let sleep wash me away.

I woke up with the carriage stopped and the other women out of the carriage, and around me, I could hear the tents being put up and a makeshift camp for the night starting to come to life in a new place. Outside, Marshall shouted directions. When I crawled out, I spotted Alma over with the band, talking with Clarence again while Constance and Temperance looked like they were asleep, leaning against the outside of the carriage. Looks like the booze had caught up with them; they'd probably sleep until dinner then be up and annoyed. As long as I didn't have to deal with hangovers on bath day, we'd be golden.

I took a breath and looked toward the mountains.

I'm coming, Dad. Just hold on a little longer.

THE SOUND OF SILENCE

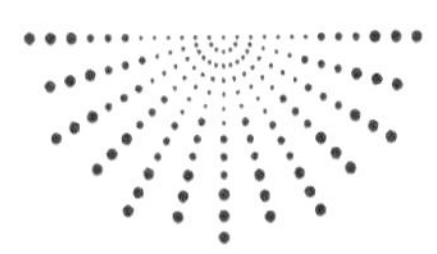

CHAPTER ONE

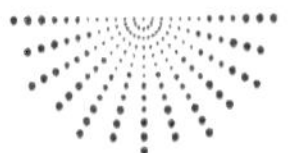

After the smooth, quick ride on the train, going back to horse and carriage seemed to take an eternity longer than it usually did. The only saving grace was the view of the mountains crested in early morning fog as we finally rolled up to our latest destination in a town just near the bottom of the Smokies. Half the caravan still slept, and the sun hadn't yet fully peaked out from behind the mountains. For the moment, peace lounged over us.

Marshall and I rode together in a carriage, both of us curled over our respective cups of coffee. It might've been summer, but that didn't mean a chill didn't hang in the air. That was one of the things I liked about the mountains: it never seemed quite as hot here as it did closer to the coast. And when you had to wear enough clothes to hide most of your skin, that heat got downright unbearable.

The town itself still seemed to be sleeping; nobody ran into the streets to greet us or sneak to catch a peek of one of the freaks from the show. Then again, they might not even know we were coming. I had no idea how far Dad had gotten with spreading the word about the show before he vanished. We might be the biggest surprise since Christmas morning. Or we might find out we didn't even have a space reserved for us to set up.

We rolled into the open fields just outside of town, and our tent team got to work. Those boys moved fast, with the memory of doing this a thousand times before guiding their hands. When you moved as much as we did, it all became an old trick, something you could do nearly in your sleep. It certainly made the trips a lot easier once you got used to it. That seemed to be the thing that stood between the people who lasted working with the show and the people who left after a week. If you couldn't handle not having a place to call home, then you weren't going to be around for long.

We were only about a quarter set up when another set of wagons started pulling up. It wasn't enough stuff to be one of the big shows, and I didn't recognize the insignia on the cart. It all looked near brand-new, and I doubted it had seen more than a month or two of travel. That caravan stopped, and a few people got out. I glanced at Marshall.

"Guess I better see what that's about," he said, putting down his coffee.

"I'll go with you," I said and got up. If there was going to be trouble, I wasn't going to let Marshall face it by himself.

We'd barely gotten out of the wagon when a familiar face began crossing the field toward us. Eclipse, the woman from the train station back in Arkansas, looked mighty happy to see us.

"I didn't anticipate running into you two," she said. "What brings you to this part of the woods?"

"This is part of our touring section," Marshall said.

"That is interesting; I'm set to be here this week. Right here in this lot where you're setting up," she said.

Well shit. No one ever came to this nowhere town; I never figured someone else would have this lot booked, but I guess that's what we got for being cocky and not having a showrunner organizing things right now.

"You've traveled a long way in a short time," I said. "That's impressive. Is this your first stop?"

Eclipse smiled and petted the side of one of her horses. "It is. We had a few dropouts along the way, but we're still ready to put on a good show."

"What kind of show you run?" Marshall asked.

"An all-in-one kind of show. We got some medical displays, and that big skeleton you gave me."

Marshall and I looked at each other. That wasn't nearly enough to be a full show, and I'd wager that she didn't know that.

"You got two things?" I asked.

"For right now. We're hoping to get more soon. But everyone's got to start somewhere, right?" She asked with a shrug.

Marshall tilted his head slightly toward the wagons with Eclipse and then toward our caravan. It only took me a second to gather his meaning. Our show was still a little down from the loss of the Duncans, and we could use a booster. Besides, we needed to be here; I felt that in my bones. Something called me here.

I gave Marshall a nod, and he looked back to Eclipse.

"I have an idea," Marshall began. "What if our shows worked together this one time?"

Eclipse looked pretty taken aback by the idea and not quite sure how to process it.

"It'd be a great way for you to see how we run our show up close and personal," Marshall added.

After a few seconds of silence, Eclipse said, "I think that sounds agreeable. Just for this one town, this one time. After that, we're going our separate ways."

Marshall smiled and offered his hand. "It's a deal."

She reached out, and they shook on the deal.

Marshall whistled, and several builders came over. "Y'all boys are going to be helping Miss Eclipse here. Make sure she gets everything laid out nicely with our show."

Eclipse looked surprised but grateful for the help. She, Marshall, and the tent builders all went over to her side of the field and started going over supplies. I headed back over to the wagon to finish off my coffee.

Alma walked out of her carriage, breakfast in hand, and motioned to Eclipse. "What's going on with that?" she asked.

"We're going to have some neighbors for the show. Shouldn't mean anything too bad."

"Isn't that the lady that bought the skeleton from you?"

I nodded. Looking over at the wagons I couldn't tell where the skeleton was. But as I thought that, several bigger wagons started pulling up and I could just make the shape of an oversized femur sticking out of one of them. "That's my boy," I said, laughing.

Alma shook her head. "I do not understand you, Hazel."

I smiled and headed into the carriage; Alma followed me and sat down across from me. I poured her a cup of coffee before sitting back with mine.

"Why exactly are we here?" she asked. "This is supposed to be one of our last stops for the season, and we're only halfway through summer."

For a second, I debated lying to her. Tell her some nonsense about schedule changes or anything like that, but there wasn't any reason to lie to Alma. Besides, she'd see right through me.

"I think Dad might be somewhere around here," I said, keeping my hands curled around the warmth of the mug.

"He still hasn't gotten in touch with you or anything? No letter, no message, nothing?"

I shook my head. "We haven't even got people who've seen him or some sign of him, aside from that trunk of his we found in Arkansas. It just ain't like him to up and vanish like this."

"I know. He might not be the most organized fella I ever met, but he keeps to the season tour schedule like a stopwatch. And vanishing in the middle of high season doesn't make any kind of sense. You think something happened to him?" she asked softly, seeming almost afraid to put the question out there.

"The only reason I can think he wouldn't get in touch with us is that he's in trouble. I just don't know what kind. Or where. Or how to help. I don't know nothing. And that's the worst part of this whole damn thing. I can think until my brain's about to sludge out of my ears, and it doesn't do me a damn lick of good."

Alma reached over and put her hands over mine. "We're going to find him."

I tried to believe that. But right now, I needed to not think about Dad anymore. "What's going on with you and Clarence?" I asked.

Her cheeks darkened just a touch. A blush didn't show much through her brown skin, but I knew her well enough to recognize it when I saw it. She pulled her hands back into her lap.

"He's a nice guy. He's the kind of guy I never thought I'd meet at a show like this."

"We do seem to attract some terrible guys, don't we?"

"We sure as sin do," Alma said.

Alma and I both laughed at the remembered series of unfortunate men that had come to the show. Jonah had by far been the best in years, aside from Marshall and Dad of course.

It always amazed me how Jonah wasn't married. Now, most of the girls who came to the show looked a lot and had been polite, but there was no way any of them could've gotten approval to marry Jonah. I never even heard him talk about a girl that caught his eye.

Then again, he had the attitude of a preacher and the holiness with it to boot, so maybe he just wasn't interested. But a godly man most of the time ended up married. I sure wasn't going to pester him about it. He'd been a solid staple in the show for way too long to start giving him a hard time now.

"Clarence is nice. He's a good guy. He's got a good head on his shoulders; didn't panic at all during that whole fire in the train."

"I suppose that's a good sign after all," I said. "Don't want someone who's going to panic over everything. This show's a little too wild for that kind of problem."

Alma shook her head. "It truly is. We're really going to team up with this lady who doesn't know what she's doing?"

"Everyone's got to start somewhere, right? We're only working with her here; it's not like we're joining our shows up for good. She didn't have enough to draw a crowd at all, but she's got the stake on this place. We'll work with her for now and move on when the time's right."

Alan nodded and stood up. "I'm going to go make sure they don't put our dressing area somewhere stupid."

I waved her off as I made myself another cup of hot coffee.

CHAPTER TWO

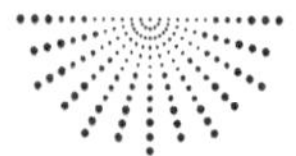

Outside the wagon, I listened to the setup continue. All the usual sounds filled the air: tent poles being driven into the ground, heavy canvas being lifted into the air, ropes and chains holding everything in place. In my childhood, it'd been the morning lullaby I'd woken up to most every morning. All the sounds of the show made it home for me. I didn't need everything in the same place every day of my life. But I liked having pieces that stayed the same: the people, the smells, and the sounds of a new day being built from the ground up.

Glancing out the side window, I saw Marshall still talking with Eclipse. The conversation didn't seem to be antagonistic or heated. I guessed they'd agreed or at least found a good compromise on tent placement and show layout. The only real question that I imagined would bring up some trouble was the one around money.

I wasn't sure how we'd divide the cost of the show in two. And it wasn't like anything could be a half-and-half split. Our show had much more going for it, and several more acts. But Eclipse had us over a barrel in a way. We needed the space, and if she did have claim to the land, there wasn't another field available anywhere near town.

The next nearest piece of civilization meant hours of travel. We were at her mercy, and I hoped she would play nice.

After I finished my cup of coffee, I walked over to the conversation between Marshall and Eclipse.

"You didn't bring me another cup?" Marshall asked.

I shrugged. "Wasn't sure you'd want one."

"I'll let you ladies chat while I fix myself a cup. Miss, you want anything?" Marshall asked Eclipse.

"I'm fine, thank you." She waved him off.

Marshall disappeared, and I got the distinct impression he was foisting this conversation off onto me. I didn't play a negotiator, but hopefully he already made all those deals.

After a brief moment of silence, Eclipse asked, "You've been in the show your whole life?"

"Yes. Basically born here, me and Marshall both. Most of the acts have been here a while too. The twins damn near raised me."

"A whole little family for you then. That's nice. It seems like you and your brother have built a nice group. Anything ever gone wrong?"

I laughed. "Only every day of my life. Things go wrong all the time; canvas gets split, someone starts a fight, we get rained out, police bust our nuts, and we spend a lot of time just trying to break even. The Ringling boys might make it look like this kind of thing is an easy way to make money, but most of us ain't anywhere near where they are."

She looked a little taken aback, and I regretted my words. Too many people trying to jump into the circus business because they'd seen a good show once or twice and thought they could do the same easily. They thought it was easy, quick, and simple money to make. And those people just ruined it for the rest of us. I wasn't sure where Eclipse fell in all of that, but if she moved on for a quick buck, I'd rather let her down fast and soon.

Finally, she laughed. "You tell it like it is, don't you?"

"There's a reason I'm not the one talking up the shows."

"Maybe you should. I think you could tell a mighty fine story. Something most of these folks have never heard of. Like, what's the real story behind that skeleton you sold me?"

Now, this moment meant telling it like it was couldn't be an option anymore. I couldn't very well reveal to this stranger that I hunted monsters, fairies, angels, and devils and let her know that all those things were real. My people only knew because it'd been impossible for Dad to keep it a secret when my powers started developing. Besides, I trusted the folk I performed with, not this stranger in front of me.

"Like Marshall said at the train station, just something we stumbled upon during some archaeological dig out in Africa. Don't know exactly what it was, but some of our scientist folk say that maybe humans were once that size. Big as the mountains."

"Is that really where it came from?" she asked.

I forced myself to not shift my feet; Marshall always told me my feet gave me away in poker, and I got the impression that Madame Eclipse might be good at reading people. She was testing, seeing if Marshall and I said the same thing. I knew Marshall would've kept the story straight, after so many years of learning the facts and the stories we made up for all of our shows, there was no way he'd stumble over something simple like this, even with a newer lie.

Part of me busted at the seams to tell her the truth, to say I killed it. To let someone know what I'd done, someone to see how much work I put into this. But that wasn't the way it was meant to be. Besides, I didn't want to deal with Dad when he got back and found out I blabbed my mouth.

"Marshall handled all of it," I said, nearly wincing at that lie.

"Does he handle most of the show? Are you just a performer?"

"We handle a lot together. Marshall runs front of house, and I run inside."

"The little lady of the show?" she asked.

I seethed at that comment. I was no one's little lady, not even the show's. I forced my hands not to curl into fists, and instead smoothed my fingertips over my dress. Compared to the elegant blue silk gown she wore, my cotton and patchwork dress made me feel like a bug, but I kept my spine straight and stood taller.

"We do the things we're best at. Marshall has a way with people and telling a good story."

"What are you good at?" She asked.

"Putting on a damn fine show."

Eclipse smiled. "I bet you are. I look forward to seeing you perform."

"What got you into doing the shows anyways?" I asked.

"Probably the same as everyone else. Saw a show as a kid and couldn't get it out of my head. Got tired of being the secretary, of being the old maid. When my folks died, they left a little money, and I decided I'd rather die broke chasing that silly dream than ever go back to how it was. I quit my job, bought up some wagons, and started finding help. It was like fate itself smiling on me when I bumped into you and your brother at the train station. Like divine intervention showing me that I'd chosen right."

I nodded, not sure what to say to that kind of confession. I couldn't blame her. I couldn't imagine living that kind of life. Even the show didn't keep me totally isolated from those expectations. Every performance, there was someone wondering why I wasn't married or why I was not a mother, a homemaker, a decent sort of lady.

Eclipse and I sat at one of the mess tent tables and watched as the show sprung to life around us. We had only been here maybe an hour or two, and already you could see the shape of it all unfolding like a wide-open book. Luther came over to grab breakfast; he paused when he saw Eclipse sitting at the table with me.

"Luther? It's been a while," Eclipse said.

He just nodded his head real low, almost like a bow. "Madame Eclipse, I didn't expect to see you here."

"That's what I imagined you'd say. You left before we finalized our schedule."

I looked between the two. "You used to be part of her show?" I asked Luther.

Before he could answer, she said, "He did. The very first person I hired. It's been, what, a few months now?"

Luther nodded. He had the face of the schoolboy who had been caught ditching class. His eyes kept darting back toward the carriage he'd ridden in, and I could imagine as soon as he got the chance, he'd vanish right back in there.

I tried to break the tension. "He just joined our show. Helped us out of a real bad spot when one of our acts up and left."

I didn't want to admit to this woman the truth of what had happened, or even really to myself. We had lost the Duncans because I had been sloppy, and Gunther had died because of it.

"I'm glad you found another job," Eclipse said. "I hope you do a little better this time at least."

I expected Luther to blow up, call her names, say something nasty, or otherwise make a fool of himself, but instead, he seemed to almost curl up inside himself, like a wounded animal.

"Thank you, ma'am."

Before anything else could pass between them, he grabbed a plate of grub and vanished back to his carriage.

"Is there something I should be worried about with him?" I asked after he disappeared.

Eclipse just waved her hand. "We just had a…personality disagreement."

"And what exactly does that mean?" I asked.

She smiled and shook her head. "I'm sure it won't be an issue for you. Luther likes pretty girls."

I'd hoped with another woman that I wouldn't have to worry about the unnecessary comments on my looks; I took a deep, long breath before slowly standing up. "It's been lovely chatting with you, but I really ought to go help get the ladies' dressing room set up."

"You don't have help that does that?"

I shook my head. "No, we keep things pretty hands-on. I'll see you later." I walked from the table before she could say anything else.

With her eyes trailing me, I wouldn't go storming straight to Luther's carriage to demand answers. But as soon as we were inside the performer's tent this afternoon, I would find out what had happened.

I walked into the ladies' dressing tent and found Alma helping braid Constance's hair while Temperance worked at patching a dress.

"We working with another show?" Constance asked.

"Just temporarily. Don't be making too many new friends." I said as I started moving boxes of supplies into their appropriate places.

"I was getting to that," Alma said.

"That's alright. You look like you got your hands full." I shoved my box into the corner. When I walked back over, I noticed a dress I didn't recognize in Temperance's hands. "Whose dress is that?" I asked. "I didn't think Eclipse had any performers."

"Alma's," Temperance said, not looking up from the delicate stitches in the dress in their hands.

Looking closer at the dress, I recognized the pale blue cotton number that Daddy had gotten made for Alma the one year we decided to do a spring fling of our own for the whole troupe. Those outfits were probably the prettiest, nicest thing most of us had ever worn. I still had my light yellow gown tucked away safely, hoping maybe one day I'd have another reason to wear it.

"What's the occasion?" I asked Alma.

"It ain't no occasion. I just needed a hole patched."

"She's going out with that boy," Temperance said.

The hand Constance controlled popped the top of the hand Temperance controlled. "She asked us not to tell anyone."

"Hazel doesn't count. We all know that."

I grinned at Alma. "And when is this date happening?"

Alma glared daggers at me. "That's not important," she said.

"If you're getting that dress patched now, then I bet it's tomorrow," I said.

Alma's skin darkened slightly. This was the first time I'd seen Alma this flustered before. It was a bit charming to see my friend looking like this. I hadn't seen her this happy in a long time.

"When were you going to tell me?" I asked.

Alma crossed her arms and sighed. "In the show tonight. Don't go getting all twisted up about it."

"I ain't. I think it's sweet."

Alma groaned.

"How long are we staying here?" Constance asked to change the subject.

I shrugged and wished I had a solid answer. Making the schedule based on a feeling didn't go real well or lend itself to solid dates and timelines. "Probably not too long," I finally said. "Y'all are getting dolled up a little early today. Wanted braids tonight?"

"My hair is bothering me." Constance said, "And Alma offered to help with it if I fix up her dress. When do you think our first audience will be?"

"Tonight. Everything should be ready for a trial run by lunchtime. We just gotta figure out where all these other folks are going to go."

"What kind of folk?" Temperance asked.

"So far all she's talked about is some dead stuff. I don't know yet. Not a lot. But we might have that skeleton back," I said.

"Is it haunting us?" Alma asked. "I thought we left that thing in Arkansas."

"It's back for round two. Hopefully it will make us some good money, though," I said.

"You need any help getting everything set up?" Alma asked.

I shook my head. "No, I'm good. I just wanted to make sure we all got our spots in the dressing room before anyone new got added in."

The twins laughed. "Always looking out for us, aren't you?" Temperance asked.

I grinned. "Someone has to."

I figured I would leave them alone and not tease Alma too much. I wanted her to have a good time with this boy. But I would be getting all of the details from her as soon as I could. I couldn't believe she'd been holding out on me like that. Then again, since Dad left, we hadn't had a lot of time to catch up like we used to.

I walked out of the dressing tent with the sound of the twins and Alma laughing behind me. At least everyone seemed to be in good spirits after the disaster of Tennessee. Guilt still lingered on my shoulders for setting fire to that train, for Gunther, for the Duncans, and even for the death of that damn Red Cap. I hunted her down and felt every inch like a monster she'd claimed me to be before she lit herself up like a bonfire.

I opened and closed my fist, testing the grip and strength behind it. It still felt normal, exceedingly average, aside from the burning lingering around the hound tattoo. No matter how cold the rest of me might be, that tattoo always felt like it burned with fire. At least the hound had mostly quieted down in my mind; but the next time I encountered blood or got real mad, I wasn't confident I could keep it in check. None of the other spirits ever caused me to lose control like that before, and I didn't have anyone to ask for advice.

"You must be Hazel."

I turned and saw a woman I didn't recognize walking toward me from Eclipse's side of the camp. She wore men's trousers and a blouse, and she kept her thick dark hair in a tight bun. Her lips were painted red, making them a striking focus against her pale, white skin.

"And you are?" I asked.

The woman smiled and offered her hand. "My name is Ruby," she said. "I'm the talker for Madame Eclipse. She's told me all about you. You're the one that skeleton came from, aren't you?"

I took her hand and shook it before letting go and stepping back. "My brother and I are where that skeleton came from."

"It's the most amazing thing I've ever seen," she said.

She talked fast, like everything had to make it out in one single breath. I wondered if she'd ever passed out talking before. I could imagine the petite woman in front of me giving an intriguing introduction to the show. I wasn't sure how Marshall would balance that with his talking style.

"Thank you. I'm glad it found a good home. Did you need help with anything?" I asked.

She shook her head. "No, ma'am. I just really wanted to meet you. I'm quite excited about working with your show. I've heard you have some of the most amazing exhibits this side of the Mississippi."

I wasn't sure who had told her that or why she felt the need to butter me up, but I had to admit the compliment felt good. I didn't get too many of those about the show in my line of work; most people just wanted to comment on my body and lack of clothing.

"I appreciate you all letting us encroach on your location."

"I think it's just fortune we found each other. I've been telling Eclipse that we don't have enough for our show yet. But she won't have it. Do you think you and your brother can talk some sense into her?"

"She's welcome to watch how we run our show and see if there're any changes she wants to make to hers. But I'm not in the business of telling people how to live their lives. I figure that's best left to every individual."

"You're just as nice as I heard," Ruby said.

Now that had to be the biggest bald-faced lie I'd ever heard. No one on God's green earth had ever called me nice. And I was just fine with that.

Instead of smart mouthing her, I smiled. We needed this to work out, and that would mean dealing with nonsense attempts at buttering me up. My best guess was this girl wanted a job out of Eclipse's show. We had no need for a talker; she definitely barked up the wrong tree in every sense of the word. I wasn't even the one who did the hiring for our tent. But I did have some questions for her.

"I think we just hired on one of your old coworkers. Luther. The name ring a bell?"

"Of course! He got hired right before me. Didn't stick around very long, though. Surprised he managed to get a job with a show like yours."

"He just started. I'm wondering what kind of a worker he is."

Ruby put her finger to her chin like she was thinking. "He's a nice guy. Clean, mostly watches his language, and doesn't drink too much."

"Those are all good things. But that doesn't answer what kind of worker he is."

Ruby shifted on her feet a little bit; it looked like she shared my habits when it came to lying. "I don't like to badmouth anybody, ma'am."

No one who said that ever really meant it, and I knew there was more bursting to come out. "But?"

"But… he didn't much seem to like having to listen to a woman. He and Eclipse used to get into terrible arguments, and I'd step in to calm things down. But one day I guess the fighting just got too bad, and he decided to leave. Eclipse stayed mad for a while, but I think now she's realized it's probably for the best. I'm sure he'll do just fine in your show though."

Of all of the things I expected Ruby to say, Luther having a problem with women in authority was not one of them. I hadn't gotten that sense from him at all, but I believed her. When a woman told you something about a man, it was best to listen to what she said.

"I'm sorry to hear that," I said.

"Maybe it was just Eclipse was new and still trying to figure out how to run things. I think they both have strong personalities, and they didn't work well together. Kind of like if you try to put out an oil fire with water, it just makes it worse."

"And what was it he did in your show?"

"Firebreather," she said. "He put on a mighty fine show. But we usually had to keep him outside, so he didn't burn everything down."

"He didn't do anything else with fire?" I asked.

"Anything else? No, not that I recall at least. We never really had any shows, all just practice stuff."

I got the impression Ruby lied to me about a lot; I just wasn't sure what the lie might be. Maybe she thought I didn't know what Luther could do with that red right arm of his. Or perhaps she was telling the truth, and I just misjudged her. Regardless, I decided to take what she said at face value instead of trying to find reasons to mistrust a stranger. After all, Luther was still a stranger too.

"What do you think your role should be in our combined show?" I asked.

"I hope to do what I usually do. Stand out front and help bring in the crowd, of course. I understand you guys have your own talker. But I would be interested in learning from them. I'm still new at all this and always willing to study."

Another sales pitch. Either she was desperate to get out, or just trying to show off. Regardless, I was immune to whatever she sold. I spent way too long around carnival barkers, talkers, and smooth criminals to be taken in by some kind words and a wily smile. But I could already see that she probably did a fine job at getting men into the booth. With a pretty girl up front, what more could be in the tent?

"I suggest you talk to Marshall. He's the one you'd be working with anyways. He's probably finished his coffee by now."

"Thank you! I'll talk to him and figure all this out. I'll see you later, okay, Miss Hazel?"

I offered a wave as Ruby scurried off toward Marshall's wagon.

She had potential, and with a little guidance would probably become one hell of a show woman.

I glanced around the area and saw no signs of Eclipse lurking about, and that meant time to confront Luther.

CHAPTER THREE

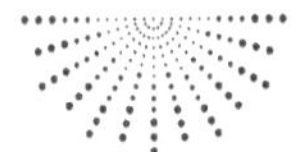

I knocked on the door of Luther's wagon and didn't get an answer. "It's me," I said. "Open up."

After a moment, the latch lifted, and Luther peered out. He looked around before opening the door wider and motioning for me to come inside. I walked in as he adjusted the lantern on his table. With his one and only window covered, that was the only light in the whole place.

He hadn't had a chance to make the space his own yet, but a few pieces of him stood out. Books I didn't recognize lay sprawled across the floor, and Luther's traveling trunk stuck out from under the bed. A half-eaten plate of breakfast sat on the table beside what looked like an abandoned cup of coffee.

"Some reason you're hiding in here?" I asked.

"I'm not hiding. I'm just… getting ready for the day," He said. Even he didn't sound like he believed that.

"And what exactly are you getting ready for?" I asked.

He stammered then sagged into a seat. "Are you firing me?"

"I'm not doing nothing until I have a little more information about what exactly went on. If you'd care to help out with that, adding some details wouldn't hurt your case."

He traced his finger along the rim of his mug and sighed. "I just didn't like her management style. Just… personality conflict," he said.

Using almost the same words that Ruby had sounded mighty suspicious to me. No one ever talked about personality issues for anything good. Usually, all that meant was that someone was an asshole. Now, I just needed to figure out who it was and what happened. I was not going to bring in a troublemaker to be a part of our show. No matter how impressive their showmanship skills were.

"See, that's what Ruby said. Almost with those exact words. Y'all come up with a story before you left?"

"No, no, no! Nothing like that. Just the easiest way to describe it."

"So what? You just woke up one day and decided you couldn't stand working there anymore and left?"

"All we did was practice. We never put on the show. I got frustrated, sitting around doing nothing and making no money. It's hard practicing when you know you're never going to see an audience."

"How long did that go on?" I asked.

"Over a month. I just couldn't take it anymore at some point, and I left. I imagine she's still pretty unhappy about that."

I licked my lips, not sure I could trust the words coming out of his mouth. But for now, we needed a show to fill the spot the Duncans had left behind. Luther was that. But with Lady Eclipse and Ruby here, part of me figured he'd probably bolt again.

"Well," I said as I stood up. "I'll leave you to finish getting ready."

"You don't have to go."

"Yeah, I do."

I walked out the door and didn't look back. A man asking you to stay in his wagon for no good reason never lead to anything I wanted. And staying in a small space with a man you weren't even sure you could trust? That was an even worse decision.

I spotted Marshall across the way, speaking with Ruby. For once, Marshall was quiet and listening more than he talked. Ruby looked incredibly animated and excited, pointing toward the stage and the tents. Looked like they might have found the truce about who would be talking out front. I'd wager they would share the load. But if this was the first time Eclipse had put her show to work, I wasn't confident everything would run smoothly.

You could practice all you wanted, but the practices never managed to catch everything that could and would go wrong in a show. The biggest problems we ran into had nothing to do with our performances or our spaces; it was always the crowds that gathered to watch that caused the most chaos. And that was something you couldn't figure out from rehearsal. I supposed it would be for the best that Eclipse got to watch us and maybe get some real experience with a bit of backup before she went out on her own.

Everything looked almost ready to go. We combined a few spaces, and it seemed like the only thing left was the display for the skeleton. I made a few rounds to get familiar with the layout of the whole thing. The tent setup remained mostly the same: the stand for the talkers out by the ticket booths, and a path of food stands leading up to the main tent and the sideshows.

They were finishing setting up the stages and getting all the displays together. A makeshift canvas divider hung between a few of the stages. I imagined there would be two to a spot as we made room for Eclipse's show. I wasn't used to having half a stage, but my swing stayed ready, and that took hardly no space at all.

The back of the tent, where we kept the extra show that cost a nickel, had been left open with nothing overhead. Probably the best idea for a display like Luther, because as much as he claimed he had everything under control, it would only take a second to burn the whole thing down. If we could manage to get a crowd, I felt pretty confident we could put on one hell of a show and maybe even turn a profit here.

Now that I believed the shows would be set up alright, I decided it was time to venture into town and look for signs of Dad. I got dressed in some of my finer clothes, with every inch of skin covered to hide the tattoos. Then I went to find Marshall and told him I was heading into town.

"Great. Let me come with you," Ruby said. "I wanted to get some more flyers out and try to drum up some business for our first show this evening."

I glanced at Marshall, who just shrugged. Some help he was. "That's fine, but we need to get going. It's almost lunchtime."

Ruby scurried off to get cleaned up a bit. I looked at Marshall. "What's the verdict?" I asked.

"It's going to be strange. They seem oddly confident and clueless at the same time. Dangerous combination."

"Just about the most dangerous combination there is," I said.

"You going to town to look for Dad?" Marshall asked me.

"Yup. I figure there's got to be some sign of him here, maybe something that can point us in the direction he's gone."

"Something more solid than a dream, you mean?" he asked.

I glared. "I told you, you didn't have to come with me here. I could've been just fine on my own."

"No, we are not splitting the show. Besides, if Dad went missing, we don't need a repeat with you vanishing too."

"I'm not going anywhere, Marshall," I said. "You won't get rid of me that easily,"

Marshall laughed as Ruby walked back over. It surprised me that she hadn't changed out of the men's trousers—certainly one way to get attention in town. It was attention I wasn't sure we wanted, but if anyone gave us a hard time, I could take them.

"You ready?" Ruby asked.

I nodded, and Marshall waved as the two of us headed toward town.

Ruby hummed an odd tune as we walked, but I didn't pry for details or push for conversation. After a morning spent running around trying to piece together a story, I was all right not talking for a little while.

Ruby seemed comfortable with the lack of conversation as well and didn't try to ask a million questions like she had this morning. Hopefully she'd gotten all those out with Marshall. He excelled more at giving answers about the show and selling tickets than I ever would. It worked, having the responsibilities divided like that. I wasn't quite sure that Ruby and Eclipse would find that same harmony, but that fell way out of the list of the things I needed to worry about.

Instead, the only thing I wanted to worry about right now was my dad. And I didn't really care why Luther had left his first show or why no one seemed willing to tell me the truth about it. At the end of the day, that didn't matter one lick to me. Not when family was missing.

The town was small, even smaller than the one in Arkansas. Only a few buildings stood out: a single tavern, a general shop, one restaurant, and a tiny post office. But we had visited right around lunchtime, and it seemed like most of the townsfolk were out and about, so hopefully Ruby could get a crowd.

She glanced at me. "Guess I should've brought something to display," she said with a nervous laugh.

I barely resisted rolling my eyes. That was Showmanship 101, but if this was her first time doing a show ever, I couldn't expect perfect out of the gate. I had no plans on stripping out of my dress to be the showpiece of her display. "You're just going to have to sell it with your words then," I said. "I've got some business in town. I'll meet you back at the square in a little while."

Ruby nodded, pushed her shoulders back, and lifted her head up high. She took a deep breath before walking confidently into the square. I didn't stick around to wait and see what happened; I just hoped the audience here wasn't too opposed to a woman in trousers.

I headed for the post office. The building spanned the size of a double wagon and not a bit bigger. The man at the counter stood up as I walked in.

"Good afternoon, Miss," the man said." What can I help you with today?"

I put on my biggest not-threatening smile. "Good afternoon, I believe my father may have passed through her. I wanted to check if he had any mail I could collect for him."

"We don't get many strangers passing through," the man said.

"All the same, I'd like to check."

"What's his name?" the man asked with a heavy sigh.

"Harold Finnegan."

He ducked behind the counter and into the back where he seemed to dig through several satchels of mail and then to an organizational shelf. After a few minutes of looking, he returned to the counter empty-handed.

"Sorry ma'am, I don't have anything for your daddy."

"There's nothing for me or anyone else by the name of Finnegan?" I asked.

"I don't have any messages for that name. Apologies miss."

I wasn't surprised; this had been a gamble, but damn if it wasn't frustrating as hell all the same. How could Dad just up and vanish like this? Not leave any kind of note or nothing; something had to be really wrong.

"Thank you. If anything comes in over the next few days could you send someone out to the fields to deliver it?"

"The fields?"

"Yes, the circus is in town," I said.

He frowned but slowly nodded. "If anything comes in, I will. Have a good day now."

Reluctantly, I headed back to the town square to find Ruby. Even from a distance, I could hear her; she had a voice clear as a bell and quite a crowd around her. At first, I worried that she had an angry mob after her with righteous fury for wearing trousers, but instead I found a group of townsfolk looking positively mesmerized. The crowds were silent, eating up every word she said. I'd never seen a bunch like that before; there was always a doubter or a smart ass trying to get in another word. Or there were the religious folks claiming the devil walked amongst us in our shows. But not to Ruby.

She spoke with a smoothness I hadn't seen in my previous discussions with her; this took me off guard. I stayed in the back and watched the display. Even though I could see her lips moving and hear the cadence of her words, I couldn't pinpoint the exact things she said. It sounded more like music than a speech or presentation. Everything about the scene made me feel almost light-headed.

A burning in my arm snapped me out of the hazy feeling as the crowds started dissipating and moving to the side. I walked over as Ruby smiled and met me.

"Did you finish up everything you needed to?" she asked me.

"I did. Looks like you drummed up quite a crowd."

She smiled. "Yeah, the people were really excited about us being here. I think we'll have a decent audience."

"I hope so," I said.

Ruby smiled. "I can promise we will."

Something about the way she said that made the hairs on my arms stand on end. I eyed her and wished that I had some ability to tell when someone wasn't all human. Something about Ruby didn't seem quite right to me. I wondered if there was a reason she worked at a show like this. It did seem like faery folk leaned toward this kind of work.

"Ready to go back to the camp?" Ruby asked.

I nodded, ready to get away from her.

Most of the walk back we kept silent, and that made me happy. I didn't fancy another go at that strange fuzzy feeling; it was like I'd disconnected from my brain. Did she know she had that kind of effect on people, or was it something she might not be aware of? I wasn't even sure how to bring it up either. I couldn't find the words to ask if she knew what her speech did to people. If she knew, did that make her a threat?

Right now, all I wanted to focus on was finding Dad, not figuring out if someone might not be human. That had no bearing on me, and as long she didn't act like a monster, then I didn't really care. The Duncans had been faeries. I never cared that they weren't human because they were good folk who didn't cause harm, and that was all that mattered.

We made it back to camp quickly, and I left her to go wash up and get dressed. I tried to shake the strange feeling, but it lingered on my skin. I'd never seen a crowd so enraptured by anyone or anything before. I just wanted to know how she had done that and what more she could do. If she could drive people's actions, that could get dangerous quick. Especially if she didn't know what she was doing. But how did I even bring something like that up? I shook my head and started messing with my hair.

"You going to burn down this tent thinking that hard," Alma said as she walked in and started changing into her show attire.

"Sorry," I said, and turned back to shoving bobby pins in my hair to keep it up off my neck.

"Why you apologizing? There's nothing wrong with thinking. What's on your mind that heavy?" she asked.

I shook my head. "Just trying to sort this whole two show, one tent thing," I said.

"It isn't going to be too much of a problem, I reckon," she said. "They barely have any acts. Just think of it as a few new visitors for a little while. Nothing major to worry about at all. We don't have to find a permanent home for any of them. Besides, aren't you excited to be back with that skeleton of yours?"

"Yeah, course. You're right," I said. Not even sure how to tell Alma what I saw in town. "Just been a strange few weeks is all."

"It sure as hell has been," she said, and patted my shoulder. "I'm heading on into the tent. Did you need anything?" she asked.

"No, I just gotta get into my slip, and I'm ready."

"See you in there; we need to be ready for the show in fifteen so don't get stuck in thinking so hard you're late, or I will carry you to the stage."

I laughed at that image. "I'll be fine," I promised.

Alma didn't look convinced, but she waved as she headed over to the display area.

I took a breath and stared at my reflection in the mirror. Maybe the lack of sleep was finally starting to catch up with me. Constance and Temperance used to always tell me my daddy burnt his candle at both ends and that one day he'd run out of wax and wick. I kinda felt the same way right now.

Everything had been happening so fast, and I didn't have backup to call on when things got rough. Marshall helped with the show, but when it came to actually getting stuff done on the monster side of things, no one existed to even ask for advice. All I had was Dad's book, and it'd turned out to be damn near useless as far as I could tell. I didn't want to have to keep doing this on my own. I hated to admit it, but I wasn't sure I was ready to be a solo hunter.

I'd spent so much time thinking that I needed to prove myself and hunt alone, but now that it was happening, I would have done just about anything to go back to being that backup, helping someone else figure out what to do but not making the decision myself.

I didn't need that forever, but right now I just wanted some help. I needed to figure out how to do this on my own. I wanted my father back.

Surprisingly, my eyes started to water up, and I forced myself to look up to keep any tears from falling and ruining my makeup. I didn't have time to redo anything or to work on a new look. I just had to get my face together long enough for the show and to not look totally ridiculous with a melting face.

I finished my hair and makeup, wrapped up in a robe to cover everything from shoulders to ankles, and walked over to the show tent. A large crowd already formed outside, and the ticket booths looked full. Who would've expected an audience like this in a city this size?

Marshall and Ruby stood on the stage out in front of the show tent, loudly welcoming everyone to the show and preparing them for one good time. I ducked inside and headed to my stage.

On the walk to my display, I noticed the new exhibits from Eclipse's show. One was the corpse of her mermaid, something that looked more like a fish attached to a tiny monkey. An obvious fake, and I could tell that. She also had a taxidermy possum with wings attached to it, and a head with two faces suspended in a jar.

Out of everything, the jar looked like it might be real. But everything else was so obviously fake. I didn't really want to be on display with something like that. But at this point, it was a little too late to back out. Whoever had sold these to Eclipse had walked into a goldmine. Someone with that much money willing to buy this stupid crap was a con-artist's dream. If she learned nothing else from traveling with us, I could at least teach her how to avoid getting swindled.

There were a whole lot of charlatans in line with the sideshows and circuses. Usually, they just took care of the rubes outside, but if they found a wayward show owner, that was just a good a mark as any. Maybe even better. You could make some solid money selling crap to someone who didn't know better.

As I hopped up onto my stage, Alma tilted her head toward the new exhibits. "You see our new tent mates?" She asked.

"Yeah, quite a lot of lookers, huh?"

"How can someone with enough money to fling at you for that skeleton be dumb enough to buy a taxidermy monkey?"

"But that explains why she was so eager to buy from us. I mean, compared to that crap, just about anything's better."

"You know, I think that money and sense just don't go together. I have never met a rich person with a lick of sense."

I laughed. "If we could get money to match sense, we can solve a whole lotta problems in the world."

Alma smiled.

"What are you girls going on about?" Jonah asked as he walked in.

"Just discussing our new tent mates," I said." Have you met them?"

Jonah glanced at me. "You shouldn't laugh at the gullible. They say the gullible are the closest to God."

"Then Heaven is full of fools," I said.

Jonah smiled and shook his head as he got onstage and sat down to read his paper. Out of every act we had, Jonah and the twins always made me the saddest. All of them were just doing normal things: reading the paper, drinking coffee, smoking. And people flocked to stare. At least here, people paid for that privilege. But there was nothing extraordinary about a man going about his life—unless that man didn't have arms.

"Let the show begin!" Marshall announced.

CHAPTER FOUR

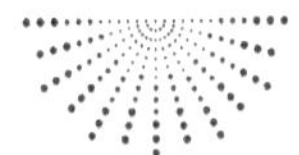

Alma hurried back to her stage and picked up some weights to show off. I hopped onto the swing display and started idling, moving back and forth in what I hoped looked like a girlish fashion.

The crowds rushed in like a dam just opening after a winter thaw. They packed in so tightly it amazed me anyone could move. I couldn't imagine Luther trying to display fire in a crowd this tight.

While a good sized group of people milled around moving from one display to the next, it stayed the quietest crowd we had ever had. I didn't get any intrusive questions. No one trying to play coy and lift my slip; no one trying to grab my arm to test if anything washed off; no one asking if I was married or looking. The stillness unnerved me. How could this be the same crowd that had just been outside making so much noise it felt like you could hear them for miles. But now silence reigned, and that didn't make any sense.

The silence hung heavy enough that I could actually hear everyone's act. Temperance and Constance were doing a song and dance number for once. Their voices were off-key, and their dance thudded in awkward and clunky ways, but the audience stood transfixed by it. Alma lifted various weights around her area, each one more impressive than the last, but even when she lifted the heaviest thing we had, a full barrel of rocks, no one gasped in reaction. Jonah sat reading a Bible verse aloud to the crowd in front of him. I could hear Luther going through his spiel outside the tent and the crackling fire, but still no gasps, no shock and awe.

The swing creaked with my movements back and forth until I felt the sound might crack open my skull. Just as I got off of the swing to get out of the silent hell, noise suddenly exploded.

Not in any screaming, startling way, but as though the sound had suddenly switched back on in the world. The crowd didn't look alarmed. It was like they hadn't even realized what happened. I looked around at the others on display, and all of them appeared a little uneasy. Of course, there was no real way to yell across the crowd and ask if they had just experienced the same thing as me, but somehow, I thought we all shared in that same strange moment. Whatever had broken the spell had left no trace that I could see.

With the crowd back to making noise, I focused on a good show, dealing with all the annoying questions, letting one or two curious boys touch my arm to prove that nothing rubbed off my ink. The crowds stayed constant in size and now in volume too, with no trace of whatever strangeness had passed earlier.

As the afternoon turned to evening and a chill started drifting over the tent, the crowds finally began to slow. Now they were small enough to pick out individual conversations and not just a cacophony of sound and fury signifying nothing.

"Did you hear they saw that big cat again?" one of the visitors said.

The man beside him shook his head. "What does it matter? Probably just a mountain cat or something. They're all over this area."

"Bigger than that. And the most silent thing you've ever heard. They say if you see it, you're going to die. And soon."

"Yeah, mauled to death by a mountain lion. That's pretty standard when you see one of them."

"You are not listening to me."

"I am not into all of that monster shit you talk about. Even the shit in here aint' real."

"I think I'm plenty real, gentleman," I said as I got off the swing and approached the edge of the stage.

"I didn't mean no offense, ma'am," the skeptical man said. "But some of the stuff in here don't look right to me."

"That's the whole point, dumbass," his friend said and slapped his shoulder.

"You a big hunter?" I asked. "I've never seen a mountain lion before, are they really all over the place here?"

"They are. I shot quite a few that come after my goats and my chickens. Got to protect what's mine."

"Of course. You're sure this death lion isn't just—"

"It's not just some normal lion. I'm telling you," his friend said. "I have lived here all my life; I know what a mountain lion looks like, and this ain't it."

"And I know your daddy makes some pretty strong moonshine," his friend muttered.

The first man flushed. "It isn't because I'm drunk. I haven't seen it, just heard about it. Makes the world go silent, and that's how you know death is coming."

"Isn't that how it always is?" I asked. "No one's actually seen it, they just know a friend of a friend who has."

"When that thing shows up, y'all'd've wished you'd listened to me."

"Why? I'm a better shot than you, and you haven't even told us anything good. There's a big cat that you die when you see. Sounds about like everything else in these woods. Don't piss it off, and it won't kill you."

I liked this skeptic guy.

"What's this about silence, though?" I asked.

"That's how they say you know it's close. The whole world goes silent; nothing makes a sound like it's supposed to."

"You sure that's not just the woods at night? It's a whole lot quieter then." His friend crossed his arms.

"If you would get your head out of your ass, and listen to what I'm saying—"

"If you would stop talking out of your ass, then maybe I'd listen to half of what comes out of your mouth."

While the two men bickered, I frowned and thought. If this guy was right, did that mean this strange cat thing had been close? I didn't have time to go on a hunt again. I still had to figure out where Dad had gone. I didn't need to be chasing after some cat. By the time I snapped out of my thoughts again, the two men had left and the tent sat mostly empty.

By the chill in the air, night had arrived. The giant crowd had made the day go faster, even with the strange silence that had first greeted our show. But if that had been the sign of this lion thing, then how had I still been able to hear my coworkers going on with their presentations? Shouldn't it have silenced everything and everyone? And why did the audience seem unaware of this sound difference? I wish that guy and his friend were still here so I could question them more, but they were long gone. Outside, I could hear Marshall closing up the show for the night.

I hopped off my stage, and before I could say a word, Alma approached me. "What the hell was that silent nonsense?"

CHAPTER FIVE

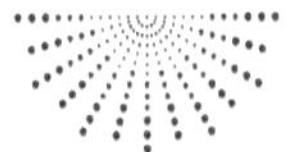

You noticed it too?" Jonah asked. "Thank the Lord; I thought it was just me."

"I sensed it," I said, and looked toward the twins.

Constance and Temperance glanced at each other before they both nodded.

"Never realized we sounded that bad with our singing before. Guess there's a reason we don't perform in fancy, silent showrooms," Temperance said.

"What was it?" Alma asked.

"I don't know. And I honestly don't know if I want to know," I said after a moment.

Everyone shifted on their feet, strange discomfort settling over what should have been a successful evening. I knew we made a lot of money, but that silence still lingered. It made me feel a little better to know that everyone else recognized it too. I wasn't alone in what I had thought might have been a hallucination.

"The audience didn't seem to notice anything," Jonah said.

Everyone but us seemingly had been unaffected by the strange silence that wrapped around the entire tent. I leaned back against one of the larger support beams and let out a long sigh. Was it too much to ask for nothing to happen?

Trouble seemed drawn to me and the show like a moth to a flame. I didn't have time to suffer fools or troublemaking monsters causing chaos.

"There was a man here who talked about some cat, a big one, and if you looked at it, you die. Said it made the whole world silent when it got too close." I said.

"Are you sure that's not a mountain lion?" Alma asked.

"He seemed pretty sure of that," I said. "And I imagine someone living in these mountains would have a pretty good idea about what lives around here."

Alma nodded while the twins pulled a big bottle of whiskey from behind their curtain. Before I could even say anything, Constance took a long swig.

"If there is some death causing lion hunting around here, then I am not dying sober," Constance said and offered the bottle to Temperance.

Temperance took a long swig as well before Alma managed to pull the bottle from them.

"What'd you do that for?" Constance asked.

"Because every time y'all get drunk, I'm the one who has to carry you back to your tent. And I am not doing that tonight." Alma said, keeping the bottle firmly in her hands and away from the twins.

"I'm going to see if Marshall had the same thing happen out front. If it was just in the tent…" I didn't know what to think if that was the case.

How could something presumably as big as that man described be close enough to the tent to affect all of us but not the front? And that still didn't clear up why the audience didn't get affected at all.

"If there is some beast hunting around, we ought to stick together," Jonah said. "How about we all go talk to Marshall and then go to dinner together?"

"Sure," I said. He had a good point.

Our group headed out of the tent and out front where Marshall had started to pick up trash left behind by the crowds. I didn't see any sign of Ruby or Eclipse anywhere around the show. Maybe they'd already gone off to get something to eat or to split up the expenses.

"Now that's a group of trouble if I ever saw one," Marshall said. "What are all of you doing out together? Usually, once the show's done you guys can't wait to get some distance."

"Did anything strange happen out here during the show?" I asked.

Marshall looked at me like I'd grown another head. "Strange? Like what?"

I glanced at the rest of the performers who all looked about as alarmed as I felt. "There wasn't any time that got real quiet out here?" I asked.

"Quiet? No. There were a few lulls but nothing bad. How was it in there?"

"In there was strange," I said. "There were a few minutes when the whole world went silent. Nothing making a sound even though there were loads of people. Nothing like that happened out here?"

Marshall frowned. "I think you need to get some sleep, Hazel. Sounds like you're starting to hallucinate."

"We all heard it happen, Marshall." Jonah spoke up. "It wasn't just Hazel."

Marshall looked around the group before running a hand through his hair. "It's been a rough few days. Things will make more sense in the morning."

"You don't think this is something we ought to be worried about?" I asked.

"I think it's something that can wait until tomorrow. It's been a long couple of weeks, Hazel."

I stepped toward him. "And what if this is some kind of monst—"

"I think whatever this is, whatever happens, is something that our new neighbors don't need to know about right this second. Understand?" Marshall looked pointedly at me.

I hadn't even thought of that. Ruby and Eclipse had no idea what I did. Me going off in the dead of night to hunt something that may or may not exist would be hard to explain away. And if we wanted to stay here and keep using the land rightfully reserved by them, I would have to stay low if I wanted to investigate this.

I nodded in understanding. "Let's just all go get dinner and call it an early night then," I said.

We all walked to the mess tent together with Marshall walking right at my side. "You're sure you didn't hear anything?" He asked softly.

"Positive."

Marshall frowned, but he kept pace beside me. "After dinner come by my caravan, and we can talk about it more, alright?" he said.

Hardtack and some potatoes greeted me for dinner, but we did at least have warm coffee and tea around to drink. For all the cooking they did, the chefs only seemed to excel during breakfast. Every other meal was just one layer of disappointment after another.

As everyone finished eating, I watched people leave in pairs or small groups. At least I knew this little makeshift family looked after their own, even against things that we all didn't quite understand yet. As Alma left, she clapped me on the shoulder.

"Good night, Hazel," she said. "Don't do anything stupid tonight."

"I never do anything stupid," I said.

Alma rolled her eyes with a laugh as she joined Clarence, Jonah, and the twins. They all left the mess hall together and headed for the sleeper cars.

"Mind if I join you?" Luther walked up to the side of the table opposite Marshall and me.

I had honestly forgotten that he had performed tonight. With all the changes going on and the strangeness of the night, it had somehow faded from my mind. I wondered if he heard anything or the lack of anything from his vantage point at the back of the tent.

"Sure thing," Marshall said.

Luther sat down and ate his dinner. Marshall and I were both giving him a hard stare down, trying to find some indication on what he might have experienced during the show today.

"I have something on my face or something?" he asked.

"How was the show?" I asked.

"Good. It was real good."

I glanced at Marshall before asking, "Nothing strange happened?"

Luther slowly put down his spoon and looked at me. "That weird quiet spell, you mean?"

"Spell?" I asked.

"You know, it was real quiet for a time, for about a minute."

It had felt like much longer to me, but honestly, I didn't know how much time had elapsed in that silence. It could've been minutes, seconds, hours; I just didn't know.

"You experienced it too?" Marshall asked.

"Wait, it happened to you guys?"

"Inside the tent. All the performers heard it happening, well I guess we *didn't* hear anything, and that's what was strange."

Luther looked to Marshall. "And you?"

Marshall shook his head, "Nothing strange happened out on the stage."

"What the hell was it?" Luther asked.

"I don't know, but I aim to find out," I said, unable to help myself.

Even when the last thing in the world I wanted to do was spend time investigating a strange silence-creating cat, I knew I couldn't just walk away and leave this alone. Besides, if some monster cat, something not of this world, existed here, it was part of my job to get rid of it. How much of an excuse of Dad being missing would work with something like Lady Death? She didn't seem like the real familial type, but I didn't really know her to be honest.

Luther finished eating and stood up. "I'm going to get some sleep."

I watched as he left the tent, strolling to his wagon.

"Have you seen Ruby or Eclipse?" Marshall asked.

"No. I thought they were with you during the show."

"They were, but they vanished as soon as the show ended."

"As long as they didn't vanish with all of our money, I don't care where they went. There is only one missing person I can care about at any given time, and right now, that position is taken."

Marshall sighed. "I'm going to go check on them. I'll meet you at your room once I'm done."

"Don't take too long. I am not waiting up all night for you."

"I won't. See you in a minute," he said before leaving the tent.

Left alone in the mess hall with no one but a few of the tent builders and one or two of our ticket booth workers, I rubbed my temples and let out a heavy sigh. How did I keep winding up in these messes? Dad being missing threw everything off. I still felt totally off-balance, like I was trying to learn how to ride a bike without a foot. I could still manage somehow, but I constantly felt like one breeze might knock me over.

For right now, I enjoyed the fact that I could hear low conversations in the background, the soft rumbling of other people existing in this world with me instead of that strange, awful silence. Right now, that was all that mattered and all I wanted to consider. The rest could come later.

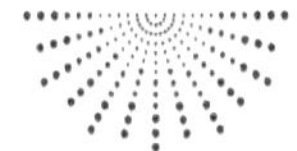

W hat happened exactly?" Marshall asked.

He sat at the table while I perched cross-legged in bed. "I already told you. Everything went silent except for all of us."

"Silent? Hazel, that crowd was big enough to drown out half the damn town."

"I know. But all I could hear was the twins' bad singing. Nothing made a noise in there for…I don't know how long, but it was weird."

"Alright, alright, I believe you. But what do you want to do about it?" he asked.

"I don't know."

"Look, Hazel, you don't have to go hunting down—"

"Don't I? That's Dad's job. He's not here—that makes it mine now."

"Hazel…I don't think we can keep that hidden from our new coworkers."

"I can be subtle!"

"You set a train on fire last time you hunted something," Marshall pointed out.

"That was…a bad decision, and one I don't appreciate you bringing up."

"And the one before that, you brought a giant skeleton to the show!"

"Marshall—"

"Hazel, you don't need to try to save the world right now. You need to sleep," Marshall stood up. "Just go to bed."

"Yeah…sure," I said. "Turn the lantern down on your way out."

I got under the covers. The caravan went dark before Marshall closed the door and left.

As I laid in the darkness, I couldn't get what Luther had said out of my head. I knew he meant it as a spell of time, not a magic spell. But what if it was? I hadn't dealt much with magic; I didn't have a solid grasp on how it even worked, but this seemed like something that would fit. But if that were the case, I'd still have to figure out who or what had cast that kind of spell.

Magic had never been my forte, and I didn't imagine that changing overnight. Was there some rogue, evil spellcaster wandering out there, maybe disguising themselves as a cat? Because if someone had enough magic to cast pure silence, shapeshifting would be easy.

No, I was not getting involved in this.

I closed my eyes and counted sheep. I got to nearly 200 before I realized sleep wasn't happening tonight. Not when something roamed out there causing chaos, something not natural messing with the order of things. Even though all I wanted was a good night's sleep, there would be no rest until I had answers. Reluctantly, I got out of bed, and I pulled on a pair of Dad's old trousers, tied them tightly around my waist with a belt, and grabbed a warm sweater.

Grabbing the lantern from my desk, I lit it as I headed out the door and into the night.

CHAPTER SEVEN

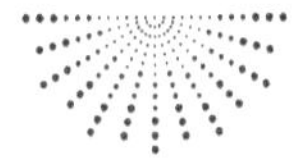

The camp stayed quiet; all of the lights were low or out, and the caravans were dark. I glanced toward where Eclipse and Ruby camped, grateful to see everything still and dark on that side of the set-up. I didn't know how I'd be able to explain my being out and about at this hour in any way that would make sense to a stranger. And trying to explain everything, well, that was just plain off the table. Marshall's place stayed dark too as I crept past the perimeter.

Inching past the horse corral, one of our older mares, Cookie, gave a whiny and moved toward me, looking for a biscuit.

"Shhh…" I hissed and scratched the horse's nose.

She nuzzled into my hand, and I patted her before scooting past.

"Quiet, girl," I said to the puzzled horse as the camp faded behind me.

With a lantern guiding my way, I headed out into the thickest area of woods near us. If something wanted to hide, it wouldn't be in an obvious place, so that left the part of woods that were hard to travel. The fewer the people that went that way, the easier to stay hidden. The lantern only cast a little bit of light, but it gave enough for me to see and step over roots, rocks, and twigs without tripping myself up too badly.

This was stupid. I didn't even know what to look for, yet here I was in the dead of night, wandering through woods that I didn't know. I was just asking to get lost or killed.

After I got far enough from camp, I unhooded my lantern and started looking for tracks. Hunters wouldn't be out this late, and there shouldn't be anyone else in the woods, so hopefully the light wouldn't draw too much attention to me. At best, it would probably scare off anything I looked for, and at worst, I'd just set a big target on my back in the pitch-black night.

I knew how to follow things; Daddy taught me that. When things got real lean for the show, we would hunt game for dinner, something to get us through until that next pay hit.

I found a few deer markings easily. They were not what I hunted. When I stumbled across bear tracks, I turned around and moved the other way. I was not messing with a bear, especially one that might have cubs. A mama bear protecting her babies was worse to deal with than any demon or troll.

I found a small stream and drank a bit of water from it before sitting on a rock and looking around. The woods were so dense and thick that, at this point, I wasn't even sure which way led back to camp. I really should've done a better job marking my trail. But if worse came to worst, I could always summon Puck to fly above the tree line and show me which way to go. The stream ran clear and strong, a peaceful melody against the cicadas, birds, and trees swaying in the cool evening breeze.

I decided to start following the stream. This time of year, we usually saw droughts, but everything flowed like it might be fresh from the winter thaw. Lucky for us, we didn't have to try and pay to get extra water brought in, because towns going dry meant they didn't care to share what they had with strange outsiders.

As I got further upstream, I caught sight of a strange figure slumped against the banks. With my lantern in one hand and my dagger in the other, I approached and found a deer carcass. That wouldn't necessarily be something to write home about; lots of people hunted in this part of the world, but this deer didn't look like it had been taken down by any gun or bow.

I moved closer to the body to examine the wounds. The slashes across the side and chest were caused by some sort of cat, and a big one at that. What struck me as strange was that it didn't seem eaten. There were no chunks of meat missing, no parts of the skin ripped open—just a dead deer with some big claw marks on it. The blood had just started to coagulate, so I knew this had to be pretty fresh. The scavengers hadn't gotten to it yet, but they probably would soon.

I didn't see any tracks leading away from the kill. This had to be the end of the trail then. Maybe the attacker headed into the water. Cats and water didn't much mix, but wildcats were a totally different thing. *If only I had some kind of tracking dog, it would be easy to find this thing*, I thought.

I wonder if the hound could track like a normal dog. I rubbed my hand over my arm where the mark of the hound still burned. Summoning it was a huge risk. If I lost control of it in a place like this, there would be a forest fire that would burn out of control before anyone could help. I'd destroy more than just a train car; I could ruin my whole caravan, a town, and a hell of a lot of woods.

But I wasn't quite sure how else to proceed. How did I hunt something that left no track, that I had no information on, and that no one seemed to know anything about? If we weren't going to be here for very long, then did I really have time to wait and see if tomorrow brought more information?

I took a long breath and shook my head. No way could I summon that thing. Never again. I was a damn fool to consider it, and for once in my life, I decided to make the smart decision.

I summoned Puck and flew him up above the tree line. I could just make out the camp to the south of me. With Puck by my side, I started the slow trek back.

It seemed like only a few minutes passed when I noticed the silence. The cicadas had gone quiet; the frogs, owls, even the sound of me moving through the woods, none of it made a noise. I deliberately stepped on a twig, and despite it shattering under me, there was no snap at all. I looked at Puck, who just took a long drag on his cigar and shrugged.

I drew my dagger in hand and continued moving. Whatever lurked out there was close and had probably seen me. And if it followed me, I wouldn't even hear it. Moving to the trees, I tried to keep my pace steady and not drop into a panicked run.

When the silence followed me, I found that same rock by the river and parked myself there. I pulled the hood back over my lantern to dampen the light. I hoped that might help. At least this close to the stream I'd have a chance to put out any fires I might start, too.

I stayed still and waited. Puck floated back and forth, anxiously smoking through his cigar at a record pace. Being in the woods in total silence felt surreal. It seemed more like a dream than reality, but I knew that I had left my bed, and I wasn't just making this up. The rotting smell of the deer and the taste of the water were crystal clear; my dreams might've been vivid, but they weren't this realistic.

Just when I thought about giving up, I saw it: a pair of golden eyes staring at me from the trees. They had the telltale slant of a cat eye but were way larger than any I'd seen on a feline before, and I'd seen lions and tigers up close and personal.

This cat and I stared each other down, neither one of us moving an inch. Slowly, I brought my lantern up to get a better view. All I could make out was a huge shape, something closer to the size of a bear than a cat. The moment I moved though, the eyes vanished, and suddenly sound returned. The cicadas started screaming into the summer night again, and the owls sang their hunting songs.

I decided not to wait and see if the cat came back. Instead, I got up, unhooded my lamp, and hauled ass back toward camp.

Occasionally, I had to have Puck glide upward to check the path, but eventually I scrambled back to my wagon. There was some strange cat out in the woods, causing silence and mayhem. At least now I sort of knew the area it might be in if I returned tomorrow night.

Puck popped back onto my skin as camp came into sight and I let out a breath. I'd made it through without any trouble.

"Out for a midnight stroll?"

I jumped, with my dagger out and at the ready instantly, only to find Eclipse smoking a cigarette outside of her tent.

"What are you doing up?" I asked as I put the dagger away.

"I have a hard time sleeping. Find that a cigarette can help put me to sleep most nights. You want one?"

I shook my head. "No, thanks. I'm good. Just needed some air to clear my head a little bit."

"That was quite a show today, wasn't it?" she asked as she put out her cigarette under her boot.

"I didn't think we'd have that kind a crowd in a town this small," I said.

"Sometimes the small towns are more starved for entertainment than the big ones. You can make big money selling dreams to little town people."

"I don't know if I exactly call a sideshow selling a dream, but I get what you mean," I said. "We always get a few people running after us wanting to join the circus. They usually make it about a day before they realize the circus life isn't what it seems from the other side of the tent."

Eclipse laughed. "I guess I could see that being the case. I do have to say I am impressed with you and your brother's show. You have a good group and run a smooth ship."

"Thanks. We try," I said. "We both probably ought to get to bed though; we've got more shows tomorrow."

Eclipse nodded. "Goodnight, Hazel. Hope you get some sleep; you look like you could use it."

I forced myself to smile at the backhanded comment. "Goodnight," I said and walked back to my tent. Climbing into bed this time, I drifted off quickly, but those golden eyes haunted my dreams.

I woke with Marshall barging into my room.

CHAPTER EIGHT

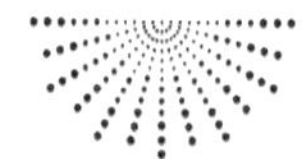

"Hazel, get out here. Cookie is missing."

I sat up, bleary-eyed and groggy. It took me a moment to connect that Marshall wasn't busting into my room at dawn looking for a snack but for our old mare.

"What? Is everyone out looking for her?"

"We don't have the money to replace a horse right now, Hazel. Yeah, we're all going out looking for her."

All I could think of was that the deer corpse I found down by the stream. If that cat had followed me back to camp…this could be all my fault. "Give me a second, and I'll be out there."

Marshal left the room, and I crawled out of bed. I stayed with the same thing I wore last night; trousers made for much easier running around than dealing with dresses and petticoats.

By the time I got out of my room, I could see most everyone else already out and about, looking around the show like the horse might be hiding in any one of the dressing rooms. Alma waved me over. "You ready to go looking out in the woods?" she asked.

"You waiting on me for that?"

"After whatever bullshit happened in the tent yesterday, I'm not going out anywhere by myself," Alma said. "Besides, you're about the only one here that's worth anything in a fight."

I couldn't disagree or argue with her on that front; we were not a group known for our brute strength, aside from Alma and me, of course.

"Let's get a move on," I said.

Alma held a lamp in her hand even though the sun had started to rise. When wandering around in the woods, it was always better to have extra light than be without. As we walked, I tried to remember if I'd seen the horse when I got home late last night. I didn't walk near their stables; I didn't know that Cookie had been there after I ran into Eclipse.

"You look like you're thinking too hard. You trying to think like a horse?" Alma asked.

"No, just trying to remember the last time I saw them. Were they there after the show?"

Alma shook her head. "I don't remember seeing them. But the things are always kind of background, you know? Don't really notice when they're there, but you sure as hell do when they're missing. I think we would've realized because we all were on high alert last night."

I nodded.

"I saw Cookie after the show," I said. "Late in the day when I was heading to bed."

I couldn't remember if she'd been there when I returned to my hunt. I'd been so sidetracked by Eclipse I hadn't even thought about it.

We walked along mostly the same trail I'd walked last night: the easiest way to move between the trees without having to forge a whole new path and chop some vines down. The bushes grew thick and heavy. In parts, the ground almost disappeared entirely under them. It amazed me that I managed to get through there last night in low light without tripping and hurting myself.

Soon enough, we came across the same stream that I'd sat on the edge of last night. There wasn't any indication that's where the eerie silence had settled. A shiver ran down my spine, but I just sat up straighter to ignore it.

"I'm not one to go wandering in woods anyways, but these are extra bad," Alma said as she adjusted the lantern and tightened her grip on her knife. With Alma at my side, I at least had a slight chance of surviving an encounter with that big cat again.

With that, it felt like I needed to give Alma at least a warning that something lived out here.

"Last night, I might've gone out looking for trouble," I said casually.

Alma stared at me. "You did what?"

"I couldn't sleep knowing something was out there. I just had to take a quick look."

"And what did your quick look find?"

I licked my lips. "I saw a big cat. I mean big, like the size of a bear. And the world got all silent and strange again."

Alma took a deep breath and let it out slowly. "Are you just stupid, or are you trying to get yourself killed?"

"You know I'm not either of those things. Hunting down trouble is my job. I was trying to do what's right."

"What's right and what's smart ain't often the same thing. I'd much rather you alive than wandering the woods in the dead of night looking for a killer cat."

"Nothing happened. I think it lost interest in me."

"It could have followed you?"

"Maybe just for a little while."

"Hazel, I swear to the Lord above—"

"Look, I saw it over this way, let's look there. Maybe the horse got spooked, ran for it, and then maybe the cat tried to get hold of it."

"You better not tell your brother about what you did last night. He'll be furious."

"Marshall doesn't have to know everything I do."

I lead the way with Alma right behind me. In the daylight, I pushed my way through the woods and toward where I had seen that giant figure. With backup, I felt a little more willing to face it. Alma and I hadn't been in too many fights together, but if there was anybody I could trust to have my back, it was her.

As soon as we got out of a section of dense undergrowth, we both spotted the tracks. Horse tracks. And moving fast away from camp. We glanced at each other before heading after them.

"Cookie! Here girl," I called.

Now that we'd seen markings in the wood, I wasn't sure we'd be seeing Cookie the mare ever again. Even if whatever I'd seen in the night didn't get her, there were a whole lot of other things out for a nice meal of fresh horse. And the longer we took to find her, the lower the odds of her survival. But if the show kept up with this kind of rate of attendance, we could probably splurge and buy a new horse and be okay.

"Cookie?" I called again.

Alma paused. "Do you hear that?"

"What?"

"Listen."

I closed my eyes to try to focus my hearing. It took a few seconds, but I couldn't deny it. "I'll be damned, that's a horse whinny," I said.

Alma nodded with a grin, and we both took off toward the sound. It only took a few minutes to find the source of it and see Cookie in a clearing of trees chewing on some clover.

What looked like long claw marks from a cat ran along the horse's flank. But they weren't bleeding, and Cookie seemed fine. The horse tossed her head at us and trotted a little bit further away to continue munching. Alma went to collect her while I just shook my head and looked around the area to see if there were any other signs of that cat.

Instead, I caught sight of a familiar set of bones. The troll bones that I had sold to Eclipse were all laid out and on full display right in the middle of the woods. They couldn't have been here for too long since the show only just arrived, but somehow clover and moss were already growing over them. In fact, if I hadn't been so familiar with what they looked like from handling them, I would have assumed it was a bunch of rocks laying around. How had they ended up in this state and what on earth drove the horse to come here?

Alma got a rope around Cookie and led her back to my side. "Guess we better get her back, right?"

"Yeah, let's go."

I scratched the mare's nose.

As we headed out of the clearing, I summoned Puck to sit and wait there for me to come back. I needed to see what happened with these bones after I had a conversation with Eclipse.

Back to the camp, I hadn't ever seen Marshall so relieved and happy to see a horse before. We got Cookie back into her little makeshift pen, and then Alma and I started patching up her wounds. Thankfully the claw marks weren't too deep, just flesh wounds. She was one lucky mare; whatever had gone after her had just missed seriously hurting her.

I ruffled the horse's mane and rubbed her nose before giving her a few slices of apple as a treat. She ate up and then wandered into her pen, presumably to nap. That's what I wanted to do, but unfortunately, life always had other plans. We had a show to get ready for, and I had a show manager to confront about what exactly she'd done with the bones she'd bought from us.

It didn't matter what she did. She owned the bones, but just abandoning them in the middle of a forest, covering them with some sort of greenery to let them disappear? That wasn't what I had in mind when I sold them to her. It was the only viable thing she had in her show, and she got rid of it like this? Why not get rid of that bullshit monkey or the stupid mermaid fake? I didn't understand it, and it pissed me off to see my hard work cast aside like that—thrown out without even a second thought, left to rot in obscurity.

Before I did anything else, I went and drank my coffee and ate breakfast. At least a little bit of time to collect my thoughts would maybe prevent me from totally blowing up at Eclipse. Everything in the morning seemed to go better after a nice cup of coffee and breakfast.

Most everyone else sat in the mess hall eating. Alma slid into a seat beside Clarence and readily joined his conversation. I smiled; they seemed like a right good match. I'd never seen Alma so happy.

I joined Jonah, Luther, and the twins at another table.

"I hear you found a horse this morning," Luther said.

"Guess I missed my calling as an animal tamer," I said.

He laughed. "Good job, I guess. I didn't realize the horse was even missing."

"That's because you could sleep through an earthquake," Constance said.

Luther smiled. "That sounds like a compliment to me."

"Good work, Hazel. I know you really helped Marshall out by finding her," Jonah said.

"And all in time to still get ready for the show," Constance said with a smile.

Temperance sighed. "Do we have to do a lunchtime show today? Can't we all just take a break?"

"I wish," I said. "The bills don't get paid if we aren't on display. You like being paid, don't you?"

Temperance muttered under her breath but didn't say anything else. Lately, the twins had been more reluctant to do shows. I imagined years of gawking got to you after a certain point. But despite being asked, they said they were happy here and didn't want to ever leave. Then again, there weren't a lot of jobs for people like us, and this way made all of us a pretty solid living.

I ate slowly, wanting everyone else to finish and get out before me so no one saw me go over to the other side of the tent. I didn't see any sign of Eclipse or Ruby joining us for breakfast, but I supposed if Eclipse stayed out as late as I did, she would probably sleep as deep into the day as she could.

Whoever or whatever had moved the skeleton out that way had some answers to give me. Maybe they didn't know the skeleton was real and just assumed it was another forgery like the ones they seemed so fond of buying. But if they kept up like that, they wouldn't be in business for very long, and as much as I sometimes hated the rival shows, I didn't want to see any woman-led venture fall apart based on bad decisions and a lack of information. I could just imagine every smooth talker and swindler for miles around coming for her.

After my second cup of coffee, most everyone had cleared out of the tent. A few people seemed to have gone down to the stream to wash up, and I saw Alma and Clarence head out on their date. As much fun as it might've been to follow after to see what happened, I knew that was a bad idea, and Alma needed her privacy. Besides, I had other stuff to handle.

Grabbing an extra cup of coffee, I made my way to Eclipse's caravan. I knocked on the door and waited. It only took a few seconds for the door to open, and Eclipse surprised me by being fully dressed and ready for the day. I expected her to still be in her nightgown.

"Miss Hazel, good morning."

"I brought you some coffee," I said.

"Thank you; I was just finishing up some ledger work."

I passed over the cup, and she smiled and started to close the door. I stuck my foot in the jamb and smiled. "I was hoping we could talk."

Eclipse looked startled for a moment before nodding and opening the door. "Of course, come in."

I walked inside and looked around. The caravan was quite plain, nothing out of the ordinary on the walls or even in her bed. Everything seemed store-bought, nothing homemade. Not that there was anything wrong with that, but usually people who traveled a lot brought some piece of home with them.

"What can I help you with?" Eclipsed asked as she sat down with her cup of coffee.

"I just was curious about that skeleton of ours that you bought. I didn't notice it in the show yesterday."

"You know, you are right, traveling with that thing is a challenge. It takes up a lot of space, and I honestly don't have a tent that size to display it properly. I guess I didn't think about that when I saw it. It's one of the most amazing things I've ever seen, but I don't think I'm going to be able to travel with it."

"Where is it?" I asked. "I saw it when we first pulled in and joined up with you, but I haven't seen it since."

She took a long drink of her coffee. "Honestly, I had some of the tent building boys take it out into the woods and get rid of it."

I nodded. That didn't explain how moss and field greens already covered it. That didn't happen overnight or in two days. Something unnatural occurred in those woods around the bones, and I needed to figure that out immediately. Things like that didn't happen in nature unless some beast or magic got involved and that fell under my responsibility to deal with—one more thing to add to my already overflowing list.

"That doesn't upset you, does it? I didn't mean to hurt your feelings about not using your incredible find. It just really is such a pain to display. I know you understand," she said.

"No, it's fine. I just was curious whatever happened to it. Where'd you get the other items you have on display?"

"I took a few trips to New York and found them at a rare antiquities dealer. He had all sorts of amazing creatures like that. Aren't they wonderful?"

For a second, I debated letting her live in her fantasy world where these things were clearly real and not obvious fakes, but that wouldn't be helping her at all. "To be honest, they look like a lot of the imitations I've seen in some of the lesser quality shows."

Eclipse put her cup down. "Are you saying they're fakes?"

There wasn't any anger radiating off of her, just a cold, calculated curiosity. I couldn't tell if the previous naïve act had been real or forged now that she looked at me like this.

I cleared my throat and stuck to my guns. "I think they are."

"That should be obvious to anyone with a brain, but do you think the audience can tell that?" she asked.

The charming, sweet façade had faded away in an instant, and I stared at a calculating businesswoman. But if that was the case, why had she paid so much money for our bones only to abandon them?

"I didn't hear any complaining about it in the tent yesterday," I finally said.

"Good. This is one of the first shows they've been out with. I was curious what the reaction would be. It's good your group came along because we get a buffer for our more subdued acts."

She picked up her coffee and resumed sipping it.

"How much did those things run you?"

"About $5 each. I've more than made up that money with just yesterday's showing. Even if they do get outed, there's nothing lost for me. Now your skeleton, on the other hand, is a lost cause. But no hard feelings."

"You and Marshall figured out how to split everything?"

"Straight 50/50 split. You may have the better acts, but we have the space. It all evens out in the end. Besides, with the crowds we are drawing, we're both leaving here much richer women."

And who was I to argue with that?

"You didn't happen to see what happened to that little mare last night, did you?" she asked.

I didn't even know Eclipse knew that something had happened to Cookie.

I could feel the accusation behind her words, and two could play that game. "No. I didn't see anything, did you? You were up pretty late, weren't you?"

Eclipse smiled. "I like you, Hazel. I know you'd never leave your brother running the show alone, but if you ever change your mind, you always have a place traveling with me."

I stared at her in shock. No one had ever offered to give me a place outside of the show. Part of me was offended that she would even put that out there. Was she trying to drive a wedge between Marshall and me, or was I just hypersensitive and sleep deprived? Regardless, I knew I wasn't going anywhere.

I shook my head. "Thanks, but I'm happy where I am."

Eclipse smiled. "That's what I figured you would say, but I couldn't help but try. You know, all of the people that work with you are very loyal. I hope you can keep it that way. Just be on the lookout that your new hires feel the same way."

I knew she meant Luther. There couldn't be anyone else. And honestly, I didn't care if he stayed or went, we just needed a replacement for the Duncans. That's all he was. Even now he still kept to himself and hadn't bothered to get to know much of anyone else. I didn't trust him, but sometimes trust didn't matter. All that mattered was whether they get the job done, and for Luther, that answer was yes.

She finished her coffee and passed the empty mug to me. "Thank you for this breakfast chat. It's always nice talking with another woman in the business. But if you don't have anything else to ask, I need to get back to running these financials."

"Of course, I wouldn't want to keep you from your work." I took the mug and left. Eclipse didn't look up from her books.

CHAPTER NINE

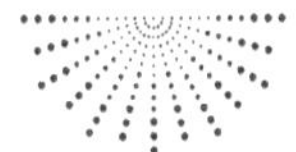

I headed straight back to my tent and spent a bit of time updating Dad's journal with the information on this cat thing: causes silence and strange sensations like trying to look through wool, rumored to look like a cat, and is living in the woods. I wasn't 100% sure if the silence and the cat were related, separate things, or one thing. Right now, it all seemed like it had to be one thing, but everything in my brain felt a little fuzzy, like I couldn't quite make the pictures out even if I could think them.

When the lunchtime show began, my body operated on its own, like a puppet controlled by strings manipulated by somebody else. Pure muscle memory of what to do, what to say, how to act, what to show, controlled me through the day. I became a well-rehearsed machine that ran without me needing to be mentally present. I stayed that way through the lunch and dinner show.

Vaguely, I noticed that we had steady crowds. It had been a long time since we'd had such consistent audiences throughout the day. Where were all these people even coming from? There was no way all of them lived in this one small town. They had to be coming from further out, but there weren't any train stations near here.

Had Eclipse sent advertisements that far out to draw traffic here? She seemed determined to make this business work. In which case, she was doing a hell of a lot better than we were with drumming up customers. Without Dad, we had no front man advertising anything. We were showing up and hoping for the best, and that was no way to run a season. Not one that left us with enough money to last through the winter.

As the last of the crowds left, I started pulling all the bobby pins out of my hair. The release of tension on my scalp immediately felt like a weight released, and I let out a long, contented sigh. The show finished for the day, and for once, I didn't feel totally drained by being on display for an entire day. It was probably because, mentally, I had been sleeping.

Once everyone went to bed, I would go hunting, and tonight I would catch a cat.

I ate dinner with everyone else, mostly keeping to myself. Alma only gave me a glance and stayed sitting with Clarence and the rest of the band over on the other side of the mess tent.

It didn't bother me, though; she looked happy. Besides, the fewer people who asked any questions, the fewer people I had to lie to by saying I was going to bed early tonight. Even Marshall mostly let me be. Marshall and Eclipse seemed to be deeply involved in a discussion over a ledger; hopefully the terms of our arrangement weren't going to turn sour this quickly. We still had no clue where to go after this, and no idea where Dad had gone.

Jonah looked from Marshall and Eclipse to me. "You think everything is okay over there?" he asked.

"Marshall can hold his own. I wouldn't worry too much about him," I said as I finished up my dinner.

Jonah nodded but didn't look convinced. He spent more time studying the conversation than focusing on his food.

"Don't worry about it. Marshall will make sure everyone gets paid properly. No matter what our show companions may have to say," I said as I stood.

"I suppose you're right. Where are you off to so early in the night?" Jonah asked.

"I was going to run to town, check the mail, that sort of thing. I won't be long."

"Did you want some company?" Jonah asked.

Jonah and I rarely spent time together, so for him to offer to be my companion for a brief jaunt to town was sweet, and a little strange. I debated telling him the truth; a man of God wouldn't be a bad thing to have on hand if this turned out to be another kind of demon. But I didn't want the added weight of having someone to look after.

"I'm good," I said.

In that entirely too preachy voice, Jonah said, "You need to work on your lying face, Hazel."

I huffed and rolled my eyes. "I'm just trying to figure out what caused that weird silence last night.," I whispered to Jonah.

"I figured as much. You want a second set of eyes coming along with you?"

"Jonah, it's fine."

"I'm going with you, or I'm talking to Marshall."

I didn't want company, but if everything went to shit, then having someone be able to run for help might not be a bad idea. "Don't breathe a word of this to Marshall."

Jonah finished his dinner and stood. "I suppose we both ought to change into more acceptable attire. I will meet you at your caravan in an hour. Everyone should be to bed by then."

"Sounds good."

Jonah nodded and left.

I watched him go and debated making a run for the woods right now before he had a chance to try and join in. If I did that, though, I knew Jonah would immediately tell Marshall when I didn't meet up with him. Instead, I just walked back to my caravan and started getting dressed in my usual hunting attire.

Right on time, Jonah showed up at my door. He wore his more raggedy traveling clothes. I resisted the urge to comment on him not bringing a Bible to lecture some monster to death. I didn't much think he would appreciate that kind of comment.

The sun hovered at the edge of the horizon as Jonah and I managed to slip out of the camp without anyone seeming to notice.

I headed in the same direction I had already been twice, toward the river where the cat kept leaving little signs of its existence.

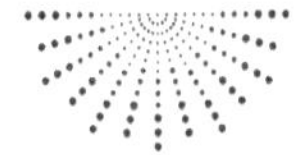

CHAPTER TEN

Y ou've been out here before looking for it?" Jonah asked.

"Last night. For all the good it did me. I didn't see what happened to Cookie."

"Maybe it's for the best you didn't. You could've got hurt, and no one would've known where you were."

"I was fine. I know what I'm doing," I said with a little more bluster than I actually felt.

Jonah chuckled but didn't comment more on that. "Where are we heading exactly?"

"This is near where we found Cookie this morning. I figured this might be a good starting point at least."

I adjusted the lantern as the sun dipped and vanished behind the horizon. The pale glow of twilight cast only a glimmer in the already dark forest. The lantern barely gave enough light for the two of us to be able to see, so we had to stick close together. With Jonah here, I hesitated on unhooding the light too much and drawing attention to us.

Having someone else here reminded me of the hunts I'd go on with Dad. Two sets of eyes were helpful a lot of the time, especially when dealing with things I didn't even know about or fully understand. But no one else in the show stood too much of a chance against any kind of monster. Bringing them out here set people up to get hurt. I glanced at Jonah and hoped that he'd be able to at least run to safety if something went wrong.

"Stop looking at me like that. I promise I'm not going to snap in half," Jonah said.

"Sorry, I'm just not used to company out here anymore."

"It hasn't been that long since your father left. And besides, once he gets back, you better not look at him like that."

I smiled a little about the thought of my father seeing me looking at him with concern. He'd laugh so hard that he'd have to stop to catch his breath. But Jonah wasn't my father.

We passed the spot where I'd found the deer carcass the night before, but only a puddle of dried blood remained. Jonah glanced at me with a brow raised in question.

"There was a dead deer here last night. I guess somebody got hungry."

"The question is, is it still hungry?" John asked.

I shook my head. "I don't reckon to know the bellies of monsters."

"I suppose not. Where to from here?"

"I figure we'll check where Cookie was this morning and see if there's anything else there."

I needed to check where that troll skeleton had been left, anyways. Something strange happened to those bones and coincidences didn't seem to happen to me, so I bet the bones growing moss overnight and this silent beast were connected.

Jonah followed right behind me, walking almost exactly in my footsteps. We both somehow managed to avoid stepping on anything that made a lot of noise, but moving through the woods in total silence was not something either of us excelled at. We were quiet, but any creature around would know someone lurked. We did not have the element of surprise on whatever might be out here.

As we approached the clearing where the troll skeleton remained, I felt the slightest electrical charge jolt through the air. The hair on the back of my neck and on my arms stood at attention immediately. I looked at Jonah, who glanced at me with a slight nod. He'd felt that jolt, too.

"Do you see anything?" I asked.

But my voice didn't show up. My lips moved, but I made no sound. I didn't even feel my throat vibrating. Nothing happened, like all the air absorbed all the noise around me. Jonah opened his mouth and moved his lips, but I couldn't hear any of his words, either. Tinges of panic colored his movements as his eyes darted around the woods for danger.

As I pulled out my knife, I moved so Jonah could have his back against a nearby tree and at least be somewhat protected from anything sneaking up on him, then I summoned the Will-o-wisp for more light. The whisper of pain against my skin freed the wisp, and it floated out with a flicker of red light. I reached out to Puck, hoping he'd obeyed my command and stayed around the troll skeleton. It took only a few seconds for the grumpy old fairy to arrive, looking at me, then to Jonah, and then to the wisp.

The wisp circled the immediate area, and at first, I didn't see anything. But when it danced closer to the dirt beneath our feet, I spotted the outline of a magic circle.

I stumbled backward and pointed to the lines. Jonah looked at me, and I gestured at the ground. He saw the markings before mouthing something to me.

It took two or three times before I could finally read his lips well enough to guess what he said.

"Hell."

I thought maybe he'd just picked up swearing, but then I looked back toward the wisp. I noticed the symbols it hovered over were almost identical to those we had found before the Hellhound appeared. In fact, the hellhound on my arm felt hungry, waiting for the chance to rip out and go to town on the area. I rubbed my hand over the mark as if to soothe an angry beast with some head scratches.

The circle this time stretched much, much larger. The wisp hadn't yet circled through the whole thing, probably because I kept it close as a light source. Even at this distance, I could tell that the summoning loomed three or four times the size of the one that had beckoned the

Hellhound. What on earth was somebody doing with a circle this size? Is this where the cat had come from? I didn't want to think about what would crawl out from a portal this size because that meant dealing with it.

"We should leave." Jonah's voice finally cracked through the silence.

I nodded. I couldn't do this with Jonah here. I needed to be able to focus on defending myself, not having to worry about protecting other people, too. I mentally commanded Puck to stay here so I could find my way back once I got Jonah home. The faerie resisted but bent to my will.

I let the wisp help with light, but I had to stay incredibly focused to keep it from veering off and trying to lead us astray. We moved faster than we had coming in, with less a concern about not making noise and more interest in getting the hell out. We passed the bloodstain from the deer carcass that had vanished, then we passed the rock at the side of the stream that had been my haven, and camp came back into sight.

Most of the caravans and tents were dark now; everyone had went to bed. I could see the light on in Marshall's caravan, and also in Alma's tent. I looked at Jonah, who offered a wry smile.

"Guess I wasn't a lot of help."

"You noticed a hell portal. I hadn't recognized the signs. See? You did help, but you should get some sleep now."

"Please tell me you're not going back out there tonight."

"I don't make promises I can't keep, Jonah."

"Be careful, Hazel. Please? If you're not home by breakfast, I'm telling Alma and Marshall."

"I always am. Promise I'll be back for coffee in the morning."

Jonah shook his head, not quite believing that, but he didn't say anything else. "I'm going to see if Marshall is doing alright and then I'll go to bed."

"You're not going to tell him about tonight?"

For a second Jonah looked confused about what I referred to, but then he shook his head and said, "My lips are sealed. I won't tell him anything about what you're doing tonight, but come morning, you need to talk to him."

"Yeah, I will. I just need a little more information to give him. Good night, Jonah."

I watched Jonah knock on Marshall's door and then head into the caravan. I walked over toward Alma and my bunk to tell her that I would be out late, but before I even walked in, I could hear voices and laughing. I was not about to interrupt late night talking after a date.

Instead, I just headed straight back into the woods and hoped that I hadn't just signed my death warrant. I needed to know what this portal meant, why they kept showing up, and if they had anything to do with my missing father.

CHAPTER ELEVEN

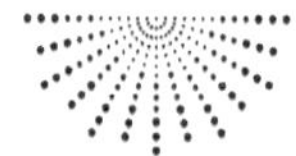

This time I moved through the forest with a focused purpose. I wanted this thing to know I was coming for it. Even if I had tried my hardest to be silent and stealthy, I couldn't sneak up on nature, or whatever this thing was. I might as well make myself clear. Part of me hoped that it would charge me. I didn't like this cat and mouse thing when I played the mouse. I'd much rather get the fight out of the way and have us both move on with our lives, or lack of life, than deal with this continuous back-and-forth.

"Here kitty, kitty," I cooed into the dark forest.

Shocking no one, the beast didn't respond. I headed right back down the same path; at this point, I knew it without being able to see. The lantern put out enough light, but I didn't want to risk pulling out the wisp, losing my focus and getting thrown off track by my own light source. For now, it was just me, my lantern, and the darkness.

Puck felt restless and uneasy, but not in any distress, against my mind when I reached out to him. The magic circle I'd left him at didn't appear to be in use. If I could wait out the night in the woods, I might be able to check out what it looked like in the light of morning. Trying to look at anything in depth when it was pitch black out didn't make a bit of sense. Even with the lantern unhooded and the wisp, it wouldn't be enough light to decipher symbols on a giant portal spell.

As I passed the pool of dried blood, I felt my skin goose pimple up; the same soft jolt set me on edge. As a test, I pursed my lips together and whistled. Nothing. The silence had engulfed me once more.

This time, I pulled out my dagger and summoned the Wendigo. I didn't want to conjure the Hellhound in a place like this, where a single second of losing control could get everything engulfed in flames. Forest fires were brutal, and I had no intention of causing one today. Besides, the Wendigo had a decent sense of smell and a hunger that would drive it toward anything it thought it could eat.

The Wendigo let out a silent roar and jumped at the pool of blood, trying to lap at it. I focused my mind and gave the Wendigo the command: *hunt what did this*. The Wendigo resisted for only a moment before starting to crawl in a new direction.

I followed after it, grateful our shared connection made it easy to track even when I lost sight of the hungry beast. The Wendigo moved with desperation, as though it felt it was on the brink of starving to death. But its hunger felt like nothing compared to the Hellhound still clawing at the back of my mind, desperate for a chance to come out and play. After everything that happened, the Wendigo wasn't even a struggle to control anymore. The whirling mark of teeth only drew a trickle of blood now instead of the gushing wound it used to be. Maybe that meant I had started to get the hang of this hunting thing.

I'd lost sight of the Wendigo but felt the thrill of battle run through me as something attacked my summoning. I ran toward the sensation and saw the beast in the light of my lantern.

It loomed easily larger than a grizzly bear but with the facial features of a cat. Its teeth were like daggers cutting through its snout. Blood pooled down its muzzle, and its eyes glowed solid yellow with a deepening tint of red. It opened its mouth in what I assumed was a screech, but no sound hit me. The Wendigo lunged at it, managing to slice across the beast's chest.

The cat thrust its paw forward and ripped through the Wendigo with one single blow. Torn in half, the Wendigo exploded back onto my skin. I stumbled backward but kept my footing as the cat and I stared each other down.

For a second neither of us moved, then the cat did something I'd never seen anything else I'd fought do before.

Slowly it dropped onto all fours and sat. Another prickling sensation ran across my skin before suddenly the night sounds exploded through the forest again.

I stared at the beast with my dagger still up.

The cat spoke. "You are one with death. Like me."

CHAPTER TWELVE

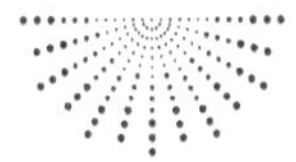

What the actual hell? You talk?"

"Only to those who speak the same language. We are of the same path. We guide and hold the hand of death."

"What are you?"

"I am a harbinger of death. To see me is to welcome her into your heart. I only approach those whose time has come to an end."

"What's with the whole silent thing?" I asked, still keeping my dagger up.

"The veil of silence keeps those whose time is not up from seeing or hearing me. I do not wish to take any out of their appropriate time."

"Then why are you here? Why have you been hunting around my show?"

"I did not know it was your show. I search for the one who shares your blood."

I tightened my grip on my dagger's hilt. "You're not taking my brother anywhere."

"I do not seek your brother."

"Then who?"

"Your father."

My heart dove into my stomach. "You're not taking my father anywhere either. He's not even here, idiot."

"But he was. I lost his track when strange things began happening in these woods."

"Strange things?"

"There is a threat of death growing here. Something that should not be in this world. I have stayed to see if I can turn the tide against this creature. This summoned thing of pain and death."

"Could you please just speak in normal sentences and stop with the riddle talks."

The cat tried to smile, but it looked far more like a sneer or a growl. I didn't get the sense it was meant maliciously but rather that a cat didn't generally smile.

"I could. But I much prefer speaking this way. You know there is something strange in these woods. You have seen it."

"Yeah. I'm looking at it."

The cat sat back and licked his teeth. "You do not behave as you should."

I tightened my grip on my dagger. "What did you just say to me?"

I couldn't believe that a cat wanted to lecture me about how to behave. Wonders never ceased.

"Your ego has no bearing or place here. If you listen to my words and do not take offense, you will realize what I am telling you."

"Plain language, please. And you could drop the insults, you know?"

The creature sighed again; its tail twitched from side to side in annoyed jerking spasms.

"What I am telling you is that something not of this world, not of the realm of death, is after you and your show. And death is looking for your father. I came to warn him but found only you and this unwelcome monster."

"Do you know where my father is?"

"I may."

I rolled my eyes. "You are just a load of help, aren't you?"

The cat grinned with all shark teeth. "I only provide help for those who can help themselves, little girl."

I took a step forward with my dagger still held firmly in my hand. "You insult me one more time, and I don't care if we work for the same person."

"I think I can see why my lady might be fond of you," the cat said, then shook its head. "I cannot help you find your father nor guide you while this monster lurks. There will be much death here. There will be much for me to collect, wayward souls lost without a guiding hand."

"Alright, I'll kill the thing, and then you can tell me exactly where my father is."

The cat made a noise that I assumed was its attempt at laughing. Only all it did was screech and chirp in a strange pattern. "Child, I doubt you could even harm a hair on this creature's body."

"That's 'cause you have no idea who I am and what I can do. How about you shut up and let me work."

The cat bowed its head. "Very well. Destroy this monster, and I will meet you here again tomorrow night and give you all the information I can about the whereabouts of your father."

"Will killing this thing mean Dad's not in danger anymore?"

"Tomorrow. Happy hunting, Hazel."

The cat stood back onto all fours and slunk away into the woods, vanishing from sight almost immediately. Showoff-y jerk. I waited for a moment to make sure it was gone, but the night noises stayed constant.

What had that thing been on about? Some monster in the woods not of death? That didn't make sense. Everything died; even the ridiculous Hellhound died, technically. I didn't do well with the riddles or word puzzles, and I hated that so many of Lady Death's instructions came in that form. If she wanted something done right, she needed to tell people what the hell it was she wanted, not give them some poem and hoped they figured out the right meaning.

But the cat said something lurked in these woods that didn't belong, and I sure as hell would find it and show that cat a thing or two. Telling me I wouldn't be able to touch it? What a cocky asshole. It had the attitude of a cat, for sure.

I summoned out the wisp for extra light to guide the way. I didn't worry too much about getting lost. I could always summon Puck to look above the—

Puck.

CHAPTER THIRTEEN

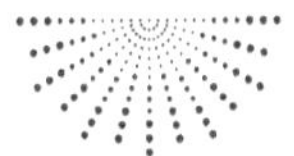

I closed my eyes and focused in on the familiar energy of my closest companion. Puck sat in a tree looking down at the bones; thankfully, his eyes saw better in the dark than mine, but still not with crystal clarity. Someone or something moved around the bones. I could see the shadow shifting from section to section. Well, shit.

I released the wisp and took off at a run toward Puck. As I got closer, the familiar, acrid smell of blood coated the air. I slowed my running as I completely hooded my lantern, blocking all light, and made every attempt to move as quietly as possible. I didn't hear any more movement, but the smell of blood only grew stronger the closer I got.

With my lantern snuffed out, it was hard to see much of anything, so I dove back into Puck's head. He still sat high up in the trees, out of reach of whatever happened on the forest ground beneath him. I couldn't make out any signs of movement anymore. How long had someone been there? Had I just been ignoring Puck? That damn distracting cat.

I held my breath as I stepped into the clearing with my dagger out. When nothing lunged for me, I chanced opening the lantern just a hair. At first, I didn't notice anything amiss. There didn't seem to be anyone nearby, but I could make out a few footprints pressed in the moist earth. I moved closer to the bones. The dirt squished under my feet like it had just rained, but there hadn't been a cloud in the area. I swallowed and slowly turned my lantern toward the ground.

Blood pooled around each bone, dripping from the very top all the way to the earth beneath it. It saturated the vines that encompassed every piece of bone. I stumbled backward, barely keeping from dropping to the blood-soaked ground.

I summoned Puck down to my side, more as a comfort than any protection. I'd seen a lot of dead things in my life, but the amount of blood here staggered me. Dozens of people's blood. Or animals.

With the lantern and Puck at my side, I moved outward from the center and back into the woods. There was no way someone had just transported this much blood; bodies had to be somewhere nearby. I thought about the deer carcass I had seen the other night. About how that corpse had gone missing this morning. Had something just been farming for blood?

Only a few dozen feet out, I stumbled across the pile of bodies. They mostly belonged to wild animals, with dozens of deer and one or two bears among the corpses. I let out a soft sigh of relief there didn't appear to be any humans among this pile, at least. I looked a little closer and, near the top of the heap, I noticed the soft brown fur of Cookie.

"Damn it all."

Whatever had done this had somehow gotten the horse out of our show and murdered it out here. Was that what they were up to early this morning when we found her? I didn't know, and that made everything worse. None of this matched anything I'd ever encountered before. But I knew that a lot of blood on a skeleton in the middle of the Hell Circle could not be anything good.

Part of me wanted to go ahead and burn all the bodies, in case they were going to come back as zombie creatures of some sort. But I didn't think I could control a fire like that, let alone get something to burn strong enough to take care of all of these corpses. Aside from being very dead, none of them seem to have been covered up at all.

I noticed a rope around Cookie's back legs and returned to the skeleton. Pointing my lantern up into the tree branches, I could see a series of cords tied from the trees far above. How in the world had anything been strong enough to tie those animals up there and then get them down and carry them this far? Let alone do it so fast. One night to do all of this? It hadn't been like this when Jonah and I had been by earlier. That meant this all happened in a few hours at most.

This couldn't be Rowan the Red Cap. I'd seen her burn to death in front of me.

I leaned against one of the trees and tried to get my thoughts together. But they ran all over the place with nothing connecting them. I barely started one idea before another one had taken its place and then both ran off course. My brain ran as a conductor-less series of thought trains, all of them going straight to a panicked hell.

When the sun began to rise, I realized that I could do nothing right now. Time ran shorter and shorter to find this thing before it caused however many deaths the cat said it would. I needed to get back to the show before everyone else woke up and Jonah ratted me out to Marshall.

Using Puck, I navigated my way back fairly quickly. But before I could get to my caravan, I ran into Ruby and Marshall standing outside of her wagon; Ruby was trying to open her door, and Marshall was preventing it. At first, I thought I'd fallen into a strange dream; Marshall would never harass a lady like that. I worried I might have to break up a fight as I heard the yelling.

CHAPTER FOURTEEN

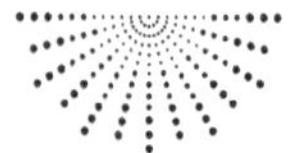

"We are leaving," Ruby said. "You can have this stupid field! I don't care, I'm leaving, and I'm taking everything with me that's mine."

"Where is Eclipse?" Marshall asked. He still wore his pajamas and bare feet. His hair stuck up in a multitude of directions that would be funny if it didn't look like he was in the middle of a nasty spat.

I walked over. "Is Eclipse missing?"

Ruby and Marshall both jumped. Marshall recovered first. "Where the devil have you been, Hazel?"

"Is that blood?" Ruby said, pointing toward my feet.

"Cookie's gone and dead," I said. "Think a cat got her, found her body this morning while I was out on a walk."

Marshall eyed me, knowing I was lying, but Ruby just stomped her foot. "That does it; I am leaving. This place is cursed or something."

"Where is Eclipse?" Marshall asked, stepping in front of Ruby's door to prevent her from going back inside.

"I don't know, but I'm done staying here. Move." She tried to push Marshall, but he didn't budge.

"You're not going anywhere until Eclipse shows back up."

"She doesn't even matter. I quit."

"That's all well and good, but I can't let you leave since I don't know what is rightfully yours and what's not. Especially not with Miss Eclipse not here," Marshall said. "And I'd appreciate it if you would listen to that."

"Are you threatening me?" She stepped toward him and shoved him again. "You better not lay a hand on me."

"If you lay another hand on my brother, it's me you're going have to deal with," I said, stepping toward the both of them.

Ruby looked from me to Marshall and let out a heavy sigh. "Y'all are both lunatics. Fine. I'll stay but only until noon. If Eclipse hasn't shown by then, I'm leaving even if I have to go on foot with nothing but my clothes. Now kindly move so I can get inside and out of this cold weather."

Marshall stepped to the side, and Ruby stormed into her caravan. Marshall glanced at me, and I nodded in silent understanding. Puck reappeared and quietly found a hidden home beneath her wagon. If she tried to leave, Puck would find a way to stop her until we could get over here.

With that taken care of, we both walked toward Marshall's caravan and stepped inside.

"What is going on?" I asked.

"I woke up positive I heard a woman screaming. When I ran out the door, I saw Ruby with the horse stable open. When I walked over to her, she got all argumentative. I suggested we get Eclipse involved, and she told me she didn't know where she was. You don't think that cat got her? Same way with Cookie?"

I shook my head. "No, I had an interesting chat with that cat last night."

Marshall stared at me as if I had somehow sprouted red hair overnight. "You hit your head or something?"

"Nope. The cat told me we both worked for the same lady, so we weren't enemies. It said something big and bad had moved in here, but it knew stuff about Dad."

"Like what?"

"It wasn't real clear on that front. But it said Dad's time is running short, that death lurked very near him. It said it would tell me more but only if I dealt with this big bad thing in the woods."

"And I'm assuming you've dealt with it?"

""'Fraid not. The only thing I found last night was a whole pile of dead animals and ground soaked in blood. It's been one hell of a night, Marshall."

"I'll say. What kind of thing would do that?"

"I wish I had half a clue. I don't know anything about what would do that and to top it all off, there's another circle. Like that one those hounds came through."

"Well, hellfire."

I couldn't help but laugh. "Yeah, that's about right."

"What do you suppose we should do?"

I sat down on the edge of his bed. "I don't have one lick of an idea. I don't know how to break a magic circle like that. Not one as big as that is, anyways. The hound one wasn't that big, and I still barely managed to deal with it."

"Maybe we ought to take a little field trip out there. See if Jonah's got an idea. We might even see if Luther would like to look. That last Hell Circle nearly burned you up, might be nice to have someone who doesn't burn checking it out."

I nodded. "Sure. Go get Jonah and Luther rounded up."

"Only if I can have at least a cup of coffee before we go anywhere."

"I'll even make you one. Meet you in the mess tent."

I went straight to fix up a cup of coffee for Marshall. I would always keep my word when promises of food or coffee were involved. But I didn't plan to wait around for him to assemble a group to come wander out into the woods with me. Whatever roamed out there I could deal with on my own. I didn't need extra baggage hanging around and distracting me.

If I'd learned anything from making that attempt with Jonah yesterday, it was that help only sidetracked me and kept me from paying attention to what I was doing or noticing the big things. Besides, if stuff went wrong, the only person who would be of any use would be Luther, and maybe Alma or Jonah. And Luther didn't even know about any of the monster hunting things yet. He hadn't been part of the show long enough to get that information.

I set Marshall's coffee down on the table, and then I walked straight back into the woods. I would deal with this on my own. That cat said that everyone who heard that silence was marked for death. My only guess was that someone used the troll skeleton as a sacrifice or portal power maybe, something to appease whatever they were trying to pull from that circle. I just hoped that Eclipse hadn't got caught in whatever it was. I hadn't noticed any human bodies, but there had been so many animal bodies it would've been easy to over-look one, especially if she was at the bottom of the pile.

Moving straight and steady, I knew exactly where to go and get ready for a fight. This Hell Circle had trouble written all over it, and this time I wasn't leaving until I got some answers or found a way to break it without burning down the entire woods. I would figure out something; I always did.

Most of the blood around the circle had absorbed into the ground, so the dirt no longer sunk beneath my feet. Now, a tarry red-brown liquid clung along the top of the bones and the vines that wrapped around them. The markings on the earth gleamed with a soft yellow light, like the beginnings of a campfire that hadn't quite caught yet.

I licked my lips and took a deep, fortifying breath. "Here goes something," I muttered to myself as I crossed the circle's threshold.

CHAPTER FIFTEEN

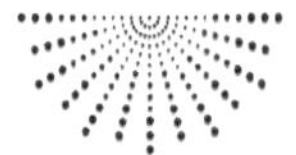

I expected fire and flames, hell and brimstone. What I didn't expect were vines pouring from the ground then upwards to the sky and connecting to each other. In a matter of moments, they had all squeezed together into a tight dome surrounding the skeleton and me. Only a tiny bit of light pierced through the vines, and I immediately regretted my decision.

With my dagger out, I summoned the Wendigo as back up for whatever was about to enter the death dome with me. I didn't notice anything at first. Then I caught a glimpse of one of the bones moving, and just like that, all of them were. The bones flew across the enclosed space, snapping together and rebuilding themselves.

"Aw hell."

I let the Wendigo fade away; it had helped against the flesh and blood troll, but I somehow doubted it would fare so well against the second version of the troll made of bones and vines. I needed a strategy for whatever this thing might be.

The vines that had been along the remains wove together like a muscular structure for the skeleton. They flexed and bent as the troll tested its new body. I moved to the edge of the circle and began hacking at the vines. I needed a way out and the chance to re-evaluate this truly terrible plan I'd chosen. Fighting this big of a thing in this tight space did not give me any advantage.

But for every creeper I severed, another one grew immediately. I couldn't even get a hand through. My own overconfidence had trapped me. But I wouldn't roll over and give up. I had been holding off on summoning the Hellhound for fear of burning the whole woods down. Now was the time to scorch everything.

I let the flames overcome my arm and pool on the ground. In the scarlet and white fire, the hound appeared. It glanced toward me before turning to the troll. For once, no rage or hunger radiated from the hound. Instead, there seemed to be curiosity and almost alarm. Maybe for once, we could be on the same page and not be fighting each other.

"Get us out of here." I forced my command to be strong.

The hound tossed its head and let out a howl. Then it charged toward me.

I dove out of the way as the hound crashed into the edge of the vines. I didn't wait for the flames to stop; I just charged through the fire and smoke and hit outside the circle at last. Scrambling back to my feet, I turned to the now enflamed dome. The hound followed behind me, stepping between me and the burning vines.

As the dome collapsed, the troll stood to its full height and swung its arm. I rolled out of the way as its fist collided with the trees around me, snapping them to the ground. Thankfully, the flames began to extinguish themselves. The dirt was too moist with blood to catch fire. At least I wouldn't be burning down the entire forest. Though, at this point, that might be preferable to dealing with this thing.

I got back to my feet; the hound rumbled beside me. It was now or never to make peace with it. We were going to be living together for a very long time, hopefully. And what better way to do that than by fighting with something else summoned from a circle from hell. I planted my feet firmly, focused, and pointed the hound toward the troll body.

The hound rebelled against me. Instead of attacking the troll, it leapt up and bit my arm. It phased through me without harm, but the heat burned against my skin, and I could feel the hairs on my arm singeing away.

"Listen here you jackhole; we're both going to die. Or I'm going to die, and that means you too."

The hound snapped at me again. Distracted by my backup betraying me, I didn't see the next troll punch coming in. It slammed into me, sending me flying backward, smacking into a tree, and then crashing to the ground. The world went woozy and spotty. Blood trickled from my lips and nose.

I expected the hound to charge at me again now that I was off balance, but instead, it planted itself between me and the troll. It let out a long, deep, rough growl, then charged the troll. It looked like all I needed to do to get the damn hound to listen to me was to put myself in mortal peril. Easy.

I struggled to get to my feet, barely able to breathe. At best, I had bruised ribs. I didn't want to think about the worst-case scenario.

As much as it pained me to admit it right now, I was in trouble. Big trouble. Against the very back of my mind, I could hear Puck alerting me about something back at the camp, but it was taking all of my focus to keep the hound summoned, and I didn't care if Ruby made a break for it or not right now. She could run to California, and I wouldn't care. I just wanted to live.

With my dagger still firmly clenched in my fist, I tried to focus on the pain to bring me back into my body, to give me a little more focus. The hound and the troll were still going at it. The smaller, faster hound avoided most of the hits but didn't seem to do a whole lot of damage. But it at least kept the troll's attention off of me and gave me a second to breathe, or at least try to.

I turned my attention into the hound, letting myself slide into its body. There was panic but rage too.

Whatever these things were, wherever they had come from, they did not get along. No sense of familiarity rang between the two creatures at all here. This magic seemed foreign to the hound; maybe this thing wasn't even from hell. Rather than make a blind attack at any part it could get to, I directed the hound toward the vines. If it could destroy the vines, maybe we could at least limit the troll's movement.

But a hound couldn't do this alone, and I didn't have the strength to focus on another summoning right now.

I slid back into my own body and pushed myself off of the tree I'd hit. I managed to hold steady on my feet. With the hound running interference in the front, now was my chance to try a sneak attack to the back.

I could take it down the same way I'd taken down the live version. If these vines worked like tendons, human body or monster body, then without the Achilles tendon, it would hit the ground. And from the ground, the hound could have a field day.

I limped as fast as I could around the broadest part of the clearing. I avoided the circle, now broken into a thousand pieces that barely resembled the original markings. The troll didn't notice me, and the hound launched itself up and onto the troll's arm. It sank its fangs into the troll's hand. Flames exploded out from the hound and burned the vines in the hand. Time to take my chance.

Forcing myself to ignore the pain, I managed to rush the back of the troll. Plunging my dagger deep into the troll's heel and ankle, I cut as deep as I could and severed the vines there.

The plants tried to regrow but sputtered into black smoke as the troll hit the ground on its knees. The hound leapt up toward the throat, grabbing at the soft bits there. Slowly, the whole thing began to catch fire. The vines burned deep inside the bones with an intensity I didn't think was possible from something as simple as boiling plant matter.

I tried to get some distance from the smoke, at least enough to get some clean air. I hit the ground and began crawling. With the fight behind me, the rush of battle began to fade from me, and my body felt heavy. Everything began going spotty; I didn't know if that was the smoke or something worse.

When I finally could take a sharp gasp of cold air, I heard the running water of the stream I had originally found. I crawled into it and let the cold water run over me. Thankfully, the shallow water didn't present any danger of my body being washed away by a current. The water soothed my aching body as I closed my eyes and just focused on breathing.

When I heard paw prints approaching, I looked up to see the cat creature standing above me with its head tilted.

"See? I told you I could kill it."

The cat tilted his head the other way. "That thing you killed was not the creature I warned you of, my child."

"What?" I sat up and crawled out of the stream.

"That was a monster in the woods, yes. And it would have brought much death with it. But what builds a thing like that? Should you fear the thing itself or the one who made it?"

I groaned. My head hurt too much for poetry again "Where is my father?"

"I will give you this answer, child. Because you have done well and perhaps delayed the inevitable. Your father traveled east, along the river. He moves toward the coast with plans of getting on an ocean liner."

"An ocean liner? That doesn't make sense."

"Your father is doing what he feels he must. But sometimes the things we must do, do not solve the problems we must solve."

"That is not helpful."

The cat chuckled. "I am glad we met, small one."

"I'm not going anywhere until you give me some answers."

"Yes, but you don't always get to choose when someone else leaves."

"Listen here. I have had the worst morning ever. I do not need your riddles right now. What city is my father in?"

"One you have visited before."

"Not. Helpful."

The cat looked toward the woods, and I half expected it to take off. Instead, it opened its mouth, but the only sound that came out was a heavy, wet sigh. Seconds later, its throat burst open and blood sprayed everywhere.

"Albemarle Sound, that is where," the cat rasped then grew still. Its entire body faded to black, then to ash that blew away. Eclipse smiled and wiped the blood from her blade.

"Hello, Hazel."

CHAPTER SIXTEEN

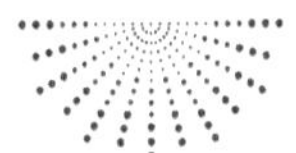

id I interrupt something?" she asked with a smirk.

I stared at her, speechless.

"I honestly thought either the troll or your lack of control would've killed you by now. I cannot believe Lady Death chose someone like you."

She circled me like a predator looking for the slaying moment. I could barely hold myself upright, but I kept my dagger raised and ready. I didn't know if I'd be able to defend myself, but I definitely wouldn't go down like that cat had.

"What are you?" I asked.

"So eager to learn, are we? What I am is much less interesting than what you are."

"I'm the tattooed beauty. I'm a little hurt that we've been in the show for a couple of days together, and you don't know that yet."

Eclipse smiled and shook her head. "That little sense of humor of yours. One of your least charming traits. You know, I've been looking for your father. And I think now I know exactly where to find him."

"You stay the hell away from him."

"Threatening me when you can barely hold yourself up? You are quite full of yourself, aren't you? You're lucky I like a woman with ego."

My forearm burned, and I glanced toward the woods; the hound hunted somewhere close by. If I could live long enough, it could reach me. For once in my life, I needed to talk and not fight.

"What do you want with my father?"

"I just want his soul. Nothing big. But now I'm wondering if yours would do."

I swallowed past the spike of fear that ran through my gut. "I don't know about that. My soul is probably all dirty. Sure you don't want a cleaner one?"

"Like your brother's?"

Without even thinking about it, I shot to my feet and took three steps toward her. My fist slammed into her face—great job on the talking and not fighting.

She stumbled backward, taken off guard by my blow. Then her sword pressed against my throat "I wouldn't do that again if I were you."

I tried not to breathe or swallow. "What do you want with my father?" I asked again.

"I told you. I need a soul like his. And now I know where he is. But maybe I'll take yours as a backup. There's always room for more souls."

I closed my eyes as I felt the blade begin to press into my throat, the slight burn of a cut just starting to happen faded as the hound burst from the woods and into Eclipse.

For the first time in my life, I turned tail and fled in terror. Only seconds later, I felt the hound slam into my arm, quickly dispatched by Eclipse. Anyone that could take care of the Hellhound that easily and kill a creature of death with little effort was not something I could take on when I'd already been beaten to hell. I needed a plan.

Eclipse appeared in front of me without warning, and I swerved to avoid slamming into her knife. I crashed into the ground. She walked toward me and as she moved, flames engulfed her sword. I was going to die, and it would be excruciating the whole time.

The flaming tip shot toward my face. As I braced for impact, somebody caught the blade. A red hand stopped it just before it slammed into me. I scrambled away, still on the ground. Luther held the blade in his hand, arm burning a bright, blistering red. Strong arms wrapped around me and pulled me further away as I looked up at Alma, and my heart twisted somewhere between relief and panic.

"Already using my gifts against me?" Eclipse asked as she pulled her sword away and stared Luther down.

"Eclipse, go," he said.

Eclipse smiled. "If I recall right, you're supposed to obey my commands."

Alma pulled me behind a tree where Marshall knelt by me and looked over my injuries. Beside him, Jonah stood looking out at Luther and Eclipse.

Luther stayed where he was, but I could see the fear curving his posture. Blood dripped from his hands where he had grabbed the sword.

To my shock, Jonah began to walk closer. Marshall tried to grab him but missed as he moved out of the protection of trees we'd hidden behind. He chanted in what sounded like Latin, but I didn't know the language well enough to have a clue. Eclipse looked amused, then startled as a gossamer dome floated around the whole group of me, Marshall, Jonah, Alma, and Luther.

"This is a space where you cannot tread. You will leave." Jonah said with more force than I'd ever heard come from him before.

Eclipse laughed. "What an interesting group you've acquired, Hazel Finnegan. I'll be sure to tell your father all about it as I rip his soul from his body."

She smiled and tapped on the glowing orb Jonah had created. With a flicker of a wince, she forced her arm through the light and patted Luther's cheek. Then she stepped back and snapped her fingers. In a flash, she vanished.

Everyone crowded around me, I could see all of their lips moving, but I couldn't hear a sound. Was this the silence of death that the cat had brought to me before? At this point, I honestly would welcome that if it meant getting a solid nap. My eyes drifted closed, and darkness swallowed me whole.

CHAPTER SEVENTEEN

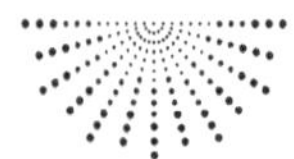

I awoke back in my caravan with Alma sitting beside me on one side and Marshall on the other.

"Don't you ever run off alone like that again, Hazel!" Marshall said. "You almost died!"

"We got to get moving," I said as I slowly begin getting out of bed.

Alma put her hand to my shoulder and eased me back onto the mattress. "We ain't going anywhere until you heal."

"I know where Dad is, and that woman is going to kill him. We have to go."

Marshall looked from me to Alma before he said, "Where and how fast can we get there?"

"You have got to be kidding me," Alma groaned. "She needs rest!"

"That thing is going to rip my father's soul from his body," I snapped. "I need to find him."

"She can rest on the road," Marshall said. "But you saw what that woman could do. If she's after Dad..."

Alma sighed.

"The Albemarle Sound, that's where we need to go," I said.

Marshall nodded and disappeared out of the caravan. A few voices echoed outside the wagon before the chaos of packing began.

"What happened to Ruby?" I asked Alma.

"She tried to run for it. We've got her locked up in an old lion pen for right now. I'm betting she knows more about that Eclipse woman," Alma said.

"And Luther?"

"He's in his wagon. Said he's not going nowhere," she said.

"You believe him?" I asked.

Alma seemed to weigh the options before she nodded. "Yeah, I do."

I relaxed back down into the bed; every piece of my body felt heavy, like weights tied me down. I closed my eyes.

"How'd your date go?" I asked.

"It was good. It was really good," she said, her voice light and excited.

I moved my arm over toward Alma, and she wrapped her hands around mine. I smiled, one good thing in a world of chaos, and I planned to hold onto it all the way to The Albemarle Sound.

Once I got there, I'd make damn sure that woman never got near my family again.

SILENCE OF SHADOWS

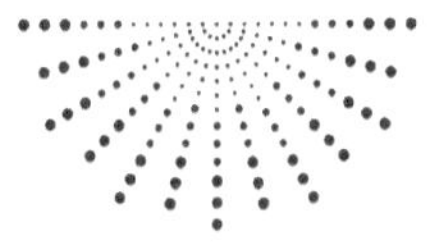

CHAPTER ONE

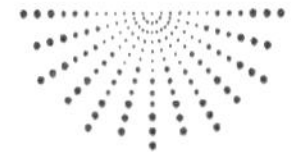

"I need to know what the hell is going on," I said as I sat across from Ruby.

We'd made good time heading across North Carolina in pursuit of Eclipse and hopefully my father, but, so far, we hadn't had much luck getting answers from the only real leads we had: Ruby and Luther.

Ruby shook her head. "Talk to Luther." Her arms stayed crossed tightly across her chest, and she refused to even look at me.

Beside her, Luther glared. "Don't you bring me into this."

"You're already in this. You worked for her too, you know," Ruby snapped. "You made deals with her just like I did, so don't try and play innocent just because we're in front of your new girlfriend here."

"I will light myself on fire before I am anyone's girlfriend," I said. "But you did work for her too, Luther. What is she, and what is she doing?"

Luther and Ruby looked at each other before he sagged back into his seat.

"You answer," she said.

Luther sighed. "I want to help, Hazel, but I don't exactly know what she is. She never really explained that. She just had these abilities. She didn't hide the things she could do, the magic." He looked toward Ruby.

"It was never a secret with her, and when I asked her about it, all she would say is 'Do you want to be able to do this, too?'" Ruby said with a faint shrug of her shoulders.

I tried to ignore the pain running along my body; I was still recovering from the injuries from my clash with Eclipse and the second coming of the Troll. I felt like I was nothing more than one big bruise, but there was too much to do while we hustled our wagons across the entirely-too-wide state of North Carolina, from the mountains to the coast.

"Let me guess; one day, you said yes, you would like to," I said.

"You wouldn't have?" Ruby asked.

"Not without knowing what I was agreeing to," I said and tried not to wince. I didn't know what I was doing right here, right now for Lady Death. I didn't understand all the terms and what this power meant, so was I any better?

Ruby rolled her eyes. "Right, you were just born with the ability to do whatever it is you do."

"What did she make you agree to in exchange for this magic?" I asked.

"All she said was that I have to promise to take care of the show. Easy."

Luther nodded. "Yeah. I said I wished I had something that would be a real crowd-pleaser. She said she could give me that. And she did." Luther raised up his right arm and let the red color shimmer in the light.

"And what did she give you?" I asked Ruby.

"A voice. A voice like a siren, she said. I don't know exactly what it was. I can draw crowds, people listen to me, and I can get away with damn near anything. She told me no one would be able to resist my voice, and I'd bring the people in, make a living for myself."

Well, that explained that strange fuzzy feeling I had when Ruby had been speaking in the last town where we stopped. "You can make people do things just by talking to them?"

"I don't think it's quite that easy or I would've talked you into releasing me by now. It doesn't work too well on you or your brother; I tried. Well, Eclipse had me try."

Now we were finally getting somewhere. "And what did she want you to do with Marshall and me?"

"She wanted you to offer us to stay on as a permanent part of your show. But I couldn't get your brother to agree to it. I couldn't get through to you at all. And then, well, everything went to shit, and before I could get out of here, you caught me. And I haven't been able to talk my way out yet."

I wondered if Eclipse had somehow taken away her gift now that Ruby wasn't by Eclipse's side anymore, but that wouldn't make sense since Luther still had his, even though he'd run away from the show.

"Luther, why did you really leave her show?" I asked. "The truth this time."

Luther sighed and looked out the window as he pulled out a cigarette, snapped his fingers, and lit it with a small flame from his thumb. Outside the little window of my wagon, the land passed by, mostly trees cutting shadows against the purple sky of twilight. We'd have to stop and make camp soon.

It took a long few moments before he spoke again. "She asked me to burn up a town where we camped. It was one of the first places we were heading to, and she couldn't get a crowd, so she wanted me to torch a part of it as punishment. She told me I'd be fine, and the fire wouldn't even touch me. I couldn't do it. I lied, told her I'd be right back after I started the fire, and I just ran. But running with no money only gets you so far. So when I found your show, I figured it was a good second chance. I didn't know that Eclipse had it out for you, or I probably would've kept on running."

This seemed like the most honesty I'd gotten out of Luther yet, and the story made sense, but why hadn't he been truthful from the start?

"Why lie to us then?" I asked.

"Would you have hired me on if you knew I came with trouble? Besides, I didn't know you were...well, that your tattoos weren't just tattoos, and I didn't know how to explain what had happened with Eclipse that didn't make me sound like a loon."

That was a fair enough excuse for me.

"Why does she have it out for us?" I asked Ruby.

Ruby shook her head. "I don't know if she has it out for you or wants you dead or what she wants exactly. She talked about some kind of contract with death?"

I stared at Ruby. How would this woman know anything about the agreement with Lady Death? That wasn't something held in public records, and I was positive Dad had never told a soul. Were there more things like the death cat from the mountain? Had one of them told her about our family? And even if it had, why hadn't she just used that to achieve whatever goal she was after? It still didn't make any sense; I couldn't piece together what she wanted aside from causing a whole lot of chaos for no good reason.

"Did you ever see a man with tattoos like mine?" I asked.

Ruby was quiet for a long while before she nodded.

My heart jumped into my throat, and my aching body forced itself to its feet. "Where? When?" I demanded.

"Just after Luther left," she said. "She brought in this man, tall, thin, covered in tattoos. She said he had something that belonged to her, and she aimed to get it back."

"Where is he now?" I asked.

"With her, I reckon. She kept him close by."

I wanted to puke. Had Dad been right there with us when we'd run into her in the mountains? Had we been sitting beside him without a clue?

"He stopped traveling with us before we joined you," Ruby said, and that made me realize how obvious my face must be at giving my feelings away.

"Where is he, then?" I asked.

"I don't know for sure, but Eclipse had hired these sketchy looking guys to travel to the coast. There was a separate wagon, a big black one I never stepped into," Ruby said. "They left, and I haven't seen them again in weeks."

"Do you know why she didn't go with them?"

Ruby chewed at the edge of her lip before looking to me. "She was looking for you."

"Why?" I asked.

"The only thing she ever seemed to focus on was that skeleton and you. She heard about it in the show and wanted to know who had done it. When she realized you were a Finnegan, she became obsessed with hunting you down. First, she just wanted the skeleton, but then she wanted you."

If what she had done to that skeleton was any indication of what her plans were, then we could expect some shambling monsters made of vines and bone coming after us at any moment now. But that didn't explain why Eclipse had fixated on me.

"When did she send my dad away?" I asked.

"After she heard about the skeleton. I helped get the wagon sent off while she went to the train station after you," Ruby said.

We had just crossed paths with Dad right when he'd started. My fists clenched.

"What are you going to do to me?" Ruby asked.

I sat in silence, trying to think past the rage circling my head. Dad had been within grasp, and this woman before me had been part of keeping him from me.

"I don't really know yet," I finally said.

"What about me?" Luther asked.

I wasn't real keen on the idea of letting either of them go and do whatever they wanted. I wasn't going to kill them, but keeping them around the show didn't seem like a great idea, either. Ruby could potentially talk her way into people's heads, and Luther had the ability to burn the caravan down. The options were slim, and I was running out of ideas fast. What were we going to do with these two?

"We can still work on the show," Luther said.

"Yeah, I don't know if the show needs you," I said.

Luther swallowed and licked his lips. "Look, I had nothing to do with her plans or anything."

Ruby shot him a glare. "And you think I did?"

"You stuck around with her longer than I did," Luther said. "That says everything that needs to be said."

Ruby shook her head. "Just because I'm not as big a coward as you are doesn't mean I was communing with demons or monsters or whatever the hell she is. It just means I have a better self-preservation instinct than you do."

"Both of you can just be quiet," I said as I rubbed my temples.

We weren't going to get a whole lot of information like this with them playing the blame game and bickering more than answering any questions.

"Neither of you heard her say anything else about my dad?" I asked.

"No. Never even heard his name, or I wouldn't have joined your show, no offense," Luther said. "She wasn't talking about that when I was there. I got in and out fast."

Ruby chewed on her lip before saying, "Before I answer anything else, I want to know what you're going to do with us."

The caravan began to shudder to a slow stop as I heard Marshall let out a sharp whistle, signaling time to stop for the night. The wagons circled up together and came to a halt.

"That's a discussion my brother and I will have to have," I said.

Ruby just sighed heavily and looked down at the ground.

"Now wait here," I said and left the wagon.

CHAPTER TWO

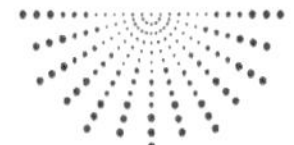

Stepping into the ring of wagons as everyone got out of their carts filled my heart with joy and fear. All of these people depended on me to somehow keep us safe against a demon-like creature. But all of them were ready to stand with me, and it scared me to think of losing any one of them.

Marshall walked over to me with a cup of tea in hand. "Everything alright in there?" he asked.

I nodded as Alma stepped closer to the wagon to make sure neither of our captives made a break for it.

"Put some cotton in your ears so you can't hear them," I told Alma.

"Why?"

"Just trust me on this," I said.

Alma nodded. It took her only a second to find some cotton to shove into her ears. I hoped that would be enough to keep the siren-voiced Ruby from getting through to our strong woman.

"They saw Dad. He got shipped off just before we sold off the skeleton. Eclipse has been hunting for us. For me," I said.

"Why?"

"That, no one is real sure on," I said and then looked to Marshall. "What are we going to do with those two?"

Marshall looked back at me with the same *I have no idea* expression that I wore on my face. We were not here to be prison wardens. I had no interest in keeping these two against their will and being responsible for figuring out how people were supposed to clear their names when they've messed up and made deals with a demon. If we held Ruby here, we were for sure kidnapping. And with her siren-like voice, I wasn't sure how long it would take before she could turn the whole show against us.

"Well?" I tried.

"They help us find Eclipse. They can stay on as far as I'm concerned," Marshall said.

"And if they don't want to do that?" I asked.

Marshall sighed. "I don't know. We let them go? We don't have the supplies for extra mouths. Especially not moving at this pace. We aren't normally traveling this hard."

"Just let them go?"

"What are they going to do?" Marshall asked.

I looked around. Aside from the dim light of our fires as dinner was cooked, not a light flickered around us. Civilization was miles away. "We can't just set them loose in the wild, Marshall; we're in the middle of nowhere. There's not even a town nearby."

Marshall considered. "The next town we get to, we drop them off and move on."

"So, the options we're giving them is either help us or get out with no consequences?" I stared at him.

"Hazel, they got taken in by a demon. They'll have consequences the rest of their lives."

I let out a long breath and then slowly sipped my tea as I mulled it over. I hated when he was right.

"Fine, let's talk to them and get this out of the way," I said. "You coming with me?"

He nodded and walked back to the wagon. I followed him.

Alma stepped to the side with a wary glance at me as we stepped into the wagon they were being held in. Ruby and Luther both sat up straighter when they saw my brother walk in. It was nice to know I commanded so little respect. Then again, right now, I probably looked like a strong breeze could knock me over.

"I understand you have some concerns about what is going to happen to you," Marshall said.

"Drop the niceties and just tell us," Ruby said.

"We'd like your help to find Eclipse and stop her," Marshall said.

"Fine with me," Luther said. "I work for you now, not her. I'm not leaving."

"And if I refuse?" Ruby asked.

"Then we drop you off in the next town."

"What's the catch?" she asked as she narrowed her eyes.

"No catch. You can go when we get a town. Unless you want to leave now."

"Out here?" Ruby looked out the window.

"Your choice."

"Why are you letting me just leave?" she asked.

"There's nothing else we need from you," Marshall said.

She hesitated. "Even if I help you all catch her, it doesn't mean I'm going to stick around to work with you."

"That's your decision. I just hope Eclipse doesn't have people who work for her, or other creatures like her, that might find you very interesting," I said casually.

"Are you threatening me?"

"Not at all, just pointing out that it's probably not going to be safe for you until Eclipse is dealt with," I said.

Ruby looked like she was thinking hard and fast. "If I stayed, what would I do in the show? I'm not going to be a peepshow girl or a stake driver for the tents."

"You'll do what you're good at. Bring the crowds to us," Marshall said.

Ruby's eyebrows inched up her face in surprise. "And why should I believe anything you're promising right now? You're kidnapping me. I don't want to be here, and you're keeping me here."

"We haven't harmed you," I snapped. "We even defended you when creatures attacked the camp. Right now, you owe us your life."

"Once we stop at the next city, you can take off," Marshall said. "No one will stop you, but if you leave, you're not coming back."

Ruby sunk into the seat with her arms across her chest.

"I'll do it," Luther said. "Y'all run a better show than I've ever been in before, so count me in to stick around for the long haul."

"You've only been in what? Two shows? One of those belonging to a monster?" I asked.

Luther cleared his throat. "Well, yeah, but that doesn't mean I mean it any less. I'm sticking around."

Great. We now had to contend with how to incorporate someone who literally lit themselves on fire into the show without burning everything down. That would be a really fun challenge to add into the mix once we found Dad. I couldn't even imagine what he was going to think when we found him and brought him back into the show; suddenly we had two new performers, and the Duncans were gone. I wasn't looking forward to that conversation.

"Fine," Ruby finally said. "I'll stay until we get to a city. That's as far as I am going with you."

Marshall nodded. "That should just be a few days. We'll have to resupply soon."

Gratitude flooded me that the show in that nowhere town in North Carolina had brought us a surprising number of visitors, because otherwise, we wouldn't be able to afford to do this. Putting the show on pause in the middle of busy season? That was a recipe for disaster, and I didn't know how we'd be able to pull this off. Something was going to give, and I didn't want that to be me.

Ruby surprised me by continuing to speak. "Eclipse did talk about your father. She talked about the pact your family had made with the demon. She was fascinated by how you keep things on your skin. I didn't realize what she meant until...well, the troll and the camp attacks."

Eclipse knew specifics about our powers. Things no one else on earth was supposed to know. I ran through my brain, trying to think of any time I might've seen her face. Could she have come to the show before? Maybe she scoped us out or caught Dad in the act of a hunt? But I didn't remember that face or that voice or anyone even vaguely resembling her ever showing up at the show before. So how had a stranger cracked our family's biggest secret?

"You don't know what she wanted with that information? Plans she had?" I asked.

Ruby shrugged. "As I said, she was really excited about getting dead things, whether they were skeletons or not. She talked a lot about that line between life and death and how thin it is. She was a little creepy about it. Which wasn't surprising once I knew she wasn't a human, but she did spend a lot of the nights drinking and talking about that. She was obsessed with death."

Great. A death-obsessed demon had stalked my dad and figured out he had a connection to Lady Death, and now she was after him? But even if that were the case, it didn't explain why Dad would just take off without a word. He would've left a message or something telling us what was going on and what to be on the lookout for. He wouldn't have just left me to deal with whatever obsessed weirdo was out there.

And if she had managed to capture Dad, why was she after me now?

"She didn't say how she knew this or anything?" I asked. "Did she hear it from someone?"

Maybe an old employee of the show had shared this information. Much as we tried to keep it secret, people in the show saw a lot of strange things in the dead of night.

"I thought she was a crazy, rich lady and didn't pay much attention to her ramblings," Ruby said.

"And after you realized what she was?"

"I avoided the hell out of her after I realized what she was, and what I had done. So no, I have no idea what or how she knew any of the stuff about your family."

"She followed us after Arkansas?" Marshall asked.

"She bought some fancy new caravans to fit the bones. Then we took off across the country after you. She knew what train you were on for Memphis"

How had she known where we were heading? We weren't following the usual trail routes, and not even Dad would have been able to guess where we'd be next. She'd have to have someone on the ground, trailing the show and sending messages to her by phone or telegram.

Marshall tapped his fingers on the desk before looking at Luther. "Did you really run away because you had a disagreement with Eclipse?"

"What? Of course. That's what I told you."

"So, you weren't out in the dead of night following me for any nefarious reason in Memphis?" Marshall asked as he crossed his arms.

The truth slammed into me with all the force of a troll punch. "You traitorous sonofabitch!" I slammed my tea mug on the table.

Luther held up his hands. "It's not like that."

"Then what is it like? Eclipse sent you to follow us, didn't she? That way she knew exactly where we were going. How did you communicate with her?"

Luther looked around the carriage. Seeing no way out, his shoulders sagged as he let out a heavy sigh. "We didn't even tell Ruby. Eclipse sent me on ahead to Memphis to meet up with you there. Soon as I knew where we were going, I used the phone at the local store and left her a message."

"Of course you did." I let out a long breath and clenched my fist beneath the table. I wanted to get up and punch the daylights out of him, but that wouldn't do anybody any good right now.

"And how long were you going to keep up that charade?" Marshall asked.

"I...I don't know. Not forever. To be honest, I was planning on getting the hell out of your show, too," Luther said.

"Well, that's comforting to hear," I muttered. What an upstanding guy this Luther was. How could we be so stupid to hire an actual spy onto our show and not notice a thing?

"So, let me get this straight," I said. "Eclipse was fascinated with dead things and my family. But you have no idea why or what she even is, only that she granted you supernatural gifts."

Ruby and Luther both looked at each other then nodded.

"You seriously made a deal with something, and you don't even know what it is? You could've made a deal with Satan himself, and you're just fine with doing that. Did you sign an agreement? A contract of any kind?" Marshall asked.

"Look, I didn't sign anything. That thing has nothing on me," Luther said.

I took a deep breath as I realized people could be that dumb—seriously thinking that some supernatural creature would gift you with extraordinary abilities and there would be no cost. Lady Death was a merciful being to have a deal with, but there was still a cost. The cost of my skin, my very flesh and blood was the price for this power. The more I used it, the more I would bleed out with every summoning. Whatever Eclipse was, I doubted she would be quite so generous.

"The devil doesn't need a contract to have marks on your soul," Marshall said, sounding for all the world like Jonah.

"Are you just going to keep us locked in here?" Ruby asked.

"Would you rather be tied up and running after the carriage outside?" I asked. "Because I can arrange that."

"I meant once we got to town," Ruby said as she rolled her eyes.

Marshall shrugged. "I already told you, you are free to go. But if you leave, don't expect to come back here and get any kinda warm welcome."

That about summed up my feelings on the matter, too. They'd made their bed, and now they had to lie in it and deal with the consequences. Even a child could comprehend that making a deal with something you didn't understand was a bad idea, but somehow these two had gotten blinded by the idea of easy power or riches.

"But we will be allowed to leave this carriage, right?" Ruby asked.

"Will I be performing still?" Luther asked.

"You can leave the carriage. You aren't a prisoner. You still work here as part of our show until you choose to leave," Marshall said sounding a hell of a lot nicer than anything I wanted to say right now.

I was willing to bet everything I owned that these two knew more than they were letting on, but I didn't know how to force the information out of them. Right now, I just had to hope the information we had about the *Albemarle* was right and that we were going to get there in time. If Eclipse was anything like any other supernatural critter I'd dealt with, she moved a whole lot faster than I did, even on a carriage.

CHAPTER THREE

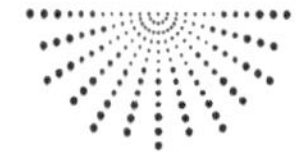

"Are you done questioning me?" Ruby asked.

Marshall nodded, and I reluctantly went along with it. I could question them for a little longer and see if we got any more information out of them, but I figured Marshall was probably right. We weren't going to get much else of use from them.

"I'll get you both dinner," Marshall said and walked out of the wagon.

Luther pulled out a deck of cards and started idly shuffling from one hand to the other. All I could think was that it looked like he was auditioning to be a stage magician. I half-expected him to ask me to pick a card, any card. But he didn't; he kept silent.

I stepped out after Marshall and Alma moved back in front of the door. Easily catching up with Marshall, I grabbed his shoulder. "We are not just letting that spying little—"

Marshall easily jerked away from my hand. "We are not in a position to be making demands, Hazel. They have all the information," he said as he continued to grab two bowls of the stew that had been put together.

"We kept them alive and are not abandoning them to die in the middle of nowhere. They owe us," I said.

"I am not arguing with you, Hazel. Go get something to eat and rest. You look like hell," Marshall stated calmly.

"That lying snake is the reason we all almost died in those woods! We are not just letting him stay here and be part of this show!" I didn't care that people turned toward my raising voice.

Marshall took a deep breath as he turned to face me. "I am not arguing with you right now," he said, and then he walked past me and back to the wagon the two were housed in.

"Well I'm arguing with you," I followed right after him.

He stopped and sighed. "What do you want me to say, Hazel? I just want Dad back. I think this is the only way to do that."

The fight flooded out of me at the weight of exhaustion in those words. Marshall might not have had a troll knock him down, but he wore the weight of the world on his shoulders, too.

I stepped to the side and let him walk into the wagon. A minute later, he stepped back out and pulled me into a hug, but he carefully avoided squeezing too hard to not aggravate my injuries.

"How do we know we can trust anything they're telling us? This is probably just a trap we're walking right into," I said.

I didn't trust Luther or Ruby, and that meant I couldn't trust any of the information they'd given me about Eclipse, either. I had no solid idea about what we were walking into or who we were even dealing with. All I had were weird tiny pictures, puzzle pieces I couldn't get to fit together.

"We probably are," Marshall agreed. "But if that gets us to Dad… then maybe it's worth it. Besides, I've never seen a trap stop you before."

Marshall tried to give me a smile, but I just shook my head. Dad was the toughest son of a bitch I knew, and if he couldn't break himself free, then I wasn't sure what our little ragtag group of performers, not fighters, could do.

"I just wish he was here," I said weakly.

I had always wanted the independence of being out on my own and hunting by myself, but I would've given just about anything for Dad to show back up and take the reins. How did he handle all of this?

What did he do to be able to manage a show and all these hunts? I could barely keep track of either.

"Me too," he said.

"We have no idea what we're walking into. We're probably just going to get everybody killed. We don't even have a guarantee that Dad is there." I shook my head. "What are we doing?"

"You tell me. You've been the one steering the ship, Hazel. I don't know what we're doing. I don't know what to expect. But I know sure as hell that neither of us is going to leave Dad to deal with whatever this is by himself."

"Even if it means destroying the entire show?" I asked.

Marshall leaned back and pulled out a cigarette. He put it between his lips and lit it up before taking a few long drags. "Is that really what you think is going to happen?"

"I have no idea. I can't protect everyone," I said.

"Hazel, you know you don't have to. We're pretty decent taking care of ourselves."

"I couldn't stop Eclipse the first time we ran into her. Why on earth do you think I can handle it now?"

"We weren't expecting it last time. This time we know at least what she is."

"But we don't. We don't know what she is or what she's doing. We have no idea what we are doing."

Marshall smiled wryly. "Yeah. But when have we ever?"

"What?"

Marshall headed back over to the food and collecting two more bowls of stew. He handed one to me. We walked together over to my wagon, and Marshall opened the door.

He waited until we were both inside before he spoke again. "I never know what we're doing. I have no idea how to run this show. No idea how to get tickets sold or how to distribute out the paychecks to everybody. I've got not a clue what I'm doing, but I'm making it up as I go. I'm learning fast, and you're doing the same thing. Hazel, you've taken down creatures from hell, and a full-grown troll. Sometimes you don't have to know what you're doing to do a good job at it."

"Yeah, but I am imagining knowing helps a hell of a lot."

Marshal laughed. "Yeah, I imagine it does, but we don't really have time to go to school to learn about all this right now. We're in the thick of it. We'll learn as we go and make up what we don't know. That's the fun way, right?"

I wrapped my hands around the warm bowl of dinner. "You can't just let me mope for one night, can you?"

"Nope. You can mope all you want once we've dealt with whatever the hell is going on here, but right now, we don't have time for anyone to be sulking. Especially not the only person who has half a clue of what's going on. Look, I know you want to take care of the show, but the show is a family. We are all in this, and if you want to get through this, and we all want to get through this, we are going to have to work together. Whether we can trust Luther and Ruby or not, they're our best bet for information."

I let out a long sigh. Marshal would be insufferable now because I knew he was right, and I didn't want to admit it to him. We didn't have time to be moping around feeling freaked out or trying to come up with all the answers. Right now, we were in the middle of a fire pit, and if we stopped to get our bearings, we would probably burn down before we got a foot further.

"I don't want to bring anyone into this that doesn't want to be here," I said. "We owe everyone that."

The loss of the Duncans still hung around my throat.

"Staff meeting?" Marshall asked. "We'll let people decide for themselves."

"Staff meeting," I agreed.

"You eat. I'll get everyone around, and we'll figure out what we are doing."

"When this is all over, we are breaking into the twins' whiskey stash and draining it dry," I said.

Marshal laughed. "You got it."

He left my wagon, and I managed to eat about half the stew before the nerves filling my stomach became too much to handle. I left my wagon and found most everyone already gathered around the fire. I quickly joined Marshall's side.

We didn't do full staff meetings often, and most of the time when Dad called them, it was only for serious affairs. I wanted to give anybody a chance to get out if they wanted. A lot of our tent pole guys had families back home, and I didn't reckon any of them were keen on putting their lives on the line for a circus show. Everyone put up with a lot of Finnegan nonsense over the years, and nobody needed to die over this.

"As many of you know," Marshall said as I joined his side, "our dad went missing back when we first started the show this summer. We've been looking for him since, and we think he's somewhere near the coast."

"We think he's in a bit of trouble. We don't know exactly with what, but we know it ain't good," I added.

Marshall put his hand on my shoulder before speaking again. "Dad always said the show was a family. You all are part of our family, and that's why we are saying anybody who doesn't want to get into whatever this trouble might be, go home. I'll get out your last paycheck for the season, and you can be on your way. Next year, when we are up and running again, you're welcome back. No hard feelings. Just let me know before morning."

The murmurings around the fire grew to a crescendo as Marshall stood steady. A few people started walking away already. It wasn't a surprise at all to me. The surprise, however, was that it was only a few guys, not all of them. I imagined we'd lose several more by morning. Hell, maybe we ought to send them home with some of our supplies, so at least if we all died in a glorious fashion, someone would still be able to use our tents. We paid good money for those, and I'd hate for them to go to waste.

"What is going on with Mr. Finnegan?" Stacy, my main helper during the shows, asked.

Marshall answered before I could say anything. "We aren't sure yet. But we know he's in a lot of trouble to have vanished from us like this. We're going to get him home. I don't expect all of you to get into a fight for this. Just helping keep our home, our little camp, up and running would be a world of help. I know a lot of you have family back home that you want to see again. I don't know how long this is going to take, and I can't make any promises about your safety or paycheck."

I was jealous of the way words flowed so smoothly from Marshall's lips. If I tried to talk that sweet, I surely would poison myself with honey.

The group began to slowly disperse as people returned to their own tents or began packing their bags.

As much as I wanted to stay awake, exhaustion haunted my every breath.

"Get some sleep," Alma said as she collected her dinner.

For once, I couldn't argue. The fight had fled from me and left me drained. I nodded and wandered back to my wagon. As soon as I hit the bed, I drifted off to the silence of the carriage. For the first time in what felt like months, I slept through the night.

I awoke with breakfast being brought in by Marshall.

"Time to get up and eat up. We got to hit the road soon."

I stretched and got out of bed and joined Marshall at my small table to eat breakfast.

"How far are we from town?"

"We should be there by afternoon if we push it."

"How many people left?" I asked.

Marshall shrugged before saying, "We lost four wagons of people. I made sure they had enough food to get back south."

"Are they still here?"

"Who?"

"Ruby and Luther. Did they run off or did they not?"

"They're both still here."

"Well, color me surprised," I said.

Marshall laughed. "I think I made a pretty solid reason for why they need to stick around, don't you?"

"Is that how you always strike your bargains?" I asked.

Marshal smiled. "You've never gotten to see me negotiate before."

"Good job, then."

I finished my cup of coffee and leaned back in the seat to relax for a moment. Getting the chance to have a full night's sleep made me feel almost like an entirely new person. Though the tiredness still hung around the edges, I no longer felt like I was being dragged down by exhaustion. Maybe I had a fighting chance, after all.

"You sleep okay?" I asked.

Ignoring my question, Marshall asked, "You really think we're going to find Dad?" in a quiet voice.

"Yeah. We aren't going to go through all of this to end up with nothing. I'll make damn sure of that."

Marshall didn't look convinced, but I had to be. There wasn't any room for doubt in my mind. I had to totally believe that we would find Dad and put this whole nightmare behind us. Whatever this Eclipse woman was, it felt like just the beginning of what was actually going on. I had gotten my ass kicked hard enough to realize I wasn't going to be able to beat this woman by myself. I needed Dad, so I had to believe this would all work out. Otherwise, the fear and worry would weigh me down too much to let me do anything.

"I hope we do." Marshall finally said. "I never realized how much work you put into running this thing. I could use another pair of hands."

"Yeah, you and me both."

Marshall patted my back before collecting one more cup of coffee and heading out of the carriage. From the window, I watched him walk back to his coach. Then, a few minutes later, I saw Jonah walk up to Marshall's carriage and slip inside.

I guess the boys had stuff to talk about. I wondered if maybe Jonah was the backup help Marshall was using right now to handle the finances and all the show's behind-the-scenes stuff. Jonah seemed like he would have a good head for that.

I still needed to talk to Jonah and figure out the glowing light he'd produced when we dealt with Eclipse.

After finishing up the last remains of my breakfast, I climbed into bed. I wasn't sure if I could sleep for the rest of the trip, but it sure sounded promising to try.

With a faint shaking, the carriage started moving, and we were on the road again. From my bed, I could see out the window and watched as Marshall's carriage moved to the front and led the way. That was probably what Jonah was there for, to help with directions. He had a real understanding of maps, and Marshall had the directional sense of a potato.

My wagon took its place at the back, and I could just catch a glimpse of Stacy guiding the horses that pulled my carriage. Thank goodness for that, because I didn't want to go out there and deal with it.

We traveled on as quick as we could toward the nearest town.

CHAPTER FOUR

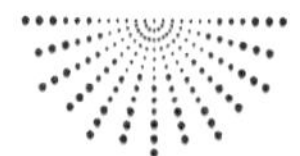

I licked my lips and looked out the window as the scenery slowly passed. We'd made good time in the wagons. We stopped only when necessary and never made a full camp. The constant moving made me feel like we were doing something, even if right now it was nothing but a lot of sitting and waiting to see what happened.

How were we even supposed to know what to do with Dad missing and us following the dying words of a quest some death-associated cat had sent us on? What was I even doing?

It was strange that when Dad had first disappeared, I'd been so positive we could handle anything thrown at us. But now I wasn't so sure I could even manage keeping myself in one piece.

I'd have to find my way sooner rather than later. As much as I didn't want to admit it or even really want the thought to take hold in my mind, I was beginning to realize that Dad might not be coming back. What would we do without him?

Marshall looked up from the papers he'd been going over with me. "Get out of your head, Hazel. Nothing good is going to come from spinning around in there."

"What are we going to do?" I asked.

"Keep on where we're going."

"I've damn near killed everyone already; maybe I should just—"

"Hazel Ann Finnegan, I swear to the Lord above if you talk about going off on your own one more time, I am going to dump water all over you," Marshall snapped, then stood up. "You went off on your own to deal with that troll, then that hellhound, then that Red Cap, and then that damn troll again. You have nearly died more times in the past few months than any time hunting with Dad. I know what you do is dangerous, but that doesn't mean you have to do it alone."

"But—"

"We helped you when Eclipse was there. If she's got Dad, we'll help with that, too. This is a family, Hazel, and that means we do things together."

Marshall sat back down like that solved everything and meant no more questions or debating, but that only made everything so much worse.

I had a responsibility to make sure that all these people, this traveling show, this family of mine, stayed safe. And I'd been failing at that even when trying my hardest. I'd barely been able to handle simple things like a single Red Cap. How was I ever supposed to be a hunter? How was I supposed to be a beacon between life and death when I could barely keep my feet on the side of the living?

My back still ached and burned in pain from my last run-in with the troll, and I didn't really have an idea when that would stop. Bruises littered my body, some of them dark enough to obscure the ink on my skin. The sleep during the travel helped, but the weight of worry still saturated every muscle and bone of my body.

"Right now, Hazel, there is nothing we can do but travel," Marshall said, still infuriatingly calm.

On the beds, I could hear Ruby and Luther snoring. The only way we'd been able to keep those two was for me and Marshall to watch them since Ruby's voice didn't impact us.

The sky outside loomed long and dark with just a sliver of moon for light.

"We traveling through the night?" I asked.

"Just for a little further. There's a river up ahead where we can wash up in the morning," Marshall said. He held out the map to show he'd already carefully plotted our route.

"How are you so calm in all of this, Marshall?" I asked. "The world has gone to hell. We don't even know if Dad is still alive and you're just...you're just fine with all that!"

"Look, we can't all fall apart, Hazel. This show has got to keep feeding people, keep moving, and if we're not going to do that, then what are we going to do? Just wait around to die from whatever that woman has planned for us? I don't know about you, but I don't plan on that happening."

I looked away, hating when Marshall was right.

"Besides, one of us has gotten the hell beat out of them repeatedly, and that isn't me. I don't want to be doing all this, but we don't get to choose what life throws at us or when it hits. Life doesn't tend to wait for a convenient time to mess things up. You rest, and you get better, because if anyone is going to be able to find Dad, it's you," Marshall said and ran a hand through his hair. "Just not when you're beat to hell like this. Get some rest; I'll keep an eye out."

I sagged into the bed, and, for the first time in what felt like months, just let myself feel all the pain and tiredness. The exhaustion that had wormed its way into every fiber of my body found a steady home beating right against my heart. I didn't know how I'd ever shake this feeling.

Something unfamiliar lingered in my chest too: fear.

Whatever Eclipse was, she had taken me down easily.

I hadn't been at my best in that moment, but I also knew that even if I had been at full strength, I wasn't confident I could take her. She'd torn through my defenses. She'd summoned that troll skeleton back to movement. She had done all of that and made a mess of my body with minimal effort. Even the hellhound, so full of fire and rage, wasn't stirring and hungry right now. Instead, it was curled back against the edges of my mind, not itching for freedom.

"I do feel like hell," I finally said.

"You look like it too," Marshall said with a smile.

I laughed even though that sent a flare of pain up my ribs. "Where's Alma? Jonah? The twins? Are they okay?"

"They are. They're in the front carriage. Jonah is keeping us on the trail and moving. Alma and Clarence are helping keep him awake."

I nodded. "The twins?"

"Drunk and asleep in the back carriage with Stacy. Everyone's okay, Hazel."

That felt like a little weight taken off my shoulders, and I sagged with relief. When I'd seen all of them staring down Eclipse with me, when I'd realized I could lose them all because I wasn't strong enough or smart enough to be doing this on my own...that had been worse than knowing I was about to die.

"How'd Jonah do that thing with Latin chanting?" I asked.

"What?" Marshall asked.

"The chanting. He said some stuff in Latin, and then that white light showed up."

"I didn't see anything."

"What did you see then?" I asked.

"She left. Jonah chanted something, maybe a Bible verse, and she paused, then pushed closer before leaving. Reminded me of a cat playing with a mouse, then letting it go because it got bored."

If Marshall hadn't seen that light, then why had I? "I must've hit my head pretty hard."

"You did. You hit pretty much everything hard."

"I can tell," I said, and rubbed my shoulders with a heavy sigh. Had everything always felt this weighty? This quiet and still? For once, all the ink on my skin had nothing to say or to reach for. The anger of the troll, the hunger of the hellhound, and the sarcasm of Puck stayed still in my mind, creating an unfamiliar silence that didn't feel soothing at all.

"When are we going to make camp?" I asked.

"Soon. We're making it by a river a few hours away. We should be there by daylight."

"Traveling in the night is dangerous," I said.

"Yep, and we're on a timetable, so dangerous it is," he said. "We got to cross the state of North Carolina as fast as possible; that doesn't mean a leisurely pace, Hazel."

"I know," I said. "We could hire a truck or something."

"We can't fit everything, and we're not leaving it alone."

I knew he was right, and I hated it. I didn't want even a piece of our show coming with me on this mission because I didn't know what was going to happen to any of us. I didn't know how I was going to keep any of us safe against something like Eclipse. I still didn't even know for certain what she was, but now I had a pretty solid idea.

If Bible verses slowed her, and she made deals with people to give them power, and runes for hell kept showing up, you didn't have to be a genius to piece together that we were dealing with a demon.

Dealing with a demon dog had been enough of a challenge; I didn't know how to handle a humanoid demon that clearly had a goal and knew all about my family. How had she known about us? About the deal Dad made all those years ago? Was that common knowledge in the supernatural world? Had that been why the Red Cap attacked on the train? Was that why trouble followed us like gnats around a horse in the summer?

Dad had better not be dead because I had a whole book full of questions for him, and I needed him around to answer them. I tried not to think about the alternative. Dad would be alive. He was smarter and a better hunter than me. He could handle Eclipse; I was sure of it. I had to be sure of it.

CHAPTER FIVE

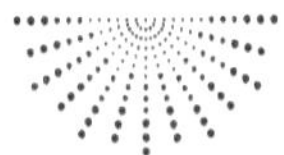

Somewhere along the next hour on the road, I drifted off again, finding an uneasy sleep in the rocking of the carriage until we finally stopped, and the sound of slow river water woke me.

Looking around the wagon, I found it almost empty. The bunk beds that had housed Luther were unoccupied, and the bunk below mine, where Marshall usually slept, was vacant. Ruby still slept in the bottom bunk across from me. I climbed down the old wooden ladder and peered out the window. Marshall, Luther, Jonah, and the other guys of the show were all in the river, washing up.

There was some hooting and hollering as they splashed around, but they mostly kept quiet. The pile of clothes to the side of the river had been laid out on rocks to dry out after a bit of scrubbing. In that case, we were probably here for a few hours.

"I suppose we get the next wash up," Ruby said from the bed.

"Marshall tries to respect privacy and all that," I said.

"How gracious of him," she said. Even though I couldn't see her eyes, I could practically hear them rolling.

Normally we all jumped in the river together, and no one cared about anyone else's parts. But since we had some strangers in our midst, Marshall must have made the call to be cautious. That worked for me; I didn't much relish the idea of being naked in front of anyone right this moment, and I'd much rather be around other ladies who wouldn't be tempted to make a snide comment. Or if they did, I'd at least have Alma to stop them.

"They should hurry up, I'm ready to be clean," Ruby said.

"If you're planning on staying in this business, you're going to have to get used to being gross on the road," I said. "Washing up real thoroughly doesn't happen as frequently as you might like."

"I doubt I'll live long enough to make a career in much of anything, so I would rather enjoy being clean with the time I've got."

"We're not going to kill you!" I said, horrified. When she didn't respond, the realization hit. "Oh, you're not worried about *us* killing you."

She sat up slowly in the bunk, her dark hair messy and frizzy. "No, I'm worried because you're taking me back to her."

"And she's going to kill you?" I asked.

"If she's feeling kind, I imagine so."

"If she's not?"

"Are you always this nosy, or am I just unlucky?" she asked.

"Considering you keep trying to sweet talk me when your charms don't work on me, I'd wager unlucky."

Ruby sighed and started trying to untangle her hair with her fingers.

I watched for a few seconds before offering. "Start at the bottom and work your way up."

"What?"

"The knots. Get the ones at the bottom and then work up. Otherwise, you're just giving yourself more work. Didn't your mom teach you that?"

"I didn't have a mother, so no," Ruby said as she moved her hands to start at the bottom of her hair.

I sat in silence for a few seconds before saying, "Me either. The twins taught me that."

Ruby paused and, for a second, it felt like it'd be so easy to cross that bridge, to offer a hand and make a friend, an ally, something. But then the moment closed as Marshall knocked on the door and walked in. He wore a damp towel around his waist and another one thrown over his shoulders.

"Water's clear for you ladies," he said.

I nodded as I spotted Alma sprinting out of the wagon and into the water with the twins following behind her.

"Towels are already out there," Marshall offered.

I nodded and headed to the water. Ruby followed me without another word.

The water ran cool and soothing against the aching bones of my body. It moved slowly enough that I let myself just float, weightless and effortless, all pressure off me for a few nice seconds.

"You alright?" Alma asked as I floated near her.

"I don't really know the answer to that, but I'm alive."

"No thanks to your stupid self." Alma splashed water at me. "I'm still mad at you for running off like that. You almost died, Hazel."

"You were in pretty bad shape," Constance said as she washed up her half of the body. Temperance was glaring at Ruby as the new woman tried to not stare at the twin's nude body.

"I'm sorry," I offered. It was about the only thing that I could say. I'd messed up, nearly died, and nearly gotten everyone else killed. Some great hero I was.

Alma sighed. "You can't keep doing that to me Hazel. You, your brother, this show. This is my family. You don't run off on family like that."

"I'm sorry," I repeated.

"Stop saying it and show it," Alma said. "You can apologize for the rest of your life but still keep doing stupid shit, Hazel."

"I'll try," I said. I meant it, but how did I keep all these people safe if they wanted to help in what may very well turn into a suicide mission against a demon?

"Yeah, I'm sure you will," Alma said with a smirk and another splash of water.

"Hey, don't beat up on me, I'm injured!"

"Then you better stop doing stupid stuff and get better," Alma laughed.

I splashed back, and soon we were diving into a full-fledged water war in the middle of the river. I felt seven years old again, playing like a kid. I remembered fights on bath day while the twins shook their head as Alma and I ran around whatever lake or river we'd found. I'd laughed so hard it hurt. Now, with my ribs bruised and aching, it felt remarkably the same.

"Can you two stop?" Ruby said. "Some of us are actually trying to wash."

I rolled my eyes and threw another splash before noticing Alma had stopped still. Right, Ruby's sweet voice didn't work on me, but that didn't mean the others were immune.

"Cut it out," I told Ruby.

"I can't just turn it off, you know. It's my voice. The only way to stop that is to stop me talking," she said.

I shook my head with laughter bubbling painfully in my chest. We were all heading to our deaths, but at least we got a bath and some humor to go with it. If we had to die, going out with Alma and twins at my side didn't seem too bad.

Rolling over and dying and giving Eclipse what she wanted? That felt all too easy. A demon on the loose, one that drew hell portals and brought troll skeletons to life, didn't seem like something to just let alone and see what happened. I needed to stop her even if it meant I didn't survive the encounter.

That's what hunters did, right? Dad told me we were the guardians of the line between life and death, the ones who bore the souls to keep the world safe from more harm by supernatural monsters. In our skins, we held the weight of death, and that came with its own price. Part of that had to mean we were ready to die, and I didn't think I was.

But if my death meant this woman would be stopped, then I could be a part of that. I wasn't going to let her do whatever she wanted. And I wasn't going to let her hurt my dad either. If the world needed a hunter like me, Dad was the better one, by far. If my death could save the show, that'd be an okay way to go, I supposed.

Alma interrupted my thoughts. "We probably ought to get out, looks like rain,"

Thunder rumbled in the distance, and dark gray clouds began to slowly fill the blue, clear sky we'd been washing under. The clouds brought a chill, and goosebumps rose along my skin as I got out of the water and wrapped up in towels. The other girls did the same, and I helped make sure to tie three towels together for the twins to be able to cover both their halves.

We all got out of the water and walked to our wagons. The boys were all outside, sitting around a fire and starting to make lunch of some sort. They were all dressed. Ruby and I returned to our wagon.

"You have spare clothes?" I asked her.

She shook her head. "No, that was with Eclipse's things, and that wagon vanished."

I riffled through my bag and tossed her an old dress. "It might be big on you, but it'll cover you up at least."

"I hate dresses," she muttered.

"Me too," I said. "But I don't have many pants. Your clothes will dry, and you'll have your pants back soon. Just deal with it for now."

Ruby slowly pulled the dress on and took a deep breath. With her towel off and the dress slowly sliding on, I could see the bare skin of her back, riddled with strange scars and circular burns that I knew instantly came from cigar butts meeting flesh. As much as my distaste colored how I saw this woman, pity burned in the back of my mind. What had happened to Ruby to bring her to this point? She didn't look much older than me, and yet our skin told very different stories about life.

She grumbled as the dress hung off her shoulders and down her waist. It fit her the way a potato sack fits a single carrot. I'd not realized just how thin Ruby was, but now that the emaciation was so apparent, I wanted to offer her food, help, anything.

"Dinner smells ready," I said.

Ruby nodded. "Are you eating in a towel?"

I shook my head and dropped my towel to put on a dress as well. The dirty, stained, ripped, and pieced together again dress looked a mess, but I didn't really care. There were no rubes to impress out here.

"Your ink didn't wash off," Ruby said.

"Yeah, every single one of them is real," I said as the dress dropped into place and I tied it up.

"There are more of them than I thought," she said.

"Yeah, well, give it time," I said. "I'm still growing my collection."

"And how do you do that?"

"That's a conversation for some other day, once we've dealt with your boss," I said. "Come on; we need to grab plates before the guys eat everything."

Ruby and I walked out and grabbed plates of food as everyone gathered around the fire. With warm food and familiar faces, I let myself be comforted by this cozy, warm scene around me. Here, I was safe. Here, I knew what to do and how to act. The rest of the world? That I didn't think I'd ever figure out.

As thunder rumbled overhead, Marshall guided Luther and Ruby back to their wagon and settled in with them. Jonah left for his own wagon, and most of the other workers found shelter from the coming storm.

I stayed on my bench with Alma at my side as we both finished our dinner.

"How's Clarence?" I asked Alma.

She smiled. "He's good. He's sticking around, so that's nice."

"He seems like a good guy for you, Alma. I'm happy."

Alma reached over and gave me a gentle shove. "Stop talking like I'm about to run off to the chapel. Y'all are my family. I ain't going anywhere. This place would fall apart without me."

I smiled. "It sure would."

Alma sighed and wrapped her arm around me. I laid against her side for the moment and let myself be supported just for this little while.

"Someone has to make sure you don't get yourself killed," Alma finally said.

I laughed as Clarence came over and slowly sat on Alma's other side. Their hands slowly entwined together, and I smiled at the relaxation I saw slide through Alma's body.

I sat up slowly. "I've got to talk to Jonah. But I'll talk to you when we get to town," I said.

Alma nodded.

"Goodnight, Miss Hazel," Clarence said.

"Just Hazel is fine," I promised him as I left for the wagon where Jonah had holed up.

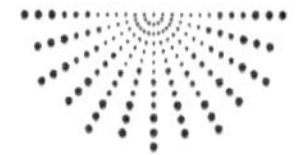

CHAPTER SIX

"Enter," Jonah called as I knocked on his door.

Steeping into the warm space, I marveled at how little he'd personalized it. The wagon looked almost the same as the day Jonah had joined the show. Jonah sat at the edge of his bed with a Bible in his lap. He turned the pages carefully with his toes.

"Are you feeling better, Hazel?" he asked, looking up from his reading.

"Good as I can."

"Then you should be in bed. Rest does an injured body good," he said as he closed the book.

"What did you do to Eclipse?" I asked.

"I'm not sure I know what you mean," Jonah said.

"I saw the light. Whatever it was you did to her or tried to do. What was that?"

Jonah shifted. "That was the work of the Lord."

"Okay, Jonah. Seriously. It paused her for a second. Almost stopped her totally for a little bit there, what did you do?"

"Faith can provide protection to those who ask. I asked and was granted it," he said.

Had Jonah been taking lessons from the damn cat about being infuriatingly vague?

"Can you do it the next time we run into her?"

"I perhaps could do that, but I'm not sure."

"You don't know?"

"In times of great danger, I seem to be able to ask for that help and get it. But I'm not..." Jonah seemed to struggle for words like they weighed too much for his tongue to form.

"You're not what?"

"I don't have powers like yours," he finally said. "I have faith, and that faith is rewarded sometimes. I don't know how much or how long it will last. How much protection or grace I deserve."

"Jonah, you're the most faithful person I've ever met. If that's all you need, then you're good."

Jonah gave a wry smile and shook his head. "Thank you for that confidence. I'll do what I can to help when we run into her again."

"Thanks, I'll make sure y'all don't get so close to the danger next time. Are you alright?"

Jonah nodded. "We're all fine. You're the one everyone's worried about."

"I'm pretty sturdy."

"No one doubts that, Hazel, but it's been non-stop since Arkansas. We haven't had many days of normal anything."

"It's been a rough season," I agreed. "But we're going to find Dad soon, and it'll be okay. Maybe we can run some late fall shows down in Florida and make up some of the money we lost this season."

"I'm not worried about the money. I'm worried about your brother and you."

"What?"

Jonah looked at me. "You've been dealing with your father's absence by never stopping. Both of you. You're both always working. It's not healthy."

"Look, as soon as Dad is safely home, I'll take a break. But until then, I'm not stopping. Marshall feels the same, I bet."

"He does," Jonah said with a little too much certainty. He carefully added, "I'm sure he does."

"Well, I don't want to keep you from your studies," I said and backed toward the door.

"Goodnight. Please try to get some real sleep."

"Yeah, you sound just like Marshall," I said and stepped out the door, only catching a glimpse of a flush running up Jonah's neck.

I headed back for my wagon and climbed into bed. Ruby already laid in bed with the covers pulled up so only a flash of dark hair showed. I crawled into the bunk beneath her and blew out the candle on the stand and hoped for sleep.

CHAPTER SEVEN

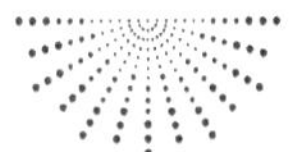

In my dreams, I floated in a ponderous dark nothing. No shapes formed a world around me, and a dense fog obscured everything. I felt entirely without any physical body; no pain, no tiredness, nothing but darkness that wrapped around forever.

The weight of the dream world slowly began to suffocate me. Something lingered in the void that watched me, that laughed at my struggles. I finally realized that if this was my dream, I could do what I wanted; I summoned the Willowisp to life to cut through the darkness.

My feet found firm ground, and I discovered myself in those woods where I nearly died at the hands of the vine and bone troll and then at the hands of Eclipse.

"Well done, little one," a familiar voice said.

I wasn't surprised to see the cat lingering about in the shadows of the trees and into the light of my wisp. Blood still soaked its fur, and its eyes reflected the darkness around us.

"Death looks good on you," I said.

The cat chuckled, or at least it made whatever sound passed for a cat's laughter.

"Always so clever, little one. I wonder how that cleverness will serve you."

Even after its death, this cat was still tormenting me with vagueness and riddles. Just my luck.

"Thanks for telling me where dad was," I said. "We're almost there now, so thank you." I at least wanted to try to be polite, even if this was just a dream.

"I'm glad you're making the journey, little one. And there will be much waiting for you when you arrive."

"Can you please just be direct and stop with the vague nonsense? Just tell me what to do!"

The cat gave a fang-filled smile. "What kind of cat would I be if I did that?"

"I don't know. Most cats don't talk anyway, so I think you'll be just fine. Besides, you're dead, so what does it matter if you don't play by those rules anymore?"

"More than anyone else, you should understand that death doesn't change any rules. Those things you command even in their death; they still must abide by the rules of their nature. Death doesn't change any of that. It simply means the playing field is different."

I didn't know why I was even bothering to ask questions of this thing, because all that was doing was annoying me by giving me more riddles to try and figure out. But I couldn't exactly stop myself either.

"Why are you here in my dream? That doesn't seem exactly like the rules."

"Now you're starting to understand. I am dead, so I cannot reach out to you in the physical world. But here in your mind and in your memories of the place where we met, I can still exist and speak to you. I can still reach you."

"So, you're bored and came to bother me rather than going into that great eternal rest or whatever?"

The cat moved to sit in front of me as I glared at him.

"Always so angry, so ready to fight. You wouldn't know what to do if someone approached you with kindness, would you?"

"You've never approached me with kindness. You silenced the

world, then gave me riddles. That's not how you make friends!" I snapped.

"The way you approach choices changes everything," it said.

"Great. Helpful. So very helpful." I rolled my eyes. "Can I wake up now, and can you stop wasting my time? I want to rest, not get lectured."

"No one is lecturing you," the cat said and licked a massive paw.

"Really? Cause this feels very lecture-like."

"So temperamental." The cat stretched and laid down near my feet.

I slowly sat down to not strain my neck as I talked to something at my feet.

"I come to help you, little one, but what I can share is limited. Riddles are a good way around the rules if you would only learn to listen."

"I listen just fine," I said.

"You listen to respond, not to understand. That is not the listening that helps anyone."

I groaned. "What are you trying to tell me?"

"There are many things you will have to deal with in the future. Things like those monsters you just faced. But things about yourself as well."

I winced as I remembered the beating from those vines.

"Those are but the beginning of what powers she brings."

"What is she?" I asked. "I gather she's a demon. But why would a demon be doing this and not just opening up portals to hell or whatever it is that demons do?"

"Demons are much like people. They do not all follow the same rules, and they do not share the same desires across the board. There are many things to want, and many ways to get those things."

"That's not helpful."

"Things can be helpful in many ways."

I groaned. "Why are you here?" I asked. "Why come and bother me? Go help Dad."

"We are connected. My death in front of you has bound us. Not on your skin but in your memories I will live. Your father and I have no such connection."

"But you know of him. You knew where he was going. That matters! Help him and leave me alone. Dad loves riddles; he'd get all these cryptic things you're saying."

"I don't try to be cryptic; I help. I give you the information that you need in the only way that I can."

"And you annoy me," I said with a sigh.

The cat stretched out and rolled over, belly up toward me. Blood matted the taupe fur, and a hole in its throat from Eclipse's blade gaped with seemingly fresh blood.

"I like you, Hazel Finnegan. You are a good choice to join our family."

"Family?" I asked.

"Those who walk with death. We are a family, you and I."

"So you know her? Lady Death? Whatever name she goes by."

"I know death, yes. Death does not appear to all in the same way."

"Of course she doesn't. What's she like?" I asked.

"What's death like?"

"That's what I asked."

"Death is quiet and still. Death is much like where we are now: a darkness that weighs down and envelops everything. It touches everything and everyone in different ways, but its heart stays the same. Death is not cruel or violent; death is simply an end. It is the constant that connects all the world together. From the tiny maggot that feasts on corpses to the troll that roams the land in a rage, all die."

I tried to keep my mouth shut and just listen, but I wanted to shake the damn cat and tell it to stop making stupid comments. To stop putting things in a way that made sense and didn't all at the same time.

"So why does death have people like us?" I finally asked.

"Because just as death comes to everything, many things try to find ways to avoid death, to escape the inevitable force that connects us all. We are the ones that stop the avoidance of our destinies. We hold the line of the universe; the universal truth is our treasure to guard."

That sounded like way too fancy a way to say that we beat the shit out of anything that stepped out of its right place and broke the natural rules of the land. We were enforcers of death, not guardians of some sacred truth.

I was already okay with not being anything special or fancy. I served essentially a bag that death kept around. I held onto the souls she couldn't collect, or that were too dangerous not to keep locked away. That's all I was: a bag with a blade.

I just nodded and looked toward where a sky should be but where only darkness hung in the air in an almost dizzying way. When the ground I sat on, the sky around me, and the trees near me all looked the same, it suddenly became very unclear what way really was up and where I was even looking.

It was easy to lose myself here, and not in a comforting way. If I relaxed too much, I could feel that suffocating weight the cat had mentioned, the weight of death creeping in.

"Am I going to die when I find her again?" I asked.

"I cannot answer that. I did not expect to die at her hands in my home," the cat said.

"But I probably will...and then what? I come here and stay with you forever?"

"If you die at her hands, then you will experience what it is you do."

"What do you mean?" I looked back to the cat.

"I mean that Eclipse seeks the souls on your skin, and if she cannot have that, she will take your soul and use you as you use your tattoos, little one."

I swallowed hard at that idea and ran a hand over my arms. I tried to not think too much about what the afterlife must be like for the creatures trapped on my skin, but sometimes I couldn't help but imagine it. Was that the future waiting for me? Was that my punishment for capturing others like this? I took a deep breath and tried to exhale the fear. I couldn't carry around that much dread with me, or I might combust somehow. At the least, I wouldn't be able to face her if I was too terrified to move. I had to be strong for Dad and for my family in the show.

"Thanks," I said, not sure if I meant it. "Any other wisdom to give?" I asked.

"Only if you can offer some head scratches."

"I'm sorry, what?"

The cat nudged its head toward me, and I hesitantly reached out to scratch behind the massive ears. The cat let out a long purring sigh.

Beneath my hands the fur felt like silk, the softest, smoothest texture I'd ever touched.

After a few seconds, the cat spoke again. "If you will have me, I would join your skin."

"You can do that?" I asked.

"Only because you and I are connected. Witnessing a death is a powerful thing. Am I welcome to join you?" the cat asked.

I thought about it only for a moment. Could I really be turning away help at this point?

"Why the hell not?"

Without warning, the cat turned and sank its teeth into my hand. I yelled and tried to jerk back, but its teeth sank deeper into me.

Pain jerked me awake with a yell. I nearly fell out of the bunk before catching myself on the railing. I curled my hand against my chest. A few pinpricks of blood slid off the top of my hand, fading away into a new dark tattoo of five tiny pinpricks, almost like a constellation of ink.

I traced the mark and reached to the edges of my mind, where I found only silence. Well played, cat.

CHAPTER EIGHT

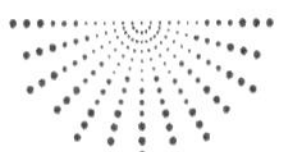

The trip through North Carolina was quiet. With most of our tent workers gone, we remained a group of just a dozen and made good time. We pushed our horses to the limit. I took to spending the time reading over dad's old entries—all his notes on trolls and other monsters. The harpy page looked particularly brutal, with a sketch of a horrible bird/woman creature with sharp fangs and claws. She was not someone I wanted to meet but was one of dad's prized tattoos. It was the biggest one, too, taking up most of his back with a pair of wings.

When we finally neared the last town before Albemarle, Ruby sat up out of her bed.

"If I leave, you won't come after me?" she asked.

"That was the deal," I said as I closed Dad's book and put it with the rest of my stuff.

Ruby looked out the window where the edge of town could be seen, and I could all but read her mind. She was getting away from us. I couldn't blame her; I didn't want to be moving after Eclipse either.

"Just get your things together, and once we stop, you can go," I said.

Ruby nodded. She packed up a few things and then balled up the dress of mine I'd been letting her borrow. She held it out, and I shook my head.

"Consider it a parting gift," I said.

Ruby snorted but shoved it into a small bag. "Thanks," she finally said.

I still had so much I wanted to ask Ruby. Despite spending so much time in a wagon together, I hardly knew her. A gulf remained between us, and I didn't know how to bridge it, or if I even wanted to.

The tiny town held maybe 100 people. Rural and isolated, this was one of those self-sufficient hamlets we so regularly visited when we needed food. We'd only been by once before, but they'd been thrilled to work with us. A lot of time they wouldn't have money to pay for a show, but trades worked out well for us all. We left with wagons full of food, and the townsfolk got to see the incredible displays we offered.

As we pulled into town, I immediately knew something was wrong. No one rushed out toward our brightly colored wagons; no children ran in the streets shouting at our posters. Not a single door or window opened, and we'd arrived in the middle of the day. Even towns that didn't like our show didn't ignore us like this, didn't just vanish all signs of life. A chill ran down my neck as the horses slowed to a stop.

"Wait a second," I said to Ruby as she hoisted her bag onto her back.

She scoffed but stayed still.

I hopped off the wagon and onto the street.

"Hello?" I called.

Instinctively I kept my hand to my side, hovering over where my dagger that waited hidden between folds of fabric in my dress.

"What are you doing, Hazel?" Alma hissed as she got out of the wagon behind me. "Don't grab that knife."

"Something's wrong," I said. "Towns are never this quiet."

Alma frowned and nodded as the silence hit her, too. Ruby came out of the wagon after Alma, bag over her shoulder and quickly walking away from us.

"Ruby, wait," I said again.

"No, I'm done," she said and kept walking.

I walked toward a small house. I knocked on the door, but no one answered; the curtains hanging in the window didn't even move in a breeze.

The saltwater air burned against my nose and cast a haze over the city that kept the streets looking foggy and strange even in the middle of the day. No matter how fast we might have traveled, I had the impression we hadn't beaten Eclipse anywhere. If she was the type of monster she seemed to be, I was just surprised she hadn't burned the entire place to the ground.

But what had she done with the people?

I licked my lips and looked at Alma. "Let's see if there's a store open," I said, glancing down the street.

Ruby still walked away from us, but her pace slowed a bit more with the silence creeping in heavier.

Alma nodded, now looking as concerned as me. I ran my hand over the newest tattoo, the silence that follows death seemed to linger here. A soft purr against the back of my mind seemed to mean my new companion, the cat, agreed.

Alma and I both got back onto the wagons and moved through the still, silent streets with a steady pace. The sounds of horse hooves and wagon wheels were the only thing making noise aside from the distant ocean breeze swinging through the city.

"What has happened here?" Jonah murmured as he looked out the window.

"Nothing good," Marshall said as we wheeled through the still city and found our way to the town square. Again, no one moved around town; shop lights were on, but nobody bustled about stocking shelves or cleaning floors. I didn't even see a stray dog or cat running the streets and scavenging for scraps.

"I think we best keep on moving," I said.

"What about Ruby?" Marshall asked.

"She left," Alma said. "We can't make her stay."

Marshall slowly nodded. "Yeah, alright. Let's move."

We kept the wagons moving, not wanting to stay in this silent hell any longer than it took to pass through. This had been our last chance to restock before we hit the Albemarle, but if we had to, we could hunt down some deer or birds and make do. We'd survived lean months before and once we got to the coast, Alma could fish up enough to keep us well fed for as long as we may have to be here.

The ache in my bones continued and lingered in a dull pain that I was starting to think might be a permanent addition, just like my tattoos. A rough life had a cost, and I'd been damn lucky to escape that last scrap with no broken bones and only a battered body. Somehow, I didn't think that I'd fare too much better moving forward. Whatever Eclipse had planned weighed heavy in the air here.

As we reached the edge of town, I slowly relaxed, moving my hand from my dagger's hilt and letting out a long breath I'd been holding for way too long.

A scream pierced the air; I recognized the voice as Ruby's.

"We've gotta go back!" I said, already jumping from the wagon. My feet had barely hit the ground before Alma landed beside me.

"Let's get her and get moving," Alma said.

I almost fought against Alma joining me, but instead, I swallowed back that rejection and just nodded. Alma and I both took off. I struggled to keep up with Alma's long legs, but soon we were back in town. Another scream pointed the way, and a streak of flesh blood marked the path.

The next scream came from above. I looked up to see a huge bird-like shape above us with a human in its claws.

Ruby screamed again, and then the bird dropped her.

CHAPTER NINE

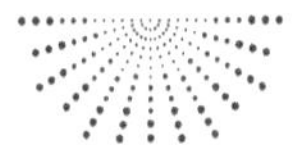

Alma sprinted forward to try and catch the woman now plummeting to the ground as I drew my dagger and struggled up some crates at the edge of the empty store then up to the roof. The old thing sagged under my weight as I ran to the central support beam and tried to keep my eyes on this creature in the sky.

Alma managed to catch Ruby, and they both hit the ground hard. Alma groaned but got back to her feet.

"Get inside somewhere," I yelled down to her.

Alma nodded and dragged Ruby toward the shop that I stood on top of. She easily kicked the door open and got inside, leaving me and the bird to stare down one another.

Giant wings moved it lazily in a circle way out of my reach, still too far away for me to make out many details. But everything I saw right now told me precisely what this was: a harpy.

Those things weren't supposed to be out on this side of the world, and definitely not unreported and this close to civilization. That didn't make any sense. Dad had only seen one once a long time ago when he was overseas. So how had one ended up in America?

I squinted at the creature circling overhead, still way too high for me to engage it or make out too many details. I could summon the troll and try there, but I wasn't sure getting up higher was the best option here. I just needed to make sure that I kept the rest of the group safe.

I glanced toward where everyone else was, the wagons just outside the edge of town. So far, the doors hadn't opened, and no one had stepped out.

Standing up as tall as I could, I cupped my hands around my mouth and shouted up toward the sky. "Hey, feather-brain!"

The harpy looked toward me with sharp yellow eyes and a screech that opened the mouth wide to show many, many fangs. Why had I thought calling it names was a good idea?

As the harpy dove for me, I resisted my instinct to duck and roll and instead held my dagger out, ready for the strike.

We collided into each other, a ball of blade, feathers, and claws. I sank my dagger deep into the bird's side, just under the wing, and its claws ripped across my arm. I barely rolled away and out of its grasp.

The harpy screamed and lunged again. This time I jumped up, landing on the back of the bird woman and immediately realizing my mistake as she launched to the sky, taking me with her as I clung to her back.

The beating wings battered against me, her flight awkward and unsteady with my weight against her back and limiting her movements. She screamed and rolled through the sky as I held on for dear life.

Beneath me, the ground grew further and further away; I was more and more certain this had been a horrible idea.

With the harpy still struggling to get rid of me, it took both my hands to stay firmly attached. I couldn't get to my knife, but thankfully, summoning didn't take any extra movement from me. All I had to do was think.

Puck popped into the world beside me, looking between me and the ground and then to the harpy.

"A little help?" I snapped.

Puck flew around to the Harpy's face, barely dodging as her claws slashed for him. She then went in for a bite as Puck threw ash in her face. A horrible scream ripped through her throat, and we summersaulted through the air in total chaos. If I didn't puke up my breakfast, it would be a miracle.

The ash-to-the-face technique hadn't helped a lot, and I wasn't sure how to coax this thing down. What did harpies prey on anyway?

I wasn't sure, but if I could get it to chase something…

I looked to Puck who was shaking his head but then reluctantly flew back in front of the harpy's furious gaze. She screeched at him and lunged as Puck took off at full speed back toward the ground.

She pursued, seemingly forgetting all about me on her back and focusing on nothing but the little faerie that had just tried to burn her eyes out of her skull. Puck moved to the ground, and as soon as we were close enough, I leapt off her back, hitting the ground hard but rolling through it and popping back on my feet. Taking the time to learn how to fall from acrobats had been worth its weight in cash.

The harpy continued the pursuit of Puck as he kept on the run, keeping her low to the ground as I positioned myself on another rooftop.

When Puck dashed by with her in pursuit, I leapt down, slamming my blade straight between her shoulder blades and then slicing down her back. When the harpy turned toward me, I yanked my knife out and went for the final stab, but she took to the sky again.

Slamming my dagger into her chest gave me the only way to hold on as the blade burned against skin, but then the flesh and body began to fade to a strange black ash. It was not the spirit I usually captured. The black ash body of the harpy continued to fly me upwards, surrounding me in a cloud of darkness.

I slashed out all around me, trying to find a pocket of air, a way out.

Panic rose around me before my arm broke from the ash cloud, and I pulled myself toward the air and light of the sky.

The harpy hung beneath me in a misshapen figure of ash. In the chest, I saw a flickering soul, but one broken in half, malformed and dark. Reaching out to accept the soul, a small pair of wings burned themselves onto my ribcage, and I groaned at the white-hot pain. As the tattoo took shape and the soul made a home on my skin, the ash around me began to fade.

My stomach rose to my chest as I began to plummet toward the ground.

CHAPTER TEN

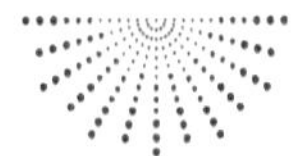

With only a few seconds to try to save myself, I pulled at the new Harpy summoning. A fragmented, dark beast formed, grabbing at one arm and slowing my fall but not keeping me in the air.

This soul kept splintering against my arm, breaking apart and then reforming on a fall that went up and down over and over again. By the time I was close to the ground, I let the summoning fade, and dropped.

Strong arms caught me, and I sighed with relief.

"Hazel, what did I say?" Alma asked.

"I know. Is everyone okay?" I asked.

"Ruby's pretty beaten up. Lost a lot of blood, but Marshall and Jonah think she'll be alright," Alma said.

I nodded and rubbed over my new tattoo. It itched and felt like it shifted across my skin in a moving pattern I couldn't see under my dress.

"I need to lay down, but I think we ought to get out of here," I said.

"What about the town here?" Alma asked.

"I bet they all ran from that harpy. They're probably long gone," I said and hoped I was right.

"Damn shame. We could use the supplies," she said.

"I know," I agreed before I headed back for my wagon.

Once inside, I pulled out my mom's hand mirror and stripped out of my dress to look at this new tattoo.

The black outline of wings against my skin looked like someone with the world's shakiest hands had inked it out. The lines started and stopped in a broken pattern while the wings themselves weren't filled in; some patches were solid while other spots were bare. The area around it glowed an irritated red as if I had just spent hours under a real tattoo artist's needle.

I traced over it, surprised by how cold it was to the touch, almost freezing and raised against my fingers. This didn't match any other tattoo I'd gotten.

Rushing over to dad's book, I flipped back to his section on harpies. His tattoo hadn't turned out like this at all. The wings across his whole back were elegant and solid, not this shaky mess I had. I frowned at the sketch of the harpy he'd drawn. While dad wasn't the best artist in the world, he did a good job catching what things looked like, and this harpy matched his drawing perfectly: the bright yellow eyes, the wide-grinned fang-filled smile, and large eagle-like wings. Even the scar over the left eye all matched. How had I just fought the twin of dad's summoning?

I swallowed as the implications hit me. If dad died, would all his summonings run loose? Wouldn't death just collect them? That's what I'd always assumed, but now, with this staring back at me, I had doubts that was the case.

Tears pricked at the edge of my eyes as my hand curled against the ugly tattoo. This couldn't be all I'd get of dad; the only way I'd get to say goodbye. It couldn't be.

I wouldn't let it.

I redressed in a looser fitting dress that didn't touch the tender new tattoo and stayed to myself as we all got back into wagons and started to move slowly, trying to keep an eye out for any of the towns-people who might've run out here to get away from the harpy. Jonah sat out front of my wagon with Alma managing the horses.

I'd barely gotten the chance to take another breath when Jonah said, "We need to move faster now."

Panic tilted Jonah's voice for the first time ever. I followed his gaze out the window and behind us I saw three lumbering shapes, each about half the size of a troll but taller than Alma by a long shot. They stumbled from the edges of the road. They were leaving the town and quickly starting to converge toward our little caravan. The fog obscured the details, but I wasn't feeling up for going toe-to-toe with three baby trolls. Running might be the only option.

The horses were urged into a run, pulling us faster from town, but as we picked up speed, so did those things, their lumbering changing to a gallop as they dropped to all four limbs and bounded toward us with an unnatural movement pattern I'd never seen before. It seemed like all four extremities barely communicated with one another, didn't coordinate to not collide. At any moment, it seemed balance would give up, but it didn't. Instead, it charged toward us with growing speed, and I knew immediately there was no outrunning whatever trap Eclipse had laid for us.

"Hazel, don't you dare!" Alma warned as I pulled my knife.

"What do you expect us to do then?" I snapped.

When Alma didn't have a quick answer, I opened the wagon door and crawled up to the top of our wooden home on the go.

Keeping low, so I didn't get knocked off, I saw the horses gaining speed but not anywhere near enough to get away from these things. With time short and limited options, I knew it was time to go big.

The troll ripped from my arm in a torrent of blood that made me glad I was already nearly laid out flat. The troll formed, a pale pink and wispy coloring to its transparent skin. It first turned toward me as I held up a hand and forced it to still its blow.

Before I had the chance to direct the troll's attention to the actual threat, the first creature found the troll. One of the beasts charged, leapt through the air, and slammed into my summoning's leg to begin trying to climb up.

The monster struggled to grab at the moving troll. I held on tight to the top of the wagon, closing my eyes and diving into the troll. The world looked strange from this high in the air, but I got the hang of it fairly quickly and managed to get a hold of the creature that had grappled my troll's knee.

I dropped it immediately once I saw the details. The thing—what I had thought might be an ogre or a young troll—was people. Not just one person, but a body made up of corpses all stitched together with thick black vines that oozed. The vines reminded me instantly of the ones that had tied the troll skeleton together. Eclipse had done this, had killed a town full of people to make these monsters.

It slammed into the ground and splattered, but the vines began stitching it back together as the other two monsters charged after us. They ignored my troll and just barreled for the wagons, gaining distance fast on the last wagon where our supplies rode with Clarence and Luther at the helm.

I sent the troll to a run, thudding across the ground, swinging at these things, knocking them backward. I pulled out of the troll's head as the troll's fists slammed downwards and a squishing, crunching sound echoed in my mind.

As the troll smashed two of the threats to pieces, the remaining one got back up, its body twisting into a new shape. Instead of charging toward us, it rolled toward the troll and the remaining bodies, and I fought back my gag reflex as the three separate masses tied themselves together and rose to meet the troll at eye level.

Well, shit.

CHAPTER ELEVEN

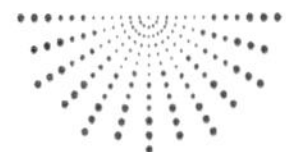

I quickly moved to the back of the wagon, which was still moving as fast as the horses could manage. The troll stumbled back, taken off-guard by something its size. Then the two giants were locked in arms, brawling like drunken men in a bar.

I tried to catch my breath, and when the horses started to slow from exhaustion, I jumped off the wagon, hit the ground, and took off running. I needed to keep close and not lose the connection with the troll.

Alma yelled after me, but I'd gotten a head start and was nearing the fray. The troll kept knocking the monstrosity down, but new vines sprang up, and it rebuilt back to its feet, more disfigured and horrifying than before.

Fire. The only thing that had stopped those vines before was the hound.

Calling out to the fiery tattoo on my skin, the hound hesitated before answering my summoning and appearing. This time it didn't rebel or resist me; it knew exactly what to do.

The hound swooped beneath the giants fighting above us both and found its way out of harm. When the troll knocked it to the ground, the hound lunged, flames searing through the vines as they tried to regrow.

The beast howled and screeched with a dozen voices as the flames consumed them, and I dropped to my knees.

The troll and the hound slowly faded back to my skin.

The smell of burning rotten flesh and the images of that monster made of humans bore into me, and I puked up what felt like everything I'd ever eaten.

"Hazel!" Alma and Marshall were instantly at my side, Alma holding my hair back as Marshall rubbed my back.

"Are you alright?" Marshall asked.

I managed a nod.

"What was that?" Alma asked.

I shook my head as my shoulders arched with another try at puking, but I had nothing left to expel.

"Hazel?"

I tried to spit the acidic taste of vomit from my mouth and wiped my lips. "That was the townsfolk."

"What?" Marshall said.

"Those things...were the townsfolk. We should keep moving," I said.

"But we could help them, or maybe—"

"There's no helping the dead, Marshall," I said and climbed back into the wagon. "We should go; we're close to her. I hope."

In truth, I wasn't so sure I wanted to be gaining on her, but we had to find Dad. I had to get answers and reach the coast and somehow stop her from doing this kind of thing to anyone else ever again.

It took a few moments before Alma and Marshall got back in the wagon with me, and we began moving again, a heavy silence among us.

I settled inside with Luther as the wagon lurched to life at a slow, steady pace.

"Not much of a welcome there, huh?" Luther said.

I glared at him. "How's Ruby?" I asked.

"She's riding with Jonah. She's unconscious but okay," Marshall said.

"So, that woman killed a whole town?" Alma asked.

"I reckon she did," I said. "Got anything to add there Luther?"

Luther sighed and looked over the edge of his top bunk bed and down at me. "I had nothing to do with what just happened. I don't even know what she is."

"But you have guesses, don't you?" I asked, crossing my arms.

"The obvious answer is she's a demon straight from Hell," he said. "Don't know what other answer you want or even think could be possible. You've seen what she can do."

"But if she can do all that, then why did she travel with a show? Why buy these fake dupes? Why hire you two? It doesn't make sense."

"Demons don't have to make sense," Luther said. "Not really my area."

"You have an area?"

He chuckled, a hollow, fake sounding laugh. "My area is avoidance. See? This whole thing? Not my area."

"You're a coward," I said.

"I'm alive," he countered. "Not all of us get special, fancy powers from birth to help us make it through the world."

"You really think this," I motioned to my tattoos, "has made my life better?"

Luther shrugged.

I was already on my feet ready to fight when Alma put her hand on my shoulder and gently but firmly forced me to sit back down.

"Let's get that blood cleaned off your arm," she said.

I took several deep breaths as Alma washed the blood from the troll summoning off my skin. I hated this feeling, that I wasn't quite whole and ready to stand on my own. I'd never had any injury knock me out like this before, and I hated every second of feeling this useless and weak. I didn't have time to feel that way; I needed to deal with a demon and save my father. I needed to be at my full power and then some, not struggling with summoning just one thing.

Marshall walked over to Luther's bed, and the two men whispered to one another in hushed, firm tones. Marshall's hands stayed clenched into fists, and I half-expected him to punch Luther's lights out. But Marshall, ever the calmer of the two of us, stayed perfectly civil. I couldn't make out the exact words they were exchanging, but the fact it hadn't devolved into a screaming match meant that he was holding his temper better than I could.

I dropped my head back onto the seat and closed my eyes.

"Just rest, Hazel," Alma said.

"I've done nothing but rest. Those people in that town are dead because I—"

"Those people are dead because that woman is an evil hag," Alma said. "Nothing to do with you, so don't add that to your shoulders, alright? You're still hurt, and sick people need rest. Best way to cure a body."

"I need to be well again."

"Yeah, and you got time to rest and get there," Alma said.

I nodded and let sleep easily wash over me without resisting it too much.

CHAPTER TWELVE

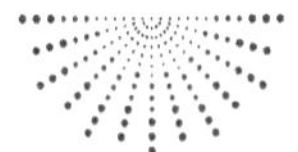

When I opened my eyes again, the familiar soft shaking of the wagon greeted me. The world around me stayed dark, but I could make out the sleeping forms of my friends. Marshall's snores came from the bed above me, and just hearing my brother near me felt like a deep breath of fresh air after being trapped underground.

I slowly sat up and moved to glance out the window. The moonless night streamed by in a slow, steady pace, and I wished we could go faster, somehow travel more quickly than this unnatural woman.

The cat's words spun around in my head like a rhythm I couldn't forget. I hated riddles; I just wanted answers. Fighting was hard enough, and having to figure out what my allies were saying just seemed a bit too much to manage on top of a battle.

I didn't even know how to prepare for this fight, either. What was I supposed to do? How was I supposed to beat someone like Eclipse, who had already bested me once?

Yes, she'd gotten me in a moment of weakness, and I wouldn't fall so easily next time, but with how easily she dealt with the cat, I had my doubts about what I would be able to do in a battle with her.

"Go to sleep," Luther's voice muttered from the darkness of his bottom bunk bed.

"I'm good," I said.

"That's fine, but I can't sleep with you moving around."

"I don't really care about your sleep schedule," I said.

Luther sighed heavily.

"What is she like?" I asked. "Eclipse."

He was silent so long I assumed I wouldn't get an answer. Then I heard the shifting of the blankets as he sat up. "That all depends on what she wants from you. She can be kind, charming. She can also be cruel and quick-tempered."

"That's not helpful."

"It's hard to describe a person who is more than one thing," he said. "I don't know what she will do when she meets you again, or what she is after. I just know she's been looking for your family."

"Then why didn't she go after us on the train? Did she send that Red Cap?"

"I don't know," he said. "That was after I'd already left her service."

"But she'd already mentioned my family before you left her show?"

"Once or twice. I honestly thought she was interested in your showmanship or business. Nothing like this."

"Really?" I snapped. "She gave you the ability to withstand fire, and you thought she just wanted to talk business with us?"

"I didn't know what she was. Only that she could give me some gifts. She wanted a show, and she was building one. I didn't have a reason to doubt her."

"But you left her."

"She asked me to burn down a town. I refused."

"But you didn't think to stop her?"

He laughed. "Stop her? Look, at the point she asked me to burn a town, I realized I was in over my head. I ran to save my own skin. I didn't look back, and I don't feel bad about that."

"But—"

"You got the ability to help people? Good for you. Not everyone's got that, alright? Some of us are just trying to stay alive."

"Then why haven't you left our show? We're just going right back to her, and that's not what you want, right?" I asked.

"Look...what I did, running, was the right call then, but now maybe there's a chance to keep her from hurting anyone else. I'll at least stick around and see. Besides, I need this job."

"I somehow doubt you're here for the job benefits," I said.

He laughed. "You really don't know the effect you have on people."

"Whatever and however people react to me is their business, not mine. I don't do anything to anyone that doesn't deserve it."

He chuckled and shook his head before flopping back into bed. "Goodnight, Hazel."

I glared after him in the darkness but got into my bed and tried to settle back in for sleep. When dawn came and the wagon stopped, it was a relief to be able to get up and out of the closed space.

Usually, I loved the trips, seeing the country pass by. But now, it all served as a reminder that Eclipse was out there, and somewhere there were other towns just like the one we'd passed. Towns she was destroying to send a message or to make a point.

I didn't know what she wanted, and I just wished she had the nerve to say it to only me and leave the rest of the world out of it. I didn't like games of cat and mouse, and I'd much rather us settle this with fists and magic rather than keep this charade up across the country.

The edge of the water glistened in an almost purple light as the sun rose. The beautiful scene only filled me with dread; I wasn't sure what we were going to be up against now, or what Eclipse might have in store next. We barely survived all her other tests, but now we were here, at the edge of the world as far as we were concerned. Boats across the oceans were not in our repertoire, and I didn't have any ambitions of sailing the world after this demon. This had to be the end of it, and I was damn sure that if only one of us made it out, it was going to be me.

Marshall stood beside me and put a hand on my shoulder. "We're going to find him," he said.

He sounded a lot more confident than he looked. After running into Dad's summoning along the way here, it was hard to believe he was still alive. How could he be? The harpy we had faced was definitely his, not just some random creature. I had recognized the scars on the harpy. I didn't know why his summonings were hostile to us or how they'd gotten free from the tattoos, but it didn't bode well for Dad's survival odds.

"We should set up camp," I said.

Marshall nodded. "Already started."

I had to smile. Marshall was always three steps ahead of me when it came to logistics.

We made our camp near the base of the rickety bridge where an old train chugged through every hour. Its piercing whistle and the rattling of the whole bridge were the only sounds aside from the soft lapping of water. It wasn't exactly peaceful, but it wasn't too bad. If I didn't think too long about why we were here, the beach was nice. The water looked cool and enjoyable. But the coast here couldn't compare to our winter home in Florida; the beaches there were beyond compare.

I didn't want to be here and at the same time felt like I was exactly where I ought to be. I couldn't turn back now, and I wasn't letting this demon get away again. However it ended, things were going to finish here.

For the first time, I felt pretty in touch with death, like she might walk out of the murky water and welcome me home at any moment. I glanced at Marshall as he moved from my side to guide the camp set-up.

Alma talked with Clarence while the rest of his band played a soft tune. What must all of them think about this? No set-up of the show, no money being made. Were we even paying them? I'd barely thought about any of those small details this whole time, and now that we were here, it felt a little too late to learn. They'd stuck with us; this group right here had chosen to come on this trip into danger.

Luther and Ruby sat near Jonah and the twins. Ruby stayed quiet, but I could see Luther telling some story that had the twins laughing. Even Jonah had a small smile. In that moment, it all felt so unfair. Why was it that I had to be the one to do this? Why did I have to bring the only family I had into this situation? Where was the righteousness in that? I'd give up every piece of ink I had if it meant that I would never have to bring them into any harm again.

Ruby still limped from the harpy attack and guilt flared heavy in my gut, like a weight had made its home in the belt around my waist.

The twins oversaw a simple meal, nothing extravagant. We ate in mostly quiet with only the occasional train whistle to pierce the darkness. I could see everyone eyeing me, and occasionally mouths opened, but no words ever came. What did you even say to a girl who was about to face a demon and probably die? No one ever knew what to say to the dying, but soon as I was in the ground, they'd find the words.

I shook my head to try to chase off that thought. Getting this pessimistic wasn't a good idea before going into a fight. I used to think I could take on anything in the world, but now...I took a breath. I'd have to find the way to beat the impossible. I was part of a sideshow; creating the impossible was our job, right?

"I'm going to head to bed," I said after the silence got a little too long for me.

"Goodnight. See you in the morning," Marshall said.

Alma stood up and pulled me into a hug. I wrapped my arms around her and held tight. It felt like when we were kids and were never far from each other. We'd run the fields hand-in-hand from sunup to sundown.

"Don't do anything stupid," Alma muttered into my hair.

I chuckled. "That's all I do, Alma."

Alma squeezed me a little closer before releasing me.

"Don't get all weepy; she ain't going anywhere," Constance said. "So drop it, you two."

Alma took a breath and nodded. "See you in the morning," she said.

I nodded, even though something in my gut told me I wouldn't see her in the morning. The quiet of the water, of the world around her, reminded me too much of the silence that proceeded death, and I needed to move that silence far away from the rest of the group.

I climbed into my wagon and laid down with dad's book. I flipped through the pages and the familiar markings: the bloody bones, the harpy, the wendigo. His handwriting made me ache for his voice, for him to tell me everything was going to be alright and that he had my back.

Forcing myself to lay down and get comfortable, I closed my eyes and tried to will sleep to come. When it wouldn't, I pulled the faerie from Noc from my thigh and used the sleeping dust on myself. If I were going to fight a demon, I'd at least get a good night's sleep.

"Hazel..." a familiar voice nudged me from the heavy weight of sleep.

I groaned and rolled over, pulling the covers over my head.

"Hazel, get up, girl."

Something about that phrasing made me pause and crack open an eye.

"Dad?" I sat up.

CHAPTER THIRTEEN

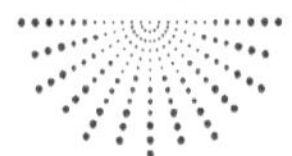

At the window of my wagon stood my father, just as I remembered him the last time I'd seen him. He wore his ill-fitting trousers and a too big vest over a bright red shirt. It was the showman outfit he put on anytime he had to make an impression in town. His thinning hair was tied back, and his beard didn't seem to have grown much longer than its collarbone length bush.

"Dad!" I scrambled to the glass pane separating us.

"Get on up, girl," he said before backing away from the window.

I scrambled to get my shoes on and rushed out after him. "Dad, wait!"

The camp was quiet. All the lights were out in the wagons, the fire dulled to nothing but embers, and a full moon pierced the dark veil of the night. Dad moved toward the lake where a boat waited for him.

"Dad!"

He climbed in and held an oar out to me. "Are you ready, my dear?"

I paused at the shore, uncertainty clouding me even though I wanted nothing more than to go wherever he was taking me. It was one of Eclipse's tricks.

I stepped back. "You're not really him, are you?" I asked.

"Hazel, what are you talking about?"

"Look demon, I've had enough of your tricks and taunts."

"Hazel Ann Finnegan, I'm not—"

"You're not Dad. He never called me his dear; he never uses my full name. It's been months, and his beard hasn't grown. It's not him," I snapped.

For a moment, he froze on the boat before the image wavered and melted into a sea of mist that faded into the surface of the water. Instinctively I reached out for him before catching myself and staying still instead of chasing after a mirage into dark waters.

"You're cleverer than I guessed," the demon said from the darkness.

"That was sloppy," I said. "Getting tired?"

The demon laughed. "Just having some fun. You should have seen that darling flash of hope you had. I wonder if your brother would have the same reaction."

I glanced back toward the camp.

"Look, you want me, you got me. Right here. No one else matters, alright?" I said.

"Full of yourself, aren't you?"

"We both know I'm the one you're interested in. None of them can do what I do," I said as Puck flared to life in a puff of cigar smoke at my side.

There was a long silence.

"Why don't we do this somewhere private? Just the two of us," I said.

"Oh?" Eclipse sounded surprised.

I took a breath and carefully eased into the boat where my false father had stood. It rocked beneath me but stayed steady. Puck helped push me off from shore, and I carefully began rowing. "The island in the center there. No one's there. Seems a good spot to me."

"Or I could just strike you down in the water," Eclipse said.

"Yeah. And you could've just struck me down any time all the way here, so let's be real about what you're after," I said.

Confidence filled my voice as the fear fled. There was no more running, no more living in fear of what the next move would be. Death was here, and I was ready to give her a hell of a time.

"How'd you do that trick with Dad's summoning?" I asked.

"He sent those," she said.

"Yeah, sure he did. They don't maintain for that long a distance."

"Maybe yours don't, but your father is the better summoner, isn't he?"

"Don't count on that. You haven't fought me lately," I said as I continued rowing, watching the shore and the wagons of my family fade away to small glimmering points in the dark all around me.

I hoped Alma and Marshall would eventually forgive me, but I wasn't losing anyone else, and I was done running scared and desperate. I was in control of my life here, and I could gamble with it all I wanted when their lives were off the betting table.

As my oars cut through the water, Eclipse appeared across from me, watching carefully. She still wore the same silk dress, her hair poised, and her eyes bright with a faint blue glow to them that was more obvious in the night.

"If you're going to sit in the boat you could at least take up a set of oars and help out," I said as I continued rowing.

"I like you, Hazel," Eclipse said.

"I doubt that."

"No, you are like me. A woman out for more for herself than what she's offered."

"Except I don't go around killing innocent people!"

"You killed plenty of innocents. The marks on your skin lay bare every one of your sins."

"Yeah, not the same as you killing a town of people," I said, stopping my rowing and weighing my options.

I could take a swing at her now, but I wasn't sure if this was her or an illusion. Besides, I was totally screwed in a water fight. I didn't even have a water beast to help me out.

"So, what are you after then?" I asked when Eclipse didn't respond.

I returned to moving toward the island. I tried to keep her talking until we got to solid ground again.

"The same as you."

"Be an independent spinster in a sideshow? That's a niche market, but I bet we could both get work in that."

A smile curled the edges of Eclipses' perfectly painted lips.

"I want more than my station."

"In hell?" I clarified.

"Yes. You know it's quite strange that the rules of your world and the rules of hell match so well. Then again, they are both filled with useless souls, aren't they?"

"What exactly are you doing here if your goals are all in hell? Get lost along the way?"

"You build your own path, don't you? You find a place to get your footing, and you dig in. I have no problems making my mark here. This world can bend to my heel first. Your world is so much easier to deal with than home," she said casually.

"Rule the world kind of thing? I thought you'd have more original goals."

She smirked. "Women do not rule in hell, earth, or heaven. A strange thing to have holding you in place, isn't it? I aim to change that one world at a time. Yours is simply the easiest to start with."

"Yeah, I don't see that going well for you," I said. "Besides, demons aren't supposed to be out here anyway. Did you get released for good behavior?"

Eclipse leaned back, and when the boat didn't shift with her weight, I realized for sure this was an illusion and not the real deal. I relaxed only a hair.

"Your father gave me my way out," she said.

"What?" I nearly dropped my oars.

She laughed. "Shocked, are you? There is so little you understand about the powers you hold, my dear. So very little you know, and so much potential lost because you lack a proper guide."

"My guide is Lady Death."

"Yes, and where is she now? Has she come around for a lesson about how to tame that beast that burns up your skin?" She motioned to the hellhound mark.

"I can figure things out on my own," I said. "She works with Dad. I'm just training."

"But you already have far more potential than your father. You tamed a beast from hell. A mortal touch should never survive that consumption. You could be great, Hazel, a legend that the whole world bows to."

I'd be lying if I said it didn't sound appealing, but I knew better than to get sweet- talked into a deal with a demon. The hairs on the back of my neck that rose when Ruby spoke were working overdrive.

"You drive a good bargain, but maybe try it again without that magic trying to force me. That's not a polite way to negotiate."

The boat bumped into the shore of the isolated island as Eclipse and I stared at each other.

"What do you want with me?" I asked. "To be your protégé or something?"

Eclipse shook her head and chuckled. "Oh, my simple little darling. There's so much you don't know, and that will all be the death of you, I'm afraid. So much wasted potential."

"You're going to kill me, so go ahead and tell me why I'm so dumb, huh?"

"Does that tactic usually work?" Eclipse asked. "I doubt it works even on the mindless creatures you fight. I'm disappointed."

"Join the rest of the world with that one," I said.

I looked around the island for what I had to work with here. There wasn't a lot of extra space on the small pile of mostly rocks, but a few stubborn trees grew that might at least give me some shelter. I'd take what I could get since the water wasn't exactly going to be my best bet. I don't know why I'd picked this as the place of battle. Not that I'd exactly gotten the choice to pick where to run into this fight. I hadn't even known this fight was coming until not too long ago, and now here I was with no plan, no strategy—a great idea all around by me.

"If I wanted you dead, do you think you would still be here?" she asked.

I didn't know how to answer that. She had a point as far as I could tell. She could have easily killed me at any time. When she killed the cat would have been the perfect opportunity. Jonah's holy barrier hadn't stopped her much at all.

So what had stopped her?

"Then why haven't you?" I asked. "What do you want from me?"

"You're interesting. Far more interesting than your father."

"Where is he?" I asked, forcing my voice to sound firm and confident.

"He's where he needs to be. Don't you worry about that," she said. Her eyes darted over to the far side of the lake, opposite of my camp.

He had to be over there. If I could just stall her long enough to get someone awake and to him... "That's not an answer, and you know it," I said.

"And I don't owe you answers, my dear. Whoever made you think that I answer to you?"

"You've kept me alive for a reason. You just said it yourself. If you won't tell me, I'm just going to assume that it's to ask questions."

Eclipse laughed, a hearty full sound that echoed around the rocky shore and trees that lined the area around us.

"What are you even hoping to accomplish?" she asked.

"Look, we can sit here and talk all night long. But we both know that's a waste of time, so let's get on with it," I said.

"In a rush to die?"

"If it means not having another conversation with you, then yes."

Eclipse chuckled again. "You're not a woman of words. You're a woman of action. I can respect that. But you will learn one day that words can be far more powerful than any violence you can inflict."

"Will you just stop your gab and let's get on with it?" I asked. If she had her attention all on me and a fight, maybe there was a chance I could get someone over to Dad.

"As you wish, my dear," Eclipse said, and I got the distinct impression that I had made a big mistake and was about to pay dearly for it.

I sent Puck scrambling, spinning in a circle to look for where this attack might come from. I knew it couldn't be far out.

"There's a lot you could learn from me, you know. So much more than you could learn from your father."

"Is it a competition?" I asked. "Didn't realize you were aiming for teacher of the year!"

I couldn't see or hear any sign of her. Even her voice bounced all around me in a directionless echo. I couldn't pinpoint any one direction to turn in, so I didn't even know what to do or where to look to deal with her. Did I summon something now or wait for her to make her the first move and react then? There wasn't a right answer, and it wasn't an easy win. I just needed to be cautious for once, on the defensive, but that wasn't my specialty.

I just wanted to disappear, but I hadn't picked up invisibility yet and needed to pay attention for a better chance to live through this. All I needed to focus on was surviving and not getting caught up in whatever mind games the demon was playing. She'd talked Ruby and Luther into deals, and I could see how it'd be easy to get caught in her webs.

"Afraid to make a move?" Eclipse taunted, trying to goad me into action. I wasn't going to take the bait.

"Just wondering how scared of me you must be," I said.

Puck stayed on high alert, his back to mine and looking around as I moved from the shoreline and further inland.

Eclipse chuckled again. "So confident. I like that in a woman," she said. "Perhaps we could come to an arrangement. It'd be such a waste to end your life."

"Yeah well, the number one rule I've gotten my whole life is don't make deals with the devil, and you're close enough to one to count, so no-can-do."

"What a pity," she said.

Puck's warning flared against my mind, and I rolled forward as a blade pierced through my faerie companion, narrowly missing what would have been embedded between my shoulder blades. Puck popped back onto my skin as I jumped up to my feet and bolted into the small section of woods. If I could keep trees at my back, I at least wouldn't get taken off guard like that again.

"Now who is afraid, my dear?" Eclipse asked.

I caught a faint glimpse of her near the edge of the water, long, thin blade in hand as she strolled toward the forest where I was attempting to hide.

"Don't worry; it only hurts for a few moments. Then it will hurt a lot as I peel off your skin."

"That's not comforting," I said before moving to another tree and finding a hold on a low branch. I pulled myself upward and into the branches above the ground. Having some distance would help, but the tree rustling didn't exactly make this a stealthy move.

"Do you really think you can climb a tree and get away?" Eclipse asked as she walked toward me.

I pressed my back against the trunk of the tree and tried to stay still. I wasn't to the top of the tree, but I was at least high enough that she wouldn't be able to reach me easily, and foliage kept me mostly hidden.

"Now, stop making this into some child's game and let's finish this like women ought to," Eclipse said as she walked past the tree where I hid and toward a nearby tree.

I covered my mouth as she pressed a hand to that tree and sent the bark up into flames.

Hellfire. I'd just trapped myself in a fireplace with all the kindling she could need. The fire didn't spread though, and these flames seemed cold. They flickered in a dark blue color I'd never seen before. I held my place, watching as this tree didn't burn to the ground but instead began to grow a thick layer of ice. A demon that didn't use fire?

What was this woman?

"Now, I'd rather not have to take the time to shatter your frozen body so just come on out," she said.

Still barely moving in my hiding spot, I summoned the wendigo. Its thin, hungry body formed on the ground beneath me. Eclipse stared at it for a few seconds before it lunged at her; it managed to get one good hit in with its claws against her side. The formal gown tore, and I saw a flash of black blood.

With her attention fully on the wendigo, I sent Puck onto the move. The faerie floated over to the boat and pushed it back into the water. Unhappily, Puck continued guiding the path back to my camp. He could get them over to Dad, and if Dad joined me, we could stop her once and for all.

After the one strike to her, I sent the wendigo charging into the woods in the opposite direction. Eclipse was quickly after it. In the moment of her distraction, I crawled to the end of a branch and took a deep breath before leaping to another tree. The branch groaned and cracked under my weight as I rushed to the trunk.

Just as I found a grasp around the trunk, the branch I'd jumped onto fell to the ground, and I cursed under my breath. So much for being stealthy. I didn't have to see Eclipse to know what was happening. The wendigo slammed back into my skin and stayed silent—one of the fastest dealings with it that I'd seen.

How the hell was I going to get out of this? What was I even supposed to do to handle a fight like this? I'd managed to wound her, but that hadn't seemed to slow her at all, and any second now she was just going to freeze this whole island.

I chewed on my lip. If she was a demon who used ice, then the best way to fight that would be with fire. I had fire to spare, and fire from her home in hell.

"Come on now, Hazel, we are just wasting time," Eclipse called.

Her hand landed on the tree where I currently hid. "I'm quite done playing with you," she said.

The dark blue flames began crawling up the tree, and I knew it was a make or break moment. I pulled the hound from my skin, wrapping my arms around its body as it dove to the ground. With the hound taking the brunt of the fall, I rolled from it as Eclipse stabbed toward us. The blade slashed across my back, but only with a superficial cut as I avoided it piercing any deeper.

The hound roared and lunged at Eclipse, jaws clamping around her hand, and bright yellow, almost white flames poured from the hound, clashing with her icy spell. The two powers of hell colliding fizzled the flames and the ice. The colliding forces spread a low mist across the area as ice melted and flames disappeared into smoke.

The hound growled low and steady, and I saw its shape step in front of me, protectively. It was strange to see how much the hound and I had adjusted to each other during this summer, that now it would protect me without having to be commanded. I held my breath as the hound gave a low, solid growl.

Eclipse chuckled. "You two finally made friends, did you?" she asked.

"This all your work? Only monsters abandon pets, you know," I said.

"Hellhounds aren't pets, and you don't know what you're doing with that thing," she said.

"Yeah, I think I do," I said, and the hound charged her.

Even if she destroyed it, I could resummon it, and this was probably my best bet against someone using ice skills. Finally, I had the beginning of a plan.

Only the hound froze in mid-leap, hovering in the air before it began to slowly fade to pieces of ash that floated in the air. A searing pain shot up my arm, and I stared in shock as the hound's bite mark, its tattoo, and its connection to me began to peel from my flesh, sending fragments of skin and ash into the air. Somewhere along the way, I began to scream as I dropped to my knees. The agony was worse than anything I'd felt, worse than any other fight or injury I'd ever had. I wanted to tear off all my skin. I wanted to die to make it stop.

The hound gave one last scream; its voice mingled with mine before it all fell still. The hound was gone, and I was left gasping for air, staring at the bloody patch on my arm. A void of skin appeared where there had once been a tattoo.

CHAPTER FOURTEEN

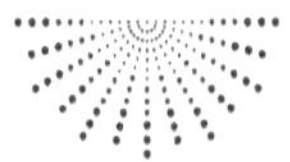

I couldn't form words, and my brain struggled to move past the shock and pain creeping along my body.

Puck's concern flared against my mind, but I forced him to keep going. *Get the boat to Marshall and find Dad.*

"See, there is just so much about this all that you don't know. It's a pity," Eclipse said. "You could be incredible, a gem. The world could bow to you, you know."

I couldn't respond as I scrambled to come up with a plan, with an escape, some way out of this. I was clearly way over my head. How could a summoning be pulled from me? Could she do that with any of my other markings? Would I survive many more of those?

"But that stubbornness of yours. It's an admirable trait, but unfortunately, entirely too strong to make you usable. Your father is much less stubborn, you know. Then again, men lead a charmed life, don't they?" Eclipse was close enough that she could have reached out and touched my face.

I struggled back to my feet, feeling unsteady and woozy as I stepped backward, barely keeping myself upright on the uneven ground underfoot.

"Where is my father?" I asked.

"Close by. Watching all of this, I imagine. Do you want to say hi?"

I gritted my teeth together and, in that instant, let rage guide me. The troll appeared arm first, slamming a fist into the demon woman as the rest of its body materialized.

Eclipse flew backward, crashing into a frozen tree she'd left behind. I scrambled into the hand and the troll picked me up and placed me on its shoulder. I was grateful my blood and spirit troll didn't smell like the living version of it had.

The satisfaction of watching Eclipse smack into a tree was short-lived as she got her footing back. Anger twisted her usually composed and perfect face, and I could see a crack forming along the pale, flawless skin of her cheek. A disguise broken in the tiniest of ways.

I swallowed hard and wrapped my fist around the troll's tattoo. I braced for the pain as I commanded it to move toward the water. If she took this summoning from me, the pain might not kill me, but the fall from on high and into the rocks below would. If I were in the water, at least I wouldn't splatter against the rocks, and maybe I could find some shelter in the murky water. I wasn't the best of swimmers, but Dad had made sure everyone in the show could at least stay afloat. We spent so much time bathing in streams, rivers, and lakes that that was a necessity.

Eclipse moved toward the troll with shocking speed, and I sent the giant creature into a leap, easily clearing the shore and splashing into the water. I couldn't go out too far from the beach or I'd risk drowning, but here the water only came up to the troll's knees, and we had a little distance from Eclipse as she paused at the shore as if unsure of crossing the water.

Vampires had a thing with running water, didn't they? Or was that demons? I couldn't remember right now, and it didn't seem like it would do me a lot of good anyway. Besides, a demon that couldn't cross water wouldn't have agreed to a meeting on an island. My thoughts scrambled, and I was beginning to see that I really, truly was in far over my head.

Glancing briefly toward the shore, Puck's boat landed and slowly lights flickered on within the wagons. With a deep breath, I tried to focus as the troll shifted in the water to block Eclipse from seeing the camp waking up.

"A lovely job you've done there with your pet. Have your ribs healed up from where he broke them all?" she asked.

I didn't even bother with a reply, but when I saw her sword flash, I changed my mind. She liked the banter, loved getting to play this cat and mouse game. And she played with her words more than anything else. If I kept her talking and taunting, then I could stall until maybe I came up with a plan to get out of this alive.

"So why summon that troll?" I asked. "And how did you do that? You animated it without its soul. That shouldn't be possible."

Eclipse paused, sword still up as she considered. "Souls aren't necessary for animating a corpse. Bones, rot, anything can move with the right motivation and engineering."

"The vines?" I asked.

"Clever and obvious, yes. The vines give it muscles, and they obey me."

"Is that a demon trait?"

"That's a me trait. You will find there are no other demons like me."

"You're the only one I've met, so I couldn't tell you," I said.

She chuckled. "So inexperienced."

"Look, hell and demons and all that stuff are not really in the area I signed up for."

"And what did you sign up for, Hazel? Do you even know what it is you do? What you've committed to? Or has your father not told you that either?"

"We take care of the supernatural things that have no business being here. We hold their souls safe from misuse until we pass them on to death," I said, reciting the lines Dad told me from the time I got my first tattoo.

"How cute," she said. "And wrong."

"Uh yeah, I think I know more about what I'm doing here than you do," I said.

Eclipse laughed. "You do, do you? Then what did I just do?"

She snapped her fingers and the hellhound that had once been attached to me appeared at her feet, growling and snarling toward the troll and pacing the edge of the water.

My surprise played out obviously on my face. "You can summon spirits, too?"

"I can do anything I set my mind too. The rules are different for me than you, of course. But that little hellhound of yours is mine now. Thank you so much for catching it for me, so helpful."

"That ritual circle where we found those hounds. That was you?"

"That is not the right question to be asking," she said.

I was getting right annoyed with all the circular talking, but I didn't really see what else to do. I didn't want to get too close, and I couldn't wade too far out. I'd trapped myself in a desperate bid to get someone to my father. Another furtive glance and I could see the boat slowly moving through the water toward where Dad had to be. Four heads appeared as silhouettes against the palest purple pre-dawn sky. Alma and Jonah's shapes were distinctive, but not the other two—one had to be Marshall, but the fourth could have been anyone.

I took a deep breath and focused. That was the one direction I couldn't bring her, not one inch closer to my family. She'd done more than enough harm wherever she was holding Dad and whatever she'd done to him.

"Then what is?" I asked as I looked around for some brilliant idea on how to keep her attention.

"Your stalling is beginning to bore me, Hazel," she said. "If you didn't want to die, you maybe should have joined a different life. Been a nice housewife for someone," she said.

"Fine. I'm not good at talking, so that works for me," I said.

I didn't even finish my sentence before the troll took another swing at her. I held onto an earlobe to not get knocked off from the movement that shook my perch on the shoulder of this giant beast.

The fist made contact again, but this time the hound was there and ready. It took the opportunity to charge right up the hand and arm, and I was soon staring face to face with my old friend, old enemy, and old problem: the dog made of fire.

CHAPTER FIFTEEN

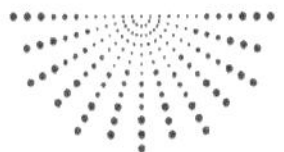

Instinctively I took a step back and nearly walked straight off the narrow support of the shoulder where I balanced. There wasn't anywhere to go to get to safety from my one-time ally now turned against me. I looked around for some kind of answer and found nothing but sky and water waiting for me.

Glancing again at the little boat, I saw that it had just reached the shore. They'd made it. They would find Dad, and we could end this.

The troll stilled with my uncertainty but stayed upright. How long until Eclipse ripped it out from under me as well? The hound's flaming body burned against even the troll's thick skin, only a few patches where water had splashed showed no sign of burning.

I took a deep breath as the answer hit me. I knew how to get rid of a monster made of fire—especially when I was standing in water.

Belly flop.

Surprise from the troll hit me first as the heat from the hellhound began to blister against my skin as it moved closer. The troll took two big steps backward before it took off at a charge and then flopped face-first into the water.

I clung to the earlobe with every bit of strength I had and gulped in a deep breath of air just before we all toppled into the lake together.

The murky water exploded with dirt, muck, plants, and fish all thrown into chaos at the arrival of a giant troll body slamming into the ecosystem of their little world. The hound struggled toward the surface, its light flickering out as it paddled upward. Launching off the troll's shoulder, I lurched forward and grabbed the hound's leg and held tight, keeping it down with me as long as I could. I was grateful I hadn't worn a dress into this fray, but no matter what I was wearing, I couldn't stay underwater forever. I had to find a way to deal with this thing.

Pulling my unicorn-blood dagger from my side, I plunged it blindly into the hound's chest. As soon as the blade touched skin, the hound flickered out of existence, and I was left floating alone.

After a few seconds of confusion, a screaming cry for air forced me to surge upward as fast as I could. We were further down than I thought, with the dim light from the sky a faraway beacon.

Help! I commanded. Almost instantly, a giant hand grasped me and propelled me upward.

I broke the surface, gasping for air, and the troll shortly joined behind me. I was surprised to see it treading water right with me, answering the question I never knew I'd had: could trolls swim?

I'd have to update Dad's book about that.

From the shore, I heard the faint sound of applause. "Well done," Eclipse said.

She took a ginger step into the lake, but rather than getting a single inch of her outfit wet, the water froze beneath her feet, spreading out with her every movement.

Damnation.

The ice began moving faster along the surface of the water, a thick layer of it rapidly taking over and reaching for me. I grabbed onto the troll and hoisted myself onto its arm and then up until I was on the top of its head. I wholeheartedly thanked God that my ethereal troll did not contain the smell of a physical, live troll. That much wet disgustingness up close would have been too much for me to handle.

I watched as the ice solidified around the troll and then began creeping up its body. I took a breath and made a leap toward a patch of already formed ice and hoped for the best as the air beneath my feet began to solidify.

Landing hard on the ice, I braced for it to crawl up my skin, but it didn't seem to touch me like it had with the troll who was now engulfed in ice and frozen in place, eyes staring straight at me.

I waved my hand to dismiss it, but the spirit didn't move. I swallowed hard and looked to Eclipse who smiled as she continued her stroll toward me. "So much you don't know."

"Yeah, you've said that a few times, but you know what? I think I know plenty about what I'm doing, and you're the one that needs to figure things out," I snapped as I tried again to unsummon the troll, but it held firmly in place; even the marking on my arm burned with cold.

"You are much cleverer than your father. But what about your brother? He seems to be the brains of your little show."

"You stay the hell away from Marshall," I said as I tightened my grip on my dagger.

On the far side of the lake, five figures in a boat rowed toward the frozen lake. I didn't know if they'd make it in any kind of time to help.

I just needed a moment of distraction, and I could stab this monster right in the heart like she deserved.

"I have no real interest in him; your father and you are the ones of interest. But I wonder, if something tragic were to happen to both of you, would Lady Death move her gifts onto him or find some other family to curse?"

"It's not a curse, it's a gift," I said.

She laughed.

From my inner thigh, I summoned the smallest thing I had, the faerie from Noct. I doubted any sleeping powder would work on her, but a blast of dust to the face would be distracting enough, I hoped.

"You're so funny in how you view things that are so obvious," she said, shaking her head.

"Alright, then tell me all about what's so obvious." I tried to relax my arms, look like I was really listening as the faerie buzzed behind me.

Eclipse and I moved around each other in slow circles, neither of us standing still or willing to turn our backs to the other.

"Your gift, as you call it, is not a present. It's a curse," she said. "A curse given to a family damned."

"Yeah, says you, a demon. Sorry if I don't believe most of the words that come out of your mouth," I said.

"But see, you are different than your father. Not the generation cursed, but the one who must pay the price. It is always such a shame that the sins of the father come on to the child, isn't it? But don't worry, I made sure he paid."

I took a deep breath and tried not to rise to the bait. Marshall, Alma, and the whole show, they needed me to be smart about this.

"I imagine he's looking out at you right now, watching you—" Her voice stopped as she turned toward the shore and spotted the figures in the boat.

In the instant that she turned, the faerie darted toward her and slammed the powder in her face.

She coughed, and I leapt forward and slammed my dagger into her chest. It cracked through her skin like breaking open a porcelain dish.

Fissures bloomed and cracked across her skin as I yanked my dagger free and stumbled backwards. Thick black ooze began pouring from the splintered facade.

"Oh, my dear, that was a bad decision," Eclipse's voice said, only she sounded like a music box that needed to be wound up again, dripping and off-tune in all the wrong places.

My foot sank into the water as I realized the ice was thawing. I scrambled back to the perch of the troll as the dark ooze spread into the water, tendrils reaching out for me.

"Up!" I told the troll, who moved with all the coordination of a drunk squirrel.

The troll wasn't fast enough. The tendrils grabbed hold of me, and I bit back a scream of pain as sharp, intense burning ripped through my body as the troll's skin turned black and beginning to slough off in thick chunks.

"Up!" I commanded again, desperately.

The ooze began to overtake the troll, climbing up its legs and toward its arms. Before the troll was completely consumed and over-come, all of it turning into this thing of ooze and hate, it grasped me in its hand and threw me.

Flying through the air, I summoned the shadow of the harpy. Her claws cut into my wrist, and she only stayed solid long enough to fly me toward the railroad bridge.

I barely managed to find something to grab onto and climbed onto the railroad bridge as the harpy vanished into ash again. I doubled over in pain as my troll tattoo began melting off me. I struggled to catch my breath as I scraped off the skin with my dagger and watched it sizzle against the blade before dropping inert to the ground at my feet. I didn't know what else to do, how to get away from this. What had I unleashed?

I swallowed hard and forced the harpy back out, sending it soaring well out of the troll's reach and toward the boat. I had to get them out of the lake before this ooze hit them, too.

Still struggling to catch my breath, I inched toward the edge of the bridge and looked down. The troll, no longer any part of me, stared up at me, or at least I thought it did; it was so consumed with this inky darkness I couldn't find its eyes, but it grabbed hold of the bridge and began to climb.

The entire structure shook wildly, and a few boards broke loose and toppled into the water below as I tried to hold steady against the pain and the tottering structure. If this thing fell, there would be nothing more for me to do, no more tricks or skills to call on. Hell, what did I think I was going to do if the troll did get up here with me? She could turn my summonings against me, so I didn't want to pull out anything too dangerous. Besides, she'd stolen my two heavy hitters. The wendigo was left, but the thought of dealing with that thing out of my control and the damage it could do made my skin crawl. I kept that summoning firmly in the do not use list.

What did I do now that a demon blob from hell was climbing up a tower after me and I had nowhere to go?

I took a deep breath, held onto my dagger, and readied myself. I'd have to come up with something.

CHAPTER SIXTEEN

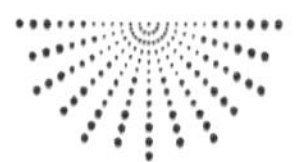

I paused when I felt a vibration on the track. Was that from the thing climbing toward me or something else?

In the distance, a burst of steam pierced through the forests and moved toward us. That was my ticket to stopping this, but there was no way this thing would stand still long enough to be killed by a train.

Against the edge of my mind, I heard the soft voice of the cat from the mountains. "You are ready now, Hazel, give me your arm."

I didn't know why a dead cat wanted an arm, but I stretched out my burned and bruised arm, still dripping black goop.

The sensation of soft fur beneath my fingers hit me first like I was petting some animal that I couldn't see. That softness began to move up my arm, traveling over the melting bits of flesh before that bite mark on my hand flared with pain. I winced as that pain rushed up my arm.

"Shall we?" the cat asked, and I nodded, watching as the bite mark began to drip blood, and the familiar shape of the cat formed beside me.

Instantly, a heavy silence wrapped around me, the sound of the train's approach gone aside from the faint vibrations I felt beneath my feet. I stepped back, inching toward the other side of the bridge with the cat at my side.

A train was my only hope, but I wanted to live through a train crash, and that meant some creative placing of myself so I wasn't crushed.

Glancing toward the boat, the harpy had just reached them and helped try to get them to the shore as the ooze rapidly approached them. As long as they were safe, whatever happened to me would be alright.

The ground shook more as the shapeless monster rose to the bridge with me. The size of the troll had melted away, and a shadow of Eclipse stood before me. Cloaked in wet darkness, two glowing red eyes stared at me and then at the cat.

What looked like a mouth opened and moved in words, but no sound escaped them. The creature bared dripping fangs at me and lunged.

Rolling to the ground, I avoided it, trying to make sure to keep the beast's back to the approaching train.

The cat shrunk down its size and perched on my shoulder as I dodged and weaved from the attacks. In the strange silence, everything felt like a dream.

A hit to my stomach knocked the breath out of me, and I doubled over before scrambling back to avoid the next hit.

The vibrations under my feet increased; the train was nearly here. I just had to hold on for a few more seconds. I moved back to try to create some distance between us, but a tendril shot out toward me and wrapped around my throat. The touch of the thing on my skin burned like acid, and I tried to break free as it lifted me from the ground. My legs kicked wildly, trying to find some support to help me breathe, but I was rapidly feeling darkness wash over me.

Behind my attacker, I saw the train's central light. If I went out taking out Eclipse, that would have to be okay.

The cat suddenly leapt from its hiding place, sinking teeth and fangs into the tendril. That loosened the grip enough that I pried myself free and jumped to the side as the tendril wrapped around the cat. I screamed as my only ally on this bridge melted to ash and burned from my skin.

As the cat faded into nothing, the roar of the train exploded into the silence.

Eclipse had only a second to turn and see the train bearing down on her before it slammed into her, splattering black everywhere. I dropped down and held onto a support beam as the train roared by overhead. I could hear its brakes screeching, but it would be miles before the train managed to stop.

As it passed by and the noise faded away again, I peered up onto the rails. The only thing remaining was a splattering of blackness, like a shadow cut to pieces. None of them moved, but I went and stabbed each piece just in case. They sizzled against the blade before fading into nothing.

I couldn't believe I'd done it.

CHAPTER SEVENTEEN

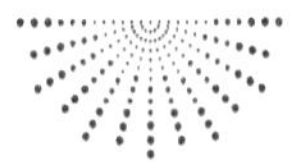

Laying on the bridge, wheezing for air, I couldn't bring myself to move. My eyes closed and the pain seemed to consume me. Raw patches of flayed skin where my troll, hound, and cat tattoos had been all burned like pure hellfire.

"Hazel!?" a voice from far away called.

Using every ounce of my energy, I crawled to the edge of the bridge and looked down. Almost without thought, Puck appeared and dove down to the figures in the boat.

The boat moved back toward the shore, and I watched the figures all run to the bridge and to me. Puck flew back to my side and tried to get me upright again, but it wasn't until Alma's strong arms wrapped around me that I found my feet.

"Hazel!" Several voices all cried out at once.

When my eyes finally focused, I saw Alma, Jonah, Marshall, Luther, and a bedraggled man with an unkempt beard and a bright smile.

"Dad?"

He looked at me, and his eyes widened. "Hazel!"

"How did you? Where is—" Dad started.

"She's gone, Dad. I took care of her," I said.

He wrapped his arm around my shoulders and pulled me close. Marshall joined in, holding me close, too.

"You stupid, brilliant girl," Marshall muttered into my hair. "You could have died. I thought you—"

"I'm fine," I said.

"You're covered in burns, blood, and weird ooze. You aren't fine," Alma said and just picked me up.

"Dad…can you call the water serpent?" I asked, wanting something to wash me down.

Dad slowly shook his head. After a moment, he rolled up his sleeve, and I stared in shock. His arm was barren of any tattoos, only faint red outlines of where they had once been.

"She took them all," he said.

I held Dad closer, even more grateful I'd killed the monster.

"You're safe. That's all that matters," I said.

"She got yours, too?" He motioned to my arm where the troll and hound marks still burned bright red in their missing markings.

"Not all of them. It's alright," I said.

Alma carried me across the bridge while Luther and Marshall supported Dad as he struggled to walk.

Back to camp, I nearly collapsed as Alma carefully deposited me onto a chair. "Sit."

I nodded.

The twins rushed over some breakfast as Dad and I sat. Blankets were draped around both of us, and I ate the offered food quietly. The lake seemed no different than when we had first arrived. The only change left by Eclipse were some black marks on the bridge's supports and a few downed trees.

Dad sat in silence as he ate and sipped water. Skin hung loosely around his arms and body from all the weight he'd lost. Had Eclipse fed him at all in the months he'd been stuck with her?

"Is she gone?" Dad finally asked, looking at me.

I nodded. "She is."

"Are you sure?"

"A train hit her. She's gone," I said.

Dad nodded, letting out a shaky laugh. "She's really gone."

"What happened?" Marshall asked Dad.

"Just after I arrived in Arkansas, she approached me, asking to help with the show. I said alright. But then she overpowered me, forced me to buy train tickets to Memphis, then locked me up in a wagon with no windows. She'd come in occasionally, and somehow, I don't know how, she could pull all the tattoos from me. She kept trying to absorb them onto her skin, but they wouldn't work; they'd turn to ash and be gone forever. It was…" Dad shook his head at the memories.

I ran my hands over the missing tattoos on my body. "Are there any left?" I asked.

Dad let out a long breath. "No. The harpy was the last one, and I sent it flying away from us before she melted the mark from my back."

"We found her, your harpy," I said and showed him my ugly wing tattoo. "But she's not the same."

Dad nodded. "So many souls lost."

"Why was she doing all of that?" Marshall asked. "She was after our show. Why?"

"She found my picture of you two in my wallet. She saw your tattoos, Hazel, and convinced herself that your souls would be different. She left me locked up in that wagon here. I don't know how long."

"You're safe now," I said. "You should rest."

"I'll sleep out here," Dad said. "I don't want to head into another wagon right now."

Marshall helped get a small cot set up near the fire. "Go to bed, Hazel," Marshall told me. "I'll stay out here with him."

"Thanks," I said.

Marshall pulled me into a tight hug. "Thank you. You found him, Hazel."

"Yeah, well you're the one who made sure we got here."

"We can argue blame tomorrow," Marshall said, wiping a few tears from his eyes.

I smiled at him before kissing Dad's cheek. "I will see you tomorrow," I said.

Dad nodded, his eyes already starting to close. "That you will."

I walked into my wagon and stripped into my thinnest nightgown. Anything touching the raw wounds from those missing tattoos hurt too much. Sitting at the edge of the bed, I looked out the window at my show, my family, all sitting around the fire, softly speaking as Dad slept. Everyone, even Ruby and Luther, were smiling and relaxed, content, safe.

I'd done it. I'd managed to save everyone, so why didn't it feel like a victory?

I thought back to Eclipse, a woman trying to carve her way in a world that wanted her to sit back and keep quiet. Maybe she hadn't gone about it the right way, but wasn't I doing the same thing?

Shaking my head, I laid back down in bed and tried to relax. I tossed and turned, unable to find any comfort. My throat burned from Eclipse's last attack, and I pulled out my hand mirror to look at the damage.

I watched as the red welt around my throat slowly began to change, turning from a wound to a solid black line that ran the entirety around my neck.

Hello, Hazel, came a familiar voice from the edge of my mind.

The mirror dropped, falling into the sheets of my bed as I got to my feet, turning around and ready for a fight.

Looks like your demon catching days are only just beginning. Eclipse said to the edge of my mind. *We have so much to do, and I have so much to teach you.*

THE END...?

ACKNOWLEDGMENTS

Thanks to my parents who believed in me and this series even when I lost my way. A big thank you to John Hartness for giving me the kick in the ass I needed to find my way back to writing. A giant hug and a lifetime of gratitude to Suzy, Carolyn, PB and Angelyn for being the best friends a gal could hope for, even when I ramble about murderous Red Caps.

ABOUT THE AUTHOR

Judy Black is a writer who makes her home in Atlanta, Ga. She loves games, books, cats, and most things with caffeine. She's a tabletop gaming nerd with several published Dungeons & Dragons adventures, including Ghastly Grins, in the ENnie nominated UnCaged anthology. You can watch her Tabletop RPG group game on Roll For Trouble on Twitch.

* 9 7 8 1 6 4 5 5 4 0 3 8 0 *